The prisoner was lowered ~~to~~ ~~the~~ ~~flooding~~ swept through Jackson. De~~spite~~ ~~himself,~~ he had to look. The leader grabbed a handful of the prisoner's hair and yanked, forcing the person's head up. The beam of light illuminated a pair of frightened blue-green eyes before they squeezed shut against the sudden glare.

Jackson's heart stopped beating.

Maya.

He jerked like he'd been electrocuted, barely managing to swallow back the cry of denial lodged in his throat. Staring into her pinched face, he felt like someone had stabbed him in the gut.

"Do you recognize your fellow guests?" the leader purred, swinging the beam of light at Doug, then at Jackson. He squinted but couldn't make himself look away, and when the light shone on her once again, she was staring right at him, her expression utterly haunted. Jackson squeezed his numb hands into fists of helpless rage.

Maya didn't answer but her devastated expression said it all. She'd seen and recognized him. From the look in her eyes it was clear she understood that whatever hell they put her through now, she'd have to withstand it alone. And somehow he'd have to endure that knowledge while battling the crushing agony that there was nothing he could do to protect her from any of it.

Jackson held her gaze, trying to give her strength. *Sweetheart, please hang on. Whatever they do to you, just hold on.* He wanted to throw up.

"No? Ah, well." The leader sounded almost disappointed in her lack of reaction. "Now that you have seen your fellow guests, I think you and I should become better acquainted." He jerked Maya's hair, forcing her to her feet, which were still bound.

She shot a look of terror in Jackson's direction that made his guts churn and it took everything he had not to call out in protest as they dragged her away. He thought he'd understood what fear felt like before? Not even close. But he did now.

Kaylea Cross

LETHAL PURSUIT

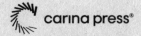

carina press®

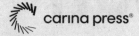

ISBN-13: 978-0-373-00300-6

Lethal Pursuit

Recycling programs
for this product may
not exist in your area.

This edition published by arrangement with Harlequin Books S.A.

® and TM are trademarks of the publisher. Trademarks indicated with
® are registered in the United States Patent and Trademark Office, the
Canadian Intellectual Property Office and in other countries.

www.CarinaPress.com

Printed in U.S.A.

This book is dedicated to the amazing men and women of AFSOC, but especially to my very favorite heroes, the selfless men of United States Air Force Pararescue, who stand ready to go into harm's way so That Others May Live. Hooyah!

LETHAL PURSUIT

I am an American Airman. I am a Warrior.
I have answered my Nation's call.

I am an American Airman.
My mission is to Fly, Fight, and Win.
I am faithful to a Proud Heritage,
A Tradition of Honor,
And a Legacy of Valor.

I am an American Airman.
Guardian of Freedom and Justice,
My Nation's Sword and Shield,
Its Sentry and Avenger.
I defend my Country with my Life.

I am an American Airman.
Wingman, Leader, Warrior.
I will never leave an Airman behind,
I will never falter,
And I will not fail.

—Airman's Creed

ONE

"TRY THAT AGAIN, and I'll break your freaking arm."

At the menace in her growled words and the way she wrenched his arm up behind his back, the drunk soldier beneath her abruptly went still. "Okay, *okay*, dammit. Lemme up!"

"Not a chance." *Asshole.* Security Forces Lieutenant Maya Lopez dug her knee harder into the back of his neck, pressing his face flat into the dirt while she secured his hands behind him with a plastic zip tie and pulled tight.

"Ow!" He twisted, only to stop when she leaned more of her weight against his neck.

She bent until her mouth was close to his ear. "You don't really want to mess with me right now," she warned softly. "I've just worked a twelve-hour shift that included taking down a bunch of insurgents trying to plant an IED in the road less than five miles from here." And the chatter said more activity was imminent, maybe even more attacks on the base like there had been before Thanksgiving. Everyone was extra vigilant these days. "Don't make me kick your drunken ass all over again, because I promise you, this time I won't be so gentle."

The man grunted, his face sweaty and red, but wisely decided not to fight. The sweet reek of alcohol poured from his skin. Had he been bathing in beer, for Christ's sake? The alcohol ban on base hadn't stopped him and his buddy from hoarding their stockpile.

Satisfied he would stay on his belly this time, Maya pushed to her feet. She rolled her shoulders to ease the soreness from where his elbow had caught her in the middle of her back during the initial scuffle. Her right hand was already banged up from her altercation with the insurgents earlier. If she hadn't been ready for it, this guy might have knocked the wind right out of her instead of merely nailing her between the shoulder blades with his elbow. Her cheek throbbed from where he'd managed to catch her with the edge of his hand in the struggle. It proved danger didn't exist exclusively outside the wire.

Beside her, Randall, the other Security Forces member she'd been paired with for this shift, hauled his own impaired suspect to his feet and looked at her with amusement. "You need a hand?"

"No." The bruise on the front of her ribs from when she'd blocked an insurgent's kick a fraction of a second too late ached with each breath she took. Her pride hurt worse though. She'd underestimated the slender, quiet teenager when she'd taken him into custody. A constant reminder that she couldn't afford to ever drop her guard, though she'd surprised the hell out of him when she'd suddenly taken him down. This drunk guy too.

"Didn't look like it, but thought I'd ask," Randall said with a chuckle.

Pausing only long enough to brush the dirt off her ACUs, Maya reached down and unceremoniously hauled her prisoner to his feet. The man stumbled and weaved a moment before finding his balance. His blood alcohol level had to be off the charts. Facing a possible discharge or criminal charges would sober him up quick enough.

"I didn't do nothin' to deserve being arrested," he grumbled, his words slurred.

"You got drunk, started a brawl in the middle of the MWR and busted someone's face open," Maya shot back. "Then you resisted arrest and tried to tangle with me. Now do us all a favor and just get in the vehicle without causing any more problems." She gripped his beefy upper arm and forcefully steered him to the waiting Humvee she'd just ridden in on. Stuffing him in the back beside his buddy, she slammed the door shut and climbed into the passenger seat.

Randall slid behind the wheel, wearing a big grin.

"What?" she demanded.

"That was so awesome." He shook his head. "Felled the guy like a two-ton tree. All five feet of you."

"I'm five-four-and-a-half." People always underestimated her because she was small. She took pleasure in making sure they only made that mistake once.

"Yeah, okay." Chuckling, he drove to the detention center. After dropping off the prisoners where they would sleep it off in a holding cell until they were dealt with in the morning, she headed across the base on foot toward the B-hut she shared with three other women. Well, technically two now, since her buddy Ace hadn't returned to Bagram yet.

One of her roomies, Honor, was reading on her bunk. She sat up and drew her shoulder-length red-gold hair to one side, eyeing Maya's face with curiosity. Her cheek must be swelling. "What happened to you?"

"Somebody took exception to me arresting them,"

she muttered, angry at herself for not blocking the blow quicker.

"Apparently. Want some ice for that? I've got a cooler with bottled water and sodas I brought in last night."

She flexed her right hand, which pulsed in time with her face. Was gonna be damn sore in the morning. "Nah, I'm good. What time does your shift start?"

"In another hour. I'm finishing up an overhaul of a hydraulic system on yet another old Chinook."

"Sounds like fun," Maya said dryly. She liked Honor and their other roommate, Erin, well enough, but it wasn't easy for Maya to get close to people. Ace had been her best friend, her only real friend. She missed her like crazy.

"Hey, don't knock it 'til you try it." Honor tossed her book aside. "By the way, any word from Ace yet on when she's coming back?"

"In her last email she said it looks like they're gonna have her come back in another few weeks to finish her tour. They wanted to let the last of the media interest around her story die down before then." God knew the media had hounded her ever since word got out that a senator's daughter and her gunship crew had gone missing in enemy territory just before Thanksgiving.

"And what about Ryan?"

Ace's man, a CCT with the ground team that fateful night, was ultimately responsible for getting her out of a lethal situation alive. "He's still here. I saw him last week over at the MWR." Maya nodded at the cooler at the foot of Honor's bunk. "Can I steal a water before I go?"

"Sure, help yourself."

"Thanks." She snagged one and stuffed a change of clothes into a bag. "Have a good shift."

With the bag draped over her shoulder, Maya chugged half a bottle of water and rolled her head around to ease the tension in her neck as she began her walk. The muscles in her upper back were knotted and stiff, as well as the knuckles on her right hand. The bruise on her ribs felt tight and sore. All in a day's work here at Bagram. A hot shower was definitely in order. Her reaction time had been too slow today. She would push herself that much harder next time she trained in the sparring ring.

The base was busy as ever this Saturday morning. The constant noise of aircraft engines and other vehicles formed a background noise she'd become accustomed to within a few days of arriving at base for her third tour in Afghanistan.

As she walked, a different sound carried over the relatively warm early March air. Faint strains of music. A piano. Passing the end of a long supply warehouse, she noticed a crowd had gathered over by where they'd set up the stage for the USO show happening the following night. She paid it only passing interest, looking forward to that shower and some rack time before she went out on patrol again tonight.

Then she heard the voice.

A man's voice. Deep and smooth, singing an old Dean Martin song.

She stopped abruptly, a prickle of awareness flashing across her skin. Something about that voice was familiar, made her heart beat faster.

It can't be him.

Pulled by some sick sense of morbid curiosity, she

pivoted and strolled toward it. The stage came into sight. Whoever the performer was, he was both playing and singing. Already the crowd was growing. Maya approached the edge of the sizeable audience, staring toward the stage. Whistles and cheers rose up to mingle with that incredible voice.

She stayed back from the throng of onlookers, only partially aware that she was holding her breath. Someone pushed their way through the horde of admirers, clearing a path, and Maya got her first good look at the singer. Her hand tightened around the plastic water bottle until it crunched in her grip.

Shit, it *was* him. That PJ, Staff Sergeant Jackson something-or-other she'd tangled with after Ace was rescued. For a moment her mind went blank in surprise, then flashed back to when he'd confronted her in the hospital hallway that day the CSAR crew had brought Ace back. When she'd had enough of his flippant attitude, she'd lost her temper. She'd muttered unflattering things about him in Spanish, and the normally silent and taciturn—and apparently Spanish-speaking—pararescueman had whirled on her, caging her against the wall with his arms on either side of her head. In that instant, she'd realized how badly she'd misread him. His long, powerful body had been only inches away from her, close enough that she could smell the wintergreen mint on his breath and feel the heat coming off him.

She might not remember his last name, but for damn sure she'd never forget his first one. Not after he'd permanently burned it into her brain with six words that had woken every feminine atom in her body and still did every time she thought about them.

My name is Jackson, he'd growled, his dark eyes daring her to defy him. *Say it.*

And oh, yeah, she'd said it. In a slightly breathless whisper that was completely unlike her. That surprising display of dominance and authority he'd shown still had the power to make her shiver.

Those deep brown eyes had blazed with a potent mixture of anger and arousal as he'd pinned her to the hospital exam room wall. The memory sent a tremor of feminine need rolling through her. That day she'd caught an intriguing glimpse of the warrior beneath that polite, Southern boy image. She was woman enough to admit she wanted to see a lot more of it, though she'd die before ever letting him know.

Watching him on stage now, she still didn't know how to read him. It was hard to reconcile the man in front of her with what she knew about his job. Being a Pararescue Jumper was one of the toughest jobs in the military. The training was so ridiculously hard that very few candidates ever graduated from the Pipeline in the first place. At just over three hundred active duty members, their tiny number said it all.

God, the man could sing. Since he hadn't noticed her, she stayed, eyeing his T-shirt-clad broad shoulders and muscled back as he played. Until that day in the hospital, she hadn't been able to envision him doing any of the dangerous things PJs did. She could now. That confrontation had been one hell of a wake-up call.

Maya was startled to realize she was smiling. His voice was incredible. Smooth and deep, with no hint of his usual Texas drawl. She'd never have guessed he had a talent like this. The man always surprised her, and it was captivating as hell.

He kept his gaze on the piano rather than the audience, hands gliding across the surface of the keys, that hypnotic voice striking a chord deep inside her. The timbre of his voice was intimate, warming her from the inside out. When the song faded away to the mad applause and screams from the female members of the audience, he looked over his shoulder at someone off stage.

Facing away from the mike, his voice barely carried enough for her to catch the words, "Get enough for sound check?"

His new fans wouldn't have it. "Encore, encore!" they chanted, even some of the men, clapping and whistling in unison until it seemed like everyone but Maya joined in.

Jackson faced the audience and offered a boyish grin, a little shy, as if he wasn't used to the attention. Hot. "One more?"

"More, more!" they chanted.

"All right, one more," he said in that gorgeous Texas drawl that made her think of long, hot summer nights spent relaxing on screen porches with pitchers of sweet tea and ceiling fans revolving overhead.

But mostly it made her think of long, lazy sex. The kind that would last all night and leave them both sweaty and too sated to move.

She shoved the thought from her head to halt the wave of arousal flooding her veins and refocused on him at the piano. A slight breeze ruffled his short, nearly black hair.

He launched into another ballad, and this time Maya recognized "Danny Boy." The sad, poignant lyrics drifted into the air, his clear, mellow voice raising goose bumps all over her skin. He had everyone there riveted, including her.

As though he sensed the weight of her stare, partway through the chorus he glanced up from the keyboard. When his bottomless brown eyes locked on hers, he faltered for the barest of moments, a single heartbeat. He recovered fast, and continued gazing right at her as he sang. It felt personal, as though he was singing to her alone. Then he smiled a little. A sexy, secret smile aimed right at her, and her heart fluttered. In that instant, she knew they were both thinking about him pinning her to that wall. About what might have happened if they'd had more privacy and he'd acted on the sexual energy arcing between them.

Damn.

Her stomach did a tiny somersault. Held by the quiet intensity burning in that hot gaze, she was trapped. Couldn't look away.

A powerful current of sensual heat swept throughout her body, making her tingle all over. The crowd dissolved away as her vision tunneled on him. He was singing to *her* as his long, strong fingers caressed the keys. Watching those lean, strong hands move, she wanted to feel them drifting over her bare skin just as smoothly, for her body to be the center of that focus. He was both protective healer and lethal warrior. Which would he be in bed? Gentle as his hands were on those keys? Or fierce and demanding, giving over to the unquenched fire she'd seen burning in his eyes that day?

The tantalizing prospect started a curious melting sensation low in her belly.

Jerking herself from her wayward thoughts, she raised one eyebrow at him and gave an impressed nod.

His grin widened a fraction before he finally looked away. A strange sense of disappointment hit her and she felt colder all of a sudden, as if the temperature had just dropped.

When the song finished, she was sad to see his performance end. This time he stood and waved at the crowd, that charming smile in place as he shook his head to politely decline their demand for more. Someone else came on stage with an acoustic guitar and set up to play. Jackson hopped down from the stage with an easy, athletic grace she appreciated, and headed right for her. She stood her ground, surprised that her heart was pounding. He made his way through the crowd, pausing only to smile and say a word or two to the people who spoke to him. Thanking them for their enthusiastic compliments, no doubt. Someone had sure taught him nice manners.

Maya waited with her arms folded across her chest and her feet braced apart, a half smile on her face as he approached. Part of her was surprised that he'd seek her out publicly after their last meeting, but it didn't bother her. She didn't give a shit what people thought or said about her. She'd learned a long time ago not to let that sort of petty crap bother her. Besides, she had a solid rep here with the Security Forces. Her superiors liked her work ethic and dedication. No one would dare accuse her of fraternization with an enlisted if she talked with Jackson here, and she was too smart to get caught if she decided to take things further with him after this.

When he was close enough to hear her, she shook her head slightly in admonishment. "I didn't know you could sing or play piano."

He gave a modest shrug, stopping a step away from

her. "You know what they say about us PJs. Jack of all trades, master of none."

She liked his self-deprecating style. Most men she knew went the other way, straight into arrogant asshole territory. He was a welcome change from the chest-beating, alpha male machismo she was so used to dealing with. "Are you part of the concert tomorrow?"

Up close he was even more gorgeous and smelled delicious—a combination of fabric softener and wintergreen. His tan skin held a bronze undertone, maybe from some Mediterranean ancestor. The cut of his high cheekbones hinted at possible Native American ancestry too.

He rubbed a hand over his strong jaw, covered with a few days' worth of nearly black stubble. It made him look rugged and intensely masculine. Sexy beyond words. "Naw, I'm just helpin' out to make sure the sound system is working right."

"Maybe you should reconsider. Looks like you've already got quite an enthusiastic fan base." And groupie base if he wanted one, she thought with a surprising bolt of jealousy.

He ignored the comment, that keen, dark gaze zeroing in on her right cheek. "So, what's with the shiner?"

She raised her battered right hand to touch the sore spot, now stinging under a new rush of blood that had her whole face turning hot. She never blushed. What was wrong with her? "It's nothing."

"Whoa." Frowning, he caught her hand in a firm but gentle grip before she could pull away. Maya's pulse leaped, warmth radiating up her arm from the innocent contact. He'd never touched her before, had never attempted it. Not even when he'd had her against that

wall and there'd been no one around to see them, and
even though he must have known she'd wanted him to.

Maya glanced down to where he cradled her hand
in his larger ones. They were broad, long-fingered, the
nails clean and short. Strong but gentle hands, capable
of saving a life or taking it, depending on the situation.
For some reason she found that extreme contrast sexy
as hell. Her heart thumped hard against her ribs while
she did her best to appear unaffected by his touch. She
wasn't sure how to read the situation. Was this his idea
of an olive branch? An unspoken truce?

"You've been fighting." He tsked.

"Comes with the territory." His touch felt way too
good. She should pull away. God knew she'd thought
about him far too often in the past few weeks, wondering what might have happened if he'd made a move on
her instead of walking away. She would have wrapped
around him and kissed the breath right out of him, buried her fingers in that thick, dark hair. He kept it cut to
regulation length, even though he could get away with
relaxed grooming standards because of his position as
a battlefield airman. It said a lot about his personality.

Raising his head, Jackson gave her a speculative
look, a hint of amusement gleaming in his eyes. He
lifted one dark eyebrow. "Just what've you been doing
to yourself, Lieutenant?"

He was only holding her hand and it was still enough
to play hell on her nervous system. "Nothing." Tingles
raced from her fingertips to her shoulder. What would
happen if she kissed him? Leaned up and pressed her
lips to that full, tempting mouth inches above her own?
She mentally shook herself. "Just a few angry insur-

gents and a resistant drunk. But hey, you should see the other guy."

One side of his mouth curved upward at her attempt at humor. "Yeah, I bet you pack quite a punch."

The admiration in his voice warmed her inside. She'd fought all her life to earn respect from others, especially men. From what she'd seen, Jackson was all about giving women respect. She had no experience with that sort of man.

He wasn't done with his inspection yet. He ran his gaze over her once again, and this time she was certain it held more than the clinical attention of a trained medical professional. Though the masculine interest was subtle, it brought more of that unnerving tingling in its wake. He still hadn't released her hand. "You hurt anywhere else?"

Why, was he offering to look her over? She almost laughed. "No, I'm all right. No broken bones, so I'm good to go."

"You sure about that? Two of your knuckles are pretty swollen and bruised."

"I've broken plenty of bones. Trust me, my hand's fine."

"Is it?" Studying her reaction, Jackson gently probed at the painful joints with his thumb, applying careful pressure until she had to fight back a wince.

Okay, so maybe the bottom knuckle of her middle finger had a crack in it or something. She stayed still, kept her expression neutral. "See? Just bruised. No big deal."

"If you say so." The look in his eyes told her he wasn't buying it. Discomfited by his genuine concern, she pulled her hand away and he let it drop. It bothered her that she immediately regretted the loss of his touch.

Jackson set his hands on his hips and studied her like he didn't know quite what to make of her. The move emphasized the breadth of his chest, the way his olive drab T-shirt pulled taut over the heavy muscles of his torso. His defined biceps flexed below the short sleeves. The man took *very* good care of himself. She liked that too. "If I asked nicely, would you go get an X-ray on that hand?" he asked.

"Nope."

"Not even if I walked you over there?"

"Nope, not even then." Maya hated hospitals. She only went if she was in desperate shape, like that time when she hadn't blocked a kidney shot and wound up peeing blood. They hadn't been able to do much for her anyhow.

A faint smile spread across his face as he shook his head at her stubbornness. "That's what I figured, but you can't blame a guy for trying."

"True." His sweet concern was proving an almost irresistible lure. No man had ever treated her with half the consideration this one did, and she barely knew him.

"Well, if you're sure I can't talk you into going to the hospital, I should head back."

To the other side of the base, where the Spec Ops compound was. "Okay. I'm glad I heard you sing, by the way. I enjoyed it. You're really good."

He smiled, making the corners of his eyes crinkle. "Thanks." A small silence ensued, and when she didn't fill the void, he nodded once to acknowledge the conversation had come to an end. "Well. Guess I'll see you around then."

"Oh, you can count on it," she replied. Pivoting, she left him to chew on that parting shot, the image of his startled smile fresh in her head. And even if it made her cheek hurt worse, damned if she wasn't smiling too.

TWO

KHALID LOOKED UP from his map when Mohammed burst into the room and announced, "They're here."

He stood and followed the teenager out into the bright sunshine. Squinting to cut the light, his gaze settled on the small convoy of trucks winding their way down the mountain road toward the valley floor. He smiled. "Perfect."

"Should I get the others?"

"Yes. Tell them to unload everything."

Mohammed scurried off to carry out the order. A few minutes later the trucks ground to a halt where Khalid stood at the edge of the village.

The passenger in the lead truck climbed out and approached Khalid with a huge smile. "My brother."

Khalid awkwardly accepted the greeting hug. He disliked forced physical contact. "Tell Rahim I thank him for his gifts."

"You can tell him yourself when you meet him in person."

His attention sharpened on the man's beaming face. "You have news for me?"

"Something big. He has written it here." The man pulled a wax-sealed envelope from his vest pocket and handed it over.

Quickly breaking the seal, Khalid scanned the document written in Urdu. His heart rate increased with a surge of excitement. "Rahim knows this for certain?"

The man nodded. "The location isn't known yet, but Rahim's source has always been reliable and accurate. He'll let us know when the time comes."

Khalid couldn't hide his smile. "The American Secretary of Defense?" Could it be true?

"I know. It's what we've all been waiting for."

No, it was what Khalid had been waiting for his entire *life*. This chance, if it really came, was something he'd dreamed of since he was a boy growing up during the Soviet occupation.

Back then he'd been too young and too crippled by the disgrace of his shameful parentage to even contemplate conducting such an important mission one day. But now, with the right planning, he would be able to achieve every Afghan boy's dream of humiliating the infidel superpower occupying their homeland. If he and the others handled it right, it might even help turn the American public's opinion of the so-called War on Terror once and for all. Their president would have no choice but to finally withdraw all American forces from the region.

Then, *then* they could celebrate the sovereignty of the Afghan people and take the fight to the enemy's shores, where it belonged. Not like before, with sporadic and poorly planned attacks on small targets. A new, deadlier and well-organized war that took many American lives and struck fear into the hearts of the American people. One waged relentlessly with endless attacks wrought on American soil by soldiers of Allah from far and wide. But especially by martyrs already living among the enemy. People no one would ever suspect until it was too late. That was where the future of this war lay.

Pulling a lighter from his pocket, Khalid lit one end of the letter and let it fall at his feet, watching the licking flames curl over the paper, devouring it. With Allah's grace, he and the others would do the same to their enemy within a few months. "Tell Rahim I look forward to our meeting. It will be an honor to meet him in person finally."

The man clapped Khalid on the shoulder. "I will tell him. Now, where shall my men take all these supplies?"

Khalid walked to the first truck, where several men were opening the canvas sides to expose the crates filled with food, medical supplies, clothing and weapons. Pistols, automatic rifles, grenades, RPGs. And ammunition. Lots of ammunition. Everything he could ever need to carry out a campaign in the region. He let out an ironic laugh. Throughout the winter his numbers had dwindled. He'd lost some men to the cold, others to their homes and villages. Now, with these supplies, he'd be able to feed and equip dozens, maybe as many as a hundred or more new recruits.

Mohammed came trotting over, a wide grin on his boyish face, partially covered with the scraggly beard he was trying to grow. "Praise Allah," he said as he saw all the equipment.

Khalid nodded. "Have the men stock everything in the caves, quickly. I don't want anything to be visible from the outside."

"Of course, Khalid-jan."

Khalid smiled fondly at the boy, feeling almost fatherly. Mohammed was his most trusted soldier, teenager or not. Khalid had done everything he could to protect him over the past few months, teaching him to survive, and to kill. He set a hand on Mohammed's shoulder, patted it. "You're ready."

The praise turned the tops of Mohammed's cheeks red. "Thank you."

Letting his hand drop, he gazed up into the clear blue sky, filled with renewed energy. "No, Mohammed, thank Allah." For it was by His grace that Khalid would slay the demons from his past and embrace the future bright with purpose and possibility.

MAYA OPENED THE gym door and stepped out into the cool air, chugging a bottle of water on her way back across the base. Today's workout had been especially intense, but she'd needed the release despite her sore right hand and other bumps and bruises. Her quads felt weak and her abs were still on fire, and she freaking loved it. With her self-inflicted torture done, she now had her weekly Friday morning date to keep.

Her little friend, Fila, was waiting for her in their usual meeting place. Maya smiled and raised a hand in greeting when she saw the eleven-year-old girl at the fence. Fila waved back, shifting a young child about three or so on her hip whom Maya had never seen before. "*Salam alekum*," Maya called out.

"*Alekum salam*," Fila answered softly, a shy smile on her young face. The boy on her hip clung to her, regarding Maya with suspicion in his teary eyes. His little cheeks were flushed an unnatural shade of red.

Something was wrong. "Is he sick?" She pointed at him then put a hand on her own forehead and stomach, made a sickly face.

Fila nodded. "Brother."

She'd brought him here for treatment, Maya realized. Fila had walked miles and miles from her isolated village, carrying her brother here in the hopes that Maya would help. Her family, as usual, was nowhere to be seen. Maya wasn't about to abandon these children too. She gestured with her arm for Fila to follow her around the fence's perimeter. "Come on."

At the gate she spoke to the guards and received permission to bring Fila inside. The Friday market always made everyone on base a little edgy, especially since that rocket attack back in November that had killed several service members and wounded a dozen more. Security had tightened considerably since then, and procedures for the market had changed.

Fila followed her inside the base. Maya flagged down a passing vehicle to hitch a ride so her little friend wouldn't have to walk across base after her long journey. Fila hesitated, her gaze uncertain. Had she never been in a vehicle before, or was it the soldiers inside it who made her nervous?

"Come on," Maya said again, giving her a reassuring smile. "It's okay." She waited until Fila climbed inside the vehicle before sliding in next to her. Her brother sat perched on her lap, his flushed, chubby cheek nestled into the curve of Fila's neck. "What is his name?" she asked slowly.

"Salar."

Maya shifted her gaze to the boy. "*Salam*, Salar."

His glassy eyes focused on her, his expression guarded. Maya understood too well what it felt like to be at the mercy of others. Even those who were supposed to take care of you. These children had more reason than most not to trust people. She'd make sure no one here abused that trust.

The driver stopped at the hospital to let them out. Maya led Fila inside and spoke to a few of the staff. A few minutes later Maya's other roommate, Erin, appeared with a clipboard, her brown hair twisted into a bun.

"Hey, who have we got here?" she asked, aiming a gentle smile at the children.

"This is my friend, Fila, and her little brother, Salar. He's not feeling very well, are you, buddy?"

He didn't respond, but his lethargy said it all.

Erin made a quick note on her paper. "Come with me so we can get them set up in an exam room, and I'll have a doctor come by as soon as possible."

Maya ushered them into a room after Erin and shut the door. Both children gazed around the room with wide eyes, their anxiety palpable. "It's okay," Maya said again, this time catching Fila's gaze. The girl seemed to relax a fraction. "Her English is about as good as my Dari, so this should be interesting. Don't suppose you've got an interpreter on staff?"

"No," Erin replied, pulling her stethoscope from around her neck and offering it to Salar so he could examine it, "but the doctor I have in mind has a pretty good handle on Dari." She showed Salar and Fila how the stethoscope worked, even allowing them to place the earbuds in their ears and listen to Erin's heartbeat.

When they smiled and seemed to be enjoying themselves, Erin gestured for Fila to raise her brother's shirt. His little tummy was distended and looked hard. With him nestled on Fila's lap, Erin did a quick exam, taking the basic vitals and finally coaxing the little boy to accept a thermometer under his armpit. After writing all the information on a chart, she spoke to Maya. "He's got a pretty good fever going. I'll get the doctor to come as soon as he can."

"Okay, thanks." While they waited, Maya used hand gestures and her limited Dari to entertain the children. Salar began to warm up to her slowly, even offering a toothy grin once or twice. The doctor arrived a few minutes later. His easy smile and basic grasp of Dari seemed to reassure Fila enough to allow him to take Salar and place him on the exam table. After another thorough assessment and some questions to Fila, the doctor glanced over at Maya.

"I'm going to need some blood and urine samples."

That should be fun. "Why, is it serious?"

"Not if he gets the right treatment, but I want to rule a few other things out first just to be sure."

The urine sample was easy enough. Salar thought it was hilarious to pee into a cup. The blood sample, however, didn't go so well. In the end, Maya had to pin the child down while Fila held his free hand and stroked his hair, speaking to him in a calm voice. A sudden memory slammed into her brain. Of her sister taking care of her during that awful, violating exam after their uncle's nocturnal activities had finally come to light. The tenderness Fila showed her brother reminded Maya so much of Pilar, a hard lump formed in her throat. She quickly swallowed it down and pushed the painful recollections from her mind before they could tear into her.

Samples in hand, the doctor left the room and returned a half hour later with the news that Salar had a bacterial infection that required IV antibiotics. That procedure didn't go so well either.

Two hours later with tears drying on his cheeks, a bandage on the back of his hand and a lollipop in his other, Salar was ready to go home. Fila had a little vial of pills for him, and the doctor checked twice to make sure she understood how the medication was to be administered.

None of them could get out of there fast enough. Stepping outside, Maya pulled in a deep breath of air, that uncomfortable pressure in her chest easing the moment she exited the hospital. After grabbing Fila and her brother something to eat, Maya took them back toward the main gate. Salar was getting sleepy, and Fila was obviously tired too. Maya held out her arms and gave Fila a questioning look. The girl immediately handed her brother over. Maya expected him to squawk but he never made a sound, just looped his arms around her neck and settled his head on her shoulder. Her heart squeezed at the feel of him nestled against her.

On the way across base, they spotted a group of soldiers playing soccer with some local kids. Salar craned his head around to watch. The ball hurtled past the players and bounced toward them. Maya paused as it rolled near her feet.

"Hey, little help over here?"

Startled by that deep Texas drawl, she glanced up into a familiar pair of smiling dark eyes. He wore a bright orange Texas Longhorns ball cap.

A sharp pang of excitement flashed through her and her heart rate picked up as she turned around fully to face the man who'd haunted her fantasies these past few months.

JACKSON GRINNED AT the flare of shock in Maya's eyes and set his hands on hips as he waited for her to respond.

"You have time to run soccer clinics?" she asked in that Latin-tinged accent he was coming to crave the sound of.

He grinned wider. "Now and then, yeah. Who's that with you?" He indicated the two children with a jerk of his chin.

"Friends of mine." She made the introductions, and Jackson stepped closer to offer his hand to them both. Fila shook his shyly, blushing and avoiding eye contact, but Salar quickly buried his face deeper into the curve of Maya's neck. Not at all offended by the rebuff, Jackson smiled. He knew from personal experience just how good Maya smelled up close. The lotion or whatever it was she used was scented with vanilla and the tart bite of tangerine. He'd love to lean in and nuzzle the side of her neck to get more of it, but the boy was getting to enjoy it instead.

She shifted Salar on her hip. "We're just leaving the hospital. Poor little buddy has an infection that needed some needles. It wasn't fun."

"Sorry I didn't see you earlier. I'd have been happy to help."

She looked started for a moment, as though she wasn't sure what to say to that. "Thanks, but we managed okay."

"I'd say you did better than okay. They both seem pretty attached to you." And damn, that maternal side looked good on her, too, confirming what he'd suspected about her all along. Beneath that tough exterior lay a big heart she didn't seem to want anyone to know about. He'd bet that very few people ever got to see that softer side of her. What would it take for him to earn her trust, get her to let him in that far?

Maya glanced down at Fila's hand twined with hers and smiled a little. It softened her whole face and lit the pilot light on Jackson's protective instincts. "Yeah. We've been through a lot together, haven't we, guys?"

This had to be the girl Maya tried to protect the day the base had come under attack in November. Ryan had told him Maya had charged the fence to shout instructions to her young friend. Apparently Maya had stayed there through automatic gunfire to make sure Fila was okay, only moving when Ryan had forcibly ripped her away from that fence and hauled her behind cover. Jackson had no difficulty whatsoever imagining her standing her ground to protect the girl. Maya might be a badass, but he was on to her now. There was so much more to her than that tough-chick image she preferred to show the rest of the world.

By the increase in noise behind him, the youngsters were getting restless to resume playing. He indicated the stalled game behind him with a jerk of his thumb. "Care to join in?"

Her expression turned startled, those big sea-green eyes staring up at him. "I don't..." She glanced down at Fila, gestured to the ball at her feet and said something in Dari. The girl shook her head shyly. Maya met his gaze. "I think they're both done for the day, but thanks. I'm going to find us a ride back to their village."

"You going with them?"

"Well I'm not letting them walk all that way again, especially without an escort. This little guy has a death grip on me anyhow, and I don't want Fila to have to be alone with any other soldiers."

Something flashed in her eyes at the last part. A spark of buried anger. That and the fierce way she said it made him think there was something more than protectiveness behind her words. Had someone abused Fila? The idea made him feel sick. He shifted his gaze to Maya's hand, locked with the girl's. "How're the knuckles?"

"Good."

They weren't. He could see the bruising and swelling from where he stood. He'd bet money she'd at least cracked one of them, yet she held Fila's hand without complaint to offer reassurance to her young friend. That sweetness pulled at him. "Your cheek looks better."

She nodded, her expression closing up. "Yeah, I'm fine. Here." She nudged the ball toward him with the toe of her boot.

"Thanks." He didn't want her to go yet, but navigating this situation was tricky. Their difference in rank didn't seem to bother her though. Thank God for that. Technically she could have reported him for rounding on her that day in the hospital. He'd been on edge, just back from a mission where he'd lost a patient on the way back to base. Normally he had a long fuse, but she'd managed to push every one of his hot buttons within the space of a few minutes. "By the way, I apologize for the way I spoke to you that day."

She shook her head, looking straight into his eyes. "I deserved it. Never realized you spoke Spanish. Guess I'll have to swear at you in Dari from now on."

Her response startled him so much that he chuckled. "No, those words I know."

"How did you learn Spanish, by the way?"

"My mom worked two jobs when we were kids, so she hired a nanny and she was Mexican. My accent's not perfect and I can't speak it as fast as you, but I understand it well enough."

"Yeah, you sure do."

He admired that she took responsibility for her attitude that day. He hadn't expected her to. "If you can't find a ride, let me know. I'll go with you." Even as he said it, he knew she'd never take him up on it.

"Thanks, I appreciate it. Come on, guys, let's get you home." She tossed him a cocky grin. "See you."

No *Sergeant* tag, so she wasn't hung up on protocol like Ace had been with Ryan. That had to be a good sign. "Yeah. Take care." He admired the sway of her hips and the lean lines of that taut body as she walked away. The woman was sexy as hell. Her self-confidence and take-charge attitude even more so. And while he liked her harder side, that soft, feminine glimpse he'd just seen was what drew him in.

Jackson pulled off his ball cap to drag a hand through his hair and shook his head at himself. Damn, he was in bad trouble here. Growing up in a household of women, he'd developed an appreciation for the fairer sex early on. But Maya was different. When she was nearby, he *felt* it. When she walked into a room, she owned it. Knowing she was interested in him made it that much harder to resist temptation and stay the hell away from her. He couldn't remember ever wanting a woman this badly, and he had no idea what the hell to do about it. Maya was unlike any other woman he'd known. It was like trying to navigate through a minefield. One false step could blow his legs off, yet he couldn't resist the lure. But he was most definitely up for the challenge she posed.

"Hey, Thatcher, you done getting shot down for the day? Cuz we're waiting to finish the game over here."

Turning around to glare at his fellow PJ, Jackson sent the soccer ball hurtling back at him.

Game on.

THREE

MAYA CLIMBED IN behind the Humvee's wheel the next morning and slammed the door shut. "Ready to rock?" she called to the gunner in the back manning the .50 cal.

"Yes, ma'am." He rapped twice on the top of the vehicle.

"Just waiting for my copilot. He should be here in a minute." She went back to checking her radio and weapon one last time, not paying much attention to the personnel milling around the line of vehicles.

"Guess this means I get to ride shotgun?"

She jerked her head up to find Jackson leaning his roped forearms on the open window frame of the passenger door, a mischievous smile on his face. Her heart stuttered. What was he doing here? And why did her heart always beat faster when she saw him? He had his full kit on, a large ruck and his M4 slung around his shoulders. "You're going to FOB Chapman?"

"Yes, ma'am. I volunteered for the MEDCAP."

Huh. The medical civil action plan was part of a hearts-and-minds campaign dreamed up by the brass in an effort to "reach out" to the people in some of the isolated villages down south. PJs often took part in them, giving medical care and other critical supplies to the civilians.

"That right?" It didn't surprise her that Jackson had

volunteered for it. She already knew he wanted to be a doctor because she'd caught him studying for the MCAT a few months ago. Of course, back then she'd misinterpreted his laid-back demeanor as passivity. Now she knew that beneath his calm, quiet facade beat the heart of a formidable fighter. The man was a sexy, walking contradiction. "I've kinda got a lead foot."

"Even better." He straightened, tall and strong and ready to rock.

Weird. She knew he could handle whatever came his way in the field, since he'd earned his maroon beret for a reason. And yet, even though he was bigger and stronger than her, for some reason she still wanted to watch out for him. Maya eyed him for a second, letting her gaze roam over the impressive contours of muscle in his chest and shoulders, reminding herself that he could be lethal in addition to a gentle healer. He wanted a ride with her? Why not? "All right, throw your stuff in the back and get in."

He did, then climbed in next to her and shut the door. And suddenly the Humvee didn't feel big enough anymore. It was like he took up all the space, all the air. Every cell in her body was attuned to him. She could smell the faint scent of wintergreen and clean male musk. Her skin prickled with awareness and he hadn't even touched her. This was gonna be a long five-plus hours drive, but an interesting one. "Okay, let's roll," she announced.

When everything was in place, the lead vehicle exited the main gate and started outside the wire into the Afghan equivalent of the Old West, driving south along the main highway toward Kabul. Maya pulled out into line, third from the front of the convoy. Behind her, four more supply trucks and another Humvee brought up the rear. The mountains rose to jagged peaks on their left, the crests still tipped white with snow that was only beginning to melt in the spring runoff. Mudslides had wiped out a few of the mountain passes recently, and there would be plenty more before the snow melted completely.

The silence in the vehicle wasn't awkward, but she still felt the need to initiate conversation. "So, how's the studying coming?" she asked Jackson.

"For the MCAT? Good."

"When do you write?"

"June."

She bit back a smile when he didn't offer anything further. He was quiet and definitely comfortable in his own skin, yet bold in other ways that continued to surprise her. No way he'd landed a ride in her truck by dumb coincidence. She couldn't figure out why he'd gone to the trouble of arranging it. Wasn't like he was planning to make a move on her or anything. He was way too polite and respectful to cross that line with her. She felt so far out of her depth with him it might have been funny if it hadn't confused her so much. "What made you want to be a doctor, anyway? I mean, it makes sense that you'd want to, since you're a PJ and all. But there must be a reason."

Jackson stretched out his long legs a bit more and leaned a forearm on the window ledge in an unconsciously sexy alpha male pose she knew he wasn't even aware of making. That made it even hotter. "My dad died of a heart attack when I was a kid. Guess since then I've always wanted to save people."

A solid reason, for sure. She respected and admired

that. Most of all, she loved that he was motivated to help people. "What sort of doctor do you want to be?"

"Not sure yet. A GP, or maybe a surgeon."

"Not a pediatrician? You seem good with kids."

"I love kids. Not sure I could handle seeing sick ones day in and day out though."

God, why did that make her heart squeeze for him? This man cared too much, felt too much. Didn't he know how dangerous that was? If he was lucky, he'd never have to learn that lesson. She let the conversation lapse for a minute but was too curious about him not to keep asking questions. He seemed willing enough to answer them. "Did you grow up in Texas?"

He nodded, giving her a half smile that made her stupid heart flutter. "Born and raised outside of San Antonio. You?"

"Born in Mexico City. Moved to California when I was three." She glanced over at him. "You part Italian, or Native American, maybe?"

He shot her a surprised look. "One-eighth Comanche, from my mother's side. You got a big family?"

Not anymore. "Just my grandmother left now." And a few other relatives she'd never have anything to do with again, lest she give in to the urge to dispatch them all to hell where they belonged. "And you?"

"My mom and three older sisters."

That made her smirk. "So you were the man of the house, huh? I hope you had lots of bathrooms in your house growing up." She and Pilar had constantly battled over time in their tiny bathroom. The thought brought a pang of wistfulness. Losing her sister had been the single hardest thing she'd ever faced. No matter where she went, she carried a piece of Pilar with her, even if the memories hurt. And she wouldn't have it any other way.

"It wasn't so bad. I just learned to be fast. Get in, get out before anyone saw me."

"So you were already way ahead of the covert ops curve when you enlisted."

He flashed her a sexy grin that made butterflies flutter in her belly. "Yeah, I was."

Grinning, she kept her eyes on the road and maintained the proper distance between her truck and the one in front of her. They reached the first checkpoint and stopped for the Afghan police to check their documents. Once the convoy got rolling again, the all clear was given and the gunner, Dawson, slid down into the backseat with a sigh.

"Warm out there for this time of year," he said, wiping a sleeve across his brow. "You got any tunes in here, LT, or what?"

"Just the hip-hop on my MP3 player, unless you like Afghan music."

"Hip-hop it is."

She glanced over at Jackson. "You like hip-hop?"

He made a face. "I tolerate it."

"Well, sorry, but I'm fresh out of Dean Martin. Unless you want to sing for us? Because I totally think you should."

Dawson leaned forward. "Dude, you sing?"

"And he's damn fine at it too," Maya put in.

Jackson aimed a bland look at her and shifted in his seat. "Nah, I'm good. Throw on the hip-hop." He turned his head away to stare out the passenger window at the bleak terrain they passed through.

Was the man actually embarrassed by her praise?

With a laugh, Maya plugged in the cable and hit play. Dawson immediately started singing along and tapping out the rhythm on the door frame. She glanced over at Jackson to find him fighting a smile, enduring it all in his quiet manner.

They were over an hour north of Kabul when the CO in the lead vehicle came over the radio. "Suspicious vehicle on the shoulder ahead. We're stopping to check it out."

Jackson instantly reached out to shut off the music while Dawson sprang up from his seat to man the .50 cal. Maya slowed with the others. A half klick away, she spotted it. An old once-white Toyota pickup, left parked at an odd angle on the right side of the highway. Something she would have passed stateside without a second thought, but over here it posed a potential deadly threat.

She halted behind the second Humvee, keeping the engine running while Jackson and Dawson climbed out to provide perimeter protection, just in case the Toyota was an IED and insurgents were waiting nearby to detonate it remotely. Her M4 was within arm's reach and her sidearm was tucked into its holster on her right thigh. She continuously scanned the surroundings, on alert and ready for anything as the minutes passed. Finally the lead team members walked away from the vehicle and the CO came back on the radio with the all clear.

Dawson climbed into the back to resume his position in the turret, while Jackson slid into the passenger seat. As he set his weapon down with another display of those muscles rippling across his back and shoulders, she was struck again by just how big and intensely masculine he was. Lord, the man tempted her.

In the civilian world she'd have handled things between them totally differently. When she was interested in a man, she went after him. They rarely said no. This time she couldn't act on the attraction, and not just because of the risk of being caught and written up for a hundred different broken military regs. She might be willing to work around those obstacles if Jackson seemed like the fling type. But he didn't, and that was all she had to offer. All she could ever offer a man.

He shut the door and settled back against the seat. She didn't look away quite fast enough. He caught her checking him out and gave her a slow smile that did strange things to her insides. Annoyed at herself, she turned her attention back to driving and pulled out behind the truck in front of them. "See anything?"

"Nope."

Neither did she. Nothing but dust and rock as far as the eye could see, right up to the base of the mountains. Releasing some of the tension in her shoulders, she drove on in silence. The lead vehicle started to pick up speed. The needle on the speedometer edged past forty miles per hour.

She'd just reached a hand out to turn the music back on when a huge fireball exploded beneath the lead truck, forty yards in front of them. A wall of flame shot into the air as the vehicle blasted off the ground.

"Fuck!" She instinctively wrenched the wheel hard to the left to avoid driving into the fire.

"Contact, front!" someone called over the radio. Jackson already had his weapon in his hands.

No shit, contact. Her heart slammed once against

her chest wall, then training took over. Swerving away hard with a squeal of tires, she hit the accelerator and raced past the burning Humvee. She screeched to a halt at a safe distance away as some of the others tore past her, their boots thudding against the hot pavement.

Jackson was already reaching for the door handle with a gruff, "Stay here." He grabbed his ruck from the back and took off, missing the angry stare she shot him.

Uh, no, she would *not* stay here.

Dawson was still manning the .50 cal, searching for further threats as Maya exited the vehicle and brought her M4 up. There were no targets, nobody coming at them. Where the hell were those cowardly fuckers? Soldiers had already formed a defensive perimeter around the convoy, all facing outward from the burning Humvee. All except Jackson. He was running right for it.

Heart pounding, Maya fell back toward him, making sure she covered his six. The stench of burning metal filled the air, along with shouts and cries from the wounded. She knew that was why Jackson was racing there. As a PJ he was trained to save lives, even at the expense of his own. That sacrifice wasn't happening, though. Not on her watch.

Maya whirled and ran flat out toward the burning vehicle.

THE HUMVEE WAS lying partially on its right side, completely engulfed in flames. Two men jumped out and ran away from it, but Jackson couldn't tell if anyone was still trapped inside. The intense heat of the fire hit him long before he reached the truck. Thick, toxic black smoke boiled into the air. Combined with the sound and shock wave from the explosion, any insurgent in the area looking for a target definitely had one now. The wreckage was now a beacon, calling militants to them from miles around.

As he ran, men converged on the burning wreck with fire extinguishers. Someone was at the back of the truck, trying to pull a passenger out. Head bent, an arm thrown in front of his face to shield it from the heat, Jackson raced up and grabbed the arms reaching out through the rear passenger window. The man shrieked as Jackson hauled him out and slung him over his shoulder, rushing him a safe distance away.

He kneeled, set him on the ground and took an initial sweep of the damage. A few shrapnel wounds to the legs, some light scorching over his lower body. Nothing life-threatening. The man's eyes were dazed but alert. "Anyone else still in the truck?" Jackson demanded.

"N-no. Just me..." He was shaking all over from the overload of shock and adrenaline.

Jackson shrugged out of his ruck as someone dropped onto one knee beside him. He glanced up into Maya's grave face. "Anyone else?" she asked.

"Negative," he answered. Damn, he'd told her to stay in the truck. There could still be more IEDs planted along this stretch. Why had he ever thought she might follow his command?

He dug some bandages out of his ruck and when he glanced up, Maya had her weapon slung across her back, her hands already clamped down over one of the more serious shrapnel wounds on the man's right thigh. "Gloves are on the top of my kit," he told her. "Put some on."

She didn't argue, waiting only until he began cut-

ting the material away before she did as he said. More
soldiers came over to help, but Jackson waved them all
back. Maya held the pressure dressings in place over
the worst of the wounds while he did a more thorough
exam. The sight of the blood didn't seem to faze her.
"Did you lose consciousness?" he asked the patient,
watching his pupils, gauging his cognitive function.

The man shook his head, telling Jackson his C-spine
was probably okay. The guy wasn't going to walk out
of here though. Jackson glanced over his shoulder to
speak to one of the other soldiers. The nearest hospital
was at least an hour's drive away, and this guy was losing a lot of blood. "Go call for a medevac and get me a
backboard and cervical collar." The soldier rushed off.

His patient was panting through his teeth, shuddering, trying to lift his head to see the damage. "My legs.
How're my legs?"

"Can you still feel them?"

"Fuck yeah, they're on fucking fire."

"Consider that a good thing."

"Lie back," Maya told him firmly. He did. She
looked up at Jackson, her sea-green eyes steady, attentive. "What else can I do?"

"You're doing exactly what I need you to right now,"
he answered, tying off another bandage then pulling
out a sphygmomanometer and stethoscope. "Keep pressure right there so I can get a baseline." The patient's
BP was high, which was to be expected, considering
his elevated heart rate and pain level.

Someone finally came back with the C-collar and
backboard. He secured the soldier's neck carefully in
case there was any spinal trauma, and Maya helped
him roll the man onto the backboard. "Any other ca-

sualties?" he asked the soldier who'd brought him the supplies.

"Two. One minor, the other one..." He glanced down at the wounded man, who was pretty much out of it now, so he kept talking. "Not so much. Another PJ is with him."

"Munro," Jackson told him.

Maya raised her gaze to his. "Cam? Devon's Cam?"

"Yeah, we're partners. Volunteered for the MED-CAP together." Cam was one of the best friends Jackson had ever made. "Any word on the medevac?" he asked the other soldier.

"En route. Another twenty minutes."

That was plenty quick enough, at least for this guy. Jackson leaned over him so the patient could see him better. His eyes were a bit glazed. "You're good to go to the hospital. We're just waiting for the helo. Want some meds for the pain while we wait?"

He gritted his teeth and shifted restlessly against the pain. "How long?" he managed.

"Twenty minutes."

He squeezed his eyes shut. "Shit, yeah. Gimme something."

"You allergic to any meds?"

"Penicillin."

Jackson administered a syrette of fentanyl. The medication took effect in seconds. With a sigh, the patient relaxed slightly, his breathing slowing.

Then suddenly he reached up to grasp Jackson's forearm. His eyes were wide, anxious. "My legs. Tell me the truth, man. Am I gonna keep my legs?"

"Your legs are gonna be fine once they heal up," Jackson assured him.

With a nod of relief, the man closed his eyes and rested quietly, enduring the pain as best he could. Jackson glanced up, wondering where Maya had gone to, and didn't have to look far. She stood just a few yards away, facing away from him. She'd stripped off the gloves, but her hands were stained with blood as she held her weapon up and at the ready. She was in profile to him, the brim of her helmet shadowing her face. Both her hands and her posture were rock steady, despite everything. Ready for action if anything happened.

"Want to clean your hands?" he called out.

She didn't glance his way, and her tense posture didn't change. "Later. After the helo gets here."

Jackson climbed to his feet. Leaving another soldier to watch his patient, he hefted his ruck and made his way to where Cam worked on the other two. Maya followed, maintaining that same distance and vigilance. Protecting him? Shit, no. He could take care of himself. If anything, *he* should be guarding *her*. "You don't need to do that. Go on back to the truck and clean up."

She shook her head, not bothering to look at him. "You can't treat patients and watch your back at the same time. Until we get the all clear, I'm not taking any chances."

With his safety. She didn't say it, but she didn't have to. His shook his head in exasperation. Though she was half his size, she would stay and guard him, with her life if necessary. The woman was turning him inside out, but her stubbornness rankled him. While he understood and respected her training and ability, he didn't want her putting herself in danger on his behalf.

The way he saw it, it was his duty to protect her, not the other way around.

Now wasn't the time for that fight. Tearing his attention away from her, he strode over and squatted beside Cam. "Need a hand?" One of the patients had an ugly head wound and the other was sitting up talking with his buddies.

Looking up from where he was still bandaging the head wound, Cam's blue eyes met his. "No, I'm good. Where the hell are those assholes hiding? A hole in the ground?"

"Have to be. Nowhere else to hide around here." Patting his friend's shoulder once, Jackson went back to check on his patient, who was resting as comfortably as could be expected in a situation like this. Maya shadowed him, staying close, weapon up and safety off. Did her stubborn insistence about guarding him mean anything other than her simply performing her duty? If he was honest, he wanted it to mean more.

Finally the throb of rotors sounded in the distance. A Black Hawk appeared in the clear blue sky, the red cross on a white background on the door becoming visible as it neared. It touched down close by and a crew rushed out. Squinting against the dust kicked up by the rotor wash, Jackson helped carry his patient to the helo. He moved back and turned to collect his gear to find Maya standing next to it. She was looking at him this time, and the admiration he saw in her eyes made his heart swell.

Crossing to her, he stopped beside his ruck and pulled out some damp towelettes. "Here."

She safetied and slung her weapon then took them

from him to wipe up. "Thanks," she said softly, seeming almost shy as she avoided his gaze.

"You're welcome." He wanted to touch her. Wrap his arms around her and hold her close, just for a minute. They could easily have been hit by the blast. If the IED had detonated a second later, it would have been their Humvee blown to hell. Maya had held it together, stayed tight despite the scare and adrenaline rush, the sight and smell of the blood. Not once had she faltered in her duty.

A fierce wave of pride and protectiveness rose inside him. She was brave and strong and professional. He knew in his gut that if the bullets had started flying, she would've stayed and defended him, putting herself between him and whatever the insurgents who'd remotely detonated that IED could throw at them.

He'd never met a woman like her. She deserved a man who would appreciate all that she was, cherish the softness locked away beneath the hard exterior. Jackson did. Something had forged her into this steely soldier. He wanted to know what it was.

Her hands shook ever so slightly as she wiped at her forearms, telling him she wasn't as unaffected as she wanted everyone to think. Without a word, Jackson gently took the wipes from her and held her hands in his. Her eyes flashed up to his, surprise in their depths. Her skin was cold. But there was heated awareness in her gaze too. A kind of buried longing he would love the chance to satisfy.

Damn, he wanted her. In a primal and possessive way he'd never experienced before.

He gently washed away the remaining traces of blood, mindful of the swollen knuckles on her right hand. He stroked his thumb across them lightly, wishing he could heal her with his touch, that he could fight her battles so she wouldn't have to. Standing this close to her, touching her soft skin and drinking in the unique features that haunted his dreams, he only craved her more. And suddenly he couldn't hold back the incautious words that flew out of his mouth.

"If we were alone right now, I'd show you just how much I want you."

Her expressive eyes widened a fraction. The flare of shock morphed into molten heat in the space of a heartbeat. And she didn't pull away. Didn't break eye contact. One dark brow rose in challenge, all that attitude confronting him full force. "Is that right?"

Oh, hell yeah, that was right. All fucking night long. Until she couldn't breathe without wanting him against her, inside her. "Yes, ma'am."

Her lips quirked, her bold gaze holding his. Direct. Unflinching. Full of confidence and interest. "Well, I'll definitely keep that offer in mind."

He went rock hard at the verbal taunt. Before he could reply, one of the other soldiers called out to them. "Let's saddle up. Plans have changed—we're going to Kandahar."

FOUR

THOUGH IT HAD taken them the rest of the day to reach Kandahar, at least they'd made it there without further incident. And while the prolonged trip had seemed like a drag at first, now Maya was thankful they'd come to a large base like this, rather than the FOB they were originally headed for. The anonymity it afforded her made it that much easier to carry out her plan.

She'd almost been blown up today, and Jackson with her. Tonight she was going to ease the ache of arousal she'd been suffering with for so long. Because if Jackson thought he could say blatantly sexual things to her and then walk away without following through, he was sorely mistaken. She was about to rock his world.

She passed several groups of Spec Ops guys sitting on camp chairs around bonfires as she strode to the other side of the compound. One was strumming a guitar while the others chatted. They watched her with curiosity but didn't comment, and she kept walking like she owned the place. This was a secure area, but she'd already gotten past the guards easily enough, and without stooping to using her blue beret as cover. She knew people who had abused their authority as Security Forces personnel to manipulate certain situations and it disgusted her. The trick to avoiding questions was acting like she had every right to be here. From her earlier recon she knew her quarry lay on the quiet outskirts of the compound: second tent from the end of the third row.

It was dark now, the faded illumination from the overhead lights throwing faint shadows as she approached the canvas tent with her heart beating fast. Her treads were quiet on the two wooden steps leading up to the closed flaps. Easing one aside, she peered in. Her eyes adjusted to the sudden darkness quickly, confirming what she'd already suspected. Jackson was asleep in his bunk, and his tentmate Cam was nowhere to be seen. If she'd done her recon properly, she figured she had at least a half hour until he showed up. Plenty of time to accomplish what she had in mind.

Stepping inside, she let the flap close behind her and tiptoed over to the bunk against the far wall, heart pounding in anticipation. Jackson's quiet, steady breathing filled the otherwise silent tent. Biting her lip to hold back a chuckle, Maya crossed to his bunk and stopped beside it. He was on his side facing her, those incredibly thick lashes resting on his cheeks. When he woke up, he was in for one hell of a surprise.

Without giving herself time to think about it, she carefully crawled onto the inflatable mattress.

The moment it shifted, he woke. His eyes snapped open and he reared onto his elbows. Frozen, he blinked up at her, while she prowled up his supine body and tried not to laugh at the look of startled incomprehension on his face.

"Hi," she whispered, straddling his hips and leaning forward to cage him in with her hands on either side of his head. There was no way he could miss the parallel between her position and what he'd done to her that day in the hospital exam room.

"What are you doing here?" he blurted in a sleep-husky whisper.

"Came to tuck you in."

He glanced over to the other bunk as though he was worried they had an audience. "Cam is—"

"Busy for the next little while," she answered, adoring his sleepy befuddlement. She leaned down so her lips were an inch from his, until his breath washed over her face gently. It was scented with peppermint this time rather than wintergreen. Toothpaste? "Unless you didn't mean it earlier when you said you'd show me how much you wanted me if we were alone."

He huffed out a rough laugh. "Hell yes, I want you—"

That was all she needed to hear. Leaning down to close that tiny gap between them, a thrill shot through her as she put her mouth on his. Slowly. Softly. So she could feel the exquisite give of his lips beneath hers. They were warm, supple. And they parted ever so slightly under hers in silent invitation for her to taste him.

Then Jackson's hands came up to cradle her face, taking her off guard for a second. A quiet groan escaped him as he raised his head from the pillow to fuse their mouths together. Her lower belly fluttered in response. She loved the way his hands cradled her face, the gesture hungry and possessive.

Maya settled in closer, adding more pressure and a hint of tongue as she explored his response, his flavor. He must have showered before turning in because the man smelled deliciously of soap and shampoo. She made a low sound of appreciation in her throat and deepened the kiss, caressing and sucking at his tongue. She couldn't wait to find out if he was that delicious all over.

One of his hands moved from her face to slide into her hair and cup the back of her head, holding her close. Satisfied at his reaction and enjoying herself immensely, Maya nibbled at the corner of his mouth and down his strong jaw to his throat. When he shifted and tried to turn them over, she resisted.

"No," she whispered against his skin. "Like this."

For a moment she thought he'd argue, then he exhaled and relaxed beneath her. Jackson tilted his head back to give her more access and tightened his fingers in her hair, his other hand reaching up to press between her shoulder blades. He was clearly fighting the need to take over, so the fact that he was *allowing* her to take the reins made it hot as hell. For all his laid-back nature, she sensed he didn't give up control easily.

Her breasts made contact with the hard muscles of his chest. Even with their T-shirts dulling the sensation, a shiver sped through her. Her nipples tightened to hard points against her sports bra. Every brush sent a bolt of pleasure straight to the empty ache blooming between her thighs.

Growing bolder, needing some pressure there to relieve the empty sensation, Maya sat up to peel her shirt over her head and lowered her weight onto the unmistakable ridge of his erection beneath the blanket. Jackson sucked in his breath and slid the hand on her spine down to the small of her back, his warm palm burning her naked skin. With a naughty little smile she pulled off her bra and tossed it aside, then bent to shimmy out of her pants and underwear before he could catch more than a glimpse of her. With her face nuzzling the side of his neck, she breathed him in. "Hmmmm," she murmured, licking her way down his throat.

Like he was too shocked to move, Jackson froze in place, one hand in her hair and the other just above the cleft in her buttocks while she teased his skin with tongue and teeth. "Jesus, Maya," he whispered. "You're naked."

"Mmm-hmm," she agreed. "Now it's your turn."

He didn't protest when she sat up suddenly and grasped the hem of his T-shirt, but his hungry gaze immediately zeroed in on her bare breasts poised just above his head, her dog tags nestled in the valley between them. She didn't miss the way his throat bobbed as he swallowed. She smiled. "Lift up," she ordered quietly.

Jackson immediately raised his upper body off the bed, allowing her to peel the cotton up his chest to expose the muscular planes of his torso to her avid gaze. Oh, he was gorgeous. With a hum of appreciation, she bent and nuzzled the pad of his pecs, pausing only to push his dog tags away and press a kiss over his thudding heart before she leaned down and settled the soft weight of her breasts against his hot skin. Tiny shocks of pleasure radiated through her body at the contact.

He shifted restlessly beneath her, lifting into her body. "Your hair," he murmured, tugging at the elastic holding her bun in place. "Take it down."

Amused by the command, she did as he said, adding a little shake of her head so the cool weight of her hair tumbled around her shoulders. Jackson's stare was so hot it all but singed her naked skin. A surge of triumph swept through her. His hands trailed reverently through her hair, his fingers tangling gently in the waves, following their length to where they ended against the rise of her breasts. Maya bit back a gasp as her nipples hardened even further, eagerly awaiting the touch of his hands, his mouth.

She shook herself out of her sensual haze. This was about making him lose control, not the other way around. She would never let her guard down that far with a man.

Oblivious to her thoughts, Jackson let his hands drift down to cup her breasts. Judging by the look on his face, he didn't mind that they were small. But when he leaned up and forward, making all those defined muscles on his torso stand out in sharp relief, and tilted his head like he intended to taste her, she stopped him with a solid hand on the center of his chest. She pressed back firmly. "Lie down."

His lust-glazed eyes flashed up to hers and held, assessing her for a long moment before he at last relaxed and slowly complied. When he was settled, once again sprawled out on his back for her enjoyment, Maya rewarded him with a string of nibbling kisses across the broad expanse of his chest. She rubbed her face against the thin line of dark hair in the center of his chest, pausing to leisurely lick at a tightly beaded nipple. Jackson hissed in a breath and threaded his fingers into her hair, flexing them against her scalp. The feel of his hands there, holding her close and urging her on, was sexy as hell. Using teeth and tongue, she continued to tease him, nipping her way down the shallow valley that delineated his abs until she reached the hem of his boxers. His fingers contracted against her scalp.

"Mmm." She set her hand over the thick ridge of his cock, pleased at the way his eager flesh flexed against her hold. With a soft sound of approval, she licked the smooth skin just above his boxers and squeezed the solid length of him, while her other hand slid into the waistband and tugged downward.

Jackson lifted his hips to help her, hands still wound in her hair as she drew the boxers off and grasped him with both hands. His cock was hot and hard, kicking in her grip.

"Maya—" His voice cut off abruptly as her cheek brushed against the thick length of him. She wanted to taste him so badly. Drive him out of his mind with pleasure. A long, low groan tore from his chest when her tongue stole out to lap at him. The salty tang of him exploded on her tongue, increasing the insistent throb between her own legs. Hungry for more, she parted her lips and took the swollen head into her mouth, wrapping her tongue around that sensitive spot beneath the ridge.

"Oh, Jesus, Maya..." His back arched, head rolling back in ecstasy.

Oh yeah, just like that. Exactly like that. His husky plea, her name on his lips, sent a shiver through her.

His hands bunched in her hair, a little less gently now that his control was fraying, his fingers rubbing against her scalp in a drugging caress that made her eyes close in enjoyment. The muscles in his belly were rigid and his breathing was erratic. She sucked him slowly and firmly, working him with her mouth, wanting to make him writhe. And even that wasn't enough. She wanted to hear him moan in release and know she'd pushed him past any resistance into pure need. But she wanted him inside her when she did.

Without releasing him, she reached beside her for her pants beside the bunk. A few fumbling seconds later she had the condom. Giving him one last luxurious suck that made him hiss out a breath, Maya sat up to tear the packet open. Jackson let go of her hair and wrapped his hands around her waist instead. He licked his lips, breathing unsteadily as she smoothed the condom down him and quickly straddled him. Before he could do anything more than grasp her hips, she stood his erection up with one hand and eased down on his length, taking him in. He was hot and thick, the delicious stretching sensation making her clit throb. She ignored it, focused solely on her objective. Watching his face, she sank down until he was fully embedded inside her.

His nostrils flared, eyes glittering with raw hunger as he stared up at her. He reached up to touch her breasts, but she blocked him. With a frustrated sound he gripped her waist again, but the sound dissolved into a groan as she began to ride him. "Baby, just..." Jackson reared up, both hands splaying over her back to hold her close as his mouth latched on to one of her sensitive nipples. He did it with such absorbed hunger that she let him for a moment.

No man had ever touched her the way he did, with such care for her pleasure. For just a second, her control wavered under the temptation to give in to the warm pull of his mouth, his caressing tongue. It felt too good. Though she ached for more, she pushed at his shoulders and tried to lean away. Jackson held her tight, keeping his mouth right where it was.

Sensation swelled, sending a trail of fire from her nipple to her pulsing core. His mouth was hot, his tongue like warm velvet against her sensitive flesh. A tiny gasp escaped her as the pleasure bloomed hotter. She rocked faster, using her hands on his chest for leverage as she pushed him toward the peak. He sucked at her with an erotic greed that made her heart squeeze.

Unable to stop herself, she clasped the back of his head with one hand and held him close for just a little longer, reveling in sensation. It would have been so easy to forget herself, lose herself in the moment and forget her purpose here. Her body wanted the release he offered.

No.

With effort, she drew away from his mouth and shoved at his shoulders until he once again lay on his back beneath her. His dark eyes glittered with frustration, those strong hands wrapped around her pumping hips, his fingers digging deep. Having the sheer leashed power of him beneath her and at her mercy made it even better. She picked up speed and his head rolled back on the pillow, eyes squeezed shut, lips parting in ecstasy.

Two seconds later, footsteps sounded outside the tent. Jackson went rigid, his fingers biting into her hips to hold her still. A boot hit the first stair outside the tent. Maya paused, turning her head toward the tent flap. She had every intention of finishing what she'd started, and let Jackson know it by squeezing him with her inner muscles.

"Cam, hold up," Jackson called out, his voice strained with need and arousal.

"Huh?"

"Hold up," he repeated roughly, staring defiantly up at Maya the whole time.

"Uh, okay..." Cam's other foot hit the top step, then the stair creaked but no further sound came. Was he sitting there, waiting for the okay to come in? She smothered a laugh.

Meeting Jackson's annoyed gaze, Maya again tightened around his captive flesh, wanting to push him beyond the end of his control. More than anything she wanted to see him let go, surrender to the need she sensed burning in him. He felt so good inside her. Too good. It made her yearn to give in to sensation, find out if he could make her climax. Instead she ignored the urge and circled her hips. "Gonna come for me?" she whispered, her voice a wisp of sound in the stillness.

The look in his eyes changed instantly. The glittering hunger retreated behind a wall of cold determination. Before she could even guess what that meant, he flipped them and she suddenly found herself beneath that powerful body, at his mercy instead.

BREATHING HARD, MUSCLES bunched in an agony of need, Jackson stared down into the shocked depths of Maya's eyes. Even in the dimness he clearly saw the flicker of unease as she realized she was no longer in control. In those first few seconds he watched the knowledge sink in that he was stronger and could force a response out of her if he chose. The primal part of him wanted to. She was as turned on as him; he could feel it in the slickness between her thighs and hear it in the little gasps of pleasure she tried to hold back. What the hell was this? A sexual power trip? Because he didn't appreciate being on the receiving end of it. And he hated it more that he couldn't stop his physical reaction to her.

As much as he fought the pounding hunger, his body wouldn't allow him to stop. Not now. He was too close, too on edge and he'd wanted Maya for months. He'd be a goddamn idiot to pull out now, and he knew she'd disappear once he did.

That didn't mean he was ready to go down without a fight first. If she was hell-bent on unraveling him completely, then he was taking her there with him.

Her hands were flattened on his shoulders as though to push him away. The wary edge in her expression ate at him. The aroused glitter in her eyes was now locked behind a blank wall. If she hadn't been so wet, if penetrating her sultry flesh hadn't been so easy and he hadn't caught those telltale sounds of pleasure earlier, he'd have been convinced she wasn't even turned on. He shifted his weight and she sucked in a breath, her body going rigid as though she was about to fight him. As if she was afraid of feeling the pleasure. Screw that.

Uh-uh, sweetheart. You wanted this, you're getting it. Every last fucking inch of me. Until she cried out his name and came around his cock, whether Cam got an earful outside or not.

Braced on his forearms, watching her eyes, he pulled back slightly then pushed forward. Her gasp of startled pleasure was the sweetest music to his ears. But before he could do it again, she'd wrapped those toned legs around his waist and clamped her hands on to his back, holding tight as she swiveled her hips in a slow circle calibrated to make him lose his freaking mind.

Jackson bowed his head and fought to breathe. Christ, she fought dirty. And she was fucking strong for her size. He started to pull back; she followed, gripping him even tighter. Jackson bit back a curse. No matter how he tried to twist away, she wouldn't let go. There was no way he could dislodge her without truly hurting her and he'd rather die first. He stilled, breathing roughly, so frustrated he wanted to scream.

Why? Why was she doing this? He shook his head once, a tight movement of denial, of defiance. She stared up at him, just as implacable. A low growl of warning rumbled up from his chest. He was a heartbeat away from losing it and pounding into her until he exploded. And then she'd not only have won whatever fucked-up contest this was, he'd have lost his only chance with her. Because he knew in his gut that once this was over, she'd walk away for good.

He wasn't letting that happen.

As though his futile efforts at resistance amused her, Maya laughed softly against his ear and nipped the lobe, sending sparks of sensation tearing across his skin. "Just let go," she whispered, a seductive, beguiling caress over his pleasure-drenched senses. Her scent enveloped him, tangerine and vanilla and warm, aroused woman. She drew him closer, her wicked tongue playing at his ear while those erotic hip circles shredded what was left of his control.

"Wait—"

"Uh-uh," she breathed, and swiveled her hips once more in a devastating arc.

Fuck. *Fuck.* It was too good. He couldn't stop it.

With a muffled curse, Jackson fisted one hand in her hair and drove deep. He barely heard her quiet gasp as he plunged into her body, the pleasure spiraling out of control. Burying his face in the curve of her neck, lost in the heady fragrance of her scent, he clenched his jaw to keep from shouting out as his orgasm slammed into him. Wave after wave coursed through him until it felt like he was being wrung inside out.

He shuddered against her, every muscle locked and straining until the pleasure finally began to ebb. Sucking in precious oxygen, Jackson couldn't hold back the low groan that escaped as he let his weight settle atop her and kept his face against the perfumed skin of her neck.

Maya surprised him by making a quiet humming sound and then kissing the side of his jaw, her hands smoothing gently across his slick shoulders as though she savored the closeness. And goddammit, but that unexpected show of tenderness from her almost undid him. Lying naked and tangled in the cradle of her arms was so much sweeter than the release she'd just given him because he knew she rarely showed this tender side of her. He cuddled even closer, until his body touched every inch of her skin it could, and nuzzled the soft skin just below her ear. His only satisfaction was the goose bumps that broke out beneath his lips.

She stiffened, her fingers stilling on his back for an instant. Then she sighed and relaxed once more, running her hands up his shoulders and neck to thread into his hair. Her fingers stroked through it gently, and it seemed like she was enjoying petting him. Jackson all but purred his satisfaction.

Her quiet chuckle gusted against his temple. "*Dios*, and on top of everything else you're a cuddler too?"

He didn't know what to make of the wonder in her tone so he nodded. "You're not?" She felt pretty damn cuddly to him right now. He never wanted to move again. Why hadn't she let him please her?

"No. But you do tempt a girl." There was a wistful note in her voice.

Dammit, why? Why would she deliberately deny herself the pleasure and affection he was more than willing to give her? Couldn't she tell he was dying to? It didn't make any sense. Frowning, he lifted his head and met her eyes. "So? What about you?" For emphasis, he rocked gently against her where they were still joined. She'd been right there with him before he'd rolled her beneath him. Had the position freaked her out? She had to want to come. Hell, *he* wanted to make her come. Needed to.

She put a hand on his shoulder to push him up. "I'll take a rain check."

What the fuck? She was seriously going to walk away from the orgasm he was freely offering? The rain check comment was bullshit. They both knew the moment she walked out of this tent she'd be gone forever. "Hey, what—"

"I gotta go." She pushed at him again, avoiding his gaze and making his gut sink. "Cam's outside."

"Cam can wait," he said tightly.

She pushed harder, her jaw set. "Let me up."

Everything in him warned not to let her go.

Though moving was the last thing he wanted to do, he reluctantly eased off her and withdrew, immediately missing the warmth of her body. She climbed out of bed without another word and gathered her clothes.

Staring at the gorgeous silhouette of her body, Jackson tried to think of what to say or do but came up blank. He had no fucking idea what was going on in her head. He was sure he'd seen the heated arousal in her eyes, heard it in those breathless little gasps when he'd had her nipple in his mouth and flipped her beneath him to drive into her. She'd been hell-bent on holding back. Had someone hurt her in the past? Abused her, maybe? The idea filled him with anguish. His gut said pushing her right now would only distance her further, when he wanted the exact opposite.

Biting back more protests that he already knew would be futile, he flopped down on to his back and drew the covers over himself as she dressed. It was hard to not say anything. The tense silence was like sandpaper on his skin. He caught only flashes of that smooth golden-toned skin as she hurriedly dressed and laced her boots. Lying alone in the rumpled blankets with the evidence of her unfulfilled arousal drying on the condom and his inner thighs, he felt cold. He felt...used.

She didn't look at him until she was securing her hair into a bun at the back of her neck. Her closed expression gave him no clue as to what she was thinking or feeling. "See you."

Pissed off and at a loss about what to do about it, all he could say was, "Yeah."

Without another word or even a backward glance, Maya strode to the tent flaps and stepped through with a calm, "Hey."

A second later Cam stepped inside, rubbernecking Maya's retreating figure. Jackson blew out a long breath, and his buddy turned around to gape at him with a stunned look on his face. "So, I didn't see anything," he blurted, hands raised in self-defense.

Jackson was too tired and annoyed to manage a laugh. "Nope."

Cam crossed to his bunk and sat down, his boots landing with a thud as he tossed them onto the wooden floor. A moment later the covers rustled, and then all was still. "Night." Jackson could hear the grin in the bastard's voice.

"Night," he grunted, and scrubbed a hand over his face. What the fuck had just happened? Why had Maya sought him out—and here in the so-called "secure" confines of the Spec Ops area—just to fuck him and get him off without getting anything out of it in return? Except power or control, or whatever the hell she'd been after. For the first time that he could remember, he was completely out of his depth with a woman. Wasn't that a kick in the ass?

Though he'd just had the best orgasm of his life, he'd never felt less satisfied.

FIVE

Climbing down from the cab of the old Toyota pickup, Khalid took a cardboard box from the front seat and carried it to the rear of their camp. His men were gathered around a small fire, cooking their evening meal when he approached.

Mohammed glanced up, a wide smile breaking over his face when he saw what Khalid carried. "You have them?"

Khalid nodded and surveyed his troops. Mostly young men in their late teens and early twenties. There had been more in the fall, but the majority of the older ones had been sacrificed in the previous operation to eliminate Nasrallah. Those remaining were motivated, fair marksmen and, more importantly, completely loyal to him.

A cool wind picked up, ruffling his hair and making the flames crackle and leap within their stone pit. "I have received word from Rahim's people that tomorrow's operation is a definite go. Are you all ready?"

A chorus of excited voices answered him in the affirmative.

He held up a hand for silence. "We leave an hour before dawn, in the groups I've divided you into. Mohammed will lead the last group to ensure our escape route is clear." Across the fire, the boy's eyes shone with pride at being given command of his own group. "We have only one chance to execute this properly. You all know what is expected of you—what I expect from you as men and soldiers. Prepare yourselves accordingly with prayer."

He paused to let his gaze carry over the circle of men, the rise of excitement warm in his veins. "And now for those of you who will accompany me into the village, something to help you on our journey to rid our land of the unbelievers." He opened the box flap and reached inside for the item on top. Smiling, he held up the first of five camouflage-patterned jackets of the Afghan National Army for everyone to see.

ABOVE THE POWERFUL pulse of the Black Hawk's rotors, Jackson listened to Cam and his other fellow passengers bullshit over their headsets as the helo flared above their LZ and hovered a moment before touching down. The pilots shut down the engines, and everyone took off their headsets and collected their gear in preparation to disembark. Just as well, since he didn't much feel like talking to anyone anyhow.

Shouldering his heavy ruck and a duffel he'd stuffed full of medical gear, he hopped out of the helo and headed across the empty expanse of dun-colored ground to where the SF guys had already set up shop at the village's perimeter. Doing a MEDCAP with an A-team helped on several levels, especially since they were all linguists and could speak Pashto. A real bonus out here, where none of the villagers spoke any English and what Pashto Jackson knew wouldn't fill a coffee cup. Two more H-60s landed behind the bird he'd just exited, remaining on the ground only long enough for their passengers to disembark before powering up and lifting off again.

As he neared the SF guys, he noticed Maya off to the right with some other Security Forces personnel, likely setting up last-minute security details for the upcoming press promo op for an unnamed senior U.S. official. Nothing better to show the voters back home how much the current party in power back stateside loved to help the Afghan locals. At least this setup saved him from an awkward episode with Maya. They both had jobs to do here, and there was no doubt in his mind Maya would let nothing come between her and her duty.

It still shocked the shit out of him that she'd sought him out last night. He'd never encountered a woman so sexually aggressive, let alone have one be so detached from her own pleasure during sex. It not only bothered him, it made him want a repeat so he could make sure this time ended differently for her. Things felt too unfinished between them.

Cam caught up with him, carrying his own load of gear. A group of villagers had already assembled near the SF troops. Mostly women and children waited, standing a short distance behind the village elders to await permission to come forward.

"You got enough stuff for the kids if I run out?" Cam asked.

"Should have. Let me know if you need it."

The SF Team Sergeant directed them to the two small tents set up at the eastern end of the village. Maya was farther down, directing a few of her soldiers into place. Even if her rank hadn't been displayed on her uniform, there was no doubt as to who was in charge there. The woman wore her authority like a Kevlar cloak.

"You know anything about her background?" he asked Cam, still watching her.

Cam followed his gaze and answered. "Some. Dev told me she didn't get to know her real well at Bagram, but apparently she was raised by her grandmother in L.A. Tough neighborhood, lots of drugs, gangbangers. She must have learned to kick ass early on to make it out of there without getting sucked into that kind of lifestyle."

"Makes sense."

Cam shot him a sideways glance. "Why do you ask?"

"No reason." It was just that he couldn't fucking figure her out. He'd always prided himself on being able to understand a woman and how her mind worked. God knew his mother and sisters had tried their best to get him to understand them while they'd raised him. What happened with Maya last night had left a bitter aftertaste in his mouth. He wanted to be the one to make her let go of all that hard-won control, watch her melt in his arms when he got her underneath him next time. And there *would* be a next time. He'd make sure of that.

"She's stumped you, huh?"

Cam knew him too well. He didn't bother denying it. "I think maybe, yeah."

"Well, that's one for the history books. I can't wait to tell Went." His eyes sparkled at the prospect.

"Yeah, I'll bet." And once Ryan heard about that, there'd be no end to the ribbing he'd take. The "woman whisperer" had finally met his match and lost? It'd be all over the Bagram Spec Ops compound by morning.

"I'd tell you to send her flowers, but she doesn't seem the type," Cam continued with a wry grin.

Jackson wasn't so sure about that. Back in November, when he'd hand-delivered a bouquet of wildflowers on Ryan's behalf so Maya could give them to Ace, she'd seemed stunned by the gesture. No, he was pretty sure that flowers and good old-fashioned courting might be exactly the way to go with her, even if she'd never admit to wanting it.

"Maybe a fancy knife or a tactical flashlight might be more her style," Cam suggested with another grin.

Jackson's lips curved at the irony in his friend's tone. "I was thinking maybe I should write her a song." Though he said it half-jokingly, part of him was serious.

Cam must have known it, because his eyebrows shot up. "Yeah? Wow, okay then. Damn, you're pretty into her, huh?"

He nodded, since there was no harm in confiding in Cam. After last night, Jackson guessed Maya figured things were over between them. For him they weren't. Not by a long shot. He knew he could find his way underneath all that attitude and bluster if he looked for the answer carefully enough. With her, patience was the key. Only he didn't know how much patience he had left when it came to her.

"Which tent you want?" Cam asked as they approached the hastily set up medical area.

"Doesn't matter."

"You take the far one, then. It'll give you the nicest view." His blue eyes danced with laughter.

Grinning, Jackson passed him and carried on to the far tent, closest to where Maya was positioned. She didn't glance his way, but he knew she'd seen him. He ducked under the low tent flap and stepped inside. Someone had set up a small table and cot with a pillow and blankets on it. Setting his gear down, he got to work unpacking what he needed—BP kit, syringes, bandages and swabs, some OTC meds and a few mild narcotic analgesics. The analgesics were sort of ironic, since he was currently sitting in the middle of the opium poppy capital of the world. The villagers he was about to treat probably had enough opium to keep them high and pain-free for several lifetimes.

Just another fucked-up thing about this war.

One of the SF sergeants came into the tent, a short, stocky guy with a thick ginger beard. "You all set up?"

"Ready to rock."

"Okay, the deal is for me to stay and help translate. If for any reason I need to step out, you'll be on your own. You know any Pashto?"

"Pretty much nil."

"I'll stick around as long as I can then." He left and returned a few minutes later with one of the village elders, a man in his seventies if Jackson had to guess, dressed in traditional garb of the flat-topped hat, loose shirt and pants with a vest. The soldier acted as translator as the elder thanked Jackson and they exchanged polite courtesies. After he exited the tent, Jackson's first patient was brought in. A young girl around four, the same age as his youngest nephew back home in San Antonio. The girl's mother wore a veil that covered everything but her eyes, and from the lack of wrinkles around them, Jackson guessed she had to still be in her late teens.

Staying silent, watching him and the SF soldier

warily, she sat on the cot and placed her daughter in her lap. The girl clung to her, staring at Jackson with wide, dark eyes.

Jackson smiled and dropped to his haunches in front of the little girl. "Hey, sweetheart. You got a sore hand?" The cut running the length of the side of it looked sore and, from the discoloration, infected. He asked a few questions, which the other soldier translated for him. All he picked out was the word *Taliban*, and it was enough to make his lips thin in disgust. He put it all together even before the translation came.

"She says it happened a few weeks ago when some Taliban fighters came through. The little girl got too close to one of them, and the asshole slashed her with his knife."

Tamping down his sudden surge of anger, Jackson held his hand out toward the child. "Can I see it?" It took a while for the girl to let him take a good look, and with the back and forth translation it was a few minutes longer before Jackson could actually start cleaning the wound. It was deep and definitely needed stitches. It surprised him the girl wasn't running a fever, though the mother reported there had been one for a few days after the injury.

Irrigating the wound and cleaning it out didn't go quite as smoothly, but once Jackson got the local freezing injected, the girl stopped squalling and watched in amazement as he sutured the gash closed and bandaged up her hand with a sterile dressing. After a shot of antibiotic just to be safe, the girl and her mother left.

He saw a dozen or so patients after that, some having walked miles from other nearby villages when they'd heard about the opportunity to get free medical care. Or maybe just to see the big, bad American soldiers up close. Winning hearts and minds from the locals wasn't easy this late in the war, though he hoped to change some minds among the villagers today. He treated a barrage of minor cuts and scrapes, handed out vitamins and antihistamines, put an old man's arm in a sling to take the strain off his damaged rotator cuff.

He was alone in the tent reorganizing his supplies when urgent, raised voices came from outside. Jackson glanced up at the sound of shuffling feet coming closer, and the SF soldier stuck his head in.

"Got a sick little guy here for you. He's in pretty bad shape."

Jackson stood, grabbing a fresh pair of gloves from his pocket. "Bring him in."

An old man entered the tent, carrying a boy around seven or eight. The boy was listless and pale, lying in the man's arms like a limp doll.

"Put him down," Jackson instructed, helping settle the boy on the cot. His face was gray but for the bright red fever spots on his smooth cheeks. "How long has he been sick?"

The soldier translated. "Four days. He had severe stomach pain and he's been vomiting a lot. Then this morning, when the family woke up, he was like this."

Already putting the symptoms together, Jackson grabbed a tongue depressor and his scope. The boy stared up at him with dark, fever-glazed eyes. After a bit of coaxing, Jackson managed to get him to open his mouth. His tongue had a grayish tint and there was a film on it. Not good.

When he palpated the boy's abdomen, it was rigid, but he didn't flinch or give any indication that it hurt.

Jackson was certain he already knew what the problem was. Finding the point halfway between the boy's right hip bone and his belly button, he pressed his fingers deep, watching for any signs of pain. The boy shifted but remained quiet. Then, with a silent apology, Jackson yanked his hand away.

The boy blanched and came up off the cot with a shocked gasp, grimacing as a strangled sound of pain came from his throat. One hand automatically came up to shield the spot Jackson had just touched, and his breathing was fast and choppy.

All dead giveaways confirming what he'd feared.

Jackson tossed his stethoscope aside and strode for the flap. "Don't let him move," he said tersely to the SF sergeant.

Exiting the tent, he immediately looked for Maya and found her a hundred yards or so away, manning her post and supervising her airmen. "Lieutenant," he called.

She glanced over and raised her brows in question.

"Got a situation here."

She strode over fast, giving him a terse jerk of her stubborn chin when she neared. "What's up?"

"I've got a young boy in there with a ruptured appendix. Peritonitis has already set in and he needs immediate surgery."

Her alert gaze sharpened even more on his face, and there was no trace of awkwardness from what had passed between them last night. "What do you need?"

He freaking loved that she offered assistance without hesitation or questioning him. And he was grateful, because the kid needed them to act *now*. "I need an emergency medevac to get him to a base hospital ASAP, or he's not going to make it."

THE MOMENT HE said it, Maya immediately got on her radio to request an emergency medevac. After giving her the nine line to pass on to the dispatcher, Jackson rushed back into the tent to tend his young patient. His word was good enough for her. If Jackson said it was urgent they get the boy to a hospital, then it was. End of story.

Once she got confirmation and the ETA for the helo from Bagram, Maya strode quickly over to Jackson's tent. The SF sergeant at the entrance nodded to her and let her pass without a word. She stepped inside just in time to see Jackson handing a fluffy brown teddy bear to the sick little boy. The huge duffel in the corner had several other stuffed toys poking out of it along with the medical equipment he'd brought.

"Helo's on its way," she told him. "Should be here within a half hour."

Jackson met her gaze. "Can they move that up any faster?"

She shook her head. "I made it clear the situation was urgent." She spared a glance at the boy, then the old man with him. "That his grandfather?"

"Yes. He'll go to the hospital with him." He grabbed a bag of fluid and something else from his supplies. An IV kit. "Can you hold the bag for me once I get it hooked up?"

"Sure." She slung her rifle and took the fluids, hovering close by. "Need any help with that?"

"Maybe. His BP's so low, I'm not sure I'll be able to find a vein open enough to get this IV in."

The grandfather stood at the head of the cot and watched, his face impassive, though there was no doubt he was anxious and wasn't leaving the boy's side.

It took Jackson three tries to get the needle into the boy's vein. The child barely flinched at all the pokes, a sign of just how ill he was. Jackson got the IV locked in place and hooked the tube from the bag into the line. "Okay, we're good to go." He opened the valve and set the drip running, one hand resting reassuringly on the boy's thin shoulder. "There ya go, buddy. That should help a bit."

His bedside manner was spot-on. Calm, professional, but most of all, it was clear he cared. That kind of thing cut through language and cultural barriers. Though the boy and old man were no doubt anxious about being here surrounded by American soldiers, there was no way they could doubt that Jackson gave a damn and was doing everything he could to help the child.

"I think you'll be an amazing doctor," she said without thinking.

His head came up in surprise, and then he smiled. "Thanks."

She looked away, battling the blush trying to steal into her face. Why had she just blurted that out? She sounded like she was crushing on him. Pathetic.

Cam stepped inside the opening and took in the scene with a single glance. "Need a hand?"

"No, we're good. Gonna get this young fella outta here shortly." Jackson put a blanket over the boy.

"Give me a shout if you need me."

"Will do."

Cam ducked out. Maya's gaze landed on the open

duffel in the corner and couldn't help asking what was on her mind. "Are stuffed animals standard on a MED-CAP? Or was that your idea?" A box of Lifesavers candy lying among them solved the mystery of why he always smelled like wintergreen.

He shrugged. "We like to give stuff out to the kids. Just little things like rubber balls and crayons, pads of paper, teddy bears. They don't have much out here and they always really appreciate the toys."

She bet they did. And she also bet that the toys had come out of Jackson's own paycheck and not the military's budget.

Watching him work with the boy, she was struck again by his genuine kindness. She shook her head, part of her worrying about him. He had so much skill and compassion to give the world. Those were attributes to be cherished and protected. She hated thinking about something happening to him.

They sat in silence next to the boy on the cot, while the grandfather stroked the boy's hair every so often. When they finally heard the steady *whump whump whump* of the rotors, she and Jackson stood.

"I got him," he said, bending to carefully scoop the child into his arms. Protective yet gentle. The combination turned her to mush inside. He would make an amazing father. It was stupid, but she couldn't prevent the little pang in her chest at the thought of him settling down and having a family someday. If she were a different sort of woman, she'd have fought for that kind of future with everything in her. She didn't regret last night, only the way it had ended. Either way, she'd hurt him, or at least his pride. That hadn't been her intention at all. She felt badly about it, but there was nothing she could do to fix it now.

Holding the bag of fluids up so it dripped properly, Maya kept pace with him to the Black Hawk. The medic on board helped load the boy onto a stretcher and handed the grandfather in after him, while Jackson shouted the particulars over the noise from the engines.

She and Jackson stood back as the pilots powered up the engines and the helo lifted off, its nose tilted downward slightly as it cruised forward and up into the cloud-studded sky. "Think they'll operate in time?" she asked him.

"Hope so. That's one tough little dude. Peritonitis is really damn painful."

Maya covertly drank in his profile. To her, he was amazing. What would it feel like to be able to help save a boy's life like that? "If his grandfather hadn't brought him here today, he would have died. He's lucky."

"Yeah. Glad I was here."

Gah. The man was so unbelievably sweet and humble it killed her. Mentally shaking her head at herself, she pulled her weapon around, holding it across her body with the muzzle pointed down. "Looks like you've got another patient waiting." An old woman stood at the tent entrance. "Better get back to it before the guest of honor gets here to start the dog and pony show—"

The sound of another incoming helo broke the quiet. She gave a sardonic smile. "Speak of the devil."

"Enjoy the show," Jackson said with a wry grin.

"You know it." She got on the squad radio to make sure everyone was in position, part of her concentration on Jackson as he walked away.

After last night, she hadn't known what to expect from him today, though in hindsight it shouldn't have surprised her that he hadn't brought it up or been anything but the consummate professional he was. Had he lain awake after she'd gone, thinking of her? She hadn't slept worth a damn. Leaving that bunk had been one of the hardest things she'd ever done, but also one of the smartest and most necessary. Because if things had been different—if *she* had been different—she'd have given anything to stay snuggled up in his arms. That, more than the fear of discovery or reprisal for all the regulations she'd broken, was what had driven her back to her own tent.

The incoming Black Hawk finally landed and the star of the show got out, along with the remainder of his personal security team. Glimpsing his dark skin and military bearing, Maya immediately recognized Doug Haversham, the U.S. Secretary of Defense. They'd told her to expect a high-ranking official, but it surprised her they'd send someone this high profile. As one of the men responsible for the war effort in the region, he wasn't exactly a popular choice for these locals.

That wasn't her concern though. With her principal on the ground and a serious duty calling, thoughts of Jackson disappeared. "All right, gentlemen, get your game faces on," she said into her helmet mic. "It's showtime."

SIX

Hours after the boy had been airlifted to the hospital, Maya stood talking to one of her airmen as the publicity stunt finally started to wrap up. The SF team and the PJs had all packed up their gear in anticipation of their trip back to base. By all accounts, the MEDCAP had been a huge success. That was great, but to Maya, the best thing about the whole day was when Jackson had helped save that kid's life by diagnosing him and getting him evacuated to base.

All day long there'd been a steady trickle of patients coming by to see one of the "doctors," Cam and Jackson. Most of them were women and children or old men, and a large percentage had come from neighboring villages, some many difficult miles away. Word traveled surprisingly fast out here among the people. Another reason why she and the others had to stay vigilant. There'd been no incidents of any kind at the security checkpoints, and keeping the Secretary of Defense's arrival a secret to everyone but the higher-ups made the entire event that much more secure.

Haversham was far off to her right next to a cluster of mud-and-brick houses, wrapping up some photo ops with a small group of local children who were making good use of the toys the PJs had brought along. She hoped he was truly interested in them and what they were playing with, rather than just pretending to be for the cameras' sake. She hated two-facedness in general, but especially in leaders and officials who were supposed to represent and look out for the best interests of the people they served. If someone was tasked with protecting others, then said person better damn well take it seriously. Including the Sec Def.

"Helos are inbound. ETA thirty-five minutes, Lieutenant," an army major said over her headset.

"Roger that." Since she hadn't slept much last night, she was actually looking forward to getting back to Bagram and crawling into her snug little bunk between Erin's and Honor's. It also meant she'd get a reprieve from having to see Jackson again. All day long, part of her had been aware of him, her subconscious pinpointing exactly where he was at any given time. Right now he was back inside his tent, packing up all his gear and supplies.

It was best for both of them if they simply avoided each other, but part of her still wanted to be near him. He had a calm, confident energy that drew her in. In his presence she now felt admired, rather than annoyed. Deliciously feminine, and maybe even beautiful. She'd never felt that way before. She liked it too much for her own good.

Maya shifted her grip on her weapon and turned her attention back to what was happening around her. Everyone seemed to be relaxed, talking among themselves or watching Haversham with the kids. The Sec Def's protective detail remained at ease but watchful near the LZ, where the inbound helos would touch down. The SF team brought in for the MEDCAP was near them, the lieutenant and team sergeant talking to a couple of village elders, and she spotted a few Afghan troops mixed in among them. They must have arrived only recently because she hadn't noticed them before. No one seemed to be paying them much attention.

"Hey, LT, we outta here soon?" one of her airmen called out to her left, at his post beyond Jackson's tent.

"That's affirm," she called back. "Our ride should be here within the next twenty-five minutes." Looked like there was nothing more for them to do here anyhow. Haversham's security detail had things under control, and there were only local civilians remaining.

The words were barely out of her mouth when a sudden explosion rocked the ground behind her. She crouched and whipped around in time to see the small fireball erupt into the air less than a hundred yards down the hill from the designated LZ.

"Report," she said tersely into her mic. The civilians around her were all shouting, rushing their terrified children back into their primitive dwellings.

"Didn't see anything, LT," one of her airmen replied. The others reported the same.

There was nothing moving on the side of that hill and no one moving on the ridges above them that Maya could detect. That explosion was too big for an RPG strike. Someone had to have planted explosives there ahead of time. *Bastardos*.

"Probably remote detonated. Do a perimeter search and report back to me." Whoever had blown that thing up was close by, and there might be others. Maya moved closer to the edge of the steep hill. Behind her, soldiers rushed into motion, others remaining hunkered down in defensive positions around the village, scanning the hills for further threats. Jackson had come out of his tent to stand beside Cam, taking in the situation, weapon at the ready.

She glanced back at the Sec Def's security detail, already rushing to surround him while he walked quickly toward them with a calm expression that belied the tense situation. He was halfway to them when one of the SF troops shouted something and went to one knee, bringing his weapon up. The security detail whirled to face the threat. She did the same, her gaze landing on some newly arrived ANA troops near the LZ.

They were all in the middle of pulling masks up over the lower part of their faces.

Her stomach dropped. Everything went into slo-mo. Her gaze instantly flew to their hands as they raised their weapons, and there was no doubt who their target was.

"Ambush!" She shouted the frantic warning into her mic and raised her own rifle to return fire, but it was too late. The bastards had already taken aim and fired at the Sec Def's security detail, the sheer volume of fire dropping three of the five men before they fully realized what was happening. The remaining two had reached the Secretary and thrown themselves on top of him, acting as a living shield.

Chaos erupted. More insurgents dressed in Afghan army uniforms rushed at them, converging from different directions. The assholes had been biding their time, waiting for just the right moment to strike when everyone's guard was relaxed.

The air was alive with screams and shouts, the crack of rifle fire. Maya took aim and squeezed the trigger in a double tap, hitting one of the insurgents in the back. He went down with a cry and rolled over, aiming his rifle in her direction despite the debilitating wounds. A bullet zinged past her shoulder, close enough for her to hear it sizzle through the air.

She took aim, applying pressure to the trigger when another larger explosion rent the air, much closer this time. Maya felt the concussion deep in her chest, her bones vibrating like a tuning fork. The powerful shock wave rippled through the ground like an earthquake, knocking her feet out from under her. Her helmet and back slammed into the hard earth with enough force to knock the breath out of her.

Struggling up on to her elbows, she blinked and shook her head to clear it, gasping for air. From the corner of her eye she saw Jackson running toward her flat out, an expression of naked fear on his face, his mouth open as he screamed a warning at her.

His weapon was gone. It took a moment for his words to register over the roar in her ears.

"Maya, run!"

Reading the urgency in his gaze, she whipped her head around. Two men were rushing straight at her, rifles aimed. They wore ANA uniforms and had masks covering the lower parts of their faces. She instinctively reached for her M4, now twisted behind her.

No time. Her hands flashed down to where her sidearm was strapped to her thigh. They were only steps away. The pistol's weight barely registered as she grabbed it. It didn't even clear the holster before they caught her.

One hit her in a flying tackle. He drove her back into the ground with a bone-jarring thud that rattled her teeth. His hands were locked around her wrists. He twisted the weapon out of her grip. A low snarl erupted from her. She fought him, arching her body with all her strength to throw him off. He didn't budge, and increased the force of his grip on her wrists.

Her fingers were already going numb but she didn't let go. She could *not* relinquish her weapon. The man straddling her was too strong to dislodge. She snapped her head forward to bash him in the face with her helmet and caught his shoulder instead. He cursed something at her and held her wrists, while the other man grabbed her web gear and flipped her over, the kicks and punches she dealt having little effect.

She lashed out blindly with her boots in an attempt to break free. One of them slammed the butt of their rifle into the right side of her back, just below her shoulder blade. The force of the impact drove right through the plate in her body armor. Something cracked.

She went down with a soundless scream, white-hot pain sweeping through her, stealing her breath. Spots danced before her eyes. For a long, frozen moment she couldn't breathe. She fought to stay conscious. Her fingers slipped around the pistol grip. They wrenched it from her grasp.

No! The agonized scream of denial echoed in her head.

Hard hands flipped her over roughly. Her injured ribs hit the ground, sending another searing shock of pain through her. Through the haze of agony and fear, she realized something.

They could have killed her easily a handful of times by now. Instead they'd disarmed her, were pinning her down. Because they wanted to take her prisoner.

Rage and terror sent her into pure survival mode.

She would not be taken. She would not be a victim. Not ever again.

Maya screamed in rage and twisted hard, despite the bright stabs of pain in her back, managing to dislodge one of her attackers. She flipped on to her hands and knees and had almost made it to her feet when the other knocked her down. She brought her knees up and slammed her feet into his chest, knocking him back a step.

The initial wave of strength from the adrenaline rush was still driving her survival instinct, but it wouldn't last. The pain was so bad she didn't get to her feet in time. One man grabbed her upper arm, narrowly avoiding the elbow she threw at his throat, and caught both wrists behind her back, wrenching upward.

She caught a glimpse of Jackson through the panicked stampede of civilians racing past him. He was down, lying on his side facing away from her, rolling over with difficulty. Had they shot him? *No. Not Jackson.* Rage and sadness pulsed through her, fueling her strength to fight.

The man struggling to subdue her didn't let up with his grip. *¡Cabrón!* She yanked at the hands holding her prisoner, thrashed with all her might. The man gave an angry grunt and hauled her up against him, so close she could smell the cloying stench of his body odor.

Panting, blinded by sweat and dust, Maya dropped to her knees in a last-ditch effort to break free. Instead of releasing her, he followed her down, rapidly securing her arms behind her. A screech of pure fury ripped free when one of them threw a hood over her head, enveloping her in blackness. She wrenched her head from side to side, to no avail.

The dark intensified the terror slithering inside her, made it a living, breathing thing until she all but choked on it. Her heart galloped, pounding against her ribs. A wave of nausea rolled in her gut. She could not let them take her. Her best chance of escape was now. Maybe her only chance. With her strength dwindling and her body immobilized, she was left to face the terrible realization that she was powerless.

Gathering her strength for one last defiant bid for freedom, she bucked and then gasped at a hot sting in the side of her neck. A needle.

No, por favor, no!

The sedative burned as it spread through her bloodstream, paralyzing her muscles. The pain in her ribs began to recede into the background. Her head lolled, eyelids drooping, too heavy to force open. She fought it, but the drug was too strong.

Someone hauled her limp form upright and dumped her over their shoulder. The shouts and now sporadic gunfire around her faded into nothing as the blackness took her.

MAYA SURFACED WHEN someone yanked her upright and hauled her into the air. Her stomach did a slow roll and her head pounded sickeningly. Her hands were secured behind her back.

Weak, fighting through the drug's effects, she struggled to make out the sounds of men's voices, distantly registering the bobbing motion that meant she was being carried somewhere. Air caressed her bare arms. They'd taken her jacket and body armor off, leaving her in only her T-shirt and pants. There were no more screams or shouts, no gunfire. She could feel the material of the hood pressing against her face. They'd managed to abduct her.

Focus, she commanded herself. Every wasted second meant she was losing the precious opportunity to fight for her freedom and possibly her life.

Her body remained limp, uncooperative, despite her attempts to move. Her head felt fuzzy, like she was drifting through fog, but her brain was fully functional. It was like being buried alive. She could do nothing but suffer the indescribable frustration of lying draped over someone's shoulder as they took her inside a place that was much cooler and smelled musty and damp. A building? There was a scraping noise ahead of her, a few grunts. She didn't understand what the men were saying, but they were dragging something heavy along the ground near her. Other prisoners?

The Sec Def, she thought with a jolt of horror. They couldn't have gotten the Secretary and Jackson too. A lump formed in her throat, almost choking her. Was Jackson still alive? He'd been lying in the dirt, unmoving. The thought of him dying like that tore her up inside, filled her with fury.

A male voice behind her said something, and the man carrying her bent to slide her off his shoulder. She hit the hard floor and sprawled on to her back. Shards of pain radiated up from the right side of her back. Someone ripped the hood off her. Her eyelids felt like they were glued shut. She managed to force them open a bit and got a vague impression of a dirt floor, a small, black space beyond where they'd dumped her surrounded with iron slats covering the opening.

A cell.

The sour bite of terror filled her mouth. Someone prodded her sharply in the back with a boot, right against her injured ribs. Agony splintered through her, stealing her breath. She barely had time to gasp in a tortured breath before she felt someone shoving her forward into the black hole awaiting her.

Her mind screamed in protest but her body remained unresponsive, heightening the horror threatening to suffocate her. She'd taken basic SERE training. She was fully aware of what male captors did to female POWs and knew firsthand how cruel a man could be to a woman.

A cold fist squeezed her heart as she envisioned being tied up and helpless while she was beaten and raped, humiliated. Would she break? That terrified her the most. Succumbing to the pain and torture, shaming herself and defiling the oath she'd taken when she'd sworn to defend her country. She mentally recited Article 3 of the U.S. Code of Military Conduct.

If I am captured, I will continue to resist by all means available. I will make every effort to escape and to aid others to escape. I will accept neither parole nor special favors from the enemy.

The floor was hard and cold beneath her. Metal squeaked and clanged as they shut a cage door nearby, then her captors' footsteps retreated, abandoning her to her fate.

It was almost a blessing when the drugging fog returned again, stealing her awareness.

Her last conscious thought before she went back under was that she would rather die than endure what her sister had in order to help them both survive.

KHALID TURNED OFF his handheld radio and attached it to his belt as he entered the complex where the prisoners were being held. Tunneled into the side of the hill, the structure was deceptive. From the outside it looked like just another village dwelling. They'd been careful to leave the trucks at the base of the hill and used ATVs to bring the prisoners up the steep trails. A few of his men were out destroying any evidence of tracks now.

His eyes adjusted to the dimness inside the tunnel entry. It was much cooler here, and damp. He walked through the anteroom disguised as a simple living quarters and pushed aside the heavy carpet covering one of the hidden entrances that led to the holding area. Down the narrow corridor, he could hear his men dragging the prisoners toward the cells. His heart raced with excitement. He could hardly believe they'd done it. With only three of his men lost in the initial firefight, they'd managed to kill or wound dozens of Americans while taking hostages. Including the biggest prize of all, whom Khalid was now going to check on personally.

They'd slipped across the border into Pakistan without a single incident and melted into the hills, thanks to a little help from some of Kahlid's most powerful allies.

Up ahead, Youssef, a hardened soldier in his late thirties who had come to him through the Pakistani ISI, glanced back at him from where he observed the containment of the prisoners. In the darkness, Khalid could barely make out the other man's profile. "They're all still out," Youssef reported in Pashto. "Their pulses are strong. Should be waking up within the hour."

"Good." While he wasn't overly concerned with their comfort or health, he had to be careful to keep them all alive long enough for him to get what he wanted. Khalid strode forward to oversee the Secretary of Defense being loaded into his cell and nodded in satisfaction when his men placed the American official in a cell made up of carefully spaced iron bars. "Keep him where the other men can see him. I want them all to know what has happened when they awake."

"What about the woman?" Youssef asked, indicating the heap lying at his feet.

He gestured to the farthest cell with a jerk of his chin. "Put her in there against the far wall. Keep her away from the others. And I want you to remain here until she wakes up."

Youssef bent to pick her up without a word and disappeared into the darkness. A moment later, a metallic clang echoed throughout the corridor as the door to her cage shut.

Perfect.

Khalid had commanded his men to take her alive because she provided him with a huge advantage, and he planned to use it against the prisoners at every opportunity.

A few months ago, General Nasrallah had set his sights on a different American female soldier, intending to use her for publicity and to earn a hefty ransom.

Khalid had a far better motive for taking a female prisoner than his inept predecessor.

A shaft of light penetrated the dimness as someone pushed aside the carpet covering the entrance.

Khalid turned, squinting at Mohammed. "Yes?"

"Rahim wishes to speak to you, Khalid-jan." He held up a satellite phone.

Smiling, Khalid headed back through the entrance

and took the phone from Mohammed. "It is done," he said.

"Praise Allah," his mentor replied. "You know what to do?"

He knew *exactly* what to do. "I will begin as soon as they awaken."

SEVEN

A DANK, DAMP, musty odor overwhelmed by the slightly alkaline scent of dirt hit Jackson's nostrils as he struggled toward consciousness.

His eyelids felt like they were weighted down. He struggled to open his eyes, registering the near-darkness, the hard surface he was lying on. His hands were bound behind him and bruises throbbed across his back and shoulders from when the three men who'd attacked him had finally taken him down. As far as he could tell, nothing was broken. Faint male voices floated toward him, too far away to identify or discern what they were saying.

He rolled stiffly to his back and forced his body into a sitting position, all the while fighting to slow his pulse rate. Whoever had grabbed him had stuffed him into the equivalent of a cell carved into rock. The floor was bare dirt with sharp stones in it. They dug into his hip and shoulders as he propped himself against the back wall. He stared through clearing eyes at the crude iron bars forming his cage, his mind racing.

This wasn't SERE training. This was real.

Shifting to his knees to get a closer look, he examined the bars and where they connected to the earthen floor and ceiling. There were no gaps that he could see in the construction. None of the bars gave way when he tested them with his weight, leaning his shoulder against them. The lock on the front held solid against his kicks.

"There's no way out. I already checked."

Jackson instinctively crouched and swiveled around at the tired male voice behind him. His eyes had adjusted to the dimness enough for him to make out the shape of another prisoner slumped against the wall of the cell beside his. The man's body was swallowed by shadow but if he squinted, Jackson could make out the basics of his facial features. His dark skin made it harder to see him. When he realized who it was, Jackson's heart sank.

They'd captured the fucking Secretary of Defense.

"Sir," Jackson began quietly, his voice still groggy from whatever they'd drugged him with. "Are you all right?"

"As all right as the rest of us. And I think you'd better start calling me Doug. What's your name?" he asked quietly.

"Jackson."

"You're a PJ?"

He nodded, glancing down at his uniform, which they'd left on him for some reason. The reflective patch bearing the letters *PJ* was still there on his left arm. His body armor was long gone. "Are you hurt?"

"Only roughed up so far. Whatever they knocked us out with gave me a pretty good hangover, but otherwise I'm okay." He sounded tired, strained.

Hangover was the perfect way to describe the pounding in his head and the dryness in his mouth. Jackson twisted his fingers, trying to increase circulation, despite the tight plastic zip tie around his wrists.

The damp interior of their prison created a chill in the air that made goose bumps break out over his skin. He kept his voice low, uncertain if more guards might be close enough to overhear him. "Any idea where we are?"

"Side of a mountain someplace, best I can figure."

Yeah. It looked like some sort of cave, or maybe an underground bunker. "How many of them there are?"

"At least five that I've seen, but there are probably others."

Jackson turned his upper body to peer past the Secretary down the carved-out corridor. It seemed like there were more cells down there, though he couldn't see or hear anyone else. Didn't mean they weren't there. They could be unconscious or keeping quiet. "How many of us?" he whispered, careful to ensure his voice didn't carry.

"Four. Unless they brought in more while I was out of it. I think there's a female," he added grimly.

Maya? Jackson's gut clenched. They couldn't have taken her. Last he'd seen her, she'd been fighting off two attackers and other soldiers had been rushing to her aid. She was smart and strong.

They got you and the Sec Def, didn't they?

Goddammit, he didn't want her to be one of the prisoners.

Whether it was Maya or not, throwing a female into the mix made a bad situation that much worse. Back in SERE school when the "captors" had roughed up a female airman during an interrogation had been bad enough. He and the other male "captives" had gone crazy trying to take the "captors'" attention off the female, bargaining to take her place. They'd been ignored, of course.

Watching them hurt that woman and not being able to stop them was one of the hardest things he'd ever had to endure. Even though they'd all known on an intellectual level that the interrogators wouldn't do any worse than rough her up, the male captives had reacted on a primal level. The lesson had stuck with him ever since, all the more horrifying since he came from a home with a single mom and three sisters.

Jackson wasn't sure what he'd do if something like that happened here. And if it was Maya? *Christ.*

Because this time, there was no guarantee they'd stop at kick and punches. The thought made him feel sick. Where he came from, real men didn't beat on women. And these fuckers sure as hell wouldn't abide by the Geneva Convention.

A thousand thoughts whirled through his mind as he struggled to come to terms with this new reality. Waiting in the dark, anticipating the unknown, was almost worse than having the shit kicked out of him.

The Sec Def was silent beside him. Jackson knew he'd served in the Marine Corps back in the day, but that had been a hell of a long time ago. How the hell had they managed to take him with all his security detail there? He wanted to ask more questions, but each time either one of them spoke it increased the risk of attracting their captors' attention. And right now they had to preserve whatever hope and morale they could. It was critical for their survival.

A flicker of light came from the far end of the corridor. Jackson's heart began to thud as it came nearer, bringing the sounds of measured footsteps with it. His palms turned clammy. *Stay focused. Remember your training.*

But no amount of training ever prepared a man enough to face this for real.

The beam of light intensified, and low male voices drifted toward them. He heard Doug shift against the back wall of his cell, trying to make himself as still and small as possible. They both had to be the "gray man" here, the guy who blended into the background so well that he all but disappeared. The best-case scenario for a prisoner of war, second to escape.

A silhouette appeared, outlined against the light. Then two more. The men's strides were purposeful, drawing nearer with every heartbeat. Jackson stayed frozen in position against the damp, rough wall.

The man carrying the flashlight stopped in front of his cell and said something to the others. He sounded surprisingly young, but Jackson refused to look up lest he draw attention to himself. A second man halted beside him, wearing the typical baggy pants and sandals common to men in the region. The third man hung back, as if he wanted to watch what happened next. Jackson's muscles tensed when the first man squatted down but he managed to keep his gaze on the dirt floor just inside the metal bars rather than look up.

The bright beam of the flashlight hit him in the face, blinding him. He squinted and turned his head, gritting his teeth in annoyance that he'd reacted at all. The beam traveled down his body, and the second man grunted something to the one standing in the shadows. A few seconds later, they moved on to the Sec Def and did the same. Checking for life-threatening injuries maybe, since a dead hostage was no good to them.

Two of the men moved on to a cell farther down and started talking among themselves. The squeak of metal hinges reached him, and then came the sound of something heavy dragging across the floor. The younger one called out to the first man standing near Jackson's cell and he walked toward them. Jackson had only a quick impression of someone tall and lean as he passed by. More low words, then a grunt followed by the groan of the iron door closing once more.

The latch clanged into place and the men came back. This time they stopped directly in front of the Sec Def's cell. Out of the corner of his eye, Jackson watched as the flashlight illuminated the body draped over the second man's shoulders. Whoever he was, he was already dead. Blood covered his face, head and the light blue oxford shirt he wore. One of the Sec Def's personal security detail.

The tall man whispered something, and the one carrying the dead man shuffled off down the corridor. Then the tall one, who had to be the leader, hunkered down so that his face was lit by the flashlight beam. Unable to stop himself, Jackson risked a glance at him. He had a full dark beard and a light complexion. His eyes were a strange yellow-hazel. Jackson forced his gaze back to the floor as the leader spoke, in English.

"Hello, Mr. Secretary. I am honored to have you as our guest." His heavily accented voice was pitched low, but what really upped the creep-out factor was the maniacal gleam Jackson had seen in those hellish eyes.

When Doug didn't answer, the leader let out a low chuckle, as though his prisoners' silence delighted him. "We have important plans for you while you stay with us."

White noise. It was all just white noise, Jackson reminded himself. He had to tune it out and focus on reinforcing his will to survive.

"Eventually we will expect you to tell us about coalition operations in the area and make a recorded statement denouncing the war for the world to see, but you would obviously be unwilling to do so at this point. Unless I am wrong?" Silence was his only answer, and Jackson swore he could hear the smile in the bastard's voice when he continued.

"Then instead I believe I'll start with a less worthy opponent. Mohammed," he commanded and rose to his feet as the young one hurried down the row of cells into the darkness. Another screech of mental hinges, then the sounds of a scuffle, quickly ended. The metal latch clanged into place, and Mohammed returned with another prisoner draped over his shoulders. Jackson could hear the prisoner's harsh breathing, a stifled, painful moan.

The leader said something, and Mohammed lowered the prisoner to the floor. A sense of foreboding swept through him. Despite himself, Jackson had to look. The man grabbed a handful of the prisoner's hair and yanked, forcing the person's head up. The beam of light illuminated a pair of frightened blue-green eyes before they squeezed shut against the sudden glare.

Jackson's heart stopped beating.

Maya.

He jerked like he'd been electrocuted, barely managing to swallow back the cry of denial lodged in his throat. Staring into her pinched face, he felt like someone had stabbed him in the gut.

"Do you recognize your fellow guests?" the leader

purred, swinging the beam of light at Doug, then at Jackson. He squinted but couldn't make himself look away and when the light shone on her once again, she was staring right at him, her expression utterly haunted. Jackson squeezed his numb hands into fists of helpless rage.

Maya didn't answer but her devastated expression said it all. She'd seen and recognized him. From the look in her eyes it was clear she understood that whatever hell they put her through now, she'd have to withstand it alone. And somehow he'd have to endure that knowledge while battling the crushing agony that there was nothing he could do to protect her from any of it.

Jackson held her gaze, trying to give her strength. *Sweetheart, please hang on. Whatever they do to you, just hold on.* Fuck, he wanted to throw up.

"No? Ah, well." The leader sounded almost disappointed in her lack of reaction. "Now that you have seen your fellow guests, I think you and I should become better acquainted." He jerked Maya's hair, forcing her to her feet, which were still bound.

She shot a look of terror in Jackson's direction that made his guts churn and it took everything he had not to call out in protest as they dragged her away. He thought he'd understood what fear felt like before? Not even close. But he did now.

MAYA WAS TRAPPED in a waking nightmare.

They'd bound her hands and feet to a metal chair and left her alone in the middle of the small earthen room. The waiting was almost worse than the pain she knew was coming. Old fears rose up like specters to haunt her. In the dark, heart thudding in terror, she was nine years old all over again, locked in the closet when her uncle's footsteps came down the hall toward the bedroom she shared with Pilar.

Don't come out, whatever happens. Her sister's urgent whisper was still razor-sharp in her memory. *I'll let you out once it's safe, but stay hidden and stay quiet.*

Even at nine, it had been perfectly clear to her what Pilar had endured to protect her. Those masculine grunts and muffled cries of pain from beyond the closed closet door of their bedroom had painted a vivid picture in her brain that she'd never been able to erase. The hand-me-down double bed she'd shared with Pili had squeaked ominously, the oak headboard banging against the wall in a relentless rhythm until Maya thought she'd go mad.

Many times her fingers had curled around the handle of the wooden baseball bat in that closet, prepared to burst through the door and cave his skull in to save her sister. But time after time, she'd done as her sister said and stayed hidden in the safety of their closet. And she'd never be able to forgive herself for her cowardice as long as she lived.

Instead of acting, doing something, *anything* to save Pilar, night after night she'd remained locked in that stygian closet with her hands clapped over her ears and silent tears streaming down her cheeks. The other adults in the house had ignored those pitiful cries tearing from her sister's lips, either in denial or because they were passed out somewhere next to an empty bottle of wine. It had gone on for nearly two years until Pilar had finally agreed to run away because she'd at last deemed Maya old enough to endure life on the streets.

But no one can outrun the past. Though they'd escaped, in the end it hadn't been enough. The memories had killed Pilar as surely as the coarse rope looped around her slender throat when Maya found her hanging lifeless from the shower rod in the dingy bathroom of the apartment they'd shared. The note Pilar had left on the kitchen counter was permanently etched into her mind.

You have to live, Maya. Living is the only way to get revenge on the bastard who did this to me. Swear to me you'll never give in. Swear it.

She'd dedicated her life to upholding her sister's dying wish. Here in this dark prison, that final promise was about to be tested to its limits.

Male voices came from outside the small room they'd placed her in. Maya swallowed but it did nothing to ease the tightness in her dry throat. Her heart thudded a hard, pounding rhythm and a cold sweat broke out over her skin.

These men lived by their own laws, their own code of conduct. Islam was supposed to be one of the most peaceful religions, but these men twisted it into an extreme, violent facsimile. That they were Muslims didn't necessarily protect her from rape, though she hoped it would. They perverted their religion to suit their own agenda, so it was possible rape wasn't an aberration to them.

Maya's skin crawled. Having to endure that cruel degradation at their hands would be almost as bad as dying. All the SERE training in the world couldn't prepare her for the brutal reality of that.

Her mind wandered back to a conversation she'd

had with Pilar shortly after running away from their *abuela's* house.

How did you stand it, Pilar?

I left my body and went somewhere else in my head. Someplace he could never find me or touch me again. A place where fear and pain don't exist.

Maya·had mentally prepared herself for the possibility of capture and rape as much as any female service member could before deploying. It had been something she'd thought about only in passing, telling herself the chances of it ever happening were miniscule. Now that the moment was here, could she take it? She would rather die than break under torture.

Someone swept aside the corner of the carpet covering the entrance and two men strode in, carrying a lantern. One remained by the doorway, while the other set the lantern on a crate close to her and came to stand directly in front of her. She fixed her gaze straight ahead, staring at nothing, careful not to bow her head or give any outward sign of fear. Given how frightened she was, it wasn't easy.

A hard hand flashed out and gripped her jaw, forcing her head up. She didn't bother resisting because she didn't have much choice and it would be a waste of energy, but she refused to meet his gaze. His hold was forceful, bordering right on the edge of painful, his long fingers digging into her flesh like talons.

She stared stubbornly at the V in his throat, where his thick dark beard stopped a few inches above the collar of his shirt. She could see the edges of his defined pectoral muscles there, sensed the raw power in his arms and shoulders, his formidable will. This man was hard as steel inside and out. He radiated a cold, controlled anger she had no desire to see unleashed on her. It took everything she had to keep from trembling.

"Name."

The cold rasp of his voice sent a chill down her spine. She drew in a breath, ready with the standard name, rank and serial number response, surprised at how steady her voice came out. "Lieutenant Maya Lopez, five-seven-two—"

"Enough." He dropped his hand.

She clamped her jaw closed and waited.

He circled her slowly, like a wolf stalking its prey. He was tall, around six feet or more, somewhere in his thirties and built lean. The traditional baggy clothing he wore did nothing to disguise the raw power seething inside that whipcord body.

A shiver crawled through her as he spoke again. "It sickens me how weak Americans are to let women wear a uniform. Tell me, Lieutenant Lopez, why you are fighting this war." His voice dripped with disdain at her rank. When she didn't respond, he paused in front of her. "Answer me."

"I can't answer that question." Now her voice shook.

"You will. *Now.*"

Here it comes. She tensed, preparing as much as she could for that first blow. It didn't fall, and eventually Maya allowed herself to relax a fraction. All her senses were tuned to the man in front of her, locking on him with a kind of hyper-focus she'd only ever previously experienced during combat.

He shifted again, and Maya could feel the frustration pulsing off him. His hands flexed once, his fingers curling into fists of rage. Then he turned to the man at the doorway and barked something at him in another language. Pashto, maybe. The rug covering the opening lifted as the man rolled it back, then his retreating footsteps echoed until they faded into silence.

In the midst of that suffocating void, the waiting, the anticipation of pain was almost unbearable. She didn't understand why he'd asked the man to unroll the rug and leave. Unless he was coming back with something. Another prisoner, or maybe a weapon? A torture tool? A list of possibilities ran through her mind. Pulling out her fingernails. Gouging out her eyes. Cutting her. Her breathing sped up, despite her effort to control it. Shit, she didn't know if she could withstand whatever he had in store for her.

A low chuckle filled the vacuum of silence. "Very good. You should be afraid," the man said softly, the satisfaction in his tone making her skin prickle.

Half hidden in shadow, she didn't see his arm move. His open palm flashed out and hit her cheek with a resounding crack that swung her head around. Maya gasped and clenched her teeth together to keep from crying out. Her heart gave a terrified jolt as she collected herself. The left side of her face stung and her eyes watered.

During the brief SERE course, they'd told her to cry out, to vocalize her pain and fright if a captor beat her, because it usually made them go easier. Now that it was actually happening, that stubborn part of her demanded she stand her ground and refuse to give in. And she knew in her heart that crying and begging would do no good anyway. This man had no mercy in him.

Another blow landed on the opposite cheek, this one with more force. She flinched and instinctively cringed away, but her arms were tied too tightly for her to move much.

"Why are you fighting here?" he demanded ruthlessly, towering over her.

"My country asked me to," she answered in defiance, breaking the protocol of only giving name, rank and serial number.

"It is not your place to invade and occupy our sacred homeland. We will expel you as we have all the other occupiers." This time his fist slammed into her stomach.

Though she'd tensed her muscles, the punch still caught her off guard. She doubled over with a grunt and sucked in a shallow breath as the blow set off a blaze of fire across her damaged ribs. Her face was clammy with perspiration when she managed to open her eyes and force her body upright. In the light she saw him unbuckle his belt, heard the leather slither through the loops holding it around his waist and wanted to vomit.

You can take this. You will *take this. Pain and humiliation won't kill you. You have to survive. You promised.* She was shaking so hard her teeth were chattering. The gnawing fear, the sense of disbelief that this was truly happening, were paralyzing.

He lowered his hand and waved the belt slightly, making the leather strip come alive, slithering along the ground like a snake waiting to strike. Her stomach rolled.

But he didn't drop his pants or make a move to undress her. Instead he raised his arm and brought the belt down sharply across her thighs. Maya arched under the bite of the leather through her pants as pain exploded in her nerve endings. A jagged gasp ripped from her throat before she could control it. She strangled on it, fighting to hold it back, not let him see how frightened she was or how much it hurt.

"Say it."

Say *what*? What the hell did he want her to say? She could barely breathe, much less speak.

He brought the belt down again and again in angry yet controlled movements, lashing her thighs, her upper arms, across her upper back, wherever he could reach. "Say it! Tell me how much it hurts."

Maya squeezed her eyes shut and bit down hard on the insides of her cheeks, something primal in her refusing to cry out. She was a lieutenant in the United States Air Force. It was her duty to fight. She'd vowed it to her fellow airmen, to her country. Her only power now lay in resistance. She couldn't give in, couldn't show fear now, because it would only fuel his cruelty.

His open hand slapped her across the face again, and this time she tasted the metallic tang of blood in her mouth. A strange roaring filled her ears, her heart racing too hard, too fast. Sparks of light flickered behind her closed eyelids, her body fighting against the agony sizzling along her nerve endings.

The man was panting now, and she knew it was more from rage than exertion. Not only was she his enemy, she was a woman. In his mind, that made her lowlier than an animal. "Infidel whore," he spat, and punched her beneath her left eye. His knuckles plowed into her cheekbone with a sickening crack.

She screamed, her head snapping backward with the force of the blow, the momentum throwing the chair back. She hit the floor with a thud. The back of her skull smacked into the hard ground, her left wrist taking the brunt of her weight as she fell, crushing it beneath the chair back. She felt the bone snap. Shards of agony splintered through her arm, ribs and across her damaged face.

A strangled cry tore from her, her lungs compressed against her ribs. Gasping for air, whimpering now, she turned her head weakly to spit out a mouthful of blood, wondering if she would die in this room.

And he wasn't done with her yet. Without raising her up, he wrenched at the laces of her boots and tossed them aside. Disoriented and nauseated from the blinding pain encompassing her, Maya tried to lash out with her feet, but the bonds held her ankles to the tipped chair's legs. He yanked off her socks and before the cool air on her feet registered in her whirring brain, he raised the belt high in the air and lashed it down with a loud crack on the tender soles of her feet.

The first blow tore through her nerve endings like a blowtorch. Maya forgot how to breathe, her whole body going rigid with the hot shock of it. He did it again. And again. The merciless leather bit into her ultra-sensitive skin with each lash. It was electric, unlike anything she'd ever imagined. Every cell in her body was on fire, writhing in agony.

She dimly realized she was screaming and gritted her teeth to stifle the noise. Her body arched and twisted with each cruel lash of the belt in an effort to escape the torment, despite her other injuries. The pain was hideous, inescapable, hitting her everywhere at once, overloading her nervous system.

Maya shook and fought for each desperate gasp she drew into her aching lungs. When he stopped, she pried open her wet, swollen eyes a fraction of an inch to stare up at her tormentor with undisguised loathing.

Her show of hatred seemed to amuse him. One side of his mouth curled up in the midst of that heavy beard. "Scream," he taunted piteously, the amber glow of the lantern transforming his face into a terrifying mask of hollows and shadows. His yellow eyes gleamed like a demon's. He was getting off on her pain, she realized distantly as she fought the despair swamping her.

"I'll keep going until you give me what I want. Scream to your infidel God to save you. I want them to *hear* you in their cells, woman," he snarled, once again raising the belt.

Something inside Maya shriveled and died at his words. In that terrifying moment, waiting for the next vicious lash of the belt, she finally realized what he was after. More than just her suffering and degradation. He had a more malevolent intent in mind.

He was going to use her as a weapon to break the male captives.

Tears of horror and pain stung her eyes and she managed to shake her head, a last show of defiance. "N-no." *Please let me make it through this. Please don't let him break me.*

Those hellish eyes glowed in the lantern light. "Scream," he commanded and brought the belt down on the tender soles of her feet in another cruel, whistling arc, this strike harder than all the others.

She screamed. She couldn't help it. The agonized cries tore out of her without her permission and she couldn't stop. Time and space lost all meaning. Her entire existence shrank into a red haze of pain. The uncontrollable sounds of her suffering rang unchecked off the cavern walls and down the corridor to where the other cells lay.

EIGHT

JACKSON WAS IN hell and there was no way out.

As a battlefield airman at higher risk for capture, after basic SERE school he'd been selected for advanced training, which amounted to "advanced beatings." He'd hated every moment of it. He'd surprised himself with how well he'd handled the pain, but part of him had always known the handlers would stop short of life-threatening damage.

The captors here had no such limitations.

The sounds of Maya's terror and agony slowly stripped away his resolve to stay detached. Locked in his cell with his hands and feet bound and forced to sit idly by while they tortured her was almost more than he could bear. He'd give anything for the chance to charge in there and kill the man responsible, set her free, bargain for her life with his own.

Her screams raised the hair on the back of his neck and made his gut twist. They'd started out low and muffled, but now they echoed down the corridor, filling every atom of space with her terror and suffering.

He couldn't block them out. Couldn't stop praying. Those screams were real, not staged. He knew they were because she was yelling in Spanish, begging for mercy. Her voice was choked, hoarse. Desperate. And still the man torturing her didn't let up. He'd pause for only a few minutes, as though to let the worst of the pain recede, then start in all over again. Jackson took a deep breath and released it slowly, fighting back the red haze of rage. He wanted to kill that motherfucker for hurting Maya.

He could hear something striking her flesh repeatedly. His mind conjured up dozens of horrific scenarios, each one of them as terrible as the last. He dug his numbed fingers into the rock wall and clenched his muscles until his body trembled. Nothing helped.

"Fucking monsters," Doug muttered under his breath, shifting in agitation against the wall of his own cell. He'd been silent since the interrogation began, but obviously it had taken a toll on him too.

Jackson didn't respond. He couldn't because he'd either choke on the words or puke, he wasn't sure which.

The kid standing in the corridor began pacing again, back and forth down the length of the cells, fidgeting and running a hand through his hair. It was clear he was uncomfortable with what was happening in the other room, though he did nothing to try to stop it. He was too afraid of his leader.

Jackson had already tried to get the kid's attention, but either he was ignoring him or didn't speak English. He hadn't responded when Jackson had spat something at him about whether beating an unarmed woman was the true practice of Islam. From the kid's increasing agitation, he damn well knew it wasn't.

When the last scream faded into stillness, Jackson held his breath, praying it was over. Nothing came from the room now but low moans, sobs. His lungs constricted at those heartbreaking sounds. He had to squeeze his eyes shut and think of something else to erase the image of Maya spread out on the floor naked, beaten and bleeding. Or worse.

Fuck.

"Mohammed." The sharp command came from the room Maya was in, followed by something in Pashto Jackson couldn't understand.

The boy snapped to attention and took a halting step in that direction then hesitated, as though he had no interest in seeing what his leader had done to Maya. He swallowed audibly and began walking down the corridor. A few minutes later he returned, carrying her across his shoulders.

Jackson sat up, heart pounding. The lighting was poor at best, but his eyes remained riveted to her. She lay limp across Mohammed's shoulder, her head lolling with each step. She was dressed, but that didn't mean she hadn't been violated sexually. Her shallow, rapid breaths shuddered in and out, telling him she was still conscious. Every few seconds a pained, pitiful whimper cut through the silence.

The pressure of tears filled his throat. He swallowed them down, keeping his blurry gaze on her as Mohammed took her to the empty cell next to Jackson's and placed her gently inside. Even that seemed to cause her a great deal of pain, because her breath caught and she gave a throttled cry that ripped through the quiet.

Mohammed froze in uncertainty, laying her down only when his leader snapped something at him. He stepped away and closed the cell door behind him.

Soft treads approached, and the man responsible for her suffering paused in front of the partition between Jackson's and the Sec Def's cells. He carried a lantern in one hand, the candle now burned down to a stub. But it gave just enough light for Jackson to see Maya's body.

She was curled on her side in the middle of her cell, facing toward him. The light glinted off her unbound coffee-colored hair, and Jackson got his first glimpse of her face. He sucked in a swift breath and bit down so hard his molars ached. Fucking Christ, the bastard had beaten her to a pulp.

One eye was already swollen shut. Her cheeks were wet with tears and blood trickled from a wound in her mouth. She cradled her left wrist against her body, and her shallow breathing told him it hurt to draw a breath.

The primal male in him howled in agonized outrage that they'd done this to her. The medic in him was terrified she might have internal damage and bleeding. Every single muscle in his body was rigid to the point of snapping, rage and horror flooding his system so hard and fast it made him dizzy. Only his bound hands prevented him from reaching for her.

Holding the lantern, the leader stood there quietly for a time, as though he wanted them to see exactly what kind of damage he'd inflicted upon her. When he spoke, there was a quiet smugness to his voice that only intensified Jackson's hatred. If he got the chance, he'd kill him with his bare hands.

"Your female colleague had nothing of value to offer me. But you do," he said pointedly to Doug. "For her sake, I pray you cooperate with our demands. If not..." He let the sentence dangle for a moment, purposely building the tension. "I am not sure she can withstand much more of that." With that, he turned away and strode back down the corridor, taking the light with him.

The instant the rug swung back down over the opening, Jackson was on his knees, crawling up to the bars that separated them. "Maya." His throat was so tight it came out as a croak. "Maya, can you hear me?"

"She's in shock," Doug said, as if Jackson couldn't tell that for himself. "Maybe she's better off that way."

Jackson's hackles rose and he ignored the man's advice. "Maya, I'm here. I'm right here, can you hear me?" His heart was in his throat and for a long moment he didn't think she would respond. Then he heard her shifting ever so slowly in the darkness, a little gasp of pain falling from her lips. "Maya..."

"H-hurts," she whimpered, a bare whisper of sound that told him the effort of speaking was too painful to bear.

His eyes stung hotter. "I know. Can you tell me where?" If he suspected she had internal injuries, he'd yell for a guard and keep on yelling until they let him treat her and agree to release her. He didn't care what they did to him after that.

He'd made the decision after the ordeal of advanced SERE school that in the event of being captured, he'd rather die fighting than live on his knees. But he'd live on his knees if it would save Maya. He'd do goddamn anything for that, including sell his soul.

"Maya?" He kept his voice low and steady, despite the tearing pain in his chest. She needed calm now, for him to anchor her. "Tell me where it hurts."

She sucked in another shallow breath, bit back a cry. "R-ribs. Wrist. Face. Feet."

Feet? Had that fucker pried her toenails out or something? The sense of vertigo returned. He closed his eyes and pulled in a deep breath to steady himself.

"What about your chest or stomach, somewhere inside? Does it hurt inside anywhere?"

"Mmm-hmm." The response was uttered from between gritted teeth.

His pulse shot up. "Where, honey?"

"Ev-everywhere..."

Jackson closed his eyes. He couldn't fucking *do* anything. It tore him up inside to know that. Even if he started shouting for the guards and by some miracle they let him tend to her, he had no equipment or supplies. Taking a calming breath, he opened his eyes and tried to see her in the darkness. She was quiet, but he could hear her shivering and those soft, little choked noises she made, as if she didn't want anyone to know she was crying and was doing everything in her power to hold them in. Having seen firsthand just how strong and formidable she was, it broke his heart.

Lying down on the cold stone floor, he stretched out against the bars of his cell and pressed against them as hard as he could, desperate to get closer to her. When he spoke again, he did so in Spanish so that if any of the captors were listening they wouldn't be able to understand. This was for Maya alone. His voice was an aching whisper. "Maya. I'm right here, baby. Can you touch me?"

She took a shuddering breath and then those heartbreaking noises stopped as though she refused to let any more out. Was she ashamed? God, he wanted to hold her.

"Come here and touch me," he urged softly, trying to give her the compassionate human connection she needed.

He heard her shift in the darkness, followed by the

swift intake of a pained breath. He gritted his teeth against the urge to tell her to stop and willed her to come closer. There might not be anything he could do to alleviate her suffering, but he could at least try to give her some kind of solace.

He tracked every torturous inch of her progress with the sliding noises along the floor, her throttled groans of pain. All the while he kept urging her softly in Spanish, hoping his voice at least anchored her. At last she was close enough for him to register the warmth of her body on the other side of the bars. She reached through them to place a shaking hand against his face. Jackson's throat closed up. He leaned into her touch, pressing his cheek hard into her icy palm, and rubbed gently. Her breath hitched on a sob.

"I'm here," he whispered hoarsely. At that moment he'd have given anything to be able to make the bars disappear and have his arms free so he could hold her, soothe and warm her. "You're not alone."

She shifted those last few inches until she was laying full length against the bars. The only places they touched were her hand on his face and a few inches of their thighs, but he could feel the heat of her body and hoped the shared warmth would stem the worst of her shivering. Every time her muscles shook, it jarred her body, hurting her even more.

He turned his face into her palm and kissed the center of it, not trusting himself to speak. Then those trembling fingers traced over his face like she was trying to see him with her touch and traveled down to curl into his uniform, clutching the fabric as if it was a lifeline. He thought his heart would crack in two. "Just hang on, baby. Hang on to me."

She expelled a rough breath and held on.

Doug spoke for the first time, his low-pitched voice carrying the English words from the cell behind him. "We're here for you, Maya. You're not alone. We're going to get through this together, all of us."

She said nothing, only shuddered and kept breathing in a shallow pattern that alarmed him. It killed him to be so close and yet be unable to help or touch her more than he was. An unknown amount of time passed, and her breaths evened out so much he thought she must be asleep. But her grip hadn't relaxed on him and when she shifted, a ragged cry slipped free. The sound sliced through him like a scalpel. He pressed harder against the bars. She needed to feel him, feel his body up against her, his heartbeat beneath her cheek.

Lying as close to her as he was going to get, he did the only thing he could think of to soothe her.

He opened his mouth and began to sing softly.

MAYA'S FINGERS HAD long since gone numb from clutching Jackson's uniform shirt, but she refused to let go. The bars keeping them apart dug into her flesh, though she barely noticed the discomfort through all the other pain. Her ribs, face and the soles of her feet throbbed and burned until she wanted to scream from the relentless onslaught. Everything else just plain hurt.

Crawling to Jackson had been almost unbearable, but being able to touch him took the sharp edge off the fear and despair. The slight heat she could feel coming from him helped warm her a little. Yet the black void of hopelessness was there, waiting for her, ready to swallow her. She'd almost fallen in.

With that single session, that fanatical *malparido*

had managed to break her. She'd screamed for him, endlessly. Her throat was swollen from it. It shamed her.

In the midst of her despair, Jackson's low, melodic voice filled the darkness. It rolled over her senses like a caress, penetrating the shock and cold inside her. Singing. He was singing to her because he couldn't touch her and it was the best he could do instead.

Closing her eyes, she allowed herself to drift, holding tight to his uniform and his voice. That low, beautifully modulated voice brought a sudden rush of tears to the surface. Her heart swelled until it felt like it was jammed against the inside of her bruised ribs.

Maya let the sound of it stroke her battered soul, vaguely recognizing an old Rat Pack song. She didn't really hear most of the lyrics and they didn't matter. The sentiment behind them did, and his effort to reach out to her. Somehow he'd known she needed him to ground her, keep her from going too deep in her head. She didn't care that the Sec Def was in the cell next to Jackson and could overhear everything.

Jackson sang two more songs to her softly before falling silent.

A long pause followed before she could find her voice. "Thank you." Saying the words made the cut in her lower lip bleed more, but she didn't care.

"Anytime, *querida*."

That endearment wasn't fake, or said because he was desperate to make her hang on. He meant it. Knowing that flooded her cold body with a frisson of warmth.

He shifted against the bars once more, pressing harder into her touch as though he wanted more contact. Once again, he spoke in Spanish, the words slow and measured. "You've got to keep fighting, baby. I know it hurts and I know you're scared, but you have to fight and get through this."

She swallowed thickly. "My sister said that to me."

"Your sister? What's her name?"

"Pilar." She fought the tide of memories rushing at her. "She died."

"I'm sorry."

She managed a nod, though of course he couldn't see her. Her fingers relaxed their death grip on his uniform as she cradled her injured wrist against her body. It hurt to breathe. Taking shallow breaths didn't seem to help. The pain in her ribs, face and wrist was worse than lingering burning in her abused feet.

Jackson. Focus on Jackson.

She stroked her hand over his chest, comforting herself with the feel of all that strength and vital heat beneath her exploring touch. He moved against her like a big cat, trying to touch her in return. There in the hushed darkness with a fellow prisoner listening in, it still felt intimate. His thoughtfulness meant so much. Jackson was safety and security, a solid link to reality.

"Tell me about her," he murmured.

With his patient coaxing, she found herself telling him about her sister. Haltingly at first, then more easily, she gave him an abbreviated version of events in their upbringing and the horrific sexual abuse Pilar had withstood. Things she'd never told another living soul. That was how much she trusted Jackson. And a part of her she didn't want to acknowledge was afraid she wasn't going to make it out of here alive, so she needed to tell someone about her sister. She didn't care if anyone else overheard.

"She took it so that I wouldn't have to," she managed hoarsely. The darkness helped. It made her feel less exposed, hid the guilt and torment that had to be all over her face. She hurt all over but nothing was going to ease it, and talking about her deepest secrets made her feel closer to him than she had to anyone else since Pili died, even Ace.

"Where did you go when you ran away?" he asked. His tone held no judgment, only concern.

"The streets."

His silence said everything.

Maya changed the position of her right arm, wincing as the slight shift jarred her left wrist, balanced on her hip. She paused until the worst of the pain had faded before going on. "For a while I thought she'd make it. We didn't have any money, and she started turning tricks at night so she could earn enough to get us an apartment." Maya would never forget the horror she'd felt when she'd first found out. "She wouldn't let me get a job, no matter how much I argued. Said I was too young and insisted I go to school every day. She was my hero." Looking back, it was obvious now how much braver Pilar had been than her. To sacrifice so much for someone you loved, give up your pride, your body and your future? That was how much her sister had loved her.

"God, Maya..."

"Before long, she started drinking. To numb the pain, I think. Then came the drugs. I couldn't do anything at that point. It was too late." She drew a slow, shuddering breath, fighting the fiery splinters of pain that shot through her ribs as they expanded. Wincing, she continued. "My junior year, I came home one day and found her. She hanged herself in our bathroom."

Jackson made a low, sad sound and was silent a beat before asking, "What did you do after she was gone?"

"I stayed there using the money she'd left me and finished school. My school counselor and social worker told me about the Air Force Academy and helped me get ready to apply in my senior year. Being accepted was the best thing that ever happened to me."

She'd needed to get the hell out of her old life, and the Air Force had seemed like the perfect way to do that. It gave her a bachelor's degree in behavioral science, allowed her to travel and armed her with the skills to defend herself and others. "I made up my mind at Pili's funeral that I would make a difference. Be in the FBI or CIA someday, make the world a safer place." She'd dreamed of making it into one of those agencies, of hunting monsters and making a real difference in the world. And now she'd wound up here.

"So you became a kickass warrior," he finished. "I'm glad you made it out of there."

But not kickass enough. The bleak thought stole into her mind before she could block it. She owed it to her dead sister and to her fellow prisoners to keep fighting. If she gave up hope, she was as good as dead.

"Your sister would be proud of you." He sounded convinced.

A sudden lump clogged her throat. She hoped Pili would be proud. If she somehow survived this and made it home in one piece, she'd make it into one of those government agencies or die trying.

"Tell me your favorite memory of Pilar," he coaxed, dragging her back to the present.

She thought about it and, despite the pain in her face, smiled a little. "Mostly dumb things. Dancing around the kitchen together in our place after we ran away. The sad little Christmas tree she bought at a discount lot and dragged home. We decorated it with strings of popcorn and bits of fabric because it was all we had. That was the best Christmas ever," she whispered tightly. Blowing out a shallow, painful breath, she swallowed back the tears that threatened. "What about you?"

"Christmases were always a big deal at our place. Big dinner, lots of laughs." He sounded wistful, but she could hear the edge of a smile in his voice. "Mostly just my family. They're my happiest memories."

Maya blinked away the sudden moisture in her eyes. His love for his family was so strong she could practically feel it. A small part of her envied belonging to that kind of tight-knit security, but she just wanted him to return to his loved ones safely. The chances of them escaping on their own were almost zero. Their only chance lay in a rescue. She prayed for a miracle.

"They're..." She paused to gather herself, found the courage to say it aloud. "They're all out looking for us by now. Right?" She hated the uncertainty eating at her.

"Yeah. And with the Sec Def being involved, the entire region has to be crawling with SOF personnel right now."

She clung to the tiny spark of hope those words lit inside her. Maybe someone would find them before it was too late. Otherwise their chance of escape—of survival—dwindled by the minute. Even if they managed to get out, in her condition she'd be a liability to the others now. No way could she keep up on the run with her injuries.

They were silent a long time. To stay calm, Maya focused on taking shallow breaths and feeling the steady throb of Jackson's heart beneath her palm. "In your training," she began, in English this time, "you must have been good in the water. Scuba diving and whatever."

"I wasn't at first, but I got real good eventually. Why?"

A beat passed before she answered. "I've always wanted to scuba dive." The wistful words trailed off into silence, and he didn't break it.

She was just drifting off into a light doze when the sound of footsteps snapped her to rigid wakefulness. Her bloody lips pressed together to stifle a cry of pain and fear. Were they coming back for her?

No. No! Her heart beat a hard tattoo against her ribs.

Jackson heard it too. He tensed, seemed to hold his breath for a few seconds until it became clear the person was headed toward them. She forced herself to pull her hand away from him, her mind screaming in protest at the loss of her only anchor in this sea of agony and suffering.

"Maya," he whispered, regret and urgency lacing his voice.

Forcing back the cries clawing at her throat as she inched her way to the middle of her cold cell, Maya gathered what was left of her courage. If the guards suspected she and Jackson cared about each other, they'd exploit it at every turn. She refused to allow that to happen. She was the ranking military officer; her duty now was to protect Jackson and the Sec Def.

If that meant taking more beatings over the next few hours or days to spare them, she'd do it.

I am an American Airman.
Wingman, Leader, Warrior.
I will never leave an Airman behind,
I will never falter,
And I will not fail.

She repeated that part of the Airman's Creed over and over during the long seconds while those dreaded footsteps approached. The beam of the flashlight finally washed over her and for one terrible moment, the panic rising inside her was so strong she didn't think she could hold it back.

But the man holding it merely shone it over her still form as though he was looking her over or making sure she wasn't dead yet. Apparently satisfied by what he saw, he clicked it off and shuffled back toward the opposite wall. His knees cracked as he sank down and settled himself there.

Aware of Jackson lying close by and that her captors would be returning for her soon enough, Maya closed her eyes and drifted into a fitful doze, desperate for the escape.

NINE

THEIR JOINED VOICES floated into the cool spring air as Khalid and his men said their dawn prayers. The air was chilly, his breath rising in a silver vapor into the sky. As one, they kneeled together, facing Mecca, touching their foreheads to their prayer carpets while the first rays of sun filled the valley below, painting the harsh and barren landscape with tones of pink and gold.

A beautiful morning for reflection and an entire day full of promising opportunity ahead.

He and his men finished prayers and gathered together for a light meal of tea, bread and dried fruit. Everyone was quiet but in good spirits, though Khalid could sense nervousness in some of the others. He'd done what he could to calm their fears, but there was no escape from danger now. Their high-profile prisoner guaranteed that a full-scale rescue operation was well underway now. Every last man had to maintain increased vigilance and be ready to move location at a moment's notice, using one of the various evacuation plans already in place.

He spotted Mohammed sitting away from the others, wrapped in a heavy woolen shawl. The teenager's gaze connected with his for a heartbeat before he looked away. Expelling a deep breath, Khalid approached him. This had to be dealt with. "Did you sleep well?"

"Yes, Khalid-jan." He wouldn't meet Khalid's eyes and his expression was guarded.

Khalid lowered himself to the ground and squatted beside Mohammed. Together they watched the sun rise, spilling more of its warm light across the valley. "Taking those prisoners was an important thing. You understand what we must do now, yes?"

The boy nodded, looked away and shifted his feet. Khalid knew why he was so uncomfortable. It was the reason he'd sent Mohammed away from the room before beginning the physical part of the female's interrogation. From the corridor he'd have heard everything, but at least he'd been spared the sight of it.

"Our prisoners are well-trained soldiers," he continued. "It is my duty to break them, to find out what we need to know. That is the only way to help our people now. It is how we will begin the end of the American occupation."

Mohammed nodded again, still staring out over the valley.

Khalid harbored no anger or impatience toward the boy for his reaction to last night. He had no doubt that Mohammed was one of Allah's warriors, but this boy would serve the war effort in a different way. There was no urgent need to expose him to more of the uglier truths of this war. Khalid knew it wasn't the mistreatment of the female Mohammed objected to. The boy simply had no stomach for torture, let alone to watch it performed on a bound captive, regardless of sex or age. Khalid understood that.

"You don't have to watch that part of it," he said in a low voice. "Not if you don't wish to."

Mohammed lowered his gaze to the ground, a flush

staining his cheeks above the scraggly beard he was trying to grow, as though he was embarrassed by his reaction. "I will do whatever you require of me."

"Witnessing the interrogation is not necessary for you to prove your loyalty to me." And in truth, Khalid would prefer that the boy not see it. There was something so unspoiled and pure about Mohammed, Khalid was loath to see it ruined.

That same innocent light had been stomped out in Khalid's soul when he was just a child, because he hadn't been given the choice. In its place a deep, burning anger had been born. Now nothing could extinguish the flames that hungered for justice and acceptance. He'd battled that unquenchable fire his entire life and would until the day Allah chose to take him home. He didn't want that for Mohammed, this half man, half child he'd been entrusted with. In this at least, Mohammed would have the choice Khalid had been denied.

"Do not fear that I see your aversion to witnessing suffering as a weakness, Mohammed," he added, feeling protective of the boy. "You have a great capacity for mercy. That is a rare gift."

The boy's lips thinned in displeasure. "Mercy is for the weak," he mumbled.

"Not always." He wished someone had shown him mercy when he was young, other than the initial gift of allowing him to live as a babe swelling his mother's belly when his true origins had been revealed. If he could help Mohammed retain that inner purity for a while longer as he trained to be a warrior, perhaps it would remove some of the deep stains on Khalid's soul. Time would harden the boy eventually anyway.

If he lived long enough to reach full manhood.

He pushed the thought from his mind. "Has Jihad returned from his patrol yet?" Rahim's liaison had left at three o'clock that morning to do a security check of the area with two of Khalid's men.

"No. He should be returning soon though."

Khalid rose and stretched his back. "Come. The prisoners will need water. You may take them some."

Mohammed jumped up to do his bidding. A few strides from the entry, he paused and looked back over his shoulder. "What about...food?"

The boy's naïveté and the concern in his eyes made something inside Khalid ache. Something he'd long thought dead. He kept his tone firm but kind. "No. Water only. These prisoners are different from any others. I need every advantage to get them to tell me what I need to know." He left the rest unsaid.

Whether he understood his intent or not, Mohammed didn't argue.

Following him to the entrance of the cave network, Khalid paused when the radio on his hip squawked. He pulled it from his belt. "Yes?"

"I am with Rahim," Jihad said without preamble. "He wishes to meet with you."

Rahim was here? Khalid's pulse tripped. "When?"

"The sooner, the better."

"Meet me at the designated place. I'll wait for you there." Khalid replaced the radio, hardly able to contain his excitement. If Rahim was close by, it meant the Americans had not yet found their hiding place. There was no way he would ever have ventured here otherwise.

Khalid took three men with him to the prearranged spot, all young and loyal men in their early twenties who would lay down their lives for him without hesitation. They maintained extreme vigilance as they descended the steep rocky trails to the rendezvous point, too aware of the rising sun exposing them and the ever-present threat of American satellites or drones in the area. Behind the cover of some large boulders and a screen of brush, they waited.

A small group of men appeared a few minutes later. There was no mistaking the great leader among them, though Khalid had never seen him before. Rahim was tall and broad through the chest and shoulders, his bearing and muscled frame broadcasting his previous life in the military. His light gray pakol covered most of his hair, but seeing the man's coppery beard glinting in the sunlight was still a shock. As were the light blue eyes that met his when Rahim came close enough.

They crinkled at the corners as he smiled. The morning sun displayed the freckles covering his face, testament to the amount of time his pale skin had been exposed to the Afghan climate. "Khalid. Peace be upon you," he said in Pashto.

"And on you, peace." They shook hands.

Rahim placed his free hand over their clasped ones and regarded him warmly. "Praise be to Allah that we meet at last."

He inclined his head. "God is great."

Rahim released his hand. "You have done great work with this operation. You do your mujahideen brothers a proud service. Now." A hard glint entered his eyes and he switched to the flawless English of his birth so that only Khalid would understand what they were saying from then on. "I understand you have some prisoners for me to meet."

JACKSON ROLLED STIFFLY on to his side and forced himself into a sitting position when he heard the footsteps approaching. Beside him, he could hear Doug shuffling in his own cell. Maya had finally slipped into a light sleep, a little under an hour ago as best he could tell. He hoped she stayed asleep for a long time, if for nothing else than to spare her from the pain of her injuries. She was breathing shallowly, her body self-splinting to prevent further damage.

The lantern in the man's hand bobbed, making the softly glowing light bounce with each step. Jackson could make out the figure of the teenager, Mohammed, who'd brought Maya back to her cell after the interrogation. He passed by to Doug's cell, setting the lantern on the floor with a metallic clink. He held something up—a canteen—and held it through the metal bars, raising it once by way of offering. Doug didn't respond. The boy tried again and waited, hunkered down at the cell door, but after a minute or two passed without an answer, he moved on to Jackson.

The lantern light gave just enough illumination for Jackson to get a good look at the boy's face. Mohammed had to be under twenty. His black beard was thin and scraggly, his upper cheeks soft and smooth, no wrinkles around the eyes. He offered him a drink from the canteen, frowning when Jackson didn't acknowledge him. He said something in Pashto that Jackson didn't understand and poured a little of the water into his hand to drink it, showing it wasn't poisoned or tainted in any way. Jackson ignored the offer, despite how dry his mouth was. He was so thirsty he craved even a mouthful, but he would never let his captors know it. He could go another day or two without water if he had to.

Mohammed offered the canteen again, making a re-assuring sound in his throat as though saying, "Come on, it's okay."

Maya stirred.

Jackson tensed as she moaned and gingerly shifted on to her back. In the lantern light he could see she'd squeezed her eyes shut, her lips pressed together to stifle sounds of pain. She had to be even thirstier than him and Doug after what she'd gone through last night. If she had internal injuries to her GI tract or internal bleeding, drinking could cause even more damage. He licked his dry lips and got to his knees close to the bars separating their cells.

"She's hurt," he said to Mohammed, who stared at him in surprise. The language barrier was a problem, but there was no way he could misunderstand what Jackson was saying. "I'm a medic." He raised his shoulder a few inches and looked pointedly at the reflective patch on his upper arm. "I can help her. Let me check her, see if there's anything I can do."

No response, though the kid glanced between him and Maya, frowning in uncertainty. Looking at Jackson for confirmation, he held the canteen up and gestured toward her with a questioning look on his face.

"She's hurt," he repeated, looking in her direction then shaking his head. "No water yet. I need to see if it's safe for her to drink."

Mohammed lowered the canteen and stared back at him with a worried frown, and Jackson realized what was going on.

It wasn't the language barrier. He didn't have the authority to allow Jackson to enter Maya's cell, let alone free his wrists. Probably because the kid knew Jackson could kill him with his bare hands if given the chance. Mohammed might be brainwashed and fighting for the wrong side in this war, but he wasn't stupid. And right now he was Jackson's best hope of helping Maya.

"Let me help her." Urgency thrummed through him. If he could just convince Mohammed to let him in there, make himself seem nonthreatening, maybe Jackson could earn his trust enough to get him to remove the flex cuffs around his wrists.

A sudden image of breaking the kid's neck appeared in his head. He dismissed it with a silent growl of frustration.

Fuck.

Even if he convinced Mohammed to let him into Maya's cell with his hands free, moving her without knowing the extent of her injuries might prove fatal for her. And he couldn't kill the kid, grab her and make a run for it while leaving the Sec Def still locked up. Even if he got them out of here, the chances of them surviving the attempt were slim at best.

But the innate urge to escape was powerful.

He glanced over at Maya's pinched face, his mind whirling with different options. The entire countryside had to be crawling with soldiers out looking for them, along with every technological advantage the U.S. had over the enemy. He had to consciously slow his heart rate to calm himself. His paramount concern right now was Maya. She was the most at risk and the one in immediate need of care. He tried again to plead his case. "Let me help her. I need to see how badly she's hurt." He kept his expression neutral, trying like hell not to give away how much she mattered to him. If Mohammed picked up on that, he'd tell his superiors.

Mohammed seemed to hesitate a few seconds before meeting Jackson's gaze, and stared at him for a long moment. He pointed at Jackson then to Maya, his eyebrows raised in silent question.

Jackson nodded emphatically. "Yes. I need to see her." If he found the serious injuries he feared he would, he'd make a lot more noise until they gave him some medical supplies to work with, or at least something he could give her for the pain. Bastards had to have access to some opium.

Mohammed eased back on to his haunches and chewed his lip as if he didn't know what to do. The fact that he hadn't up and left the moment Jackson had issued the first request gave him hope. Maybe there was some decency left in this kid after all. If so, Jackson had to capitalize on it before one of the others came back.

As though he'd come to a decision, Mohammed leaned the canteen against the cell bars and met Jackson's gaze, holding up a finger in the universal sign for "just a sec" then rose, leaving the lantern where it was. Jackson bit back the shout of denial on his tongue.

"Where's he going?" Doug whispered from beside him, his voice full of anxiety.

"Either to ask permission for me to look at her, or to get the others," Jackson answered, a new dread churning in his gut. His turn in the interrogation seat was coming. He knew that. Had he just guaranteed being next? With renewed urgency, he focused on Maya's inert form. "Maya? Can you hear me?" He'd gladly take the coming beating if it saved her from another.

Her eyes opened, one nearly swollen shut. He could see the light reflecting in the other one. "Yes." The answer was so soft he barely heard her, and it made his heart squeeze.

He didn't have much time. "When they come back, just stay quiet and still. Don't do anything that might draw attention to you, okay? Try not to react, no matter what they do." Whatever happened next, he wanted her out of the line of fire. If—when—they came to take him away, he didn't want her reaction to make her a target again.

"Okay." Her eyes slid closed as if the effort of keeping them open was too exhausting.

They lapsed into a tense silence until Doug spoke at last. "They'll come for me next."

Jackson swiveled his head around to look at him.

"It's me they want answers from. I'm the reason we're all here."

"They're going to use us against you," Jackson corrected, stating the obvious. "The reasons behind all this don't matter. We're all in this together now."

Voices floated from the far end of the corridor, where Mohammed had disappeared. Then footsteps. The strong beam of a flashlight lit their way, and Jackson's stomach sank when he recognized the bastard who'd beaten Maya walking in the lead. Mohammed trailed behind at the end of the group, with two more big men following behind the leader.

Jackson quickly dropped back to the wall of his cell and drew his knees up. Maya didn't move from her position on the floor, but her breathing had turned shallow with fear. With every step the men took, his muscles drew tighter and tighter, his body suspended in a hellish flight-or-fight mode. Only he could do neither.

The leader stopped directly in front of Jackson's cell and handed the flashlight to the man next to him. Whoever he was, he was taller and broader than the leader. The man passed by to pause at the Sec Def's cell, raising the beam of light and taking his time perusing their most valuable captive. He said something in Pashto to the leader, who answered him with a clipped response. The new man spoke again, and there was no need for Jackson to understand the words to recognize the smile in his voice. He was well pleased with what he saw in that cell.

The beam hit him next. Jackson squinted and focused on a spot on the floor between his bound boots, while the man looked him over for what seemed like an inordinate amount of time. He asked another question and received a response from Mohammed this time. Jackson knew they were talking about letting him check Maya. His heart leaped in relief when the light slid away from him, but he held his breath as it swung toward Maya.

From the corner of his eye he watched as it slid over her body, lying still on the cold floor. There was dried blood smeared on the left side of her face, and she had one arm curled over her waist protectively. The light beam froze on her like a spotlight, and all at once a deathly stillness stole through the chamber. Jackson's nape prickled in warning.

The man holding the flashlight said something sharp and curt. No one answered. He shifted and faced the leader, saying something in a deceptively quiet voice that was no less lethal for its lack of volume. The leader answered in a clipped tone and fell silent. The tension in the room was palpable.

It seemed like hours before the light at last slid away from Maya and pointed toward the floor at the man's large boots. Military-style boots. Then he squatted down in front of Jackson's cell door. "You're a PJ?"

The flawless English shocked him so much that his head snapped up before he could stop himself. When he saw the face reflected in the beam of the flashlight, he went cold all over in sudden recognition.

A copper-tinted beard glinted in the light, covering most of what were definitely Western features. Below the fiery eyebrows, a pair of brilliant blue eyes gazed back at him. "I'm called Rahim."

That name exploded in his brain like a claymore. Holy fuck. The man who'd beaten Maya wasn't the leader at all. They'd been abducted at the command of this man, who every intelligence agency allied with the U.S. had been searching for over the past three years. And here he was, safe and sound.

Shock reverberated through Jackson, holding him paralyzed for a few seconds until the man spoke again, this time with less patience. "I'll ask you one last time. You're a PJ, correct?"

Jackson gave a tight nod.

"Lieutenant Lopez does need medical attention. I understand you asked to provide it?"

He wanted to say yes. But he was worried now that Rahim and the others had figured out the truth between him and Maya. He prayed he was wrong. He had to hold on to whatever hope he could find.

"Well?"

He gave a hesitant nod, daring to meet those pale

eyes. He almost welcomed his turn with the beatings. It would be better than being forced to sit idly by and watch Maya suffer for a single moment longer than necessary.

Rahim assessed him for a moment with those intense eyes before nodding once to himself. Then he rose. "I'll be back with some medical supplies in a little while. Mohammed will stay here and watch you." With that, he strode away, the others following him except the kid, who slid down to sit against the far wall of the corridor.

Jackson let his head drop back against the wall and closed his eyes, struggling to understand the enormity of what was happening. Rahim's words rang in his head, bringing mingled relief and shock. That unmistakable Midwestern accent told him without a doubt that the impossible was true.

The United States's number-one high-value target was a fucking American.

TEN

KHALID STEPPED INTO the room he'd used to interrogate the female prisoner with an uncomfortable stiffness in his muscles. He was not looking forward to the reprimand he sensed was coming.

Rahim entered next, followed by his most trusted man, Jihad, who dropped the heavy carpet back into place behind them. The small windowless room was immediately plunged into darkness, save the beam of the flashlight Rahim held. He swept it around the tiny space, lingering on the metal chair and the blood spatters marking the hard-packed floor.

Jihad stood back near the wall with his arms crossed over his chest, observing Rahim's inspection. Reaching back, Rahim placed the flashlight on the small metal table with a quiet clang that seemed to echo in the stillness. The light washed across his face, and the livid expression in his eyes made Kahlid's hands turn clammy.

"What were you thinking?" The low words sliced through the tense silence. He spoke in Pashto, no doubt so that Jihad would understand. That added humiliation only increased his resentment.

Khalid fought the urge to shift his stance under the power of that angry stare. "She is the weakest and the one with the least training," he said defensively. "I can use her to make the others talk."

"You can't use her if she's dead, can you?" Rahim snapped, his tone dripping with disgust. "As it is, she may be too badly injured to be of any further use to us."

He bristled at the rebuke, especially in front of an audience. Jihad's black stare was every bit as disgusted as Rahim's. "I have to show them what I'm capable of."

If possible, Rahim's eyes turned even colder. "It's only day one. You went too far."

Kahlid's immediate reaction was to argue, but the logical part of him knew it wouldn't do any good. And he was walking a very perilous path now. Months before, he'd tricked an American soldier on the battlefield into calling in the airstrike that had killed Khalid's former leader General Nasrallah, whom he had regarded with irritation and disdain. Not so with Rahim. He was a powerful and charismatic leader, battle tested, and he had a true vision of how this war needed to be waged.

Khalid had fought long and hard to have the freedom and opportunity to lead his own men in this fight. The last thing he wanted was to lose everything he'd finally won.

And if there was one man he feared crossing, it was Rahim.

Khalid cleared his throat and lowered his gaze in deference, forcing back the tide of anger rising inside him. "Shall I finish it then?"

"No. I'm going to let the PJ do what he can for her. It will be a show of mercy, and if she lives, it will help our cause with the others. If she dies, you've lost whatever advantage she brought us."

She wasn't going to *die* from what he'd done to her. "I didn't beat her that badly," Khalid protested. "I made sure of it."

"You lost control," Rahim accused flatly. "And I'll bet you weren't even aware of it until you saw her just now."

Unease curled inside him. Had he lost control? At first he'd tempered the blows, trying to wear her down bit by bit. But once he'd started lashing her with his belt, his memory became fuzzy. "I had to break her will in order to use her against the others."

"And in doing so, you've hardened their will against you. Now is the perfect time to show mercy."

Strange how he'd just had a conversation about that with Mohammed this morning.

Rahim sighed and folded his arms across his chest, mimicking the same stance as Jihad. Individually they were very intimidating. Together, they made for an imposing display of power and authority. One that made Khalid's heart rate accelerate. "This is about your past."

Khalid stiffened in shock, unable to form a response. Mortification crawled through him. Just how much did Rahim know?

One side of the man's mouth lifted in a sardonic smile. "You seem surprised. Don't be. I know the secrets of every man in my circle, no matter how dark or distant. I was warned about your temper. Don't make me regret my decision to overlook it."

Khalid's hands balled into fists. How dare anyone say such things about him. Who had done it? Nasrallah? One of Nasrallah's men? "My past has nothing to do with this."

Rahim raised one coppery brow in silent dispute. "I think it does. You still carry the anger and shame of your upbringing and have not yet learned how to control it. That is something you need to do immediately if you want to continue performing operations for me. I won't risk failure because one of my men doesn't know how to control himself." His cool blue eyes seemed to look deep inside Khalid, finding the lonely and angry young boy he'd once been. "You've executed this operation extremely well up until this point, and I'm willing to give you another chance."

Khalid exhaled the breath he hadn't realized he'd been holding, embarrassed that he'd been chastised this way, resentful of the way his cheeks flushed. What did Rahim know of that kind of shame? Of being an aberration, hated by the entire village because his mother had traded her body for food from some Russian soldiers to keep her starving family alive during one bitter winter? He was grateful for the semidarkness that hid his reaction. Finding his humility wasn't easy, but it was necessary. "I understand. Thank you."

Rahim picked up the flashlight and motioned for him to start moving. "Bring me what medical supplies you have. Jihad will take them to the prisoner and let the PJ do what he can. Then he'll stay to observe your future interrogations with the other prisoners."

More blood rushed to his face, pulsing in his ears in a dim roar. He did not require supervision. He wasn't a misbehaving child. Clenching his hands into fists, he made himself nod. "If that is your will."

"It is. I cannot risk you losing your temper again and killing the Secretary of Defense. I need his information and a recorded statement, Khalid. This sort of opportunity only happens once. I intend to capitalize on it."

It was on the tip of his tongue to tell Rahim to carry out the interrogations himself from now on then. Self-preservation made him choke the words down. "And how do you suggest I get that from him?" he demanded, an edge to his tone.

Rahim didn't bother casting a glance at him as he walked back through the opening, where Jihad had pulled the carpet aside. "Any way you can, short of injuring him to the point that he can't give the statement. And believe me, if you cross the line again, I'll know."

JACKSON LIFTED HIS head when the men came back down the corridor. Only two this time, Rahim and that other guy, probably a bodyguard. He carried something in one hand—a large bag. No freaking way. They were actually bringing him medical supplies?

He remained where he was, not daring to believe it until Rahim hunkered down in front of the cell door once more. "I've brought you what we have. Jihad will take off those flex cuffs and give you fifteen minutes with her. After that, you and Secretary Haversham are going to have a little talk with Khalid."

Jihad? Nice fucking name, asshole. Jackson made sure his expression gave nothing away, doing his best to ignore the cold knot of dread in his gut. He stared at the bridge of Rahim's nose as he'd been trained, giving the impression he was making eye contact while decreasing the risk of displaying emotion.

"And don't do anything stupid. Jihad is former ISI, partially trained by us—you," he amended with pleasure. "If you try to escape he'll kill you. Is that clear?"

Jackson nodded, knowing he wouldn't be able to escape even if he did kill Jihad and Mohammed before they raised the alarm. A suicide mission would end *his* captivity but would make the others' much worse. And part of him feared that Maya would give up if he died.

Rahim pushed to his feet and said something to Jihad in Pashto. The big man unlocked the cell door and motioned for Jackson to approach. Jackson's muscles tensed, a surge of adrenaline whipping through his body. He stood, bending at the waist to avoid hitting his head on the low ceiling. Following their commands went against every ingrained instinct, but what choice did he have? If it meant being able to help Maya, he'd do damn near anything they wanted. He just hoped he didn't seem too eager.

The muscles in his arms bunched as Jihad took his bound wrists and cut the zip tie with a sharp knife. One snick, and his hands fell apart. He shook them, relieved when the burning pain seared his skin because it meant the blood was flowing again. Jihad motioned with his head for him to follow and Jackson did, shuffling awkwardly with his bound feet. He ducked through the low cell door and waited while the other man unlocked Maya's cell. His heart was pounding when he at last stepped inside.

"Mohammed," Rahim said, and the boy scrambled over from where he'd been sitting against the wall. He held the lantern up, providing more illumination as Rahim spoke. "Jihad has some medical training. He'll help you if you need a hand."

It was too bizarre to hear the most-wanted terrorist on the planet talking to him in perfect American English.

"Do what you can to make her comfortable. They'll report to me on her injuries after I'm gone." With that he walked away, his footsteps retreating into the darkness beyond the glow of the lantern.

Jackson clenched his jaw as he waited for Jihad to

set the medical stuff down and shine the flashlight on Maya. Make her comfortable? Was that asshole serious?

Smothering the anger boiling up to the surface, Jackson kneeled beside Maya and set a hand on her right shoulder, careful to hide his feelings for her. "I'm going to help you."

She nodded weakly, eyes open to slits, battered mouth pressed into a thin line. Taking the flashlight from his observer, he got his first good look at the damage. He barely stopped himself from swearing. Her left eye was swollen almost shut. From the size and color of the bruise along her cheekbone and the amount of swelling, he suspected she might have a facial fracture. His fingers were cold, but at least he had sensation back in them. He placed two beneath the angle of her jaw to check her carotid pulse. It was rapid but strong, and there was no fever that he could detect.

Her good eye was okay and the pupil responded properly to the light stimulus, telling him there was no significant head injury. He slid a hand beneath the back of her neck, applying gentle pressure before stroking his thumb across her skin, a hidden caress to comfort her and tell her how much he cared. "What's hurting you the most right now?"

She swallowed, a jerky movement of her throat. "My wrist, ribs and face."

The ribs worried him most. "In your back? Can you show me?"

Taking a shallow breath as though bracing herself, she shifted and froze with a gasp.

He reached out to steady her immediately, careful to place his hands on her hip and shoulder so he wouldn't cause her any further pain. "I'll turn you. Nice and slow, okay? Just lie still for me."

She was motionless and rigid, breathing in shallow bursts. Though he didn't want either of the captors touching her, he couldn't hold her in position and do a thorough exam at the same time. He glanced over at Mohammed and gestured for him to come closer. The kid balked, looking scandalized by the thought of touching a woman, and Jackson was forced to give up and allow Jihad to support Maya. She flinched when he touched her, but at least the guy was being gentle and his hold was steady.

Jackson raised her T-shirt to get a better look, careful not to expose any more skin than necessary. This time, the sight that met his eyes had him uttering a low curse. An inch or two inside her right shoulder blade, a dark bruise showed where something had slammed into her ribs. The deep blue and purple spread out in an ugly blotch along her back. He tested the bones carefully one by one, easing up when she arched and bit her lip. The ribs had to be at least cracked, if not completely fractured. "Does it hurt when you breathe?"

"God, yeah."

A lot, going by her shallow breathing and muffled sounds of pain. "Any sharp, poking sensations inside?"

"No. Just hurts outside."

He continued palpating her ribs, following them around her side to her stomach. When he applied gentle pressure there, she grimaced. "Sore there?"

"Tender," she corrected.

"What happened?" He forced himself to ask the question, fully aware he wasn't going to like her answer.

"Just a few punches," she managed, a light sheen of

sweat covering her face, popping out across the skin of her belly.

He hated the mental image that evoked.

Determining she most likely did not have internal injuries, he let out a relieved breath and took a look at the wrist she had cradled protectively against her. She made a sound of protest when he took hold of her arm and hand, her body guarding against more pain. The light showed swelling and discoloration along the side of her wrist up to her thumb. Her hand was cold, her fingers trembling in his grip. "Can you move it?"

She shook her head, mouth pressed into a tight line, not even attempting to bend it. That told him everything he needed to know. From the position of the injury, it looked like she had a scaphoid fracture, and maybe the distal end of the radius was involved too. He set her arm down carefully against her body. "Where else?"

"My...feet."

What had the bastard done to her there? Shifting down her body, he took her icy feet into his hands. Her toenails were intact and the bones were as well. The soles were mottled red and white, covered with livid welts.

Jackson bit down on the inside of his cheek to keep from snarling. Goddammit, how had she endured all this? If they somehow escaped, she wouldn't be able to walk for at least a few days. "Okay," he said, keeping his voice calm and steady, despite the sick rage pulsing through him. "Anywhere else?"

"No. That's it."

It was more than anyone should ever have to fucking endure. Unable to rein in his anger completely, he shot a lethal glare at Jihad before reaching for the medical bag.

MAYA CONCENTRATED ON taking shallow breaths while Jackson looked her over. She was ashamed for him to see the evidence of what had been done to her because she knew it would eat him up inside, but having him next to her and feeling his touch were comforts she desperately wanted. She soaked it all up like a drought-stricken flower, desperate for a drop of rain.

The shivers that stole through her sent searing shocks of pain out from her damaged ribs. She hated that the other men were here, that the one named Jihad was touching her. He made her skin crawl. All of those bastards did. Since there was nothing she could do but endure, she allowed herself to drink in the sight of Jackson's stubble-covered face as he bent over her. She wanted to reach out to him so badly, tell him how she regretted using him that night in Kandahar.

Hell, if she wasn't going to make it out of here alive, she even wanted him to know she was falling for him. With his every touch, he made the ache in her heart grow worse until she had to close her eyes, lest she give herself away. She lay quietly while Jackson worked, gathering supplies from the bag they'd brought him.

"I'm gonna tape your ribs now. I can't wrap right around your chest because the compression could cause positional asphyxiation, but the tape should help with the pain a bit."

"Okay." She trusted him and was grateful for his help. His manner was so calm and sure, it was a comfort in itself. In her mind she imagined the others leaving, and Jackson gently lifting her into his arms to hold her in the cradle of his body.

Large, gentle hands lifted her shirt higher, easing the bottom band of her sports bra up to expose her sternum. With practiced care, he began ripping lengths of tape and applied them from her sternum outward along the right side of her rib cage. Gasping when he reached the fracture site, she bit back a growl of pain.

"I know. Sorry. But it should be better after this." He secured the last pieces and pulled her T-shirt down before moving on to her wrist. That too he wrapped up, using a piece of stiff cardboard from something in the bag as a splint. She bore the pain the best she could, swallowing back the nausea that welled up. Man, she was thirsty, and starving. Were they ever going to be fed? Or was this part of the plan—to beat and starve them into submission?

She opened her eyes to peer up at Jackson, trying to memorize every detail of his face. He leaned over her and set a hand behind her neck once more, checking her lip, which had started bleeding again from all the talking. He put a small butterfly bandage on it to help seal the edges. "Could probably use a stitch or two there, but it should heal as is if you keep your lips still."

As in, keep her mouth shut? She might have laughed if she hadn't been freezing and in a shitload of pain.

Something wet touched the corner of her mouth and she glanced down to see him cleaning her face with a moistened pad. She swallowed automatically, the touch of that cool, wet cloth triggering a powerful thirst.

"Want some water?"

She nodded. Mohammed handed the canteen to him, and she allowed Jackson to support her head while she took a tentative sip, almost moaning at the feel of the cool liquid sliding over her parched tongue. Jackson held her steady while she took several slow sips and held her good hand up to signal she'd had enough. He handed it back, and she shot him a pleading look. Wouldn't he take any?

She shivered again, and this time Jihad said something to Mohammed, who left. Jackson gave her nape another covert caress as he finished checking his work, and she fought the sudden sting of tears. Right now she'd give anything for him to lie down beside her and hold her in his arms. Any pain it caused would be worth it to have him up close against her, feel his steady heartbeat beneath her cheek.

A minute later, Mohammed returned with a blanket and set her socks and boots next to Jackson. Jihad released her and positioned her on her left side with surprising care before stepping back and holding the flashlight so Jackson could see. He eased her socks on, then her boots, and she was grateful for the immediate increase in warmth they brought. The soles of her feet felt swollen and bruised, throbbing inside her boots.

Rummaging through the bag, Jackson came up with a syringe and two small vials. He squinted at them for a second before looking down at her. "You allergic to fentanyl?"

"No."

He inserted the needle into the bottle, filled the syringe. "I'm going to give you enough to take the worst of the pain away, and some ketamine to knock you out for a bit. Your body could use the rest."

He wasn't telling her the whole truth. She'd heard what that American-turned-terrorist bastard had said about them having a "visit" with Khalid, the man who'd beaten her. Jackson might want to ease her pain, but she knew what he really wanted was to shield her from seeing whatever they did to him.

Her heart constricted in fear. She flung her good hand up toward him, grasping his wrist tight. "Don't. I don't need it."

Regret and apology flashed through his eyes but he went back to preparing the syringe, adding the ketamine. "I'm putting you out, Maya."

She tightened her grip. "Please don't."

He didn't answer, his face an implacable mask as he pushed the plunger up to rid the syringe of air. He wasn't going to listen. A single tear escaped, rolling down her temple.

Jackson stilled for a moment, then murmured, "It's gonna be okay."

Please, she begged with her one functioning eye, *please don't.* She couldn't bear the thought of him enduring what she had, or worse. It made her want to throw up.

Something cool and wet swabbed over the side of her hip, and then the brief sting of the needle registered. He covered her with the blanket and tucked it around her, watching her face. She shook her head, afraid to let go, her fingers digging into his arm like talons.

Reading her distress, he took her hand in his and set his other against her unhurt cheek, gazing straight into her eyes. "Don't fight it. It's okay, I'm right here."

A sob built in her throat. Already she could feel the drug stealing through her veins, weighing her eyelid down and making her limbs heavy. The pain receded and she began to float away on a warm sea. She struggled to keep her eye open, afraid she'd never see him again.

The last thing she heard was his low voice washing over her. "I'm here."

But she knew that the next time she opened her eyes, he wouldn't be.

ELEVEN

JACKSON KNEW THE moment Maya checked out. Her head lolled to the side and her breathing evened out. Deepened. The ketamine would black out everything that happened between now and when it wore off.

The guard, Jihad, said something to him. Jackson braced himself, knowing what was coming even though he didn't understand the words. He was thankful Maya wouldn't remember what happened next. For a second he almost fought when his arms were roughly yanked behind his back and another zip tie tightened around his wrists. His muscles corded, ready to spring. He had to consciously relax them as Jihad jerked him to his feet and shoved him through the cell door.

He stumbled, barely catching his balance before he fell. The dark corridor yawned before him. He might not have a choice in going down there, but he sure as hell wasn't going easily. Jihad propelled him forward with one hand wrapped around his upper arm and the other shoved between his shoulder blades. Jackson resisted, forcing the man to muscle him with every shuffling step.

At the end of the corridor, someone pulled away a rug covering a doorway. Jihad shoved him through the opening. The tiny space was lit only by a single lantern on a low table opposite a metal chair. It was something right out of a SERE school scenario, but there were no built-in safety nets here.

He dug his feet in, refusing to move another step. The militant kicked the back of Jackson's knees, making them buckle. He fell into the chair with a jarring thud. They were on him instantly, binding his feet and hands to the chair frame. Jackson's heart slammed. He could see the spatters of blood on the floor and knew they were Maya's. The sight of them, combined with the foreign feeling of being powerless, filled him with a dizzying rage.

He stared straight ahead as Khalid stepped forward from where he'd been standing against the far wall. Jihad and the other man who'd tied him to the chair retreated into the shadows, where they remained, watching. Jackson was more than ready for a fight. He'd gladly take them all on if the cowardly bastards would untie him and let him defend himself.

Khalid walked up until he was close enough for Jackson to see his yellow eyes and read the fury burning in them. He met that eerie gaze head on, refusing to be cowed. Khalid's lips thinned. "Who are you?"

"Staff Sergeant Jackson Thatcher," he responded in a flat voice and started to give his serial number when Khalid interrupted with another demand.

"What were you doing with the Secretary of Defense yesterday?"

So they'd only been captive for a day? It felt like longer. "I can't answer that question."

Khalid circled him, staying close enough that Jackson could smell his body odor. "You're not his bodyguard, you're a medic. What were you doing in that village?" His voice dropped to a sneer. "Did you think you could win the hearts and minds of my people by giving out medicine and stuffed toys?"

Beats the hell out of terrorizing them like you assholes do.

"You were on a specialized operation. You must know about others. What are they?"

"I can't answer that question." Even if he knew the details of other ongoing operations, he'd never sell out his SPEC OPS brothers by divulging them.

"What *are* they?" he snapped behind him. Jackson could feel the impatience in the man, the seething anger below the surface. He could already tell this guy had serious control issues.

"Answer me!" A hand flashed out and cuffed him across the side of his head.

"Jackson Thatcher, staff sergeant," he answered, and gave his serial number. He was ready for the blows, but even so he grunted when a fist connected with his jaw, snapping his head back. Stars danced before his eyes for a moment until his vision cleared. Khalid was back in front of him. He refused to meet that hostile glare, staring at the wall beyond him instead. Maya had withstood her beating. He could do no less.

Another punch to the face, this one slicing open his lower lip against his teeth. He closed his eyes and tensed, his only protection for the blows. Another to the side of the head. A vicious kick to his shins that hurt like hell, and one square in the chest that knocked the chair back with a metallic shriek against the floor. He bent over, struggling for breath.

"Where are they attacking next?"

Gritting his teeth, swallowing blood from his cut lip, he remained silent. Name, rank and serial number were all he was required to say. Talking would do him no good and he sure as hell wasn't telling this asshole anything he wanted to know.

A hard hand gripped his hair and yanked his head back. Jackson instinctively resisted the motion, the muscles in his neck screaming with the effort. That seething, accented voice rolled over him once more. "You saw what I did to the woman. I will do far worse to you, and then I will bring her back in here and kill her, slowly, while you watch. Is that what you want?"

His mind screamed in protest at the threat. He couldn't give in. Not even to save Maya. If he survived and she didn't, he'd have to live with that somehow.

"Does her suffering not matter to you?" Khalid sneered. "You could save her if you wanted to. Tell me what you know, and I'll let her live."

The offer tempted him, though he could never trust it. He clamped his teeth together to hold back a snarl. His only comfort was knowing that Maya would understand his decision to stay silent. She would realize that he didn't have a choice. She'd stayed strong for them. Jackson would do the same for her and Haversham. His honor and protection of his fellow POWs were all he had left to fight for.

Khalid released his hair with a rough yank. A second later his booted foot caught Jackson in the stomach, despite the way he was hunched over, driving the air from his lungs. Pain tore through his torso. When he opened his eyes, his captor was holding a knife in his hand. The wickedly sharp blade glinted in the lantern light.

Even with his training, Jackson's insides withered at the sight of it. This was about to get ugly and he wasn't going out quietly. If he died, it would be fighting every step of the way, bucking and struggling against his bonds. He might even get lucky and free an arm or leg to protect himself. His nostrils flared as he drew in a deep, fortifying breath, praying for strength, trying not to think of all the things that knife could do to him.

Khalid raised the blade. Jackson tensed, a guttural snarl building in his throat, his body preparing for the worst.

Shouting suddenly erupted outside the room. Khalid's head snapped around.

The kid, Mohammed, burst through the carpet-covered doorway, breathing hard, his eyes wide. He babbled something to Khalid, who seemed to pale, his posture rigid with shock.

Khalid barked a few words at Mohammed then snapped an order at the other men in the room. The knife in his fist lowered. Before Jackson could breathe a sigh of relief, Jihad stalked across the room and yanked a hood over his head, engulfing him in darkness. Someone untied him from the chair and began shoving him forward, he assumed toward the door.

What the hell was happening?

Men raced past him, some already ahead of him. He could hear the groan and scrape of metal as they unlocked the cell doors, more angry shouts and the noise of scuffling while they hauled the Sec Def out. His yelled protests rang through the corridor. Were they getting Maya too?

He couldn't slow his heart down. Though he resisted, whoever was pushing him kept forcing him onward. Disoriented, hampered by the bonds at his ankles, he fell to his knees. Impatient hands hauled him roughly upward and another man came over to help, the two of them picking him up and carrying him. The temperature warmed suddenly, and he knew they'd taken him outside into the sunshine. Was it morning or afternoon?

An engine started off to the right. The men carrying him rushed toward it and dumped him into the bed of what had to be a pickup. Someone else was thrown in beside him, and from the masculine grunt he knew it was Haversham. Another body landed half on top of him a second later. Maya. She was completely limp and he hoped still unconscious. He doubted the bastards had thought to place her on her uninjured ribs or worry about her fractures.

Someone climbed into the back with them, and the tailgate slammed shut. More shouting, more running feet. Men rushed past to the cab and climbed inside, jostling the truck. The front doors shut and the driver gunned the engine, spinning the tires.

"What's going on?" Haversham shouted above the noise.

"Dunno, but I'm hoping it's because one of ours had a lock on our position." It was the only thing that made sense. They bumped and bounced along the road, tossing Jackson and the others around the truck bed. Cursing, he shouted to Haversham, "Help me brace Maya. She's unconscious." *And she's got enough broken bones already.*

The hood blocked out all the light and made him feel claustrophobic. He battled with the feeling of suffocation, focused on slowing his breathing. Feeling their way to Maya, together he and Haversham wiggled toward her and pinned her between them, doing what they could to keep her from slamming into the metal bed every time the truck bounced. She was out cold, her face pressed against his chest as best he could tell. She seemed so small and fragile up against him like this, unable to defend herself.

They drove for a long time, well over an hour, the steep upward pitch of the truck and the cooling temperature telling him they were going uphill. They had to be in the mountains somewhere. The hood was too opaque for him to see even a glimmer of light, so he had no way to tell where the sun was or what direction they were traveling in. Were they still in Afghanistan? The MEDCAP had been in a village only a few hours' drive from the Pakistani border. They could've crossed over while they were still out from whatever they'd been injected with.

"Can you see anything?" Haversham asked.

"Nothing through this hood."

"Me neither. Any idea where they're taking us?"

"No."

The guard in the truck bed with them kicked Jackson's thigh in an order for silence.

He and Haversham did their best to cushion Maya's body for the duration of the journey. His arms, hips and back were bruised all to hell by the time they arrived at their destination. They had only a few seconds to rest before the tailgate dropped and men started dragging them out.

Shouting and shoving, the captors herded them into someplace cold and quiet. A rattling of keys, the squeak of metal hinges and rough hands shoved Jackson forward into his new home. He pitched forward and landed flat on his face on some metal wiring. When he rolled to his side, he came up against more metal. Struggling on to his hip, he tried to get to his feet but his head hit more metal. The hood was snatched off him, and he got his first look around as his cell door slammed shut.

He was in a fucking cage now. He couldn't see Maya—it was too dark to see any farther than beyond the perimeter of his cage. Curses and struggles came to the left in the darkness, and he recognized Haversham's voice as they hauled him away, presumably for his turn in the hot seat.

Jackson scurried backward until his shoulders hit the back of the small enclosure, straining to see in the darkness. He was alone. Nobody was guarding him now, and he still didn't know what they'd done with Maya.

Giving vent to the adrenaline racing through him, he lashed out with his bound feet, slamming the soles of his boots into the lock mechanism. The captors had moved them because they'd feared the U.S. military had found their location. Soldiers had to be in the vicinity. The men holding them captive would be twitchy, anxious and prone to acting without thinking. That made them ten times as dangerous.

Focused on his goal, he kicked repeatedly at the lock, not caring about the amount of noise he was making. He was determined to get out of this fucking cage and fight for their freedom.

KHALID WAITED IMPATIENTLY for Jihad to finish tying the Secretary to the wooden chair someone had dragged in for that purpose. Fear was a living thing inside him, writhing in his veins. He hadn't taken a full breath from the moment Mohammed had burst in, saying that Rahim had been alerted and their hideout's location had been leaked.

The mole Rahim had spoken of aiding the Americans was real. Khalid was suspicious by nature and had mentally reviewed each of his men during the drive to this new location. He'd come up blank. None of his men had the education or contacts necessary to pull off such a thing. They were all ignorant villagers and farmers. That left only Rahim's men, but the three he'd left behind with Khalid had been present the entire time and there was no way they'd have been able to alert the Americans without one of his men overhearing.

Jihad removed the Secretary's hood and stepped back to observe the interrogation. Khalid hated that he had someone monitoring his work, but there was nothing to be done about it. And if the Americans truly were in the area, Khalid was running out of time to get the information he needed. He might have only hours left before the Americans found them and staged a hostage rescue attempt. And Khalid would never be taken alive.

"No one knows where you are now," he taunted his prisoner, towering over him. "I am growing short of both patience and time." It was possible they might have to move the captives again soon. Urgency gnawed at him. "You have many things to tell us, but you will give us that recorded statement before the rest of it. You will tell your people that this war is unjust, and why. You will tell them that you and your military have no right to be in our country and that they should put pressure on their politicians to withdraw from the area. If you do not, you will suffer for your defiance."

Khalid stepped aside enough to allow the man to see the sharpened knife on the table, as well as the electrical box waiting there. "Whether you say it of your own free will or because you merely want the pain to stop is irrelevant to me. I only care that I get what I need."

He paused for effect, not expecting a response, and he didn't get one. The dark-skinned man's deep brown eyes glittered with hatred as he stared back at Khalid.

"I don't plan on killing you yet," he added. "You are no good to me dead. But if you somehow withstand what I do to you, I have others I can kill in your place. Remember that. The woman has already had a taste of what I can do, and I am prepared to do far worse to her and the PJ with you for an audience. So. Will you make a simple recording to save them? Or will you sacrifice them to keep lying to your people about the truth of this war you wage against my homeland— against *Islam*?" The thought of it sent a fresh bolt of fury through his body until his hands shook. This man and others like him were responsible for this war and all the blood and suffering it brought. For that alone, Khalid wanted to kill him.

"There is no oil here," he spat, riding the edge of his temper, barely holding it in check. "Your military is here waging a continuation of the Crusades of old, to try to rid the world of Islam. You unbelievers will *never* rid the world of Islam, the only true religion. And you will never rid the world of Allah's soldiers who are about to carry out attacks on their rightful targets— on *your* soil." It gave him tremendous satisfaction to know what was about to happen in America. That it would happen regardless of the outcome of this operation. The Secretary's video statement would make it that much more terrifying for their enemy.

Spreading his feet apart, Khalid curled his fingers into a fist, ready to strike. He already knew the answer he'd receive and welcomed the coming beating he would inflict. His blood pumped hot and fast through his veins. "Well? Will you make the statement?"

The Secretary remained silent, looking through him rather than at him. Staring into that determined face, the elation faded. Instead of a surge of power, Khalid was suddenly filled with a hollow fear that he would not be able to get what he needed from this man. And if he didn't, his usefulness to Rahim was over. Then it would only be a matter of time before Rahim had him killed.

He was not afraid of death, only of dying the worthless half-Russian bastard everyone had viewed him as his entire life.

Tamping down the rage and fear inside him, Khalid raised his fist and hurled it toward the prisoner's face.

TWELVE

Maya woke from a troubled, pain-ridden doze to find herself still caged like an animal in this new place.

It might have been hours since she'd last woken here, or it might have been days. The constant darkness made it impossible to tell how much time had passed and increased the sense of disorientation. Any pain relief from the injection Jackson had given her had long since worn off. Her mouth was totally dry now. A while ago, the teenager, Mohammed, had come with her only meal, a thin piece of nan bread she'd been forced to bend over and eat off the floor without the use of her hands, the position making it feel like her ribs and the left side of her face would explode from the pressure.

They still had one of the men in the interrogation room. Every few minutes, a new set of hoarse screams would echo down the corridor. If her hands had been free, she would have clapped them over her ears to drown out the sound. Each cry of pain made her stomach clench and her skin ripple with chills of terror. It might be Jackson in there. The captors had taken turns torturing the male prisoners, so she knew he'd been tortured at least once already. It made her ill to think of them hurting him.

They had to be coming for her again soon. Could she withstand that sort of punishment again? A few days ago, before all of this had happened, she would have said yes without hesitation. Now she wasn't so sure.

She allowed herself to retreat from the present and slip into the past. She'd kept Pilar's memory close all these years and right now she needed her sister more than ever.

Her mind flipped through the catalog of stored memories she kept tucked away, for some reason settling on one of the last days she'd seen her sister. It was a Friday night, and she'd just come home from a study session at her high school to get a jump-start on her final history paper. She'd walked into their crappy apartment to find Pili getting ready in their room.

Maya stopped dead in the doorway, that familiar sick feeling washing over her. Her sister stood before the mirrored closet dressed in a short, tight black leather miniskirt and a red halter top that barely covered her breasts. Her thigh-high black high-heeled boots sat on the floor next to her bare feet.

Maya lowered her backpack to the floor, hating the mingled shame and anger warring inside her. "I thought we were going to hang out together and watch a movie tonight. You said you weren't working this weekend." She couldn't help the accusatory note in her tone.

Pilar glanced at her in the mirror before turning her attention back to applying the ruby red lipstick on her mouth. There were purple smudges beneath the carefully applied concealer under her eyes, and her ribs now showed below the hollows of her collarbone. Because she would rather do the drugs she was addicted to—even if she refused to admit it—in order to escape her shameful reality rather than eat the food selling her body bought them. "I have a client."

He wasn't a client, Maya thought in disdain. He was just another john willing to fuck her sister for money. Maya bit back the angry words rising inside her. "Will you be back tomorrow?"

"I'm not sure." Her sister wouldn't meet her eyes.

She swallowed, the pressure in her chest expanding until she thought she'd burst. When Pili reached for those fuck-me boots, she couldn't hold it in any longer. "We can move away from here," she blurted, desperate to make her sister listen. "We've done it twice already—we can do it again."

Pilar drew the zipper up the inside of one bare leg. "We're not moving this close to the end of the school year."

"I can go to a different school."

"You're on the honor roll and about to take finals. We're not moving." Her tone was implacable, and it made Maya's heart sink.

"You don't have to do this," she pleaded, her voice breaking. There were tears in her eyes as she watched her sister zip the other boot and straighten to fluff her hair, carefully styled over one shoulder to draw attention to the deep V in the low-cut top that showed off her cleavage. Advertising the merchandise for sale. "Don't go out tonight. We can get by another way. I can get a part-time job or—"

"No." Her sister whirled around to face her, her expression set. "You're staying in school and that's final, and all I want you to worry about is your studies. You're going to make it out of here. I swore it when we left that monster's house."

The knot in her throat threatened to choke her. She hated it that her sister was selling her body to provide a future for her. Hated even more the weakness and shame she felt in standing by and allowing it to continue. And she loathed the judgmental part of her that disapproved of what Pilar was doing. Her sister had taken the abuse for two years to shield her, was now doing a job she hated just to keep them off the streets. She should be grateful, not condemn Pilar's decision, no matter how uncomfortable it made her. Yet she couldn't ignore the reality that her sister had sold her soul along with her body.

Emotion tightened her throat. "You don't have to do this. I don't want you to, especially for me. We'll get out of here together and make a new start. We'll—" Her words cut off when Pilar set her hands on her shoulders, squeezing gently. Her smile was warm, the worn look in her eyes making her appear far older than her nineteen years.

"Don't you worry about me. You hear me? I'm fine. There's nothing more important to me than making sure you finish school and get a scholarship to get out of here for good. I know you'll do it."

It frightened her that Pili hadn't said they'd both get out, together. She pressed. "And then you'll come with me, right?" That was the real reason Maya had busted her ass these past two years, putting all her effort into her schoolwork. From the day Pilar had begun turning tricks to keep food on the table so that Maya could stay in school, she'd vowed to herself to get a full-ride college scholarship and take them far away from this life, start fresh in a place where no one would know about Pilar's sordid past.

The dimple appeared in Pilar's right cheek as her smile deepened, even though Maya knew it was forced.

"Sure." She kissed Maya's forehead and grabbed her purse that held condoms and lubricant. Pulling out a wad of ten-dollar bills, she handed them to Maya, who took them reluctantly. To her the cash was tainted—might as well have been blood money. "Go buy yourself a pizza down at the corner. Don't wait up, I'm not sure when I'll be home. But when I do get back, we'll watch that movie together. Okay?"

Maya tightened her fist around the cash, doing her best to hide the dread curling inside her. "Promise?"

"I promise."

It was the last promise Pilar ever kept, because less than a month later she broke the most sacred one of all by taking her own life, abandoning Maya forever. In the years since, she'd never fully recovered from that wound. The scar had long since healed, but the hurt was still there.

Surfacing from the difficult memory, she opened her eyes in the darkness and swallowed hard. She could feel herself beginning to losing hope. The continual pain and anxiety were already taking their toll on her, wearing her down by the hour. It disappointed her to realize she wasn't stronger than that, yet in a weird way it made her feel closer to her sister. For so long she'd been angry with Pilar for taking her own life, thinking she was a coward to give up.

Now, for the first time, she finally got her sister's desire to escape from the pain and misery her life had become. She'd sacrificed everything for Maya, but in the end the shame and despair had been too much. Facing her own grim reality, Maya couldn't help but wonder if she was more similar to Pili than she'd ever realized. In the end, would she welcome death rather than keep fighting?

The moment she thought it, a fierce denial ignited deep in her gut. *No. No way.* She couldn't dishonor herself or her sister's memory that way. And she couldn't let down her fellow prisoners. The Air Force had trained her to withstand this, expected her to. Somehow she had to get hold of her fear and find a way to be strong.

She gave herself a mental slap, trying to bolster her resolve. She might be weak and suffering, but she wasn't out of the fight yet. Quitting wasn't an option. It was *never* an option. *Hang in there. Baby steps. Take things one at a time—don't look ahead.*

"Maya?"

She twisted her head toward the low voice, heart tripping. "Jackson?"

"Yeah. You okay?"

Knowing he wasn't the one being tortured in that room down the hall flooded her with relief. "Yeah. Are you... How bad are you hurt?" There must not be guards around to overhear them, or Jackson wouldn't have dared speak in the first place.

"I'm all right."

He was lying. She could tell from how strained his voice sounded. And from the Sec Def's agonized cries, she suspected they weren't using just fists and a belt on him. Nausea rolled in her gut as she battled to block out those screams. "What did they want?"

"A video statement denouncing the war. They'll never get it."

She tried to ignore the way her heart sank at that, since they'd already threatened to kill her if Haversham didn't cooperate. "How long have we been here?" Her cut lip and swollen cheek hurt from talking, but she didn't care. She needed this connection to Jackson, tentative as it was.

"Couple of days, I think." He grunted as though something had caused him a great deal of discomfort. She tried not to think about what they'd done to him. "Are your ribs a little better?"

"A little."

"Liar."

She could hear the smile in his voice and closed her eyes, her lips curving in response, despite the apparent hopelessness of their situation. His touch and presence were the only comforts she'd had throughout this whole ordeal. "I appreciate what you did for me." The memory of how carefully he'd tended to her, those stolen caresses meant to comfort her made her ache inside.

"I didn't do anything," he replied. "I wish I could've done a hell of a lot more. Like get you out of here, for starters."

"We'll get out together," she said firmly, flinching when Haversham let out a shriek that made the hair at her nape stand up. Her skin prickled, her subconscious reminding her it was only a matter of time before it was her turn in there again. She turned her attention back to Jackson and mulled over everything she hadn't said to him. "Now's not the best time, but I have to tell you something."

"Well, I'm a captive audience right now, so go ahead," he said dryly, emphasizing the pun.

She decided to say it straight out. "That night in Kandahar?" she began, her voice surprisingly controlled. The practical part of her knew there was a good chance she wouldn't live much longer and while they had this rare moment of privacy she wanted him to know how she felt.

She heard his wistful sigh from down the hall. "It was the best night of this whole damn deployment."

The smile pulling at her cracked lips hurt. "Well, good. But now I wish it had been...different." It was stupid to blush when it was nearly pitch-dark and he was too far away to see her anyhow.

"Different how?" he asked after a brief pause.

It wasn't easy for her to talk about, let alone admit to, but she owed him at least this much. She let out a long exhalation, wincing as it pulled at her ribs. "I didn't mean to make you feel used. I wish it hadn't been like that." Well, more like she wished *she* hadn't been like that.

If she could go back in time and do it over again, she'd find them privacy, a locked room with a wide bed and plenty of hours to kill before they had to report for duty. Then she might even have tried something other than having one-sided sex with him. She'd never made love with anyone before. She wished she'd done it with Jackson. He would never hurt her or use her. Without a doubt he'd have made it wonderful, if she'd just found a way to let herself go for once.

His dry chuckle carried to her. "Okay, I forgive you. But next time? You're going to be the one at my mercy instead."

She appreciated his attempt at lightening the mood. She only hoped they got the chance to have a next time. Although at the moment, she'd settle for getting free and being able to feel his arms around her. She cleared her throat, trying to think of something else to say, but everything she came up with seemed stupid. Really, what was there left to say?

"So...know any good jokes?"

Swallowing past the restriction in her throat, she found her voice. "Only one comes to mind. Gallows humor."

"My favorite kind. Hit me."

Her voice shook ever so slightly. "Three prisoners were taken to the execution chamber."

"Awesome. I like this one already."

A laugh shook her. Oh, shit that hurt. "Don't make me laugh," she admonished. What the hell was wrong with her? None of this was even remotely funny. The exhaustion must be getting to her.

"Sorry. Carry on."

"So they haul the first guy to the front of the room. They're getting ready to shoot the first prisoner when he suddenly points out the window beside him and yells, 'Avalanche!' All the guards whip around to look out the window, and the prisoner runs away."

"Smart. I'll have to try that."

"The second guy saw how well that worked for his buddy, and when it's his turn, he yells, 'Earthquake!' then dives under the table. The guards scramble for cover under the other tables, and in the confusion the prisoner escapes."

She drew a shallow breath, licked her sore lips. "Now the third guy, he's watched all this happen and has planned his distraction out real carefully. He waits for his turn at the front of the room while the firing squad lines up with their weapons aimed at him, then at the last second points out the window and yells,

'Fire!'" She fought a hysterical giggle because it hurt her ribs like a bitch. "And so they shoot him."

A pause, followed by a dry snicker floating to her. "That's the most depressing fucking joke I've ever heard in my life, Lieutenant."

She fought the continued urge to laugh, even though she knew it was crazy. "Yeah. Sorry. I'll try for something lighter next time."

"You sure know how to lighten the mood." He was still laughing at her. "You know what?"

"What?"

"When we get outta here, I'm taking you on a vacation."

She liked the thought of that. Her last vacation had been a long weekend down to Miami from Hurlburt. And it had been completely forgettable. "Hmm. You're paying, right?"

"Of course."

"So that means you'll probably expect me to put out, huh?" Her voice was rough and weak.

Another laugh. "Oh, believe me, I'll make sure you *want* to put out. A lot. I'm real attentive."

God, he was so freaking adorable. "I might be interested," she said, playing it coy, loving the distraction of this whole conversation. She shifted gingerly and winced at the sudden stab of discomfort in her back. "Plus, last time I didn't get to see the green footprint tattoos on your ass. You've got 'em, right?"

"Honey, I'm a PJ. And you'll like my tat. It's special."

She bet it was. "So where do you have in mind?"

"Someplace warm. You said you want to scuba dive. Ever been to Hawaii?"

"No. Just California, Colorado, Texas, Florida, Germany and here." Mostly military towns. Pretty sad, when she thought about it.

"Well, then I'll take you to Kauai. It's my favorite place in the world."

She'd love to see it, especially with him. What was the harm in dreaming about it? "Okay, but now that you've brought it up, you'd better not renege on your offer."

"Hey, I'm a man of my word," he said, his tone full of mock insult. "And I'd never renege with you, since I'm already thinking about all the things I'm gonna do to you when we're in bed together next time."

They should not have affected her under the circumstances, but his words made her lower belly flip anyhow. "Why, you into kink, Thatcher?" she asked with mock suspicion.

"Maybe. You scared?"

She snorted, keeping up the banter to cover the pain and helplessness. "In your dreams, Sergeant."

"Naw, I'm pretty sure my dreams are too X-rated for the likes of you, Lieutenant," he fired back.

"I'll consider myself forewarned then." She was smiling now, in spite of her torn lip and throbbing cheekbone, feeling lighter inside. God, she wanted to get them out of here. But how? There was no chance if they kept them confined and isolated like this. Both she and Jackson had tried kicking at the locks of their cages and gotten precisely nowhere. She'd almost vomited at the pain of the effort.

A hollow silence settled between them, and she realized with a start that Haversham had stopped screaming at some point during the conversation. Had they finished torturing him, or had he...

She blocked out the horrific thoughts threatening to bombard her, the continual pain streaking along her face, ribs and wrist, the low-grade nausea and the incessant noisy gurgle of her ravenous stomach. Instead she closed her eyes and conjured up an image of her and Jackson lying on the beach while the surf rolled in. Just like a scene out of a postcard she'd seen. The breeze would be warm and salt-tinged. She could almost feel it on her face, hear the rustle of the palm trees swaying overhead.

Except it wasn't the sound of rustling palm trees she heard now. It was shoes shuffling over the dirt floor. Someone was running down the corridor. She could hear muffled shouts from outside, loud voices as they swept into the corridor and down to where the interrogation room lay. At least two men were barking orders, others rushing to do their bidding.

Her eyes sprang open when she recognized the thud of booted feet heading their way. She held her breath, making herself as still as she could, praying the person wasn't coming for her or Jackson. But the rapid footsteps came nearer. Two sets. They passed Jackson's cell.

She was the only other person down this far.

Her heart hammered as alarm streaked through her, her bravado evaporating under a rush of sheer terror. *Not again.* She couldn't do this again. Sweat broke out across her skin, panic clawing at her insides.

The man at her cage door flicked on a flashlight, and everything in her went icy cold when she recognized Khalid's yellow eyes staring down at her. They gleamed with resolve and barely concealed anticipation.

"Your Defense Secretary is a very brave man," he said, loud enough for Jackson to hear him, "but now we have run out of time. Since he refuses to give us the statement even under torture, it seems I must try a different approach. I've decided we'll play a little game. One I learned from my infidel father's people."

Her mind whirred too fast to make sense of that chilling statement, but her gaze locked on his right hand as he brought it to his waist and patted something at his belt. In the glint of the flashlight, she recognized the shape. An old revolver. She recognized it as Russian.

Her mind rewound his words and rapidly replayed them, trying to decipher what he meant. A game he'd learned from the Russians? What the hell did that mean?

He began unlocking her cage door, and finally the pieces suddenly fit together into a single, terrifying realization.

The crazy *hijo de puta* thought he was going to make them play Russian roulette.

Any bravery she'd managed to build back up drained out of her in a terrified riptide. She scrambled back against the rear of her cage, baring her teeth in helpless defiance as he reached in for her.

She reared away when he grabbed her right upper arm and started dragging her forward. Maya dug in her feet and snarled, swallowing down the jagged scream rising up her throat. He yanked. She lashed out with her boots, enduring the knifelike agony in her ribs and wrist to catch him in the gut. But there was nowhere to go and her satisfaction was short-lived. He hauled her out with one fist, yanking his head back just in time to avoid the back of her head when she flung it at his chin.

His quiet chuckle brushed against the back of her neck as he brought her flush against his body. It felt like he was made of pure steel, and she didn't have a prayer against him with her hands and feet bound. He propelled her in front of him almost effortlessly, her struggles futile. *No. No!*

Something inside her snapped.

"No más, no más!" Her frantic scream shattered the darkness, the terror suffocating, dragging her down and stealing her breath. She panicked, fought for air.

"Maya!" She heard Jackson's desperate shout, couldn't find the breath she needed to answer.

Khalid muscled her down the corridor past Jackson's cell, and she caught only a glimpse of the naked fear on his face before she was dragged past him toward her death.

THIRTEEN

Cam trudged into his barracks in the PJ area of the SPEC OPS compound at Bagram and dropped the remainder of his gear beside his bunk. It was the middle of the night and even though he was exhausted after being out on an op for the past thirty-two hours, he knew he'd never be able to sleep. Not now.

"Hey. What's the word?"

He turned to find Ryan Wentworth coming through the doorway. Went was dressed in full kit and his face was cammied up, ready to head out on his own mission. "No joy," Cam said. "We were close though." Like, less than an hour close to Jackson and the others. "Must have just missed them."

That was the most frustrating part. The fire pits in the militant's camp had still been warm, their cooking utensils left behind in their haste to escape. They couldn't have gone far, yet despite the CSAR team's best efforts and high-tech equipment, they'd managed to elude them. How the hell had they done it?

"Fuck, that sucks," Went muttered.

"Yeah." It weighed heavy on Cam's shoulders. He'd already lost one of his best friends over here, at the end of last summer. He'd been part of the honor guard at the ramp ceremony and had accompanied Ty's body home stateside. Cam never wanted to have to do that again, let alone with the guy he'd worked beside for the better part of a year now. Jackson was one of the best guys Cam had ever met. Wentworth too, despite his penchant for being a pain in the ass. "You guys heading out soon?"

"Mission brief in twenty minutes. You going out again tonight?"

"I asked my commander to let us have another go, but he shot me down until at least tomorrow night. The way things are going, it looks like I'll be part of the rescue but not part of the search." He wished like hell it could be otherwise.

"One of us will find them," Ryan said, the "us" referring to one of the American units either en route or already out looking in the area where intelligence had pinpointed the prisoners' supposed location.

Cam knew a unit would eventually find them. He just prayed they found them before the bastards who'd taken them started killing the prisoners to gain fame and political status. "Hope you have better luck hunting than we did. Thatcher's sisters have been emailing me every few hours since they were informed last night that he's missing." And he couldn't tell them a goddamn thing, due to OPSEC and a lot of other reasons. Best he could do was reassure them the American military was doing everything possible to bring Jackson back safely.

Ryan leaned against the door frame, arms crossed over his chest. "Sucks all around, man. I know they're a tight family."

Cam nodded. He was beat and in need of some rack time but he still planned to call Dev. He just needed to hear her voice, even though he couldn't tell her what was going on. She'd have heard something on the news by now and know something was up. She also understood that most of the time he couldn't tell her anything. It was a big part of the reason he'd fallen for her so hard.

"Command's got everyone out looking for them," Ryan said. "They won't stay hidden for long."

Yeah, but running clandestine ops across the Pakistani border was a giant pain in the ass for all involved. All they needed now was for the Pakistani government to find out and throw up a bunch of political red tape to slow their progress. And if that happened, the captors would have plenty of time to vanish out there in no-man's-land. With every hour the prisoners went undetected, the chance of that happening increased exponentially.

"Bring 'em all home," he said to Ryan.

"Do our best. Later, man," he replied, turning away from the doorway.

Flopping back on his bunk, Cam rubbed a hand over his gritty eyes and pulled out the sat phone he'd borrowed to call Devon. "Hey, gorgeous," he said when she answered.

"Hey! You okay? It's the middle of the night there."

"Yeah. Just wanted to hear your voice."

A pause, and he knew she'd put it all together without him having to say a word. Dev knew him so well already. "Okay. Want me to distract you for a bit?"

"That'd be awesome." He cast a quick glance about the room, making sure he was alone to keep the ribbing from the other guys to a minimum. "Hey, Dev?"

"Yeah?"

"I love you." He made sure he told her every time

they spoke, just in case. Life was unpredictable as hell over here, something they all were aware of.

A soft chuckle. "I know, and I love you back. So, I saw the news about the Sec Def. You getting any sleep over there these days?"

She had no idea that Jackson and Maya were two of the hostages. He could picture her so clearly, stretched out on the couch beneath her living room window at her place near Seattle. She'd have her left leg propped up on some pillows, the brace wrapped around her healing knee. Her chin-length black hair would be tucked behind her ears and the Pararescue mug he'd given her would be on the coffee table beside her. "Some."

"Uh-huh. Well, you watch yourself out there. Okay, you wanted a distraction, so lie down and close your eyes while I tell you about my latest physio appointments. If that doesn't put you to sleep I don't know what will, so if you nod off, I won't hold it against you."

She was so low maintenance. "Sounds good to me."

A short pause. "Cam?"

"Yeah?"

"I know you guys'll find them and get them out of there."

The absolute conviction in her voice made him smile. "Damn right, we will." He only hoped it would be a rescue mission rather than a recovery.

JACKSON'S HEART WAS in his throat when someone returned for him a minute after Maya had passed his cell. He wasn't afraid for himself. He was afraid for what would happen to her. That stricken look on her face had twisted an invisible knife embedded in his chest.

"Come." Mohammed beckoned to him, standing back from the door.

For the first time since they'd captured him, Jackson couldn't get to the interrogation room fast enough. He shot of out his cage, nearly falling when the ties around his ankles hobbled him. Following right on Mohammed's heels into the other room, he breathed out a sigh of relief and said a silent prayer of thanks when he saw that Maya was still okay. She blanched when he entered, her eyes wide. Doug was slumped against the wall where the men had left him after cutting him free of the chair. His eyes were closed, both swelling shut, and blood leaked from his nose and mouth to trail into the black stubble covering his dark face. His white undershirt was soaked through with blood, sweat and vomit. He seemed to be barely conscious.

Shit, what were these assholes going to do to them now? That Khalid guy had mentioned something about a game, but Jackson had no idea what it meant. He was pretty sure this was a last-minute invitation to the party, and they hadn't intended him to be present for whatever they had planned.

Preparing himself for the worst, he waited to find out what they wanted from him.

Khalid stood in the center of the room, watching him with intent, hostile eyes. The other four men in the room all wore black balaclavas to hide their faces, but not him. He indicated Haversham with an impatient nod. "Do what you need to wake him up. I need him alert."

Alert for what? So they could torture him all over again? Fuck that. Locking his jaw, Jackson cut a quick glance at Maya before turning his attention back to

Haversham. Mohammed stepped up behind him to cut his hands free and for just a moment Jackson seriously contemplated attacking. He held off only because he worried about what would happen to Maya after they killed him. Because if he tried anything now, he'd be shot down in seconds.

Instead, he made himself take a calming breath and sank to his knees in front of his fellow prisoner. One of the other men dropped the medical bag next to him. The first thing Jackson did was check Doug's carotid pulse, finding it fast and thready.

Peeling off the stained shirt, he stilled when he saw the burn marks on the man's chest. They weren't serious in medical terms, but they had to hurt like hell, and any open wound in this filthy environment could easily lead to infection. Jackson had scorch marks of his own on his chest from the electrical instrument they'd used on him, but nothing like these.

He did what he could for the burns, applying topical antibiotic cream and taping bandages in place over the raw skin. Haversham's lids barely flickered in response. When Jackson lifted them to check for a pupillary response, he was relieved to see them react to the light in the room, constricting quick and evenly. They hadn't damaged his brain, at least. And the captors expected Jackson to revive him? They were all dehydrated, starving, exhausted and dealing with the aftereffects of the torture they'd been subjected to. Would be better for Haversham to stay in a near-unconscious state, rather than wake up and go through more hell.

"He's not responding," he told Khalid flatly.

"You will wake him. Now."

"What do you expect me to do? He's practically unconscious."

Khalid yanked a pistol from the man closest to him and pulled the slide back, raising it to point directly at Maya. "Wake him, or I kill her." His expression was implacable, and Jackson knew he'd do it.

Fucking pathetic asshole. The threat against Maya was enough to take his attitude down a notch. He cupped Haversham's bloody, scruffy cheeks in his hands. "Hey, Doug. Can you hear me? Wake up. You gotta wake up, man." His nape prickled with the knowledge that the weapon was still pointed at Maya's head. He gave Haversham a little shake, spoke louder. "Come on, Doug, you have to open your eyes." When that didn't work, urgency drove him to smack one hand against the stubbled cheek he cradled. *"Wake up."*

Haversham's eyelids fluttered. He struggled to open them, blinking up at Jackson in confusion. A pained groan escaped his cracked lips.

Thank God. "That's right, come on back."

His eyes focused slowly, taking Jackson in first. When he looked to the side and saw all the masked men standing around the room, he went rigid, a sheen of sweat breaking out over his face.

Jackson hated being responsible for making him endure more of this bullshit. "Sorry, man." He eased back and threw a pointed glare over his shoulder at Khalid, who lowered the weapon and handed it back to the man next to him. Jackson's heart rate slowed. He didn't dare look back at Maya as a suffocating silence filled the room. Jackson refused to let them see his anxiety. They'd feed on it, ramp up their efforts to break him in front of the others.

Khalid kept staring at him, and Jackson stared right back. It was the only show of defiance he could give right now. So, he challenged him with his eyes, wanting whatever the sadist had in mind to be done to him, rather than Maya or Haversham. Compared to them, Jackson was in perfect health. He held that evil gaze. *What now?*

A cold, cruel light entered Khalid's eyes. He jerked his head to the side, indicating a spot between Maya and Haversham. "Get over there and sit down."

Though everything in him rebelled at following the command, he had no choice. Rising from his knees, he stopped when Mohammed approached and reached for one of his wrists. The muscles in his arm tensed, wanting to strike. Needing to. His nostrils flared, a molten anger igniting in his blood. It took everything he had to remain still and allow the kid to secure his wrists behind his back yet again.

Once it was done, he shuffled stiffly to his place against the wall, filled with loathing for the men holding them and for the powerlessness he felt in that moment. Sinking into position a few feet away from Maya, he could feel her fearful gaze on him and the rage faded, replaced by growing despair. He stole a glance at her with his peripheral vision. If there was a way to save her by offering his life for hers, he'd do it.

That others may live wasn't just a motto he lived by as a PJ. It was everything he stood for. And if he was going to die saving a life today, he wanted it to be Maya's.

Cold settled over him. Whenever he'd thought about the end over the past couple of days, he'd always envisioned himself fighting right until his last breath.

Sitting on the hard-packed floor waiting for whatever happened next, he was filled with the awful realization that he'd just submitted to his death instead.

THE PJ'S DARK eyes blazed with loathing and defiance as he lowered into position between the other prisoners. Though he was bound, Khalid watched him closely, trusting him least of all. This soldier was the biggest threat to them, with the Defense Secretary practically senseless and the female so battered. She sat rigidly against the wall, definitely afraid, dried tear marks staining her face, raspy breaths catching in her throat. No threat to him in a physical sense, even if she hadn't been restrained.

And yet she remained impressively strong, despite her injuries. She'd fought him every step of the way down the corridor, somehow understanding what he intended for her and the others. Khalid took note of the dried blood on her mouth and chin, the end of the crude cardboard splint supporting her bound wrist, the guarded way she held herself.

As they made eye contact, the look that flashed in her eyes took him by surprise and gave him pause. It was more than hatred. It was pure determination. Perhaps he'd underestimated her, with her smaller size and weak female body. Aside from the physical damage and fatigue, she was still willing to fight and would do so the second she had the opportunity. Khalid didn't plan on giving her one. Not her, nor any of the others.

Ignoring the lingering vestiges of disquiet plaguing him, he paused a moment to collect himself and clear his mind. The camera was recording on the other side of the room. He'd ordered his men to cover their faces so they couldn't be identified later, but the captives had already seen his own. Khalid couldn't see their expressions, but he felt his men's disapproval. It pervaded the entire room like a toxic fog. A spurt of alarm hit him, the sense that he was losing his men's loyalty making his pulse quicken.

He'd fought for the chance to lead his own men and now that he stood on the brink of clinching their support, he risked alienating them forever. "Let us begin."

Khalid did another visual sweep of the room. He could tell from their body posture and the looks in their eyes that the men were uneasy about this. They were afraid of angering Rahim with this next step, but there was no more time. The Americans were closing in, moving closer every hour, and he had to extract the confession from the Secretary in the next few minutes. His reputation, his future and the next phase of this war all hinged on Khalid getting that confession on tape.

Never taking his eyes off the prisoners, he removed his treasured revolver from his belt and handed it to Jihad, who stood behind him. "Take out all the bullets but one," he instructed in Pashto. Jihad took the weapon from him and flipped open the cylinder. The metallic sound of rounds sliding out filled the room, then a *clicking-whir* as he spun the cylinder.

"Untie her hands," he commanded, gesturing toward the female. One of the men came forward to slice the bonds holding her wrists behind her. She blanched and set her jaw before bringing both hands to her lap, cradling her splinted left wrist.

Once again, he turned his attention to the Defense Secretary. The man was watching him out of slitted, pain-glazed eyes. Khalid spoke the English words slowly, in a clear voice. "So far you have refused to make the statement I want from you. You leave me no choice but to try a different sort of persuasion." He nodded to Jihad. "Give the female the gun," he said in Pashto.

When he faced her, she turned even whiter, her features frozen like a mask. "Russian roulette. You know this game?" He could see from her reaction that she did. "There is a curious expression you Americans have. 'Ladies first.' Since you are a female and the only officer here, you will go first. Pull back the hammer, place the revolver to your head and fire one shot. If you refuse, I will shoot one of your comrades. If you try to turn the gun on any of us, the consequences will be far worse."

To ensure he was protected, he took one of his men's pistols and chambered a round, watching her closely. The metallic sound of the slide was loud in the quiet room. With the solid feel of the weapon in his grip, he spread his feet shoulder-width apart and watched Jihad bend down to hold the loaded revolver out to the female.

FOURTEEN

THE GUY WAS fucking crazy. Or high. Maybe both. He had to be if he expected her to take the revolver that could potentially end her life, let alone think she'd actually put it to her head and pull the trigger.

She reared back from the masked man holding out the pistol to her. He was taller than the others and broader through the shoulders. This close, she could smell the scent of dust and desert wind on him. His gaze was unflinching, calm. He betrayed no emotion whatsoever, even though he was essentially asking her to risk committing suicide in front of the others. What the fuck was wrong with these people that they couldn't see how warped this was?

There was no way she was touching that revolver. No. Fucking. Way.

"Take it."

She ignored Khalid's low command and cast a frantic glance at Jackson. What the hell did she do now? Her stomach plummeted when the expression on his face registered. He was pale and tense, his lips a thin, bloodless line. She tried to read his eyes, sent him a silent plea. *I don't know what to do.* She didn't have the active POW training he had. Jackson stared back at her and shook his head. The helpless rage in his eyes made her want to cry.

He couldn't help her now. She was on her own.

The man crouched at her feet gestured with the pistol again, urging her to take it. Raising her eyes to his, she let him see her hatred and disgust for all that he stood for. Her rage intensified when she caught a spark of amusement there. He thought this was funny? They were all fucking cowards, tormenting helpless prisoners. If she'd been healthy, she'd have loved to take them on one by one until she dropped. At least then she'd go down fighting. This helplessness on top of everything else was too much to bear.

The once-black revolver sat harmlessly on his outstretched palm. It was nicked and scarred all over, showing its age and use. This was no mere decoration and it held more than trivial significance for Khalid. He'd planned this whole thing out very carefully, from the video camera across the room to the air of anticipation he seemed to be enjoying so much.

"Last chance," he said. His tone was flat, hard, brimming with impatience. She didn't know if she was more afraid of seeing that impatience unleashed or finding out if the chamber she chose had a bullet in it.

Swallowing, Maya forced her right hand up.

"Stop," Jackson blurted.

Her fingers closed around the cold grip of the pistol, and the man pulled his hand away. The weight of the weapon felt strangely light, almost nonexistent in her fist. If she was in shock, maybe it would help numb her. Because she had no fucking idea how to get out of this. For one crazy moment, she thought about turning the gun on Khalid and emptying every chamber until she found the loaded one and hit him right between the eyes. She could do it if she was quick enough. Maybe if she could kill him before one of the others shot or disarmed her, they'd stand down.

"Cock it," Khalid ordered.

That cold voice was so devoid of emotion it sent fresh chills down her spine. Her fingers flexed around the grip. She didn't look at him. Didn't dare because she was afraid she'd take the chance and fire at him. If she did and the chamber was empty, her act of defiance would be useless. And then Jackson and the Sec Def would die.

Swallowing, she cocked the hammer back, her mind rebelling at each tiny movement. The metallic click was loud in the choking silence. She heard Jackson shift, caught a glimpse of movement in her peripheral vision as he tensed.

Even with her mind made up, she could *not* make herself raise the gun to her own head. The room blurred, began to spin.

"Raise it to your head," Khalid said.

"Maya, put it down!" Jackson yelled. The desperation in his voice cut straight through her.

No. It was impossible. She couldn't do this.

"You are willing to accept the consequences then?" Khalid purred in a silky tone.

Her insides contracted. Her arm felt rigid, like it was made of steel. Unbending. Her tormentor stared back at her for a few heartbeats, daring her to challenge him.

She never backed down from a challenge. Something in her simply refused to surrender—even now, when all seemed lost.

Maya locked her jaw, maintained eye contact and set the gun down in a blatant act of defiance. If the asshole wanted her dead, he could shoot her himself.

Jackson's relieved exhalation filled the tense silence.

She barely had time to blink before Khalid made his move. His eyes shifted away from her and his gun hand whipped out and up. Maya bit back an instinctive cry of protest, her body going rigid. Khalid swung the weapon around, aimed at the Sec Def and fired a bullet into his lower leg.

Haversham's dazed eyes flew open and he jerked upright, a howl of agony erupting from his throat. He bared his teeth and writhed in place, unable to escape from the pain or stop the flow of blood from his leg. A scarlet pool spread out beneath him.

Staring in horror, Maya blanched. Jackson cursed low under his breath. This time when she looked back at Khalid, she was shaking with a mixture of fear and revulsion.

He raised one eyebrow in insolent reply. "Aim the revolver at your head and pull the trigger, Lieutenant, or I will shoot him full of holes." When she didn't answer, his eyes narrowed thoughtfully for a moment. Then he glanced at Jackson. "Or maybe I'll put a few holes in *him* instead until you decide to cooperate," he finished, turning the pistol toward Jackson.

"No!" The instinctive protest came out before she could bite it back. Whatever horrors she'd endured, she couldn't take that. She'd rather die than be the cause of Jackson's suffering. Being responsible for Haversham's gunshot wound was bad enough. She was willing to sacrifice herself if it spared Jackson.

The swirling nausea peaked and ebbed, making her clammy and shaky. Her hand trembled around the old revolver. Calling on every bit of self-control she possessed, she lifted it slowly. It went against everything in her, but she did it, inch by inch, her skin crawling with the thought of what was coming. Could she actually pull the trigger? She didn't know if she had the guts.

In the end, she closed her eyes. Shut out everything in the room, locked down her emotions. It was easier that way. Digging down deep for her courage, she brought the cold round mouth of the muzzle to her right temple. Bile filled her throat, hot and acidic.

"*Maya.*" Jackson's agonized cry ripped through the room. She squeezed her eyes shut, forcing the image of his stricken face from her mind. Didn't he understand? There was nothing else she could do. If she didn't do this, Khalid would shoot him or Haversham, who was still losing a lot of blood. Friendly forces in the area might have a lock on them, might even find them in the coming hours, but she couldn't stall anymore.

"Don't do it, Maya," Haversham managed between gritted teeth. "I'd rather be...shot full of holes than... watch you do this." She could hear the conviction in his voice, the former Marine still very much alive in him. *Semper Fidelis.*

It was her turn to be faithful to them now by offering her life for theirs.

"No," Jackson said again, as though he'd read her intentions. "Maya, don't you fucking do this. You hear me? Goddammit, *look* at me."

She didn't, because she couldn't bear to. If there was even half as much pain on his face as there was in his voice, she'd never be able to go through with this.

"My next bullet goes in him if you don't pull the trigger within five seconds," Khalid snapped.

Maya bit down on the inside of her uninjured cheek. There was no guarantee friendly forces would liberate them. Even if she survived this game, there was good chance she was going to die here eventually anyway. Her captors weren't going to let her live, and probably none of the others either, especially if a rescue attempt happened. But Jesus, taking her own life? She'd sworn never to succumb to suicide after Pilar. That nothing would ever make her give in, no matter what.

It won't hurt. You won't even have time to feel it.

"Maya!" Jackson tried again.

It took an act of will not to turn her head and look at him. Clamping down on the desire to see him, she faced off with Khalid. Her voice shook. "If I do this and the shot kills me, will you let the others live?"

She could tell she'd surprised him, because he had to consider her words for a moment before answering. "I might. If the Secretary tells me what I want to know and gives the statement." He turned to face Haversham, raised his eyebrow again in that maddening way that made Maya long to shoot him in the face.

He wasn't going to give it. Maya released a shuddering breath and considered her limited shitty options.

If this shot killed her, maybe it would give Jackson and the Defense Secretary a reprieve. If they managed to escape, Jackson would have to carry him out. Either way, she had to believe that her death might help save the others. It was the only thing that gave her the strength to go through with this.

"Don't give them the satisfaction," Haversham bit out, his voice strained. "They're all...fucking *cowards*."

She shut her eyes once more. Her entire body shook.

"Fucking hell, Maya, no! *Please* don't do this."

The desperate plea almost undid her. Almost.

She filtered out the sound of Jackson's frantic voice.

Flashes of memory played in her head like a slideshow on fast-forward. She snagged one as it flickered across her mind's screen, holding on to it with every last bit of strength. Pilar and her at a playground. They were in primary school, on the swings at the school playground, flying high in the sky. Her sister's head was tipped back, her mouth wide open in a belly laugh.

Pilar. She'd see Pilar again.

She ignored the voices trying to pull her back to the present. Her index finger curled around the trigger. Tightened.

A split second, and it'll all be over. There'll be no more pain, no more loneliness. She drew a deep breath and released it slowly, savoring each heartbeat. *I'll see you soon, Pili.*

When that last breath was expelled, every ounce of oxygen pushed from her lungs, her mind went blank.

"No, goddammit—"

She pulled the trigger.

An empty click echoed in her ear.

It took her a long moment to realize what it meant. For her to realize that she was still alive. For the moment, at least.

Her eyes snapped open, her right hand falling limply to her side, because suddenly she didn't have the strength to hold the weapon anymore. The revolver clattered to the ground.

A choked sound came from beside her. "Maya, *God...* You're okay. You're okay, sweetheart. Oh, Jesus—you're okay now. Come on, look at me." Jackson's hoarse voice penetrated her chaotic thoughts.

In the wake of the shock swamping her system, her body whacked out on her. The shaking returned with a vengeance, so bad her teeth rattled. It felt like she was convulsing. Every muscle jolted out of control. She bent forward at the waist and gasped in a breath of air, then gagged from the pain. And gagged again. Nothing came up except bile, burning its way up her throat. Jackson was saying something to her but she couldn't hear the words over the roaring in her ears.

She slumped to the side, barely noticed when someone came forward to take the revolver beside her.

Jesus. Oh, Jesus Christ, she couldn't handle this. Couldn't take any more. She'd been ready to die. There was no way she could do through that again.

"Congratulations," a voice purred from directly above her.

Blinking, she looked numbly up into Khalid's face. He smirked in that oily way of his, holding the revolver.

"You won the first round."

Her lungs heaved, desperate for air. She wanted to fly at him, rip him apart with her bare hands, broken wrist or not. She'd attack him and wouldn't stop until one of them was dead.

Dismissing her, he spoke to a man off to the right. Maya seized her chance.

She launched herself at Khalid, hitting him in the chest with her shoulder. He yelped in surprise and grabbed hold of her as they fell and crashed onto the ground with a bone-jarring thud.

The surge of strength racing through her body was exhilarating. She was mindless, intent on doing as much damage as possible, kill him if she could. Fighting through the splinters of agony in her fractured bones, she rose to her knees and brought her right fist back, hurling it at the center of his face. A large hand flashed out to block the punch, catching the full force of fist with his palm.

The abrupt action jolted her out of her rage-fueled haze. Angry voices registered, Jackson's shout commanding her to stand down. A primal snarl built in her throat. She was done with standing down. If they wanted her dead, she was damn well going out fighting.

Khalid snarled something in Pashto and threw her off him. Panting, she rolled to her back and lashed out with her feet, earning a brutal kick high on her outer left thigh. Her outraged scream echoed throughout the room. He was out of reach now, too far away to get another blow in.

She came up on to her right elbow, bracing for an attack. If he'd been angry before, now he was enraged. She stuck out her chin in defiance, trying to mask the betraying quiver that ran through her. She could feel Jackson's fear beating at her, having risen to his knees, and she knew he would have dived on top of her to shield her with his own body if things had gone further.

Khalid spat at her, narrowly missing her face. His eyes boring a hole in her, he snapped something at the man who'd blocked her punch. Maya wrenched her head to the side, recognizing him as the one who'd handed her the revolver.

She didn't catch any of the heated Pashto words Khalid said to him. But when the big man came toward her, his dark eyes intent upon her in his masked face, Maya let out a cry of protest and scrambled to her feet. Her bound ankles made her stumble and she threw her uninjured hand out to catch herself against the wall, losing her only opportunity to lash out at him. Strong hands gripped her right wrist and wrenched it behind her back, the other manacling her left upper arm.

She kicked and swore as he turned her away and began to propel her toward the rug-draped opening. Out of the corner of her eye she barely caught the look on Jackson's face. Seeing the exhaustion and relief that she was safe set off a wave of determination inside her.

"Since the lieutenant is going back to her cage to serve an additional punishment and the Defense Secretary is unable to take his turn at the moment, *you'll* go next."

Maya's blood ran cold as Khalid spoke the words to Jackson. The odds were down to one in five now. A twenty percent chance that the chamber he fired would be loaded.

She would not let it happen. Would *not*.

"Fucking cowardly *hijos de puta!*" She screamed it at the top of her lungs, thrashing in the big man's powerful hold. It was no use. He was too strong, and she was too sapped of strength to do any real harm.

He propelled her forward through the opening to the corridor, but she didn't make it easy for him. She rammed her head back, catching him in the chest with a hard thud that rattled her brain. When that didn't work, she wrenched her head to the side and lunged at his wrist with an open mouth. He snatched his arm away just in time. Her teeth closed on the sleeve of his jacket, snapping hard together when he yanked it out of her mouth.

Fatigue began to creep in. A slow, insidious weakness stole through her muscles. She was out of breath, panting and sweating by the time they reached her cage. Maya dug her feet in, the heels of her boots scraping through the earthen floor. Mohammed was there behind them, hanging back as though he wasn't sure what he was supposed to do.

She kept resisting. If she disabled the man holding her, she could easily take out Mohammed and find the exit to this place before anyone raised the alarm. With her feet unbound, she might be able to make it out of here. She'd run, find someone to help her. She'd get backup, rescue the others. It was the only option for escape they had. Once they locked her in that cage again, she'd never get out. Now was her only chance, before Jackson pulled that trigger. Maybe the diversion her escape caused would buy him and Haversham more time.

With a final burst of strength, she reared up and attacked. She called upon every training maneuver she'd been taught, and some she'd learned on the streets. The soles of her feet slammed into the man's knees with a satisfying thud that made him stumble and growl in pain. Seizing upon that, she rammed her head back at the same time she drove her elbow up and at his throat. He barely managed to block it, and then he used his momentum to tip them forward. Maya lost her balance and fell, bracing for impact with the floor.

He caught her before she hit, suddenly clamped one arm around the front of her rib cage and covered her mouth with a merciless palm, cutting off her air. She screamed in rage and twisted, uncaring of the fiery shards of pain in her ribs and left cheek, through her mangled wrist. He squeezed her again once, hard, forcing the breath from her. With spots dancing in front of her eyes, she blinked to clear her vision and sucked in a breath to yell some more when he suddenly spoke.

His mouth was right next to her ear, so close she

could feel the warmth of his breath on her skin, the heat of his large body around her. He spoke in a whisper, and the perfect English he used made the scream die in her throat.

"If you want to live, shut the fuck up and listen real carefully to what I say."

FIFTEEN

JACKSON WAS SICK and fucking tired of this bullshit.

He could hear Maya yelling and cursing on her way back to her cage. The Sec Def wasn't going to crack, no way, and that meant Jackson was probably going to die in the next few minutes. They wouldn't make Haversham take a turn with the roulette. The guy was too far gone to even hold a gun, let alone hold it to his head or pull the trigger. And it didn't make any sense for them to watch him blow his brains out when what they wanted was some fabricated political statement they thought would somehow further their twisted cause.

Khalid turned his eyes on him, his mouth still pinched with anger from his tangle with Maya. Jackson fully understood her reaction. When she'd pulled that trigger, he'd been out of his mind with fear, knowing there was fuck all he could do to stop her. And when that chamber had been empty, he'd never known relief so pure. He swore his heart had stopped beating.

Now the rage was back and he was ready to let loose. Because he wasn't playing this game, no matter how many holes they put in him or the Sec Def. That was something Haversham would understand, because it was the POW code to never give in. Maya had done it to save him and Haversham, and Jackson would never forget it.

One of the three remaining masked men stepped forward to crouch next to Jackson with a knife. Jackson wanted to grab the blade slicing the zip tie at his wrists so badly his fingers twitched, but he managed to refrain, instead bringing his freed hands in front of him to rub at the raw skin and restore the circulation. "I want to bind up his leg," he said of Haversham, who was still bleeding all over the place. "He's losing a lot of blood and if he goes into shock and dies, you'll never get that statement."

Khalid jerked the bottom of his long black tunic down in an irritated motion. "Hurry up. Tie it off and nothing more."

Asshole.

Khalid glanced around the room and scowled, muttered something to one of the others, who shrugged. Khalid growled in frustration and gestured to the man, who took off the scarf wrapped around his neck and offered it to Jackson, his other hand brandishing a pistol in case he made a wrong move. Taking the filthy bandage that would likely create the mother of all infections in Haversham's flesh, Jackson shuffled on his knees to the Secretary. The guy was sucking in shallow breaths, his mouth a thin line, his nostrils pinched, skin beaded with sweat. In his weakened state, there was a chance he might not survive the shock and blood loss.

Kneeling at his side, Jackson carefully rolled up Haversham's pant leg, exposing the wound. The tibia and fibula were both shattered. He could see the edges of the fibula just below the torn skin and muscle. The bullet had passed right through the lower leg, so that saved Haversham the pain of having a bullet dug out of him—if Khalid would have let Jackson do it. "I'm gonna wrap this as tight as I can. Hopefully it'll slow the bleeding." It was better than nothing.

Haversham nodded, the movement tight with pain.

"Hold on." Jackson wrapped the sweat-stained scarf around Haversham's shin and tied it, twisting the knot tight over the wound. Haversham blanched and let out a strangled growl, eyes squeezed shut and beads of sweat trickling down his face. Poor bastard. He'd suffer worse than that before the day was out. Broken bones hurt like a bitch. With nothing else to be done, Jackson sat back on his heels and rolled his shoulders to ease the tension there. Not that it helped.

"Your turn."

Jackson looked over his shoulder at Khalid and stared back defiantly. The guy seemed edgy as hell, his eyes shifting here and there, his body posture agitated. He was watching Jackson's hands, as if he expected him to pull a weapon out of nowhere and come at him. The way he was feeling, Jackson would give goddamn anything for the chance to go after him one-on-one with his bare hands.

"Sit back down and take the revolver." Khalid gestured to where it lay on the dirt floor between him and Jackson.

Like hell. "Release the female first."

Khalid's lips curled in a sneer of contempt. "It is a fatal weakness you Americans have, wanting always to protect the women."

Because where I come from, that's what real men do. "The strong have a duty to protect those weaker than them." Maya would want to kick his ass for intimating that she was weak.

Those yellow eyes frosted. "You lie to yourself.

Your government seems to think your duty is to subject the rest of the world to its beliefs. By your own definition, that should make *you* the terrorists." He motioned with an impatient hand at the discarded weapon. "Take the revolver." He cocked his pistol and aimed it at Haversham for good measure.

Jackson's eyes slid over to the Sec Def and he got a minute shake of the head in answer. The guy didn't want him to do it, even though he fully expected to be shot again. Dude had balls. Jackson respected that.

"I will not tell you again!" Khalid snapped.

Jackson opened his mouth to tell him to go fuck himself when a sudden explosion rocked the ground, making the floor undulate beneath him. They all stilled. Khalid froze in place, barking frantic Pashto at the others, who all glanced at each other with wide eyes. The flashlight rattled on the small metal table at the rear of the room, rolling to point a spotlight on the wall behind it.

A flare of hope swelled Jackson's heart, filling it to bursting against his ribs. Had they been found?

Khalid was shouting something at the three other startled men when another blast shook the room. This one was closer, strong enough to rattle the walls and send earth cascading down on them. Jackson wobbled on his knees. The candle in the lantern flickered, its light almost extinguished before it flared to life again. The flashlight fell to the floor and rolled against the wall, blotting out most of its beam. With the room in mostly shadow, Jackson coiled in position, waiting for the right moment to spring. All he had to do was catch Khalid and one of the others off guard for a few seconds. He could snap an arm, take a pistol and even the odds within seconds.

Once he freed his feet, he could haul Haversham out over his shoulder and spring Maya so they could all get the hell out of here.

Casting frantic looks about him, Khalid continued yelling orders at his men. The dimmed light from the lantern and the flashlight cast his face in eerie shadows. With one final order, he turned his head to aim a single searing glance at Jackson before snatching up the revolver and storming out of the room. There wasn't enough time for Jackson to attack any of the others.

All three remaining men stood back near the far wall, aiming their weapons at him. If he lunged now, he'd be dead before he got to his feet.

Tamping down the frustration eating at him, he strained to hear what was going on outside. Those explosions were no accident. He could hear men shouting, but no gunfire. Had a drone fired a missile at their location to draw the militants out? It was the only thing he could think of.

A minute later, yet another explosion ripped the quiet apart. Jackson stayed on his knees, ready to shove to his feet when the ground settled. One of the three guards said something to the others, who nodded. The guy lowered his weapon and headed toward the rug-covered opening, presumably to see what the hell was going on.

He reached out to grab the flap of the rug hanging there when someone ripped it away from the other side. A shot rang out, the bullet hitting him straight between the eyes. He dropped. Before he'd even hit the ground,

Maya burst in with a pistol in her uninjured hand. Jackson didn't even have time to move.

One of the others got out a sound of alarm as he and his comrade started to turn their weapons on her. Without pause, she fired twice more in rapid succession, hitting the remaining two men center mass and dropping them where they stood before they could get a single shot off.

In the flickering lantern light, she looked like an avenging angel standing there. Her hair was a tangled mess and her face was swollen to hell, but her hand was rock steady on that weapon, even with the pain she had to be in. The deadly intent was clear on her face.

Fuck, he loved her. He shot to his feet as she approached, trying to figure out how she'd gotten loose and found a weapon. "How—"

"Shh." Shoving the pistol in her waistband for a moment, she pulled out a knife and handed it to Jackson then took the pistol again, never taking her eyes off the doorway. Jackson immediately sliced the zip tie at his ankles and jumped up to cut the Sec Def's bonds.

"We've only got a few minutes," Maya said from the doorway, peeking over her shoulder to make sure they were alone. "Can you carry him?"

"Yep." He grabbed two pistols from the fallen men closest to him then bent and hauled Haversham over his shoulder, ignoring the man's howl of agony and the pain ripping through his own body injuries.

Maya pushed aside the rug and took point, instantly assuming the leadership role that came with her rank. "Follow me."

Yes, ma'am. She took charge and kicked ass. Not only had she'd somehow gotten free of her jailors, she'd taken out three armed men to give them this chance for escape. He'd follow her fucking anywhere.

She paused only long enough to bend and grab something from the floor and hoist it over her shoulders, wincing when she stuck her broken wrist through the strap to haul it up her arm. In the dimness, Jackson barely made out the shape of the missing medical bag.

Since it was obvious she had a plan, he went with it. She turned left and took them down a narrower corridor, then right toward a light source that told him they were almost outside. Maya crouched down by the hand-dug opening, checking for threats. "Two tangos to our seven o'clock, but they're distracted. I don't see anyone else. We have to make a run for it, get to the trail he said is behind this compound to the right."

Wait, they had inside help? "Who's *he*?" he whispered, changing his grip on the back of Haversham's thigh to steady him. He'd shoved one pistol into his waistband and had the other in his right hand, leaving his left free to anchor his patient.

"The guy who knocked out the kid and told me how to escape." Her eyes stayed locked on whatever was going on outside. "We can't talk from here out, so you have to trust me. You ready?"

He trusted her with his life and was about to prove it. "Ready."

With that, she took off at a stumbling run, though it had to hurt like hell on her swollen feet. Jackson followed, expecting to hear either shouts or gunshots when someone saw them. For the moment, their luck held. No alarm sounded.

Haversham was draped lengthwise across his shoulders, gripping Jackson's shirt in his fists, trying to hold back his grunts of pain. The added weight taxed the cramped muscles in Jackson's legs and back, but the burst of adrenaline counteracted everything but the focus on getting as far away from here as possible.

He kept pace with Maya as she flat-out ran past the crumbling remains of houses and across the rock-strewn terrain. It looked like the captors had been hiding in some sort of a ramshackle village in the foothills that had been abandoned long ago. From the position of the sun low on the horizon and the red tint it threw on the landscape, he knew it was close to sundown. But the sun wasn't setting in the position he'd gotten so used to during his deployment. Rather, it was setting *behind* the mountains looming above the foothills. Since they were obviously traveling west, that could only mean one thing.

They were in Pakistan. Or fucking close to it.

He'd barely thought it when those dreaded shouts finally rose up behind them. Shots cracked through the air, some close enough to ping off the ruins and rocks around them.

"This way," Maya yelled back to him, her long, dark hair trailing behind her as she ran, taking a sharp right at the last building.

Up ahead in the wash of bloodred light, Jackson saw it. A thin trail that looked like it might once have been used by the goatherds who'd lived in the village long ago. From the wear patterns in the dry soil, it had been traveled recently but not often. The trail led straight up the hillside, disappearing from view at the crest. Was there an ambush waiting on the other side?

The shouts were closer now. More shots whizzed past, some close enough they sprayed him with dust when they impacted around his feet. The fine hairs on his nape rose in subconscious warning. A moment later, he heard the thud of running footsteps. Men giving chase. And from the sounds of it, they were gaining on them.

Maya heard it too. She risked a glance over her shoulder and must have decided whoever was back there was too close for comfort, because she ducked out of the way and went to one knee with her pistol ready in her one good hand. "Go, I'll catch up," she yelled at him without taking her eyes off her targets, face pale and drawn in lines of pain.

What? Like hell he was leaving her.

Jackson skidded to a stop just behind her, looking back in time to see Khalid and three other men armed with pistols bearing down on them. Whirling around, Jackson aimed his own, keeping his free hand on Haversham's shoulder as he writhed in place.

Khalid held that stupid fucking Russian revolver in his hand. He squeezed the trigger, even though he was too far away to possibly hit any of them, and Jackson heard the dull click that signaled he'd fired on another empty chamber. If he hadn't loaded or fired it since leaving the interrogation room, that left four chambers remaining, three of them empty.

Hesitating, Jackson started to slide Haversham off his shoulders. "Maya, get back."

Her gaze stayed locked on her quarry. "No. He's mine."

Khalid fired on another empty chamber. Then again. Only two left now, and one was loaded. Taking aim, Jackson pulled the trigger. Nothing happened. Cursing, he pulled back the slide and tried again. Nothing.

Useless piece of shit. Tossing it on the ground, Jackson reached for the weapon in his waistband and raised it. He fired, tagging one of Khalid's men in the thigh. The guy grabbed his leg and fell in a heap, screaming. Another man ran into range, and Jackson winged him in the upper arm. Next to him, Maya fired. He didn't watch to see if she'd hit one of the attackers. He fired again, but the chamber clicked empty. Fuck, he was out of ammo, and Khalid and another man were still closing in on them. Haversham muttered something in a pained wheeze.

"Go, *now*," Maya urged him, face grim and determined.

So she could stay and sacrifice herself? That was *not* how this was gonna go. "I'm not leavin' you," he snapped, furious that she'd even suggest he take off and leave her to fend off two armed men. "Give me your weapon and run," he urged. "I'll be right behind you."

"No." Her voice was so cold and resolute it sent a chill down his spine. It was plain she wasn't leaving until she cleared Khalid off their tail. "If I don't kill him, he'll just keep hunting us."

Without a weapon to help even the odds, Jackson held his breath and waited a few precious seconds, praying Maya was faster than the maniacal insurgent coming at them. All his muscles corded, a shout of denial rising up in his throat at the thought of her risking her life this way when he wanted to be the one holding the gun and protecting her.

The man beside Khalid suddenly broke away from him with a burst of speed. Maya shifted to the right, waiting two seconds before firing, hitting him through the lung. A pink mist puffed into the air. He fell and curled on to his side, his weapon lying forgotten in the dust.

Khalid pulled the trigger again. Maya ducked, but the bullet never fired.

A maniacal gleam entered his eyes, knowing the next chamber was loaded, intending the round for Maya. She had her pistol up and aimed, waiting for him to come into killing range. He didn't slow. If anything, he ran faster. Lit up by whatever unholy conviction drove him, he charged straight at her while everything in Jackson screamed at him to fling himself on top of her to shield her from the shot they all knew was coming.

Maya squeezed the trigger. Her shot went wide.

"Maya, give it to me and get *out* of here," Jackson demanded, wishing she'd just run and save herself.

Then everything went into agonizing slow motion.

With a triumphant smile flashing white in the midst of his dark beard, Khalid squeezed the trigger one last time. Jackson held his breath, praying the bullet would miss Maya.

An empty, metallic click filled the still mountain air.

It hadn't been loaded?

The stunned surprise on his face registered only for a split second before Maya's shot rang out. The bullet hit Khalid high up in the left shoulder, jerking his upper body backward. A spray of blood went up. He let out a roar and clapped a hand to the ruined joint, falling to his knees in the dirt. The useless revolver lay at his feet. Fifty yards behind him, two more men rushed toward him from the rear.

And still Maya stayed where she was, preparing to take another shot. Wanting to finish Khalid.

Jackson fully understood why she wanted to kill him, but the guy wasn't coming after them for the moment, so they needed to haul ass and take every second they had if they were going to get away. He lunged over and grabbed the back of the medical duffel with one hand, hauling her upright. "*Run*, Maya!"

She didn't. Just shook him off and took aim. She fired once more, even though Khalid was so far away the chances of hitting him again were minimal. He jerked to the right, but not in time. She nailed him high in his left arm this time. He screamed and pitched to the side. Already off balance, he tumbled over the edge of the rise and down into a wadi below.

Jackson didn't need to see more. "Go, go!" he shouted to her, gripping Haversham's back and legs, turning to sprint toward the trail.

Maya was already on her feet and running. Seventy-five meters up the hill, he spared a glance back to see the remaining men coming up on Khalid, still lying huddled in the wadi. The two newcomers spun and trained their AKs on them, but the shots sprayed low and wide, plowing into the ground behind them.

Jackson's heart slammed against his breastbone. "Move it," he growled, right on Maya's ass. He shoved a hand against it to help propel her upward, prepared to drag her over that crest at the top if need be.

She hung in there, the strain obvious on her sweaty face and the medical duffel bumping against the back of her injured ribs. Together they scrambled to the top of the rise, keeping alert for any insurgents or booby traps ahead. Once there, the trail broke into four different ones. Jackson scanned the horizon for a breathless second. Should they head west toward the Afghan border? Or south and eventually back into the foothills in the hopes of finding a way to contact friendly forces?

Maya barely paused to catch her breath, gasping, "He told me northwest from here."

"*Who?*"

"Dunno who he was, but I think he was American. He talked in English with no accent," she said in a rush.

So who the hell was he, and why was he sending them farther up into the mountains? It didn't make any sense, though Jackson was grateful for the help. But how did they know they could trust him? When Maya took a step to the right on the trail that led northwest, he reached out a hand and caught her shoulder. She glanced back at him in surprise.

He had way more training in escape and evasion tactics, not to mention combat experience, so as of now that made him the expert, despite his inferior rank. She knew it. "I'll take point. Follow in my footsteps. We've gotta cover our tracks best we can so no one can follow." Even though a blind man would be able to follow them with the spatters of blood Haversham's wound was leaving behind. The sooner the sun went down, the better.

Her jaw tensed but she gave an almost imperceptible nod as he passed her. Jackson shifted Haversham on his shoulders. "You still with me?"

"Yeah," he gritted out, sounding like he was ready to puke from the pain.

Guy was a solid bastard, felt like he weighed a ton. With the lack of food and water, Jackson was already feeling the exertion, even though they weren't at a high enough altitude to make the air seem thin. They had to keep moving. Every step they took put distance between them and the men who would surely be coming after them. The approaching darkness was a blessing, to a point, but without night vision capability, they wouldn't be able to travel far across this rocky terrain.

"I'll take the sidearm now," Jackson said, and it wasn't really a request. He hated moving out here blind without a weapon. Made him feel naked and exposed.

She didn't even look at him, her gaze sweeping the trail they'd just climbed. "I'm good. Our six is still clear."

Fine, he told himself. She'd accepted his expertise, and he had to carry Haversham. At least she was a good shot. Curbing the instinct to argue, he picked his way across the trail, choosing sturdy rocks as stepping stones to keep footprints and tracks to a minimum. He figured they had an hour or two tops until the sun set, and before then he had to find them shelter and water if possible.

Part of him was still struggling to grasp that they were actually free. He planned to keep them that way, no matter what it took.

If he'd been alone he would've gone much faster, but he didn't want to outdistance Maya and leave her vulnerable. He trimmed his pace and kept an eye on her progress. She was done in but still going, pale and sweaty and in desperate need of rest and fluids.

"Gotta keep moving for another couple of hours," he told her and sucked in a lungful of air, ignoring the slight tremor in his legs and the burning ache in his back and shoulders. "Few more klicks and we'll find a place to rest for the night, but we've gotta be on the move before sunup." It would be better to hole up during the day and move at night, but waiting wasn't an option, considering the desperate shape Haversham was in. They'd just have to be damn careful whenever they moved.

"I can make it."

"I know you can, honey." He'd seen firsthand how much shit she could handle and had absolute faith in her. She'd risked everything to spring them from their prison—now it was his turn to lead. He'd get them safely back to friendly lines or die trying.

SIXTEEN

THEY HIKED FOR what seemed like hours before Jackson deemed them safe enough to find a place to stop and rest. By then, Maya was moving on autopilot and had been for a long time. She walked in a kind of numb haze, her legs carrying her without any conscious thought on her part. Jackson was still going strong. He'd only taken a few short breaks during the climb, though he had to be exhausted from carrying Haversham, who was still conscious and in a shitload of pain. Would have been kinder if he'd passed out for at least some of the trip.

"We'll camp there for a bit," Jackson said in a low voice. He indicated a space beneath a natural overhang in the rock that he'd already gone ahead to check out. Jackson had left Haversham with her while he doubled back and conducted a listening halt to ensure they were really alone out here.

The thin crescent moon gave just enough light for her to pick out their hide in the darkness. She took the lead and once inside did a sweep for snakes and scorpions with her boots. That done, she pulled off the medical bag with a relieved groan, gingerly slipping her splinted wrist through the left strap to let it fall at her feet.

Her chest felt tight, every breath difficult. Her ribs

were killing her and there was a constant throb in her wrist and left cheek, but the sheer fatigue was the worst part. She'd never been so tired. During the in-house SERE course, the instructors had told Maya's class they'd be surprised at how much punishment the body could take, and they were right. Maya couldn't believe she was still going, but then, freedom and survival were pretty damn incredible motivators.

Jackson eased Haversham off his shoulders with a low groan and propped the man's back against the rock wall.

Haversham was panting and cursing under his breath as he stretched his wounded leg out in front of him. "Son of a bitch," he snarled.

"Yeah," Jackson whispered, reminding them to keep their voices down. Sound carried a long way at night out in the open. "Let's hope there's something in that kit to make you more comfortable."

Maya unzipped the bag and pulled the canvas sides open. Everything was in shadows, so she stayed out of Jackson's way as he rummaged inside it.

"Whoever he was, I fuckin' love the guy who gave this to you," Jackson muttered. "Here," he said to her, handing over another pistol and full magazine. "There's another one for me, but that's the only magazine as far as I can tell. And there's a canteen of water and some kind of jerky too," he said, holding a bag up to see it in the moonlight.

Maya's stomach let out a loud growl. She took the thin strips of meat Jackson handed her and Haversham and tore into them, chewing them only long enough to keep from choking before swallowing. The salty taste made her ravenous. Jackson was chewing on a mouthful of it when he passed her the canteen. She could have easily drained it in one long drink, but it had to last all three of them, and they were forced to ration it in case they didn't find drinkable water before they made it back to friendly lines. After a few sips, she savored the feel of the cool liquid in her mouth and swallowed, her parched throat sighing in relief. She passed it back to Jackson, who brought the canteen to Haversham's mouth.

"Blood loss is gonna make you damn thirsty," he told him. "Take a few slow sips for now and I'll give you more later."

"Yeah, okay," the Sec Def answered and swallowed the water obediently. His low moan of gratitude vibrated through the closed-in rock shelter.

Maya wiped her right forearm across her sweaty forehead. Now that they'd stopped and her body was cooling, the drying sweat made her shiver in the night air. It was bound to get much colder out here before the sun came up again. Being cold and uncomfortable was still so much better than being back in that hellhole. Still, the overwhelming sense of relief was shadowed by the knowledge that they weren't out of danger yet.

"So tell us more about this guy who helped you," Jackson said to her.

She shrugged one shoulder. "Not much to tell. He was behind me, and I never even saw his eyes. He told me if I wanted to live, I had to listen carefully. Then he shoved a pistol in my hand and knocked that kid out, telling me to get on the trail and head out here. Said to keep going until we hit the first village."

"What's at the first village?"

"No idea." And she didn't relish the thought of finding it, either. For all they knew, it could be a trap. But why would he release them, only to send them into an ambush? It didn't make any sense, but anything was possible. Who knew who the guy was or where his true loyalty lay?

"And you're sure he was American?" Haversham asked.

"American-educated, at least. Like I said, he didn't have an accent at all. And it wasn't Rahim. I would've recognized him."

"So that was it?" Jackson prompted.

"Yeah. He told me all that and dragged the kid away, saying there were three men in the room with you guys. So I ran straight there and took them out."

"Hell yeah, you did." There was a smile in his voice.

"I was too out of it to really see what was happening," Haversham murmured. "Wish I'd seen that though."

"She was awesome," Jackson said. "Now, let's see what I can do for that leg."

Maya kneeled next to Jackson, thankful to get off her feet, which were on fire from Khalid's lashing and worse after the long hike. "What can I do to help?" All she wanted was to lie down and sleep, if her ribs would let her. She already knew they wouldn't. Even in her sleep, the pain kept waking her, every unconscious sigh jolting her in agony. Injured ribs sucked.

"See if there's a flashlight or anything in there."

Feeling her way through the bag's contents in the dark with her good hand, she found bandages, medical tape, a pair of blunt scissors, what might have been a needle and thread, and a little vial. "I think there's some painkiller meds here," she said, holding up the glass vial to him.

Jackson took it, squinting at the label in the thin moonlight. "Must be the fentanyl I gave you. Any syringes?"

She felt around again. "One, and a pair of gloves—maybe latex." And since the needle wasn't wrapped in a sterile package, it was probably the same one Jackson had already used on her. Could he even use that on another patient now? She handed the syringe and gloves to him. "Sorry, no flashlight or matches that I can tell."

"It's okay. I can bandage him up now, then give him a dose of fentanyl—if that's what it is—at first light before I stitch him up." He snapped on the gloves, shifted around and did something she couldn't see, but Haversham's strangled cry of pain told him he was already working on the man's wounded leg. "Pressure dressing's gonna have to do for now. Can't elevate your leg with the fracture unset like that, but the good news is, the arteries seem to be intact."

"How can you tell?" Maya asked. It was so dark she couldn't see anything but black wetness on Jackson's hands where the thin moonlight reflected off his surgical gloves.

"Because otherwise he'd have been spurting blood with every heartbeat this whole time."

Oh. Right.

"Yeah, good news," Haversham grunted between his set teeth.

"I'm gonna bandage this up tight and then I want you to sleep. You too," he said to Maya. "I'll take first watch, and you and I can alternate after that. Right now though, I need you to get some rest. You've been through hell, sweetheart, and while I wish I could give you more time to relax, we're gonna have to keep moving once it gets light out. They'll be coming after us, might have other cells in these hills already out looking."

She heard everything he said but was still stuck back on *sweetheart*. The endearment sent a sudden rush of warmth through her. He really did care, and didn't give a damn if Haversham knew it. "I know. I'll be ready. But make sure you wake me so you can get some sleep before we move out."

"Sure," he answered, and from the offhanded way he said it, she knew he didn't plan to wake her at all.

"Jackson—"

"I'm wide-awake, and I'm the least hurt. You don't worry about me, all right? I've got lots left in me." He finished bandaging Haversham's leg, earning a sharp hiss from his patient, and stripped the gloves off. "That's the best I can do for now, but I'll do better once I can see what the hell I'm doing."

"Looking forward to it," the Sec Def said wryly.

Turning slightly to face her, Jackson reached out and slid a hand around the back of her neck, curling his palm around her nape in a solid grip. The heat of his touch seeped into her skin, easing some of the tension from her muscles. It felt so good she wanted to lean into his body, press her face into his neck. "Sleep now, baby. I got this."

The added endearment and the confidence in his voice put a lump in her throat. "Okay. Thanks," she whispered, grateful for the chance to lie down and sleep. Please, let her be able to sleep.

Crawling over beside Haversham, she lay on her

right side and curled into him to share body heat. The metallic scent of his blood made her stomach roll. She swallowed hard, reminding herself they were lucky to be alive. When she was settled, he threw an arm around her waist and immediately tucked her close, making her bite the inside of her cheek to hold back a gasp at the sudden flash of pain in her ribs. Jackson moved around them, staying quiet, tucking the empty rolled-up duffel beneath their heads. She sighed, wincing at the twinge in her back, struggling to ignore the smell of warm blood in the air.

With her eyes closed, every sense was attuned to Jackson's nearness. Shrouded in darkness, he put a hand on her forehead and smoothed her hair back, lingering for a few moments to run his fingers through the tangled waves. Maya savored every moment of it, yearning for so much more of his touch. Reaching up to squeeze his wrist in a silent thank-you, she swallowed a protest when he finally withdrew his hand. His hushed footsteps retreated out past the opening of the enclosure, and she knew he was finding a place to keep watch, armed only with a pistol.

Releasing a shallow, shaky breath, Maya thought of him standing guard and let her mind drift, knowing she was safe with him there to watch over her.

SOMEONE GRABBED HOLD of Khalid beneath the armpits and lifted him, while another man took his legs. His eyes snapped open as agony seared his upper body, blotting out everything else.

Letting out an inarticulate growl of pain, he struggled in the grip of the man holding his torso. "Put me down," he snarled.

"But Khalid-jan, you're hurt," a soft voice answered.

The fiery burn of the bullet wounds in his arms made him very much aware of that. "Put me down, Mohammed," he snapped hoarsely. The men lowered him to the ground. Someone brought a cushion for his head to rest upon. Khalid blinked up at the night sky, the thin crescent moon hanging over him and the countless stars in the vast sea of black. His mind was blurry, filled with fog, his world a haze of hellish pain.

Snatches of memory came back to him from that afternoon. Firing at the escaping prisoners. That female and the PJ shooting back. His revolver being empty. How was that *possible*? He'd personally watched Jihad remove all the bullets except one. He'd asked Jihad to do it for maximum theatrical effect, and so he could keep most of his attention on the prisoners. Now he wished he'd done it himself.

The last thing he remembered was the thud of the bullet in his upper arm, then falling into the wadi. All because he'd been chasing after them with an unloaded weapon. Blind fury threatened to choke him. "Where are the prisoners?"

Mohammed glanced at the other man beside him before replying. "No one knows yet. The men are out searching."

Khalid closed his eyes and ground his teeth together. "How long have I been unconscious?"

"A few hours. We're moving to the next location you told us about."

Yes, he remembered that part now. When they'd pulled his bleeding body out of the wadi, he'd ordered them to move deeper into the hills to an alternate hideout. The American forces had to be close by now. Khalid needed to stay well ahead of them. "How many men are left?"

"Fourteen. But more are coming to reinforce us in the morning," Mohammed added quickly.

Khalid fought back the burn from the wound and the fear clawing at him. He turned his head to check the blood-soaked bandages wrapped around his right shoulder, the stained sling someone had thought to place around it. The whole arm hung uselessly at his side, either numb or paralyzed from where the bullet had shattered his shoulder joint. The dressing was completely dark and glistening in the moonlight. Whatever they'd done to help slow the bleeding obviously wasn't working very well. "I need more bandages."

Mohammed cleared his throat and glanced away before responding. "There are none. The female took the medical bag. Someone from a nearby village is bringing more for us in the morning."

He wanted to howl in frustration. "How did this happen?" he demanded angrily, pinning Mohammed with a hard glare. "You were sent to watch the prisoner! She was bound hand and foot! How could you let her best you?" The blood loss and exertion from yelling sent a fresh wave of fatigue through him. He sucked in a breath through his nostrils. He had to calm down, conserve his strength for the coming march. Even in the dimness, Khalid saw the boy swallow in nervous reflex. "I—I don't know," he confessed. "I don't remember what happened. I was walking her to her cage when someone hit me from behind and when I got up, she was gone."

"What he says is true," the other man confirmed.

"We found him lying close to the cage, and he suffered a large lump on the back of his head."

The only part Khalid really cared about was that they had a traitor in their midst. Because if he'd believed that Mohammed had let the female prisoner go, he would have killed him here and now, shattered arm or not. "Get me up," he snapped. His first concern was recapturing the prisoners. Then he would deal with finding out who had attacked Mohammed and helped the prisoners escape. And his sentence would be swift and merciless.

"Khalid-jan, you are not strong enough right now—"

"Get. Me. *Up*." He said it with such menace that Mohammed and the other man rushed to help him to his feet. He swayed for a moment, woozy from blood loss and pain. It felt like flames were eating at his flesh where the bullets had torn through.

But the fear of failure burned even hotter.

"Where is Jihad?" he demanded.

Again, Mohammed seemed reluctant to answer. "He is gone."

"Gone where? Dead, you mean?"

"No," the boy answered slowly. "He was not among the wounded or dead. No one has seen him. He just... vanished."

That word rolled around in Khalid's head like a grenade with the pin pulled. *Vanished.* The sudden rush of blood in his ears was almost deafening.

He knew exactly what had happened.

Jihad had gone back to report to Rahim, inform him of Khalid's failure and ineptitude.

Fury and humiliation crawled through his veins, adding to the burn. He shuddered. "We will keep moving until we find the prisoners. I want every available man out here for the hunt, do you understand me?"

"Yes, Khalid-jan." Mohammed stayed at his side, not touching him but close enough to support him should his legs give out.

It hurt to move. Every step was its own separate torment. Khalid looked up at the night sky again. Allah was testing him. Testing his strength and his will. But why? Why, when he'd been so close to achieving his goal?

It is not for you to question Allah's will.

"No one stops," he continued, biting the words out through clenched teeth. "Not even me." Good leaders led by example. Khalid would give every last ounce of his strength to guide his men and finish this mission. They would see his conviction and follow him to the death.

A few hours ago he'd been desperate to get the recorded statement from the Secretary. Now he was frantic to recapture him. He had to get him back and safely hidden away before Rahim took over the operation for him. Khalid had risked everything to achieve this status, and now, when he'd been on the cusp of achieving his greatest accomplishment, he was in jeopardy of losing everything he'd fought for. And all because of an American female he'd grossly underestimated. It was intolerable. And she would pay. When he found her, Khalid would kill her and the PJ for this.

He tried to slow his whirling thoughts down, searching for a course of action. "The Secretary was too badly wounded to be able to walk," Khalid announced to the others. "The PJ will have to carry him, and that will slow them down. And so will the female, because she is *weak*." He spat the last word.

One of his men came loping up with a handheld radio. He passed it to Khalid. "Two of our men have just found a blood trail on a path at the top of the hill by our last location. The prisoners have gone northwest."

"Have everyone meet there immediately to begin the search," he ordered. "We will find them. They could not have gone far."

Even if they had, it didn't matter. Khalid had people scattered across these hills willing to fight for and, if necessary, die for him. He had no doubt he'd find the prisoners. He just prayed it happened before Rahim descended upon them and unleashed his wrath on them all, Khalid and his men included.

SEVENTEEN

KNEELING BESIDE HAVERSHAM while he searched through
the medical kit, Jackson paused when he heard Maya
cough again outside the enclosure. She'd woken in the
middle of the night with it and had insisted on reliev-
ing him for a few hours, and he'd reluctantly agreed because he'd been so exhausted. The dry, sporadic cough
had roused him just before dawn and it didn't seem to
be going away. One more thing for him to worry about.

"Maya, can you give me a hand here?" he called in
a loud whisper.

She came around the corner a moment later, a pistol
in her right hand and her left arm cradled protectively
against her body. The fingers on her left hand were
swollen and discolored, and the swelling in her face had
completely closed her left eye. A kaleidoscope of colors
covered her cheek and eye region, the skin stretched
so tight it was shiny. The only thing that seemed to be
improving was the cut in her lip.

"What's up?" she asked in a near whisper.

"Need you to put pressure here for a minute while I
get the suture kit ready," he said, indicating the entry
wound on the front of Haversham's shin.

Without hesitation, she tucked the pistol in her
waistband and sat on her haunches next to him, placing
her right hand over the saturated bandage. She winced

in sympathy and glanced up at Haversham. "How you doing, sir?"

"I already told you, call me Doug," he answered in a tired, weak voice. Even his dark skin tone couldn't hide the grayish cast of his face. He hadn't gotten much sleep through the night either. During the few hours he'd rested, Jackson had woken multiple times from Doug's restless shifting. "And I'm hangin' in there."

"Good to hear. Just tell me if I hurt you too much. Gotta keep the pressure up."

"I know. Do what you have to do."

Jackson filled the syringe with what remained of the fentanyl. A used one wasn't ideal but it was better than nothing, and at least with Maya having had all her shots, the biggest risk they faced from sharing needles was infection, rather than hepatitis or HIV. Since he was dealing with an open compound fracture, it would be a miracle if an infection didn't set in regardless.

He flicked the syringe to make sure there was no air in it. "Good news is, this will take the edge off while I put in the stitches and move the leg around. Once I get it sewn up and bandaged, I'll find something to splint it with, make it more stable for you before we move out." He injected Doug in the hip.

"Appreciate it."

Jackson gathered what he needed, allowing the meds a few minutes to kick in. When he was ready, he gave Maya the signal and she bent to grasp the edges of torn flesh with her good hand, pulling them together without the benefit of gloves. She leaned back to stay out of his light, applying pressure to the exit wound on the back of the calf with her forearm without being told.

It took seven stitches to close the entry wound and it

wasn't his prettiest patch job, but it would do for now. The back was trickier. They had to roll Doug on to his side while he stifled his cries of pain so Jackson could get at the larger exit wound. That took eleven sutures to close, and he tied off a small superficial vein to slow the bleeding more.

When that was done, he packed the suture kit up and gathered the bandages.

"Those are pretty neat stitches. You know, if the med school thing doesn't work out, you could always make your living as a tailor," Maya remarked.

His lips quirked. "Yeah? Maybe I'll keep that as my backup plan."

"You're not gonna need a backup plan, because I know you're gonna ace the MCAT. They'd be crazy not to give you a spot."

Her faith in him made him feel unworthy. She was the amazing one. All that strength and determination packed into her petite body. "I'll tell them you said so."

"You should." She smiled a little as she shifted around to hold Doug's leg steady for him. Padding and bandaging the wounds didn't take long, and he rose to stretch his back.

"Feelin' sleepy yet?" Jackson asked.

"Oh, yeah," Doug mumbled, eyes closed. "Just wake me up when we get back to a U.S. base, will ya?"

"Sure thing." He turned to Maya. "I have to find some wood to put a splint together."

"I'll take watch." She stepped past him and walked out to the group of boulders they'd used for concealment during the night, stifling another cough, her face pinched with pain. "Hurry though. Sun's coming up fast."

"I know." He'd done what he could to disguise their trail last night, but the blood spatters were a dead give-away. And if the men coming after them had tracking dogs—he doubted it, but couldn't rule it out for sure—they might show up at any time.

Careful to keep his silhouette to a minimum, Jackson searched around and found some sturdy branches to fashion a splint with. When he came back, he could hear Maya coughing, even though she had her face buried in the crook of her elbow to muffle the sound. And from the way she winced and squeezed her eyes shut, it hurt her like hell every time she coughed. From the deep sound of it, he'd bet money it was bronchitis and well on its way to becoming something worse if left untreated.

"Be as quick as I can," he said to her on the way by. Using the dull jackknife from the kit, he cut the branches down to size and lashed them together in groups of three. The splint wasn't the greatest, but it would give Doug's leg some stability and hopefully guard the newly set leg. His patient didn't even twitch as he bound his limb into it. Jackson shook his shoulder. "Time to go."

Haversham opened groggy eyes and flinched as he turned on to his back. "Thanks," he said, looping one arm around Jackson's shoulders and setting his other hand against the rock wall to get up on his right foot. He sucked in a breath at the increase of pain then gave a sharp nod. "I'm ready."

With Maya supporting his left side and Jackson his right, Haversham used them as human crutches. Both he and Maya were armed this time, and Jackson carried the medical bag on his back. A line of light blue

lit the eastern horizon, heralding the imminent arrival
of the sun.

"Gotta stick to the shadows and use whatever cover
we can," Jackson reminded them. Wasn't much they
could do about their tracks, except to step on rocks
wherever possible. At least the blood spatters would
be minimal this time.

They hugged the trail, staying a dozen or so yards
away from it, picking their way through shallow de-
pressions and deeper wadis. It made the going slower,
but it disguised them and their tracks from anyone else
who might come along the path. When Haversham got
too tired to carry on, Jackson passed the med bag to
Maya and hauled him over his shoulders. The man's
fingers bit into his upper arms with bruising force, but
he made no more than a groan. Jackson hoped the vot-
ing public would find out just how brave their Secretary of Defense was in the face of all this.

Maya followed a few yards behind him, watching
their backs. From her tense posture and vigilant gaze,
Jackson knew she was as worried as him that they
were being followed. She kept trying to muffle her
coughs every few minutes, but even so, the sound carried through the still air. Every time she did it, the
tension inside him wound tighter. If she developed full-
blown pneumonia, there was nothing he could do for
her out here. And if she didn't get treatment in time...
He shoved that thought from his mind.

They managed to keep moving most of the day,
taking short breaks to rest and have a sip or two of
water from the half-empty canteen. By the time the
sun sat low on the horizon, he was smoked and Maya
was worse. Her cough kept deteriorating and when he

stopped to gauge her temperature with a hand on her forehead, he wasn't surprised to find her feverish. He pursed his lips, knowing the decision he was about to make held their fate in the balance. He couldn't keep them moving like this, and there was no way Maya could keep this pace. Haversham couldn't walk on his own, and Jackson couldn't carry them both. They were almost out of water and food. That left only one option.

"I'm gonna find us some shelter and then I'm gonna have to leave you to get water," he told them when they stopped for another break.

Maya swiped the back of her right arm across her forehead, her cheeks flushed from exertion and fever. Her eyes were clear. "No. We're not splitting up."

"We have to. Our water's almost gone, and both you and Doug need more or we're gonna be in trouble."

Though she clearly didn't like it, she didn't argue anymore. "How will you find us without a compass?"

"I'm a born tracker, been huntin' since I was a little kid. I'll find you, don't worry."

That seemed to reassure her a little. She scanned the area ahead of them where the trail broke away from the rock, straying across the brush-dotted soil and disappearing into what was probably another shallow valley. "Only place with solid shelter is right beside the trail, and even I know that's too risky a place to stop."

"We'll have to find a wadi or a dried-up riverbed for tonight," he answered, stooping to bring one of Doug's arms across his shoulder.

"You two go ahead," the Sec Def managed, his face damp with a glaze of sweat and his face lined with the constant agony wearing him down. "Leave me somewhere and come back for me when you can."

"Not gonna happen," Jackson said before Maya could answer.

"I'll stay with you and keep watch until he comes back," she informed Doug. "And that's not up for debate, so make peace with it."

A ghost of a smile curved his lips. "Yes, ma'am."

Jackson stood and waited for Maya to bolster Doug's left side before starting out at a slow pace. His legs were so tired he could barely carry his own weight right now, let alone adding Haversham's. They skirted the trail to the crest of the hill, where the red-tinged mountains loomed before them. And they all heard it at the same time.

Tiny bells. Faint at first, growing louder with each passing moment, their sweet chimes filling the air. Setting Haversham down between them, he and Maya hit the deck and lay flat on their bellies, trying to make their outlines as small as possible.

A minute after that, the first bleats reached them, followed by the patter of hooves over the hard, rocky ground. *Fuck*. Jackson's whole body tensed, a surge of renewed strength exploding through him. Beside him, Maya kept her gaze trained ahead where the goats were. They sounded close and seemed to be coming closer. Haversham's face was rigid with tension.

The bells and bleating came nearer, the hooves now a constant rattle on the ground. A whole herd of goats, which meant the shepherd couldn't be far behind.

But it wasn't a human who found them.

Jackson barely had time to react when something rustled in the brush to their right and a medium-sized dog bounded out. It stopped a dozen or so meters from them, frozen in a pose that was part point, part coiling to spring. The animal was white except for brown spots on its ears, nose and a large patch on its right flank. Jackson cursed silently. Shooting it would only alert any humans in the area to their position, and there was no way he and Maya could haul Haversham out of there fast enough to evade anyone who chased them. Their only hope now was for the dog to lose interest and leave before it attracted its master's attention.

He held his breath, willing the mongrel to move on. It didn't.

The dog remained poised to spring, gaze fixed on them, ears back, a low, almost inaudible growl coming from its throat. Then a sharp, shrill whistle rent the air, and Jackson closed his eyes in disbelief at their shitty luck.

"Jackson," Maya said in an urgent whisper that barely carried to him.

He answered with a minute shake of his head. They couldn't make a run for it now. It was too late.

Another whistle, and the dog flinched, its hindquarters quivering as it kept staring at them. A man's shout rose up. The dog still didn't leave. And when the inevitable sounds of footsteps came next, Jackson's heart sank. He didn't want to have to kill an innocent goatherd. How many of them were out here? They'd probably be armed. Jackson tightened his grip around the pistol, ready and waiting.

Above the scraggly bush they were hidden behind, a pair of thin legs appeared beneath a gray tunic. Heart in his throat, Jackson watched the legs give way to a lower body, then a small torso. When he saw the young boy's face, no older than ten, Jackson stopped breathing. There was no way he could kill a kid. Not unless he was actually firing at them, and even then Jackson would only shoot to disable.

The only thing the young goatherd had for a weapon was a long walking stick.

The kid froze in horror when he came close enough and saw what his dog had cornered. His eyes went wide and his mouth dropped open, but no sound came out, as though he was too terrified to scream.

Praying he'd stay quiet, Jackson met his fearful gaze and brought a finger to his lips in the universal signal for silence.

The kid blinked once. Then, as if the motion had unparalyzed him, he opened his mouth wide and screamed something.

Jackson was already on his knees, ready to lunge for the kid and tackle him, but it was too late. An answering shout rang out, and Jackson glanced up in time to see an old man running toward them. He was carrying a rifle.

Maya cursed and dragged Haversham to a standing position, preparing to make a run for it. Jackson stayed where he was, weapon raised, ready to fire if the old man brought his rifle up. But the man stopped running and stared in shock, then held up one hand and lowered his weapon to the ground.

As their gazes connected, a shock of recognition rippled through Jackson. He slowly lowered the pistol, wondering if he was imagining things. "Maya, wait."

"What?" she snapped, whirling to face him. When she saw the expression on his face, she stopped and followed his gaze. She frowned at the man. "Is that...?"

He couldn't answer. It was all too fucking surreal.

The old man stared back at them for a moment then

beckoned for the boy, who turned and ran to him. A startled smile spread across his bearded face. He said something to the boy and took a step toward them, both hands raised to show he wasn't a threat.

"My God, it *is*," Maya breathed in disbelief.

Yeah. It was the old man from the MEDCAP, whose grandson they'd evacuated to the hospital. Jackson hoped like hell the elder was in the mood to repay that good deed with one of his own.

THINGS HAPPENED SO fast that Maya's head was spinning by the time they reached the village. She was still ter- rified they'd discover this was all a trap, but so far no one had done anything to threaten them. Only men were there to greet them, since the boy had run ahead to warn the villagers and the women and children had been sequestered. The old man had taken her place, carrying Haversham between himself and Jackson. She held her pistol tightly and muffled her coughing as best she could, making sure her body language stated loud and clear that she was still strong and would shoot at the first sign of a threat to her and the others.

The men in the village stared at them openly, some with hostile eyes, some merely curious. It occurred to Maya that many of them might never have seen a fe- male soldier before. She didn't like the attention one bit. The old man called out to them, and the boy who'd first discovered them came scampering over with a huge smile on his face. He held a large bladder of what she assumed was water, and she swallowed reflexively, longing for a drink. If a kid was running around of- fering them water and smiling at them, chances were good no one was out to kill them, right?

She glanced at Jackson to check his reaction. His face was set, his eyes wary, but his weapon was still in his waistband. Maya didn't feel brave enough just yet to put hers away, even though her wrist was killing her and every breath jarred her injured ribs. Her chest felt too tight, as if an invisible vise was squeezing her lungs.

Leading them to the largest mud-brick house at the end of the village, the old man called ahead, and someone opened the door for them. Maya hesitated and turned, not wanting to give her back to anyone. The men had followed them through the village, talking among themselves, but none were doing anything hostile or even remotely threatening. Still, she couldn't relax. There had to be a catch and she'd be damned if anyone would take her off guard again.

She was a little surprised when Jackson entered the house with Haversham and the old man without hesitation. Keeping one eye on the men outside, Maya ducked her head and followed them. Inside the dwelling, she found the boy from the MEDCAP lying on a pallet on the floor. He beamed up at Jackson, speaking excitedly with his grandfather. Then the old man helped settle Haversham onto some cushions, using more to prop his wounded leg up.

Jackson hovered close by, his back to the wall to keep his line of sight open. Maya did the same on the other side of the room until the old man looked over and beckoned to her. After glancing at Jackson for reassurance, she moved forward hesitantly. The man said something in a coaxing tone and waved his hand toward the back of the house, probably where the women were. Maya balked at the implied command. There was no way she was leaving Jackson's sight.

As though he understood her reluctance, the man sighed and gestured for her to sit. She did, probably violating all sorts of etiquettes as she held tight to her weapon, half expecting someone to burst through a door with guns blazing.

Instead, an old woman came shuffling out of the back room a moment later, babbling at the man. He issued some sort of gruff order and she returned soon after, carrying a tray full of food. Maya's stomach howled when she caught the scent of the rich spices wafting up from it. She didn't care what it was on that platter—she'd eat bark right now if it smelled like that. The lady set the tray on the floor and left without glancing at any of them, though she had to be wondering who they were and why her husband—if that was who he was—had invited them into their home.

When none of them made a move to take any food, the boy darted a hand out to snag a piece of flatbread and earned a slap on the back of the head from the old man. Their host looked up at Jackson and Haversham with an encouraging smile and took a piece of bread for himself, dipping it into a dish with some sort of orange sauce, then proceeded to eat it with great relish.

Guess it wasn't poisoned, then.

Maya's mouth watered.

Haversham stared at the food like it was the most beautiful thing he'd ever seen. "It'd be beyond rude for us to refuse his hospitality now," he said in a weak voice. "And besides, I'm starving." Reaching out to the tray, he copied the old man, tearing into the bread without another thought.

"Go ahead and eat, Maya," Jackson said quietly, and she realized he was waiting for her to eat before taking his turn. Even now, his Southern manners were still intact. It blew her away.

Not about to turn down fresh food, she finally tucked her pistol away and came forward to kneel beside Jackson. The old man cast her a curious glance, and she did her best to ignore him while she ate, trying not to look like a starving animal as she did so. God knew she looked like one with her face beaten and her hair a tangled mess, with dirt, blood and grime streaked across her skin. They looked bad, even Jackson, who was in the best condition of them all, despite the cuts and bruises all over his face. He scooped up his own portion, his gaze moving around the room, likely taking in each possible exit and entry.

The meal was silent and tense, and Maya was starting to feel like a sacrificial calf, being fatted up for the big finish. By now everyone in the village knew they were here. It was only a matter of time before someone either made a call with a cell phone or left to inform someone in another village about them.

They had to move out of here, fast.

She swallowed another blissful bite of the bread and was reaching for more when a coughing fit seized her. With her right arm up to muffle the noise, she turned away out of politeness, but the movement tweaked her ribs and the agonizing shock of pain took her breath away. Immediately Jackson had his arms around her, tipping her backward.

"Maya, lie down."

She shook her head, gasping for breath, horrified

that she'd appeared so weak and ill in front of people who might well be the enemy.

Before Jackson could argue, the old man barked something. Jackson tensed beside her, and Maya went rigid. Was this it? Was someone going to attack them? Her hand instinctively went to the weapon in her waist-band.

The old woman reappeared, this time with a teenage girl. The man said something to them and they reached for Maya. She shrank back against Jackson. Their host frowned at her and made a sweeping gesture with one hand, telling her to go with the women.

"I'm fine right here," Maya insisted, though he couldn't possibly understand her.

"I don't think you have much of a choice, lieutenant," Haversham said. "We're his guests now, for better or worse, and women are supposed to be sequestered from the men. If you stay, you're insulting him and challenging his authority."

Her shoulders went rigid, but Jackson sighed. "He's right, Maya. No point in doing anything that might make him change his mind about helping us."

Going with the women was the last thing she wanted. Not only would that mean being separated from Jackson, she also wouldn't be able to see if there was any danger to him and Haversham. Who would watch their backs if she wasn't there? "How do we know it's not a trick?"

"We don't," Jackson answered, "but he owes us and he's already offered us his hospitality. If I understand the Pashtunwalai code right, it means he and his family are honor-bound to protect us with their lives."

She knew what it meant, she just wasn't sure she believed it. Or if the old man and his family would hold up their end of the bargain. "I think this is a bad idea." She barely got the words out before another coughing attack hit her. Jackson said something she didn't catch. When she recovered and unscrewed her eyelids once more, he was holding her and had a hand on her uninjured cheek.

"Baby, you're burning up," he said softly.

She knew it. The chill and ache in her body wasn't something she could ignore. Yet for some reason that gentle tone, combined with his touch, almost undid her. The ache suddenly spread into her throat.

She swallowed past it. "So I have to do this," she whispered hoarsely.

He nodded, face solemn. "For now."

Pulling in as deep a breath as her ribs would allow, she found her center and started to push to her feet. Jackson helped her up and they followed the women to a doorway on the other side of the living space, where he stopped.

She didn't want to leave him. Everything in her cried out in protest.

He gave her a gentle nudge. "Go on. It'll be okay. I'll be right here. Try to get some sleep if you can."

Sleep here? Not freaking likely. But the exhaustion was an overwhelming weight on her weary body, dragging at her.

Gathering her courage, she stepped away from him, immediately mourning the loss of his touch as she entered the unknown of the women's quarters.

EIGHTEEN

ALTHOUGH SHE'D VOWED to stay awake, Maya finally lost the battle and dozed. The coughing woke her from a deep and dreamless sleep.

One moment she was under, the next she was hacking uncontrollably. Maya rolled on to her side and braced for the pain as it tore through her. She coughed so hard it made her stomach roll. She gagged, gasping for breath, and when she finally got a chance to breathe, she collapsed onto her side in a trembling, sweaty mess.

She heard movement beside her and snapped her eyes open to find a shadowy face peering down at her. It was dark in the room and she was disoriented enough that it took a moment to remember where she was. The thin pallet she lay on cushioned her from the hard dirt floor, and someone had placed a woolen blanket on her during the night.

A wrinkled face hovered over her, soft words that Maya didn't understand coming from the old woman's lips. She placed a hand behind Maya's neck and brought a cup of warm tea to her lips. Maya gave in and took a few sips. God, she hurt all over. Even her bones ached. And she was freezing, despite the heavy wool covering her.

Even with the coughing fit over for now, it was hard to breathe. Her chest felt tight, like her lungs were closed up. Exhaustion pulled at her, sapping the strength from her muscles until she had no choice but to relax into the old woman's care. She said something to another person in the room, and a young girl appeared at her side. Around eight maybe. The girl's face looked worried as she watched Maya.

Maya reached down to ensure her weapon wasn't within the girl's reach and discovered it was gone. A moment's panic hit her before she calmed herself. These people weren't going to kill her. She didn't think, anyway. If they'd wanted to do that, they'd had ample opportunity while she'd been sleeping. Unless they'd somehow alerted Khalid of their presence and were planning to keep them here until he showed up?

The girl continued to stare at Maya. She lifted a tentative hand and laid it on her hair. Maya stayed very still, partly from surprise and partly so she didn't scare the child. A moment later, that small hand began stroking her hair, then she felt a tug at her scalp and realized the girl was brushing out her hair gently. Maya closed her eyes, fighting the upsurge of emotion. Pilar had done this whenever she was ill, to soothe her.

She lay there, taking shallow, wheezy breaths while the girl pulled the brush through her hair, and when the old woman came back and placed a spoonful of something to her lips, Maya opened her mouth. She made a face at the sharp bitter taste of whatever it was but swallowed. The woman made a kind of encouraging, crooning sound. The rough, dry hand she placed on Maya's forehead felt blessedly cool. Too tired to stay alert, she didn't even fight it when the dark wave of sleep rushed at her and pulled her back under.

THEY HAD YET another big problem on their hands.

It had been more than a day since Maya had gone into the women's quarters, and she hadn't come out once. Jackson had heard her coughing through the night from where he'd slept off and on, lying against the wall, taking quick combat naps because he couldn't afford to let himself go deep and be caught off guard. The people in the house carried on with their normal routines and the old woman had brought him and Haversham their meals.

Once last night he'd insisted on checking on Maya; as much as it scandalized his host, he hadn't taken no for an answer. He'd found her fast asleep, the fever burning in her skin. He hadn't liked the sound of her breathing, a bit shallow and raspy. If he'd had a stethoscope, he knew he'd hear crackles and rales in her lungs.

Shifting on to his back in a shaft of early morning light coming through a slit in the door, Jackson debated what to do. The militants likely knew where they were by now, and if they didn't, it was only a matter of time before they found out. Haversham hadn't improved and wouldn't until the bones in his leg were surgically repaired, and now Maya was too sick to be ambulatory. So he either left them here with their host and hoped the old man continued to offer his protection while Jackson set out to find a way to contact friendly forces, or he stayed here with them to face the militants when they showed up.

Given how desperate things were, the decision seemed obvious.

He rose, careful not to wake Haversham, who was dead asleep after taking a dose of poppy juice their host had given him. These people made their livelihoods off their goats and opium poppies.

The old woman looked up from her mending when he passed by the doorway to a smaller room at the back. She stared at him questioningly, and he pointed to where Maya was. Frowning, the woman pursed her lips and shook her head. Jackson pointed again, less patiently this time, and she finally heaved to her feet with an irritated sigh. He stayed outside the room just long enough for her to warn the other women and give them time to scatter, then entered.

Maya was curled on her left side in the fetal position and even in the dimness he could see how red her cheeks were. He kneeled beside her and put a hand to her face, not at all surprised to find her still burning up. Her breathing had deteriorated more overnight. There were full-on crackles every time she inhaled. Noticing the spoon resting on a dish near her head, he picked it up and sniffed it, smelling the bitter tinge of the opium.

Shit.

He turned to the old woman and met her wary gaze, then lifted the spoon and gave a sharp shake of his head. "No more." Opium might ease her pain and make her sleep, but it was also a narcotic analgesic that suppressed the cough reflex in her brain stem and prevented her lungs from clearing. If she didn't have pneumonia already, she would eventually if she didn't cough up the phlegm gathering in her lungs.

Setting the spoon down, he leaned over her. "Maya. Maya, wake up."

Her lashes fluttered. She drew in a raspy breath and started to cough, jackknifing up with a grimace as the dry, hacking coughs took her. He quickly moved in behind to support her, trying to take the strain off her ribs. Her gasping breaths in between fits made his heart rate accelerate. Finally, after what seemed like endless minutes, she shuddered and collapsed into his hold, her upper body against his chest and her cheek resting on his shoulder.

"What time is it?" she rasped.

"About an hour after dawn," he responded, resting his cheek against the top of her head. He could feel her shivering in his hold and rubbed his hands over her gently. "Feeling pretty shitty, huh?"

"Yeah."

He didn't want to leave her when she was sick and defenseless, but the way he saw it, it was their only chance of getting help. "Baby, I've gotta go."

Her head tilted back and she regarded him in confusion. "Where?"

"To find a way to contact friendlies."

Her brows pulled together and she turned her attention to the doorway marking the women's quarters. "Is Haversham here?"

Jackson nodded, his cheek brushing against her hair. "He can't walk and it'll slow me down to carry him." He tightened his arms around her, letting himself hold her a moment longer. "You know why I have to do this, right?"

"Yes." It took him by surprise when she shifted around gingerly and cuddled into him. "But...in just a minute?"

The vulnerability in her voice and the fact that she'd just asked him to hold her for a minute longer shredded his insides. He gathered her as close as he could without hurting her, wishing there was another option for them. "I'm not deserting you," he promised in a whisper, needing her to believe him, to hang on. "I'll get help and come back for you. I'll come back, I swear."

She nodded but didn't answer.

"These people will protect you until I get back. Rest when you can, but don't take any more of the poppy juice, okay? I know it hurts to cough but you need to in order to clear your lungs." He pressed a kiss to her hot temple. "I'll give you your pistol—"

"You took it?"

"Didn't want you shooting someone by accident when you're outta your head with fever. You do what you need to and keep you and Haversham safe. I'll come get you as soon as I can."

"Okay," she whispered, looping her good arm around him and squeezing, the effort it cost her telling him just how weak she was.

Jackson buried his face against her tangled hair for a moment and held on, then forced himself to let her go. "Here," he said, handing her the weapon as he helped her lie back against the pallet. Once he pulled the blanket up over her, he paused to stroke the uninjured side of her face, staring down into her one open sea-green eye. Battered and desperately ill, she was still the most beautiful, amazing woman he'd ever known. "I'm coming back for you."

A small grin tugged at her cracked lips. "You better. Kick your ass if you don't."

Heartened by that show of attitude, he bent over her to kiss the bridge of her nose. "See you soon, baby."

"Bye." Her voice was hoarse.

It took an act of will to tear himself away from her, but Jackson made himself get up and leave. Haversham was awake, his gaze hitting him as he stepped out of Maya's room. "She okay?"

"No." Not by a long shot. "I have to go, Doug."

The Sec Def studied him for a second then nodded. "I'll take care of her."

"I told her to take care of you," he said on a laugh.

"Then we'll take care of each other." His dark eyes were somber. "Good luck out there, sergeant."

"Thanks." Because he was damn sure gonna need all the luck he could get.

After gathering a bladder of water and loading more ammo from the spare magazine into his pistol, he left.

He squinted against the bright early morning sunlight. The villagers were all out going about their daily lives but the ones who saw him stopped dead, eyeing the weapon in his hand. Scanning for threats and finding none, he began heading east out of the village, hyper aware of each second that ticked past. Ahead of him the mountains loomed, the peaks capped with snow that was beginning to melt. Out there somewhere lay either his salvation, or his death. Only time would tell which.

He was almost to the edge of the village when a commotion broke out ahead of him. Someone started shouting, and the women and children scattered, fleeing for their homes. Jackson ducked behind a low wall, expecting to find a mob of militants coming at him. Instead he saw his host running headlong toward the houses, long tunic flapping behind him, his protruding belly bouncing with each stride. What the hell was going on?

Jackson rose slightly, his finger on the trigger. When the old man noticed Jackson standing behind the wall, he skidded to a halt and pointed back the way he'd come, panting for breath, saying something in an urgent way that made the hair on Jackson's nape rise.

One word stood out from the others and it made every muscle in his body tighten.

Jihad.

The man said it again, his expression anxious, pointing at the entrance to the village.

Fuck. Jackson checked his perimeter. No one was rushing at him yet. Maybe he still had time to get back to the old man's house to grab Maya and Haversham and haul them out of there. He couldn't leave them there now.

He dodged the end of the low wall and took off toward the house. He'd taken two running steps when a prickling in his spine told him it was too late. Whirling, weapon up and ready, he found himself staring down Jihad.

The man stood frozen at the village entrance, maybe thirty yards away. Big bastard, probably taller than Jackson, with broad shoulders and a muscular build. His dark head was bare, he was dressed in tribal wear and he had an AK slung across his chest. With that nearly black gaze fixed on his, the man slowly raised his hands into the air in a nonthreatening gesture. Jackson didn't move. Whatever game that fucker was playing, Jackson wasn't letting him get past. He was the only thing that stood between this asshole and Maya, and he wasn't going anywhere.

Heart thudding a hard rhythm in his ears, he was completely unprepared for what happened next.

Jihad smiled and actually chuckled, the sound of his amusement carrying across the tense and deadly space between them. "You don't wanna shoot me, Thatcher, since I'm the guy they sent to get you out of here."

It took a moment for Jackson's brain to process what he'd said in such perfect, accent-free English. How many big men who spoke perfect English were running around these parts? No way was it a coincidence. He frowned in disbelief, trying to put everything together. "*You're* the one who helped the LT escape?" The bastard had stood back and watched them get tortured without lifting a finger to help them, not even during that fucked-up game of Russian roulette.

"Yeah." He kept his hands in the air, his expression totally calm, as if he stared down the barrel of a gun every day. "Now I'm here to get you guys home."

"That right? Even though you seemed happy enough to watch us get ready to blow our brains out back in that room?"

Jihad shook his head. "He handed me the revolver and asked me to take out every bullet except one. I took them *all* out instead. He just didn't notice."

So *that's* why the revolver had been empty when Khalid had tried to shoot them.

Jackson kept his weapon aimed at the center of his chest, still not trusting him for a second. If what Jihad said was true, and so far it seemed to be, it meant he was part of something much bigger than anyone else knew about. Some secret undercover sting sanctioned by the military or the government.

He was aware of the tense silence, of the many anxious eyes focused on him in the village. His host stood nearby, rubbernecking between him and Jihad with wide, anxious eyes, no doubt wondering if his village was about to be shot up. Jackson glared at Jihad. "Who the fuck *are* you?"

Jihad's black eyebrows went up. "Mind if I come closer for this conversation?"

"Yeah, I do." His index finger stayed snug around the trigger.

Another grin, but he didn't try to approach. "Name's Sandberg, and we don't have much time to talk. Khalid's group is less than five hours' march from here and they've got help on the way. Another force is coming in from the southwest, and there could be others. Trust me, you do not want to be here when they show up, especially Rahim's men. Now, Tarik, he knows me," he said, nodding toward the old man. "We go back five years now. We're buddies."

"He doesn't look very happy to see you," Jackson pointed out, his grip steady on the pistol.

"He was running to warn you so you wouldn't shoot when you saw me. I told Lieutenant Lopez to take the trail here because I knew you'd be safe here. Tarik told me all about the American soldiers who saved his grandson at the MEDCAP. I knew he'd look out for you until I got here."

Since Tarik had carried his grandson to the MEDCAP in the first place, the village couldn't be too far from where Jackson and the others had been captured. "So we're still in Afghanistan?"

His eyes danced with amusement. "Almost. Just a few miles back that way." He jerked his chin over his shoulder.

With his suspicion wavering, Jackson slowly lowered his weapon, keeping it in front of him at the ready just in case.

Jihad—or Sandberg, if he even had a real name—sighed in exasperation and lowered his hands. "Look, if I'd wanted to kill you I could've taken you out with my rifle long before you even realized I was here."

Much as Jackson hated to admit it, the guy had a point. "Okay, so say I believe you." And he wasn't saying he did, since he didn't trust him any further than he could fucking throw him. "What do you want?"

"I've got a ride coming for you all in ten hours at a pre-designated LZ to the northeast," he answered, pointing over his shoulder as though Jackson didn't know which direction that was.

"Who do you work for?" Because it wasn't the regular military, or even Spec Ops. No, this guy, if he was for real, worked for a government agency.

"The good guys."

That didn't convince Jackson in the slightest, since he knew how quickly allegiances changed in this part of the world. There was no shame in working with the U.S. and their allies one day, and pledging your allegiance to the Taliban the next. Whatever served your purpose for the moment. It was how these tribal people had survived in this harsh land for centuries, and how they would go on surviving until the end of time. "What branch did you serve with?"

"Special Forces, a long time ago. Look, man, I know where you're coming from but we don't have time for this. You might not like it, but you just have to trust me. We have to get Haversham and Lieutenant Lopez out of here right the fuck now if we're gonna stay ahead of the bad guys and make our rendezvous with that bird."

If something seemed too good to be true it usually meant it *was*, but he couldn't afford to dismiss Sandberg's words. Not if there was a chance they were true. At this point, Jackson's only options were to go with it or shoot Sandberg and make a run for it. And if the enemy really was closing in, then he couldn't abandon Maya and Haversham. "They're both too far gone to walk out."

"Then it's a good thing I'm here to carry one of them, huh?"

Setting his jaw, Jackson eased his stance and glanced at Tarik to let him know everything was okay, then spoke to Sandberg. "You do anything that smells outta line, I'll take you out." His clipped tone made it a promise.

Sandberg shrugged, his cocky expression telling Jackson he was welcome to try. "Fair enough. Now can we go to Tarik's?"

"Yeah," Jackson muttered, and waited for Sandberg to pass him before falling into line. Even if this guy was promising them a ride home, Jackson wasn't taking his eyes off him for a moment.

NINETEEN

TARIK BURST INTO the house ahead of Sandberg, the two
of them jabbering away in Pashto, and it made Jackson
even more uneasy because he had no way of knowing what the fuck they were saying. He stayed right
on Sandberg's ass as he introduced himself to Haversham—who shot an incredulous look at Jackson—and
headed to the back room where Maya was.

The instant Sandberg reached the threshold, Maya
jerked upright with her weapon aimed at his head.

Sandberg threw up his hands in surprise. "Whoa,
there. You wouldn't shoot me after I went to all that
trouble of getting you here in the first place, would
you?"

Her fever-glazed eyes narrowed a fraction at his
English. "Who are you?" she demanded in a rough
whisper.

"His name's Sandberg," Jackson answered for him,
"and he says he's one of us."

Sandberg twisted his head around to give Jackson
a bland look, taking in his pistol held at the ready. "I
am one of us." He turned back to Maya. "I've got a
helo coming in to get all of you out of here, but it's a
long ways off and we don't have much time. There're
at least two enemy forces headed this way, so we have
to move fast." He took a step forward, and Maya cham-

bered a round, the sound loud in the quiet room. Sandberg stopped and sighed in exasperation.

She didn't take her eyes off him. "Jackson?"

"Everything he said makes sense," he answered. "I don't think we have any other choice but to follow him for the time being."

She seemed to process that for a few moments and finally lowered her weapon to pull back the slide. When she put her hand down to push herself to her feet, she was so weak and shaky that her arm trembled. Sandberg stepped forward again, and Maya stopped him cold with a single, cutting look. "I don't need your help."

Throwing Jackson an exasperated look, Sandberg turned and moved past him with a muttered, "I'll get Haversham."

Half turning to keep his eye on the guy, Jackson bent and slid his arm behind Maya's back to brace her, pulling up and forward. She sucked in a breath and bent over, coughing into the bend of her elbow. He winced in sympathy. "Come on, let's get you out of here." She didn't protest when he wrapped the blanket around her for extra warmth, and that alone told him just how ill she was. With an arm around her shoulders to steady her, he walked her through the doorway.

Out in the main room, he found Haversham rolled on to his hip as though he meant to get up. His eyes met Jackson's and he jerked his chin at Sandberg, who was shrugging out of his ruck. "He's legit."

"How do you know?"

"He knew my code word."

"Your code word?"

"My government one."

Okay, that helped ease his mind a little. Actually, not really.

Sandberg was busy digging through the ruck he'd dumped on the floor. He was pulling out pieces of an M4 when he glanced up at Jackson. "Figured you could use this, just in case."

Frowning, Jackson released Maya, handed her his pistol and went to his knees to take the pieces and put the weapon together, noting the full magazine. "You got a radio in there too?"

"No, had to ditch it after I left Khalid's camp in case anyone intercepted me. We're on our own for the time being, I'm afraid."

Once he had it together and loaded, Jackson slung it across his chest and stood to gather Maya close with a hand on the small of her back. Haversham's and Sandberg's eyes both followed his move. If his actions looked territorial, too bad, because that's exactly how he was feeling. Maya was his to protect and yeah, he wanted it clear how he felt about her. Surprisingly she didn't object, rather continued watching Sandberg repack his ruck with a somewhat hostile expression on her face. A few short months ago, Jackson had been on the receiving end of that look. It felt good to know he'd won her loyalty and trust.

Sandberg's lips quirked as he tipped his ruck onto his back and spoke to Tarik. The old man nodded and rushed away to get them another small bladder full of water. "Can you carry that?" Sandberg asked her.

With a firm nod, she took it and looped the thin leather strap around her neck so that the bladder rested against her chest. "We ready?" Even worn down and ill as she was, she still wore that natural air of author-

ity he'd recognized in her from the first time he'd seen
her at Bagram. And she wore it well.

"Let's move out," Sandberg said on a grunt as he
hoisted Haversham to his feet, then across his shoulders.

"Fucking *hell*, I hate this part," Haversham gritted
out as his wounded leg got jostled.

"Don't blame you," Sandberg replied.

"Then you won't mind when I puke all over your
back," the Secretary muttered.

"It's happened before." Shifting Haversham to dis-
tribute the weight better and earning a choked cry from
his passenger, Sandberg started for the front door. Tarik
stood next to it. Jackson met his gaze and nodded his
thanks. The old man placed a hand over his heart and
bowed slightly. Jackson returned the gesture, grateful
for his hospitality, then reached toward Maya, intending to carry her.

She pushed against his shoulder and gave a tight
shake of her head. "I can walk."

He straightened to look down into her face. "You're
in no condition to walk." She wasn't in any condition
to be standing, as far as he was concerned.

Her lips pressed together for a moment. "I'm walking out of here."

She didn't want anyone to see her weak and helpless. Jackson understood that. But he also wasn't going
to allow her pride to place her or the rest of them in
jeopardy. "I'll let you walk until we're out of sight of
the village if you can get that far. But the moment you
can't keep up, you're takin' a ride over my shoulder."

She gave a firm nod. "Fair enough."

He let her exit the house ahead of him and brought

up the rear, not taking any chances in case anyone in the village had it in his mind to take a shot at them on their way out of town. Luckily no one tried anything, and soon they had passed through the village to make their way down the sloping hill into another shallow valley.

So far Maya was keeping pace okay, but he could see the effort it cost her. A few times she paused to cough, and when she walked he could hear the wheezing quality of her breaths. The accessory breathing muscles in her neck stood out in sharp relief as she gasped. Over the next thirty minutes, the space between them and Sandberg started to increase. At the top of the next rise Sandberg paused to look back, and when he saw how far behind they were, he set Haversham down to have a rest.

Maya saw it and pushed herself even harder, determination stamped all over her face. But the incline was too much for her. Partway up, a bad coughing spasm had her doubling over and going to her knees. Jackson reached out to catch her before she could topple over and waited only until she'd caught her breath before pulling her up. Her face was blanched of color, slick with sweat.

"No more hiking for you," he told her, and bent to hoist her over his shoulders. She grunted in discomfort and wrapped her good arm around his chest to steady herself but didn't try to argue. He could feel her shaking from pain and cold. Reaching the top of the hill, he took in the scene below him. The trail wound through the barren landscape like a dusty ribbon in the dun-colored soil, rising and falling with the landscape before it vanished around a bend in the distance.

"We have to hump it six klicks to the west-north-west, just before we hit that bend," Sandberg said.

Jackson studied the topography, not loving what he was seeing. In addition to the boulder-strewn terrain and steep climbs they'd have to make, there were plenty of blind corners and other places where the enemy could be hiding. Not to mention the other potential concealment spots he couldn't see.

Paying careful attention to his surroundings, Jackson started down the slope after Sandberg. The ground was littered with small rocks and pebbles, making it slippery, but he was more concerned with speed than he was about keeping his tracks to a minimum.

Small as she was, Maya was solid muscle and heavy for her size. Every few minutes he had to shift her to ease the strain on his back and shoulders, causing her further pain. He didn't let himself think about the burn in his muscles or the distance they had to travel, because that was wasted mental effort and a self-defeating mindset. In the Pipeline, they'd taught him to be mentally tough and break seemingly impossible tasks into little ones, then focus on the immediate one at hand. He used that training now, breaking the march down into smaller sections marked by each short pause they took.

At the bend in the trail, they broke left and headed west-northwest. Jackson was winded from carrying Maya. He hated moving out in the open like this, but there was no way around it. The sun was fast approaching its zenith, beating down on them with surprising intensity, considering it was only early March. Sweat soaked his back and chest, his face and neck. At one point, Maya reached out with a corner of the blanket she'd unwrapped around her to dab at his face and forehead.

"You give good piggybacks," she whispered close to his ear.

He swallowed a crack of laughter at that. "Had lots of practice," he managed, his lungs working overtime with the added demand for oxygen from his muscles.

"You carry sick women around often?" Her voice was dry, the wheeze in her chest pronounced.

"This is a first," he admitted. "Mostly guys in the field. And my nephews, o'course." Who he couldn't wait to get home to see. Had his sister found out he was missing and told the boys? They'd be devastated. He had to make it home and be with his family again. And he wanted Maya to go with him. "So, when we get back..." He paused a second to catch his breath. "Will you come visit my family with me?"

He felt her stiffen in surprise against his shoulders and she was silent for a long moment. "You want me to meet your family?"

"Yeah. They'd love you." The boys would go nuts over her, a real-life American heroine. They'd build Maya Lego figurines in her honor. When she didn't answer right away, he swore he could hear the wheels of suspicion turning in her head.

"I'll...think about it."

"You do that." With her background, he knew she'd need time to wrap her mind around that one, and he was okay with that as long as she consented in the end.

They took their next break in the shade of a small rock overhang. Sandberg looked as done in as Jackson felt. The guy was soaked in sweat as he dumped his ruck with a rough groan and bent to divvy up water and some protein bars. Jackson, Haversham and Maya wolfed them down, desperate for the nutrition and calories of any kind. Right then, Jackson was fantasizing about a big box full of Kit Kat bars he'd seen at the back of the Pat Tillman USO. He could do serious damage to that box right now.

All too soon it was time to head out again. He adjusted the M4 into place across his chest and reached for Maya, who backed up a step.

"I'll walk for a bit." Her cheeks had red flags of color on them and she'd just finished another coughing fit that had left her gasping and wheezing.

Jackson shook his head once. "Don't even," he warned and hauled her into the air, the muscles in his back and shoulders screaming in protest. She huffed out a pained breath and hung on to him with her good hand, her cheek resting on the back of his shoulder.

"Another two klicks, then we head due north until we hit the LZ," Sandberg panted, stumbling a bit under Haversham's weight. He quickly shot out a hand to steady himself against the rock wall and started off again. This time they kept to the shadows to conceal their movements, winding their way up a steep slope in their path.

Gritting his teeth, Jackson forced his burning quads and glutes to propel him and Maya upward, reaching out for a rock near the top to help get him the last few yards up. Sandberg was sucking wind too and didn't look like he had much more in him, yet he set off down the hill without pausing, carrying a sweaty-faced Haversham safely down the other side. They did it two more times before finally reaching the next change in course.

A good twenty minutes later at the edge of a dry riverbed, Sandberg slid his wounded passenger off him and all but fell to his knees in the dust beside Haversham. He shrugged out of his ruck and bent forward to rest his weight on his hands while he tried to catch his breath, smoked from carrying his heavier passenger. Jackson set Maya down as gently as he could and went to one knee, head bowed, chest heaving, grateful that she weighed much less than the Sec Def.

"How much farther?" he gasped.

Sandberg had just opened his mouth to respond when a puff of dust erupted on the hillside in front of them, followed a split second later by the report of a high-powered rifle.

"*Fuck.*" Sandberg rolled behind a rock as Jackson dragged Maya behind cover and flattened himself on top of her. She jerked and bit back a gasp of pain as another round impacted, closer this time. The report echoed too much for Jackson to get an accurate read on the location.

Maya struggled beneath him, trying to lift up on her good arm. Jackson pinned her flat. He knew he was hurting her but didn't care at the moment if it saved her from getting shot. He cut a scathing glare at Sandberg, who had his AK up and aimed. "You set this up?"

In answer, he got an annoyed eat-shit-and-die look and a clipped, "Does it look like it?"

From the way he was returning fire, no. But the timing of this new threat seemed pretty damn suspicious.

Haversham belly-crawled toward them, his grunts of pain muffled behind gritted teeth. He slid up beside them with a pistol in one hand, gaze darting across the hillside across from them. "See anything?"

Jackson scanned the horizon. "Not yet." Sniper could be anywhere out there. The ground here was too uneven and exposed. They couldn't move using any kind of cover, but staying put made them sitting targets. And whatever enemy force the shooter was attached to had to be on the move now that they had a bead on their location.

The moment he thought it, an eerie howl rose into the clear afternoon air. The hair on his arms stood up. *Holy shit.*

Beyond the far side of the riverbed where the hill curved up and away, a group of men dressed in dark clothes charged toward them, weapons glinting dully in the sunlight. Jackson rolled away from Maya and aimed his rifle just as the roar of gunfire filled the tiny valley.

MAYA SCRAMBLED UP on to her right elbow when Jackson's weight left her, using the edge of her splint to pull back the slide on her pistol. The rattle of automatic weapons fire made her heart slam, but it was the enemy's shrill cries that sent a spiral of fear corkscrewing down her backbone. Her fever and aches forgotten, she kept her eyes on the men racing toward them and held fast to the pistol in her right hand. Jackson and the others were deathly still beside her. What were they going to do? They were pinned down with nowhere to go.

"We gotta take out as many as we can and make a run for it," Sandberg yelled over the noise, firing precise bursts from his weapon.

Jackson didn't respond, focused on the attackers, methodically firing single and double taps. The sound of the M4 was distinctive among the bark of the AKs. Two men near the front of the group fell and crumpled to the ground, but the others rushed on. At least a dozen of them, maybe more. "Stay down, Maya," he ordered without looking at her.

She did, but only because the sidearm was completely useless at this range. Haversham was so close his hip pressed against hers, his broken leg bumping her foot as he waited with her, unable to do anything yet. Her heart thundered in her ears as she watched Jackson and Sandberg fire repeatedly. No matter how many attackers they hit, the rest just kept on coming, trying to overwhelm them with sheer force of numbers, splitting their force into groups that charged from different directions. Some of them ducked down behind whatever concealment they could find, making it impossible to hit them.

"Can't help at this range," she yelled to Haversham, ducking on instinct when a bullet buried itself in the rock wall over their heads. Jackson and Sandberg were damn good shots, but they had their hands full. The enemy charging on the right put their flank at risk. She had to protect their right flank. Twisting her head to look around, she spotted a group of large rocks a few yards away and got Haversham's attention. "Over there." Pointing, she started to inch away from her cover, assuming he'd follow, only to be brought up short by Jackson's angry shout.

"Don't you fucking move, Maya."

The abrupt command made her hesitate for only a second before she resumed crawling.

"Maya!"

"Shut up and shoot!" she yelled back, gritting her teeth at the sharp twinge in her ribs.

Three enemy fighters broke off and darted to her

right. The one in the lead was smaller than the others, and when he was close enough for her to see his scraggly beard, she realized it was that kid, Mohammed. Someone shouted something at him that made him stumble and twist around to look behind him. When Maya saw who it was, her blood ran cold. Then the heat of rage transformed it into a heat so molten it burned in her veins.

Khalid. He was at the rear, orchestrating this whole attack, both arms wrapped in bloody bandages. If Maya had her way, he'd be losing a lot more than blood today.

Cursing at the pain in her broken bones and the rocks digging into her flesh, Maya crawled over behind her new cover and peeked around the rock before her, her pistol up and ready. It seemed to take forever for them to come into range.

Mohammed yelled something back at his leader then turned toward her, his expression full of determination and fury. Suddenly he jerked and went down, clutching his leg where either Sandberg or Jackson had hit him. But he didn't stay down. He dragged himself up, his face twisted with pain and rage as he brought the barrel of his rifle up and fired a wild burst that went wide, peppering the rocks between her and Haversham. The others were all occupied trying to pick off the other shooters, and Mohammed was close enough now.

Maya didn't hesitate.

Rising to one knee, she took aim and fired three shots, hitting him twice in the belly. He dropped his rifle and fell clutching his middle, writhing on the ground. Another man rushed up to him. Maya fired again and again, emptying her magazine, but only managed to wing him in the shoulder. On his belly, he began dragging Mohammed back to their own lines.

Out of ammo and with her quarry too far away even if she'd had any bullets left, Maya could only watch as the survivors on her right flank hauled the wounded boy back to where they'd come from. The others followed suit, leaving their dead behind on the battlefield as they periodically wheeled to spray bullets in their direction. In the lull, Jackson and Sandberg stopped shooting. The sudden silence was almost as eerie as those terrible battle cries had been.

Maya's eyes were glued to one particular spot across that deadly space. There was no sign of Khalid, who had melted back somewhere into the shadows. But he'd been there and couldn't have gone far. He was just biding his time, regrouping for another attack.

"What the fuck do you think you were *doing*?"

She tensed at the terse whisper beside her. Bracing herself for the coming argument, she turned her head and met Jackson's enraged gaze.

TWENTY

JACKSON WAS SO fucking angry he was shaking. He'd flat-out ordered her to stay put and she'd deliberately disobeyed him, taking an unnecessary risk with her life.

She met his gaze with a maddening calm. "I just saved our right flank and mortally wounded Mohammed," she replied in a heated whisper.

Jackson shook his head. If they hadn't still been in danger and if she hadn't been so banged up, he would have grabbed her and shaken her. "Don't pull that shit ever again."

Her mouth parted in shock. "I'll do whatever I have to in order to protect our position, *Sergeant*." The last word was a hiss.

She was pulling fucking rank on him *now*? "Not. Ever. Again," he bit out. He didn't care that she was an officer and he wasn't. Out here at this moment, rank didn't mean shit. It was his duty to protect her, not the other way around. "We had the flank covered." And she'd scared him shitless by risking herself like that. They were so close to making it out of here—he'd never be able to live with himself if he didn't get her out safely. Maya didn't respond, but she didn't have to. Her one good eye and the other that was open a slit were boring holes in his face.

"Don't see any movement over there," Haversham whispered. "Think he's got more men left?"

"At least a few dozen more," Sandberg replied, crouching behind the smaller boulder. "What do you think?" he asked Jackson.

"I think we find another way outta here and haul ass to the LZ," he said to him.

Sandberg nodded. "We'll double back. Let's go." He reached for Haversham to help him up.

Staying low, Jackson rushed over to Maya's position. She was already up, hunkered down behind the pitiful cover she'd chosen. Her eyes shot sparks at him when he came down on one knee beside her. "I'm down, but I'm not out," she snapped in a harsh whisper. "You need to remember that and lose this protective alpha-male bullshit. Just because I'm the only female doesn't mean you—"

He cut her off with a single, slicing look. "Save it. I'm done arguing about this. I'm carrying you outta here, and you're gonna get home in one piece because I'm gonna make it that way. And you're never gonna put your ass on the line like that again unless the rest of us are dead. And I mean every last one of us. Got me?"

A muscle in her jaw worked as she glared at him, and when she spoke her voice was unsteady. "I don't want you risking your life for me."

His anger evaporated at the fear on her face. Though he wanted to touch her and reassure her, now wasn't the time. And if he relaxed his stance for an instant, she'd take that slack and run with it. "Too bad, because that's what I do." He'd done it for complete strangers in the line of duty without a second thought, but with her it was personal. Every single instinct he possessed was focused on protecting her, because she was *his* and she'd come to mean more to him than she'd ever realize.

Something moved in her expression, a weird mixture of wonder and apprehension before she put the calm mask back in place. Without giving her another second to argue, he checked to make sure the coast was clear and lifted her over his shoulders once again.

Sandberg was already a few paces back up the trail they'd taken. Jackson followed, half turning every few seconds to make sure they weren't being followed. The hell of it was, they all knew the enemy was still out there. They just didn't know when the next attack would come.

WHEN THE MEN dragged Mohammed into the rock crevice where he waited, Khalid took one look at the fatal wounds in the boy's belly and felt his knees give out. Denial shot through him as he reached out a hand to brace himself on the rock before he fell. The men set Mohammed down and glanced up at him in uncertainty.

"Leave us," he whispered, his throat so tight he could barely get the words out. The men left to tend to the other wounded. Khalid swallowed hard and went to his knees beside Mohammed. His young face was lined with agony, the scent of his blood strong in the air as it poured in a continuous stream from his body beneath his clutching hands.

"I am s-sorry," Mohammed gasped out, eyes glazed with pain, glimmering with unshed tears.

Khalid couldn't stand it. Ignoring the fiery burn in his ruined shoulder, he placed one hand atop Mohammed's, over the terrible wounds. With the other, he cupped the boy's bearded cheek. His own bullet wounds throbbed, sending needles of agony along his limbs until he thought he'd vomit. "Do not apologize. You have nothing to be sorry for." A helpless rage twisted inside him. So young. So full of promise and goodness. The very best of their cause and a future leader who would have shone as brightly as the sun someday. All wasted.

Because of that traitor Jihad and the female who had helped the others escape. *May they all burn in hell for this.*

"I d-didn't...listen..."

He hadn't listened when Khalid had shouted at him to come back, screamed at him not to make the reckless charge. He closed his eyes and bit down against the overwhelming tide of grief crashing over him. When he opened them, he was unashamed of the tears stinging there. "I'm not angry at you, Mohammed. You were so brave."

Those dark, trust-filled eyes stayed on his. Searching for acceptance and trust. Things Khalid had been searching for his whole life until Mohammed had given them to him. "Wanted to...p-prove myself."

Because he feared Khalid had blamed him for the prisoners' escape. The knowledge was almost too much to bear. "You already did." He stopped talking because his voice had cracked and he couldn't go on.

Mohammed's brave facade began to crumble. His legs shifted restlessly on the ground in a futile effort to escape the pain and he rolled his head, eyes squeezed shut. "*Hurts.*"

"I know, son." And there was nothing he could do to ease it for him or speed the process of dying along for him. He didn't even have anything to ease his pain—here, where opium grew more plentifully than anywhere else on earth. It could take another hour or two for him to die, maybe more. Khalid could not stay that long if he hoped to catch the enemy. But he refused to abandon Mohammed here to die alone. The boy deserved a better fate than that.

No. There *was* something he could do, he realized. He could give Mohammed one final act of mercy to repay him for his loyalty and kindness.

Fighting back a growl at the surge of pain in his left arm, he reached behind him into his belt and took hold of the knife hilt. He paused there a moment, fingers wrapped around the cool metal.

Allah, let me be swift. Let me strike true so that he does not suffer a moment longer.

"Mohammed, pray with me."

The boy's eyes opened and fixed on him, the fear and despair in them driving a different kind of blade into Khalid's heart. Holding his young friend's gaze, he began citing one of his favorite verses from the Quran. Mohammed's lips trembled a moment, and then he joined in, saying the words of the martyr's prayer. Together their voices filled the rock crevice, sending the prayer heavenward to Allah through the opening above them where the sky was a pure, endless blue.

Allah, forgive me.

Near the end of the last line of the prayer, Khalid gathered his will and brought the knife up, then plunged it down with all the remaining strength in his wounded arm, driving it deep into Mohammed's heart.

The boy lurched up with a horrific gasp when the

blade buried deep, his hands flying up to grasp at the hilt, his expression stricken, accusing.

Khalid kept his gaze locked with Mohammed's, letting him see that he wasn't alone. "Peace be upon you, Mohammed," he whispered, holding the hands grasping the knife's hilt until they went slack. The boy's head lolled back, the horror and betrayal in those wide eyes fading, softening to nothingness.

When it was over, Khalid yanked the blade out, roaring at the pain in his shoulder and in his heart. His cheeks were wet above his beard and he didn't bother wiping them dry. Rising on unsteady legs, he stumbled out of the crevice with the bloody knife in his hands to order the survivors to assemble, intent on killing every last one of the enemy.

There was no one there.

The only men left were the dead scattered before him in the distance, their lifeless hands lying empty on the ground. Everyone else had deserted him, taking the fallen men's weapons with them.

A strange ripping sensation in his chest made him gasp and double over. All his life he'd fought for the chance to matter, for the chance to lead. Now, in his hour of greatest need, no one was willing to follow him.

The blood rushed loudly in his ears, panic setting in. Rahim was coming. He knew about the traitor Jihad and wanted to exact revenge, as well as recapture the Secretary of Defense. If Khalid didn't get the prisoner himself before Rahim arrived, he was a dead man walking.

Denial and bitterness filled him, hardened his resolve. He was alone, weak from pain and blood loss and without a weapon, and he had only one more chance to save himself. He took it, striding over the sunbaked ground and across the field of dead to where the enemy had retreated. But instead of following their tracks, he skirted down the hill to a thin trail that snaked its way up and over it. Dizziness and exhaustion slowed him. The chance at redeeming his reputation gave him the endurance to push forward.

With every step, he battled the doubt nipping at him. Voices from his past filled his head, words spoken by the elders bringing fear and resentment so thick they nearly choked him.

You should never have lived.

We should have killed you while you slept in your mother's whoring belly.

Your existence is a sin against Allah and your life will be cursed because of it.

Khalid shook his head to clear those hateful voices, forcing the ugly words aside. They didn't matter because they weren't true. He was still the master of his fate. It wasn't too late. Allah wanted him to carry on, or the bullets would have killed him, rather than only wound him.

He followed the trail to its summit and down the other side, trusting Allah to guide him. And when he reached the bottom and heard the distant sound of coughing, his heart filled with hope.

Peering through a gap in the rocks, he took in the scene before him. The prisoners were on the intersecting trail, headed toward him, unaware of his presence. The PJ was out front this time, scouting out their position, because he'd left the female resting at a spot back along the trail. The traitor Jihad carried the Secretary a fair distance behind them. They were separated and exposed, as vulnerable as he could ever hope for.

He fought to slow his breathing. Aware that he had only this final chance, Khalid hunkered down to wait for the perfect moment. Exhaustion pulled at him, weighing his limbs down. He struggled through it and held fast to his purpose. His nerveless fingers tightened around the hilt of the bloodstained knife.

He still had strength enough for this.

MAYA SIGHED IN relief when Jackson set her down to rest, and the sigh immediately turned into a coughing attack. She doubled over and clamped her good arm around her ribs to shield them from the force of the coughs, though he doubted it did any good. Sweaty and shaking, she wiped her forearm across her face and opened her eyes to look up at him.

"I'm fine," she wheezed in a whisper. He didn't know why she'd bothered trying to be quiet when every living thing within a two-mile radius must have heard the coughing.

He didn't believe her for a second, but faced forward and continued creeping ahead to do some recon. It would take a while for Sandberg to make it up here, and when he did he was going to need a rest. He'd insisted they were still going in the right direction, despite the detour, and Jackson agreed. Along with the physical exertion, the constant drain of having to be on his guard was taking a toll on him. They were closer to freedom now than they'd ever been since the capture, just under a mile from the designated LZ. Right now that mile seemed more like a hundred. He wanted nothing more than to get everyone on board that helo and get the hell out of here. The minutes were dragging by.

It was too damn quiet out here. Made him uneasy.

On one knee, he paused to check his perimeter again. He could see trails leading up into the hills surrounding him. Lots of places for the enemy to hide.

Satisfied they were still okay, he crept forward another ten yards or so when something tripped his internal radar. Off to the right lay the foot of another path, this one leading up and over the hill they'd just come around. Since he couldn't see any movement, he kept going, wanting to make sure the trail was clear before the others caught up.

A flash of movement was the only warning he got.

A man burst out from behind the rocks. Jackson tracked the knife in his fist and raised his weapon. Khalid's enraged face registered just as he pulled the trigger.

His weapon jammed.

Fuck!

Khalid was steps away, knife held high, eyes gleaming with the promise of death.

There was no time to clear his weapon. Jackson threw it aside and launched himself at his enemy. They collided in midair with a bone-jarring grunt and fell to the ground on their sides. Jackson's fist wrapped around the hand holding the knife, forced it back. His muscles strained and shook at the effort.

Khalid was ranting something in Pashto and Jackson could hear Maya screaming his name in the background. Those evil yellow eyes were narrowed on him with naked hatred.

The muscles in Jackson's arm quivered as he held

the weapon at bay. In those few seconds, all his fury intensified, so hot that he couldn't contain it. This fucker had orchestrated their kidnapping. He'd beaten and tortured Maya, forced her to hold a gun to her head and pull the trigger. The memory of Maya's cries as Khalid had beaten her filled Jackson's head in a deafening roar. His heart pounded against his ribs. Instinct took over.

He reared up and drove his left fist into Khalid's wounded shoulder with every bit of strength he had left. The man went white and howled in agony, his fingers releasing their death grip on the knife. It dropped to the dusty ground with a thud. Jackson didn't even glance at it. He pounded Khalid in the face and shoulder to unleash the toxic rage seething inside him, still caught up in his memories.

He'd *hurt Maya*. Beaten her with his fists and belt. Broken her bones. Deprived her of food and water. Locked her up in a cage too small to stand up or lie down in.

He barely felt the blows Khalid managed to land with his elbow and knees in between punches. They rolled and twisted in the dirt, locked in mortal combat. One of them wasn't walking away from this. Jackson knew it. And it wasn't going to be him. He was weakened and dehydrated, but he was still stronger than Khalid and his demented fervor.

He came up on top and straddled Khalid to drive his fist into that sneering face when he caught the flash of metal out of the corner of his eye. At the last moment he saw the blade slicing toward him in a deadly arc. He jerked out of the way just as the knife swept past his chest, so close he felt the breeze it stirred.

On instinct, Jackson twisted them around and captured the bastard's head in the crook of one elbow. He added the other arm and squeezed hard, locking the choke hold down. His hands clamped around Khalid's skull. Held tight as Khalid flailed in his grip. With an enraged snarl Jackson wrenched the head around as hard as he could, snapping his neck with a sickening crunch.

The knife hit the ground with a metallic clang and the body beneath him went instantly slack, those eerie yellow eyes turning glassy.

Panting, Jackson released him and slid off to the side. The adrenaline crash hit him hard. He was shaking all over and gasping when Sandberg raced up with his AK aimed at Khalid. Maya was right behind him, her face full of terror.

She dropped to her knees next to him, grabbed his shoulder with her good hand. "Are you hurt? Are you okay?" The fear and desperation in her voice broke through the numbness.

"I'm fine." He forced himself to his feet on shaky legs and turned to block her from the sight of Khalid's body.

"What the hell were you *doing*?" she wheezed, face pale.

"Rifle jammed," he answered. "And I wasn't letting him come near you ever again." He'd *wanted* to kill Khalid with his bare hands. And he had. That shook him. He'd never known he could hate anyone that much.

He watched the words register, the truth of what he'd said sinking in. She gave a tiny nod and reached up to cradle the side of his face with her palm. "Okay. But don't ever do something like that again."

"That LZ's not coming to us, people, and it's not getting any closer standing around here," Sandberg said, returning for Haversham where he'd left him back down the trail when Khalid attacked Jackson.

He knew they had to get moving, but Jackson didn't move out right away. Instead he covered Maya's hand with his and closed his eyes to lean into her touch, letting her know what the gesture meant to him. Her hand was hot, too hot, and dry. Her breathing was raspy and labored, making him even more anxious to get her evacuated to a hospital for treatment. But that unexpected softness in her expression and knowing he was responsible for it—that was something he could easily live for.

He wrapped his fingers around hers and squeezed, keeping them to his scruffy cheek. "Almost there, baby," he whispered. "A little ways longer and we're outta here. But I think you're gonna have to walk for a bit." At the moment his legs felt too weak to carry his own weight.

A grin spread across her cracked lips and her right eye twinkled. Half turning so her back was to him, she bent slightly at the knees and looked over her shoulder at him, reaching her right arm back. "Come on, jump on," she wheezed, practically wobbling on her feet. "But just this once."

It was such a ridiculous thing to say and it was clear the effort cost her, but damned if it didn't make him grin. "Rain check."

Maya shrugged in a "suit yourself" way and stepped past him to head down the trail. Steadier now, he retrieved his discarded rifle and turned away to lead them the last mile to the LZ.

TWENTY-ONE

A FEW HUNDRED yards into the trek, Maya stumbled,
her breathing all but stopping her in her tracks. Walking uphill even for that short a distance was too much.
It felt like someone had weighed down her body with
lead bricks. Her heart was pounding out of control and
there was no way to slow it. The tightness in her chest
made it impossible to get a deep breath and when she
did, her ribs killed her or a coughing fit took hold.

Come on! she raged at her body. *We're so close.*
They didn't have far to go and they couldn't risk slowing down to wait for her to rest. She didn't want Jackson to have to carry her anymore.

Looking at him, no one would ever know that he'd
just killed a dangerous militant in hand-to-hand combat. After retrieving then clearing his jammed weapon,
he'd taken point again and was still going at a good
clip, despite the demands he'd placed on his body today.
Sandberg carried Haversham behind her, and when
she slowed they caught up fast. She waved them on,
bent over and gasping, but Sandberg didn't budge from
her side. When Jackson glanced back and saw her, he
doubled back.

"Sorry," she gasped, angry at her body's weakness.
"Can't."

He shook his head. "It's okay. Come on, darlin',

one last ride." Stooping, he offered her a hand and she draped herself over his broad back so he could lift her more easily. She hated that he was forced to carry her again. He was doing double the work to pick up her slack, had been all day. She held her breath and tensed her aching muscles when he shifted her into position. God, the constant pain was making her insane. He stood and staggered back a step, telling her just how exhausted he was, then gave a muffled groan and started walking.

Maya covered her mouth with her right forearm as she began coughing, the fiery pain ripping through her. As soon as she could breathe again, she closed her eyes and laid her cheek against Jackson's sun-warmed shoulder in defeat. "I owe you a day at the spa," she managed.

"Nah," he said between breaths. "I'll take a good rubdown from you later, though."

The thought made her smile. If she could be this ill and look like she did and he still wanted her to touch him, that had to be a good sign.

Next time she opened her eyes, Jackson had crested the small hill and had paused to rest a moment.

"Just down there in that clearing," Sandberg told them, pointing to the LZ.

Now that the end was in sight, Maya's heart was filled to bursting with hope. So close. It was hard to believe this whole nightmare was almost over. She raised her head, scanning the sky and straining to listen for the throb of incoming rotors. Nothing but the soft sigh of the wind came back, the sound of Jackson's ragged breathing.

He kept shifting her repeatedly over the final few

hundred yards, the muscles in his back and shoulders quivering beneath her. She rubbed a hand absently over his sweat-soaked chest in apology and gratitude for all he'd done for her.

At last they reached the clearing, and he set her down beside a thin, scraggly bush. She huddled into a ball on her side and wrapped the blanket around her to stave off the worst of the shivers, while he dropped to his hands and knees beside her, exhausted. Sweat poured off his face, no matter how many times he swiped his arm across it.

Sandberg set Haversham down and dropped his ruck, and the Sec Def immediately tore into it, handing both men a bladder of water Tarik had given them. Jackson drained a good amount of his before opening his eyes with a sigh and offering it to Maya. She took it and had a few sips, relishing the feel of moisture in her dry mouth. Her stomach was in knots from being exposed out here to await the CSAR team.

"How much longer?" Haversham asked Sandberg, propped on to one hip with a pistol in his hand. He hadn't released it since they'd left the village.

"Twenty, twenty-five minutes," he answered, still sucking in air.

Maya had no idea how he and Jackson had found the endurance to carry them so far in these conditions. She took in her surroundings, unable to let her guard down. They were in a natural bowl that provided some protection from the wind should it pick up. It was wide enough that a few helicopters would have no trouble setting down inside it. When they came, there'd be more than one. With the Sec Def as one of the extractions, they wouldn't be taking any chances with his safety. Wouldn't surprise her if an entire SEAL team showed up to get them. She wouldn't mind seeing some SEALs right about now.

Jackson was on one knee holding his weapon at the ready, watching the surrounding hills. No one said anything, all of them too tired and edgy to bother trying to make conversation.

When it seemed like way more than twenty-five minutes had passed, a distant sound disturbed the air. She glanced up at Jackson to see if he'd heard it too. He was tense, focused on the sky behind her. She twisted around, grimacing as it pulled her ribs. Was it their ride? Her heart rate accelerated, anticipation rising sharp and painful in her chest.

A minute later the sound increased, and it was unmistakable. The heavy beat of a rotary wing aircraft. Then Sandberg pointed. "I see it."

Everyone followed his finger. There in the distance, Maya picked out a black speck in the clear blue sky. A moment later, the speck split into three.

Oh yeah, the cavalry had arrived. The elation sweeping through her brought tears to her eyes.

She was on her feet without realizing it, shading her eyes with her hand. Part of her wanted to jump up and down and wave her arm like a maniac. She felt like a shipwreck survivor who'd just spotted their salvation. Then a series of cracks rent the air. For a moment they didn't register.

She swiveled to find Jackson reaching for her, his face tense. "Get down!"

Jesus, someone was still out there shooting at them.

She dropped to her knees and then her belly as Jackson slid up beside her. He pressed her head down until her cheek dug into the dusty ground. With her head cranked to one side, she got her first glimpse of the figures rushing down the hillside toward them. Fifty men at least, maybe more.

"Shit, they're surrounding us," Haversham muttered, returning fire.

Maya glanced the other way to see more coming at them from that side. She cast a desperate glance up at the incoming helos. They were close. Would they be able to land and stay there long enough for her and the others to get aboard?

The shooting took a sudden uptick in volume. She lay flat next to Jackson while he and Haversham fired at the oncoming enemy. Within thirty seconds, Jackson set down his weapon. "Out of ammo," he muttered, cursing under his breath.

Her stomach knotted. Before she could answer, something exploded a few dozen yards in front of them. Jackson covered her head and torso with his own while debris pelted them. That eerie howl of the militants rose up over the noise of the firefight.

"I'm out!" Sandberg shouted.

They were surrounded and out of ammo. The sound of the rotors grew louder. Maya's heart lodged in her throat. Icy needles pricked her body. Jackson lifted off her and she shifted to get to her knees, but he stopped her with an arm around her back. "Stay down," he yelled in her ear, holding her close. Unable to run though every instinct demanded she flee, she closed her eyes and clung to him, praying for help.

Bullets impacted closer, closer until she could feel them whizzing past her, thudding into the ground around them. The distant helos were still too far away.

She was holding her breath, praying for a miracle when the deafening roar of twin engines suddenly split the air. A half second later, the bark of powerful guns eclipsed everything else. Daring to open her eyes, Maya lifted her chin to see an Apache attack helicopter rise out of the valley beyond the cliff's edge and spray the attacking enemy with fire. Moments later another one appeared on its left, rising out of the abyss. It opened up its guns with a loud rattle. After about a minute of firing, they fell silent. Her ears throbbed in the sudden quiet.

Screams from the wounded enemy filled the void, but that eerie howl that signaled an attack was gone. She didn't dare look behind her or to the side as the big Chinook looming above finally came in for a landing, two Black Hawks flanking it. The Apaches gained altitude and resumed making controlled bursts at the remaining attackers. The instant the other birds touched down, soldiers poured out of them.

Dozens of them. Big men with scruffy beards and scary-ass game faces, come to send these bastards to their maker. SEALs or Delta from the look of them, maybe some of both.

Jackson's arm scooped around her shoulders. He hauled her to her feet and shoved her in the direction of the Chinook, yelling in her ear. "Go, go!"

She took off on rubbery legs, wheezing but determined to make it. The SOF troops raced past her, taking out more targets as they ran to form a protective perimeter. Another man was running toward her, and Maya finally saw the letters PJ on his upper arm.

He grabbed her and tossed her over one shoulder, ignoring her scream of agony, then turned and ran like hell back to the waiting Chinook, its rotors still turning. She bit down and shut her eyes, struggling to stay above the pain. Each running step jammed her rescuer's shoulder deep into her belly and jarred her damaged ribs.

In seconds he flipped her over and handed her off to someone else, who dragged her deep inside the belly of the helo. Just as she cleared the doorway, out in the distance her gaze landed on one of the attackers, scrambling back up the hill. He half turned, facing toward her, watching the helo. In the sunlight she caught the flash of a coppery head and beard.

Rahim.

She scrambled to twist around, searching for someone to tell. Where was Jackson? He'd been right behind her. She cried out in relief when he came flying up the tail ramp, reaching out a hand for him. He skidded to a halt in front of her and took her face in his hands. "You okay?" he yelled over the noise of the rotors.

She nodded. "Rahim's out there—I saw him."

"You sure?"

"Positive." She hadn't imagined it, and there couldn't be two copper-bearded militants built like that out here.

Another man appeared carrying Haversham up the ramp, and then Sandberg ran in. More men rushed inside, some moving backward, shooting at targets just out of view. She could hear the deeper bark of the Apache guns outside. The pitch of the rotors suddenly changed and the big helo shook under the strain as the pilots powered up. Her pulse pounded a frantic rhythm while the behemoth eased off the ground. She sensed the deck tilting as they climbed and eased forward, signaling their imminent escape.

Then a hail of gunfire erupted in the port side wall near where she was sitting. Automatically she dropped facedown on the deck, covering her head. Bullets raked the side of the aircraft, punching holes through the metal skin. Bits of insulation rained down on her. Men were yelling, swearing. The next thing she knew, Jackson had thrown himself across her. The big helo pitched to the side. Only Jackson's weight kept her from rolling across the metal deck. More shots ripped into the port side wall. Jackson jerked on top of her. Men were shouting, running, grabbing fire extinguishers. The Chinook rolled sharply to the right.

Shit, oh shit, oh shit...

They dropped so hard and fast her stomach floated up toward her rib cage. Maya thought her heart would explode. Were they going down? She squeezed her eyes shut. Jackson stayed on her like a living shield, pressing her down, one hand protecting her head. Another sharp pitch forward, and her body was shoved hard against the deck, telling her they were pulling serious Gs. She sensed the Chinook lifting, climbing ever higher. Soon the constant rattle of gunfire faded away, gradually replaced by the roar of the rotors as they sped away.

Trembling, hardly daring to believe it was over, Maya closed her eyes and went limp beneath Jackson. He rolled off with a pained grunt. The sound made her skin prickle. Lifting up on her good arm, she angled her head to see him. What she saw made all the blood drain out of her face.

He was lying on his side with a hand pressed to his belly, and his face was white with strain. Blood spilled out beneath his splayed hand.

Oh my God. "No!" she yelled, the word torn from

the depths of her soul as she lunged at him. She shoved her hand down over his, her eyes searching his face and seeing nothing but pain and anxiety he was trying to hide. She twisted around, heedless of her own suffering. "Someone *help* me!" His blood was warm against her fingers, pooling much too fast. Already it stained the deck.

"I'm okay," he managed calmly, trying to reassure her.

He was *not* okay. Terrified sobs shook her, jarring her deep inside. He'd just been gut shot. She knew what that meant.

A soldier finally came over and pulled her away from him to take her place. She fought the restraining hands but another pair grabbed her, holding her steady. "Maya. Maya, look at me."

She jerked her head up to find Haversham holding her. His eyes were earnest, shadowed with exhaustion and strain. "He'll be fine. Stay back here with me and let them help him."

They had Jackson's filthy T-shirt cut off him and she could see the ugly wound on his abdomen they were working on. Her stomach twisted at the sight of that dark hole in his bronze-toned flesh. She made a high-pitched sound of agony, and Haversham hugged her closer, pressing his cheek to hers. "Come on, sweetheart, hang tough. He's a fighter and they're doing everything they can. We'll be on base in no time and they'll get him right into the O.R."

It wasn't good enough. She wanted to be the one next to him, helping him, doing something instead of sitting there watching him bleed.

If she'd realized anything since their capture, it was

that she loved him. Unequivocally, and without reservation. She wanted him to know it.

One of the medics started an IV, while the other worked on slowing the bleeding. The second man turned his head to shout something toward the front of the aircraft, and with a start she recognized Jackson's buddy, Cam. A tiny measure of relief eased the worst of the panic. Cam loved him like a brother. He'd do everything in his power to save Jackson.

Jackson waved a hand to get Cam's attention and pointed at her. Cam and the other medic looked over at her, and she wanted to scream at them to hurry up and help him already. Cam stayed with him, keeping pressure on the wound, but the other man got up and came over to her.

"He wants you on oxygen, ma'am. Come with me and we'll lay you next to him. He'll be a lot more relaxed that way."

Beside him was exactly where she wanted to be, but *oxygen*? He wanted her on fucking oxygen when he was lying there bleeding all over the place from a bullet in his belly?

Haversham helped her up with one arm as she took the hand the medic offered her. When she was beside Jackson again, she grabbed his hand and held it as tight as she could, searching his face anxiously, feeling like she was dying inside. "You hold on, do you hear me?"

A pained half smile curved his lips in the midst of that thick, nearly black stubble. "Gonna be fine, sweetheart. Right, guys?"

Cam nodded without looking at her, all business as he focused on his work. "We'll be landing in a few minutes and I've already radioed ahead to alert the surgical staff. They'll get him into the O.R. right away. He's gonna be okay once they patch him up."

Maya didn't believe him. The bullet could have hit an organ or an artery and they wouldn't know how bad the damage was until they operated. She reached out and took Jackson's face in her good hand, cupping her palm around his jaw, holding his gaze with all her formidable will. "Don't you dare leave me." She choked on the last word, tears spilling down her face and she didn't care who saw them. If he hadn't thrown himself on top of her, he wouldn't have been shot.

Jackson's expression softened as though he understood how afraid she was of losing him. "Won't leave you, baby. Promise." His face contorted when they did something to the wound. She glanced down to where they were putting pressure bandages on him but then another medic appeared with two oxygen tanks.

"Matching set of his and her oxygen tanks, as requested," he said, plunking them down and slipping a mask first over Jackson's nose and mouth, then hers.

Annoyed, she started to bat the thing away, but Jackson stopped her by grabbing her hand and squeezing tight. When she looked into his face, he gave a sharp shake of his head and she relented, lying back on the stretcher where they'd placed her. It was so fucking stupid to be worrying about her right now that she wanted to scream at him. She was still crying and couldn't seem to stop, each sob tearing at her injured ribs and she didn't care. She wanted the pain.

The medic next to her put a blood pressure cuff on her right arm and inflated it, taking her vitals and recording them before getting on the radio, she assumed to whatever base hospital they were taking them to.

As Cam had promised, the flight wasn't long, but it seemed to last forever and Maya refused to let go of Jackson's hand. Every few minutes she squeezed his fingers to let him know she was there, and it heartened her a little when he squeezed back. Soon the Chinook's engines began to reduce power until they finally landed.

Seconds after the tail ramp lowered the medics carried her, Jackson and Haversham out. She blinked in the blinding sunshine and reluctantly released Jackson's hand with a final squeeze as they rushed them through the pulsing rotor wash and across the tarmac. Then she started coughing and lost track of everything: time, place and Jackson's location.

She was sagging against the stretcher when she could at last open her eyes and found a medical team descending on her. They poked needles into her and prodded her all over, despite her growls of pain and frantic questions about Jackson. No one would tell her anything except to save her strength and not talk. Even in the X-ray room the tech wouldn't answer her questions.

A nurse came in and injected something into her IV line that she said would make Maya sleepy. Her eyelids started to droop in seconds. With one frantic burst of strength, she fought it and snarled at the woman.

"Someone better take me to Sergeant Thatcher, or I swear to God I'll get off this gurney and find him myself."

The nurse must have realized Maya wasn't bluffing, because she reluctantly wheeled her down a brightly lit hallway into another room, where other patients lay behind curtained cubicles. One curtain was pulled aside and the moment Maya saw Jackson she cried out and half sat up, rolling to her good arm to brace herself, despite the stab in her ribs. She was woozy enough from the medication that it took two tries to rip the oxygen mask away. "Jackson!"

His eyes opened and focused on her. She saw his wan smile form beneath the clear mask. "Hey." His voice was raspy, but clear. Bloody bandages littered the stretcher and floor.

"What's happening?" she demanded of the medical staff at his bedside.

"We're prepping him for surgery so we can take out the metal fragments in his intestines," a man wearing a surgical mask and cap answered. From the authoritative way he acted, Maya guessed he was the surgeon.

But oh, shit, fragments in the intestines sounded really bad. Her stomach balled up so hard it hurt. "He'll be okay though, right?" She didn't take her eyes off Jackson, afraid they were lying.

"He'll be okay," the surgeon answered. They started wheeling him away and she panicked until Jackson pulled the mask aside to speak to her, every line of his face etched with pain he was trying not to show.

"Heal fast, Maya, and come to me when you can."

She nodded and watched with a lump in her throat as they wheeled him through the big double doors at the end of the room. The doors swung shut and all her strength vanished, leaving her limp on the stretcher. It would be okay. She'd have the chance to confess her feelings for him once he came out of recovery. When she told him she didn't want an audience, because it was no one else's damn business, and it went against military regulation anyhow. Not that she really gave a shit about that part at this point.

"Okay, now will you cooperate and lie down?" the nurse asked in exasperation. "You've got a long flight ahead and your own surgery for that wrist coming up."

Flight? What flight? She was suddenly too exhausted to form the question. Whatever drug they had her on did its job and pulled her under.

The next time she woke up, people were standing at her bedside, discussing medical things she didn't understand. Were they talking about her? What time was it? What *day* was it? She wanted to ask about Jackson but her eyelids were too heavy to keep open.

A gust of cool, sweet air hit her in the face. Her eyes snapped open and it took a moment for her to realize she was outside. A large gray aircraft loomed in front of her, its tail ramp open. Were they loading her on to it? Her tongue was too heavy and uncooperative to speak. Her heart started to race. She didn't want to leave without knowing Jackson was out of surgery and would be okay. Where were they taking her? When would she see Jackson again?

"Whoa, easy there." A steadying hand pressed down on her shoulder when she tried to sit up.

Her tongue wouldn't form the words she wanted to say. She needed to know what was happening. How was Jackson? And she had to tell someone about Rahim. Had they killed him? She hoped so. The cold night air made her shiver, despite all the blankets they'd piled on her. Everything hurt and she was too tired to keep her eyes open. Her eyelids fluttered closed. The last thing she remembered was jolting awake at the roar of the plane's engines as they powered up for takeoff.

TWENTY-TWO

MAYA SWIRLED TOWARD consciousness slowly, becoming aware of her surroundings by degrees. The quiet hit her first. The roar of the plane's engines was gone and there was a weird chemical taste in her mouth. She cracked her eyes open and instantly squinted at the blinding white light assaulting her. Trying again, she found herself in a private hospital room. She still had an oxygen mask over her mouth and nose. That was why her breathing sounded so Darth Vaderish.

She blinked, letting her eyes adjust to the brightness. Sunlight poured in from a window on the left hand side of the room. She started to raise her left arm to shield her eyes and realized how heavy it was. There was a cast from above her elbow to the base of her fingers. She'd had surgery? She didn't remember a thing after being put on that transport plane.

"Good morning."

She whipped her head to the side of her pillow to find Doug Haversham smiling at her. He sat in a wheelchair tucked beneath a rolling side table strewn with papers and a laptop. He looked exhausted. He'd shaved, revealing smooth brown skin and a strong jaw. His left leg was casted, sticking out in front of him on one of the chair's pedals.

She swallowed past the dryness in her mouth and

throat she guessed were side effects from the intuba-
tion and pulled off the oxygen mask with her good
hand. "Where am I?"

"Qatar."

What? "I thought they'd send me to Germany." She
could've sworn that was what they'd told her before
loading her on that flight. Had she been that out of it?

"They changed their minds."

Or he'd pulled strings for some reason and changed
their minds for them. Licking her dry lips, she nodded
at her cast. "Any idea what they did to me?" The ache
in her wrist was way better, that was for sure. Her fingers were still swollen though. Her cheek and ribs felt
pretty much like shit.

"They set five bones in your wrist with pins and
screws and are treating you for pneumonia. The doctors came by a while ago, but you were still out so
they'll be back in another hour or so to give you the
full rundown."

So Jackson had been right about the pneumonia.
He was going to be one hell of a doctor when he made
it through med school, she thought with a twinge of
yearning. It hurt too much to think about not seeing
him. With him in a different country for at least the
foreseeable future, she wasn't sure when she'd be able
to see him. Or if she even would. She forced the image
of his face from her mind and took stock of what was
happening with her body.

"How's your leg?" she asked.

Haversham grunted and frowned at the cast. "Hurts
like a bitch, actually, but thanks for asking."

"Sure." Now that she thought about it, it did seem
a bit easier to breathe. Her chest wasn't quite so tight.

The achy feeling in her muscles and the pervasive chills told her she must still be feverish. An IV pole beside her bed held some bags of fluids that dripped into the vein in her right arm. It creeped her out, thinking of that thing sticking out of her arm. She looked over at Doug instead. "Antibiotics?"

"I'd think so. You were one sick lady."

Yeah, but she didn't care about any of that right now. She couldn't stand not knowing about Jackson for another second. "What happened with Jackson? Is he here?" She didn't bother using his rank, since Doug knew about their...attachment to each other. Maybe it wasn't a relationship as things stood now, but she'd like it to be. Man, she wanted that more than anything. He'd gotten inside her so deep it almost frightened her. Except for Pilar, she'd never imagined caring about anyone. The thought of living without him triggered a flare of panic and grief in her gut.

"I figured you'd ask me as soon as you woke up, so I wrote down all the details to make sure I didn't miss anything. Damn meds are screwing with my mind." He flipped through a folder on the desk and removed a sheet of paper covered with his bold scrawl. "The surgeons operated last night soon after he was brought in. The operation went well and they stopped the internal bleeding. He's still in the hospital back at Kandahar and they're going to keep him for another day or two before sending him through Germany and then stateside."

Her heart sunk a little at that, because it meant she definitely wouldn't get to see him. "And what about his prognosis? What kind of damage did the bullet do—?"

"Hang on, I was getting to that part." He scanned his notes. "The bullet perforated part of his bowel but missed his bladder and kidneys. Apparently they think it was a ricochet, rather than a direct hit, and some fragments from the aircraft. At any rate, they fixed everything up and are treating him with heavy-duty antibiotics to fight any infection from the perforation." He looked up at her. "They think he'll be up and walking today, and there's no reason why he shouldn't be able to recover enough to return to active duty in a few months after some rehab."

Maya sank back against her pillow, dizzy with relief, but she didn't want to think about him returning to duty. Hell, *she* didn't want to think about having to return to duty right now.

"What about you?"

She met his gaze. "What do you mean?"

He set the paper down, pushed the rolling table away and wheeled himself over to the side of her bed. "What are you going to do after this?"

She shrugged, then the coughing spell started. Wincing, she partially sat up and ripped the oxygen mask away to cover her mouth with her right forearm. Her ribs still hurt like a bitch, but she could feel the new binding they'd wrapped around her. Once the coughing stopped, it took a moment for her to get her breath back. This time she was happy to put the oxygen mask back on. "I assume they'll send me back home to recover, since I won't do much good over here for the time being."

He nodded slowly, his thoughtful expression making her think he knew something she'd didn't. "Where will you go?"

She frowned at the question. "Home."

"You have a place to stay?"

"My apartment off base." The question threw her. Where else would she go?

After staring at her for a moment, he broke eye contact and fiddled with the blanket on his lap. "I checked into your background this morning."

Whoa, wait. Maya removed the mask and raised an eyebrow. He'd had time to dig into her information after having surgery?

A small smile played at the corner of his mouth. "Well, okay, I had my staff do that." His expression changed, softened. "They couldn't find a living relative to inform about your injuries."

So her grandmother was dead then. She'd wondered about it over the years. And she wasn't sad to hear she was gone, because that old woman hadn't lifted a finger to intervene when she'd found out what her son had done to Pilar. No, she'd done the unforgiveable and ignored it, while her granddaughter was repeatedly raped beneath her roof.

The empathy in Haversham's eyes made her angry. The only family she'd ever cared about was Pili, and she'd died years ago. So she was alone. A lot of people were. She didn't need anyone's pity. "And?"

"And so I wanted to know if there was someone who could maybe stay with you while you recover."

"It's a broken wrist and some banged-up ribs, not a spinal cord injury. I think I can handle it." And the Air Force would step in to find her extra care if she couldn't.

Now his lips quirked. "I meant being tired and weak while you fight off the pneumonia, but I figured you'd feel that way. If you change your mind, though—"

"No, thanks. I'll be all right."

He studied her for a moment. "You know, it's okay to ask for help when you need it."

"I know that." It came out a touch prickly, but she couldn't help it.

"Good, because that makes this next order of business much easier."

She gave him a suspicious look. "Meaning?"

"I hear you saw Rahim out there."

"I'm sure it was him. Did they get him?"

His expression soured. "Not yet." He shifted in his chair, and it was obvious his leg was bothering him. "You'll be debriefed up the wazoo over the next couple of days, but you'd better make peace with the idea of seeing a therapist when you get back to the States."

The one and only therapist she'd seen after Pilar died hadn't helped her at all. The mere thought of dredging up all those old wounds and adding in the discussion about what she'd just been through was both overwhelming and exhausting. "Because if I don't comply they won't return me to duty, you mean?"

"That, and it will stay on your permanent service record."

Well, that sucked. The sigh she heaved turned into a coughing fit that made her rear up in bed and double over. When it finished, Doug was close enough to shove a pillow behind her back for support. She was sweaty and weak, a little dizzy. "I'll think about it," she wheezed. This was too much for her to handle on her own. She knew that, and she had to have a clean service record to apply to the agencies she planned to target. But God, the thought of reliving all of it with a therapist made her heart rate accelerate.

"Hey, if I can do it, you can too," he said quietly.

She eyed him dubiously. "They're making you see a therapist?"

"Oh, yeah. Otherwise I think they're worried I might freak out in the middle of a big speech at a press conference or something." His grin was so disarming she smiled back a little.

They'd all gone through a nightmare. It was definitely going to leave a mark. "Maybe we could all go together and get a group rate." It would help to have Jackson there with her. She'd feel safer, less exposed with his steadying presence there. When was she going to get to see him again?

His eyes brightened. "I'll get my people on that."

The American public ought to see this side of him, because he was actually a nice man beneath that politician's image. She looked down at his cast. "So, what's the word on your leg?"

"Still attached, which makes me happier than I can say. The breaks were pretty bad, so they're not sure if I'll walk without a limp ever again, but I can live with that. Let's face it, there are a lot of people way less fortunate than me currently being treated in this building."

Yeah, that was the truth. They might have gone through hell but at least they were alive, still had all their limbs and their brains were still intact.

"I also heard that you were interested in applying to the CIA or FBI?" he added.

Damn, his staff was pretty thorough. "That was my plan once I finished the terms of my enlistment."

"You realize that in light of your captivity, that makes it even more important for a psychiatrist to sign off on your mental status?" he pointed out.

Oh, he was good. "Yeah, okay, I got it. I'll go to the therapy," she grumbled.

A satisfied grin curved his mouth. "I think you'd be a great addition to both those agencies. Especially on an FBI task force. And I happen to have a few connections there too."

She shot him a sideways glance. What was he saying?

He folded his hands atop his stomach. "It's your decision to make, but once you heal up you might consider applying for an honorable discharge. No one would think less of you for it after this."

While she didn't want special treatment, the idea of going back to work in a combat zone didn't hold the same appeal it once did. Actually it made her heart race and her palms sweat. "You're saying you think I have a real shot of getting into the FBI after all this?"

"I think you have a good shot, actually. And if you need a letter of reference, I'd be honored to write you one. I'll make sure it gets into the right hands."

Wait a minute. "I appreciate the offer, but I don't want you to feel like you have to do me a special favor just because—"

"I wouldn't offer unless I believed you should be there, Lieutenant. I meant it when I said you'd be a good addition for them. They'd be lucky to have you."

A tingling of excitement rushed through her. The end goal of working for one of those agencies had been something she'd dreamed of for years. She wanted to help eradicate any evil that would harm innocents. With a clean bill of health, a psychiatrist's signature of approval and a letter of reference from the Secretary of

Defense, her dream seemed more attainable than ever. "Well then, thank you. I might take you up on that."

"I hope you do. And if there's ever anything I can do for you, you'd better not hesitate to call me." He pulled a card out of his shirt pocket. "This is my personal cell phone number. Call me anytime."

She took it with a murmur of thanks. But the suspicion rolling around in her gut wouldn't go away. "You're not doing this because you feel like you owe me something, are you?"

"No, even though I do owe you since you saved my life out there at least a few times. I'm doing it because you're an airman, and we American fighting men and women stick together."

It made her think of Ace and Jackson. Of how loyal and steadfast friends they both were to her. She smiled. "Yeah, we do." And that made her incredibly proud.

The door opened and a nurse appeared, carrying a tray of blood-taking supplies. Maya withheld a groan. She'd been poked and prodded enough. All she wanted to do now was sleep.

"One more thing," Haversham said, lowering his voice to a conspiratorial whisper so the nurse wouldn't overhear. "There's another number on that card you might be interested in. And he also asked me to give you this." He pulled a black iPod out of his pocket and handed it to her. "You're supposed to listen to track number three, apparently." Blinking, she took it from him and he patted her shoulder. "See you later. Get some rest." With that, he swiveled himself around and wheeled the chair out the door one of his security staff held open for him.

"I need you to keep this on," the nurse said, plac-

ing the oxygen mask back over her nose and mouth
and securing the elastic band behind her head. "How's
your pain level?"

"Good." Compared to how she'd felt before, it was
nothing she couldn't handle. Her voice was muffled
beneath the mask.

"I'll just take a quick blood sample and let you get
some more sleep." She reached up to adjust something
on the IV pole.

Maya paid minimal attention to the nurse at her bedside and flipped the card over in her fingers. Beneath
Doug's cell number were handwritten numbers, along
with the words *SSgt. J. Thatcher.*

Jackson's cell number. Her heart squeezed. It
shouldn't have surprised her that Haversham had managed to dig that up too. Or had Jackson given it to him
along with the iPod? She was going to listen to that
special track the moment she was alone.

Laying the card on her chest while the nurse checked
her vitals, a secret smile spread across her face. She
didn't know when she'd be able to see him next, but at
least she'd be able to talk to him. She couldn't wait to
call him, just to hear his voice.

TWENTY-THREE

JACKSON LEANED HIS hip against the kitchen counter as he talked on his cell phone, overwhelmed by a sense of foreboding he couldn't seem to shake. Throughout their separation, he'd never felt farther away from Maya than he did at that moment. He struggled to stay positive. "So, you're sleeping better these days without your cast on?"

"It felt weird at first without it, but yeah, and my ribs are pretty much fine now," she answered. He heard her smother a yawn before continuing. "Glad you got the green light today from the docs."

"Me too." She was lonely. He could hear it in her voice, even if she'd never admit to it. He'd have given anything to be beside her right then. "I'm not sorry to be finished with all my rehab." His abs were killing him from all the core-strengthening exercises they had him doing. He needed to be in peak condition before he went back to Bagram to finish his tour, and he was getting close.

"I'll bet." She yawned again, doing her best to smother it so he wouldn't hear.

He hid his disappointment, knowing their conversation was at an end. "You sound wiped. I'll let you go so you can get to sleep." It was only eight on the West

Coast, but he knew she hadn't been sleeping well the past few weeks.

"Sorry. I'm not much of a conversationalist tonight, am I?"

"It's okay, I'll call you tomorrow night. Sweet dreams, baby," Jackson murmured.

"Thanks. You too. Good night."

He waited for her to say something else, something more meaningful, but she was already gone. Disconnecting, he stood staring out the kitchen window into the backyard illuminated by the streetlamps in the alley. God, he missed her. It was a physical ache inside him, growing every day he went without seeing her, not being able to touch her. Talking on the phone wasn't good enough anymore. When the hell was he going to get the chance to be with her?

Seven weeks, he thought with a miserable shake of his head. A whole seven weeks since he'd last seen her. His last memory of her was seeing those fear-filled eyes staring at him from across the emergency ward in Kandahar. He'd wanted so badly to erase that look on her face, stroke the furrows of concern from her forehead with his fingers before they wheeled him into the O.R. Through all the psych sessions and all the other things he was forced to recall these past two months, that frightened look on her face was the memory that stuck in his head most often.

He sensed movement behind him and knew without looking it was his sister, Angela, who'd been kind enough to put him up for this two-week leave the Air Force was giving him before he had to rejoin his unit at Bagram. He'd only arrived yesterday.

"Was that Maya?" she asked softly, her tone cautious.

"Yeah."

"How's she doing?"

He shrugged. "Same." They'd talked almost every day since she'd called him on his cell at the hospital in Germany, and yet more than ever he was convinced she was pulling away from him. He didn't understand what was happening. Whenever he tried to broach the subject of a relationship or talk about how she was handling the aftereffects of their ordeal in Afghanistan, she either closed up or steered the conversation in a superficial direction. He was worried as hell about her and it drove him fucking nuts that she was all alone. Now that his leave had started, maybe he should hop a flight in the morning and go find out in person what the deal was.

Angela came up to rest her chin on his shoulder. "Isn't there anyone to stay with her?"

He shook his head, the movement tight. Maya didn't have anyone in her life except Ace, and she wasn't going to ask her friend to stay with her even if Ace had volunteered. Because ever since Pilar died, Maya had fought her battles alone and still wouldn't accept that she no longer had to live like that anymore. She had him, and some part of her had to recognize that. But he couldn't be there for her if she wasn't willing to lean on him. He knew it wasn't personal, since she obviously trusted and cared about him a lot. Didn't make the distance hurt any less.

He rubbed a hand over the back of his neck. "Boys all tucked in?"

"They're already asleep because you wore them both

out today." She rubbed his upper arm gently. "You love her, don't you?"

"Yes." And it was more painful than the bullet wound he'd just recovered from.

Ang made a sympathetic sound. "She must really be something."

"She is."

"And she must really care about you if you guys talk so often. She's keeping in touch, at least."

He was silent for a long moment before answering. "I feel like I'm losing her somehow, Ang." Saying it aloud made the fear sharper, more vivid, but he knew his sister would understand.

Ang slid both her arms around his waist and leaned against him, both of them staring out the darkened window. "You want to rescue her."

He couldn't deny it. On a primal level, yeah, he wanted to rescue her. She'd been through more shit than anyone should have to deal with in an entire lifetime. He wanted to be there to support her. They'd both come through hell together and they could help each other heal.

Ang hugged him tighter. "I know that's how you're wired, but based on what you've told me about her, she doesn't seem like the kind of woman who would appreciate anyone thinking she needs to be rescued. She's dealt with everything else on her own, and I'll bet to her this is no different. She wants to come through this on her terms, prove she's strong enough to handle it. It's not that she doesn't trust you. It's that she doesn't trust herself enough to be vulnerable again. She's still afraid."

She said the words gently, but they still made him

wince because they were dead-on. Maya *would* hate leaning on anyone through this, even him. She'd hate it even more that he wanted to pull the whole white-knight routine. In her mind she always had to be the tough Security Forces lieutenant, take care of herself.

He understood why, but it was killing him not to take action, not be there to protect and comfort her. Getting through this hadn't been easy for him, and he'd had the constant support of his family and friends. He couldn't imagine what it must have been like for Maya, going home to her empty apartment day after day through all the grueling counseling sessions.

In the quiet of the tidy kitchen, he shook his head and expelled a loud breath. "You're right, as usual. How the hell did you get to be so smart, anyway?"

"Because I'm your big sister and older and wiser than you." She gave him another squeeze, her unyielding love and support taking the edge off the ache inside him. "Give her time to heal more. She'll let you in when she's ready."

God, he hoped so. Because the alternative was too fucking painful to contemplate and he wasn't sure how much longer he could wait for her to come to him.

WHEN SHE PULLED her bike up to the curb beside the white ranch-style house the next afternoon and shut off the engine, Maya's stomach was twisted into knots. Jackson wasn't expecting her. She had no idea what his reaction would be.

The tidy house sat in the middle of its well-manicured yard in suburban San Antonio, and she felt completely out of place. In her earbuds, instead of her usual hip-hop, Keith Urban's "For You" played, the infamous track number three Haversham had told her about.

She probably shouldn't have listened to this particular playlist on the way over, because she was already emotional enough. The song had such meaning for her, especially since it was about one teammate sacrificing himself for another. Along with it, Jackson had loaded up his iPod with tracks selected just for her. Formerly a hip-hop lover, she was now an appreciator of country music and had learned to love 50s blues because of him as well. The transformation was all his fault.

His sister sure lived in a nice neighborhood. Way nicer than Maya had grown up in back in L.A. But now she was starting to question her decision to spring this on him as a surprise. She'd almost caved and told him she was in town last night when they'd talked. Something in his voice had stopped her. After imagining this moment so many times over the past two months, it was hard to believe it was actually happening. Still, she couldn't quite force herself to walk up the path to the front door. Not yet.

Part of her was still worried that she'd built up her "relationship" with Jackson to be more than it actually was. While it seemed to her that they were in a relationship, she was about to find out whether it was true.

Whatever happened once she knocked on that door would change her life forever. She just hoped it would be the start of all her dreams coming true, rather than a continuation of her nightmares.

Pushing out a calming breath, she set her helmet on the back of the bike and took those first fateful steps toward the front door. On the welcome mat laid out on the wooden front porch, she paused to smooth back her hair and braced herself. The doorbell chimed inside the house when she pressed the button. A moment later approaching footsteps ramped her anxiety level to a whole new high.

The door swung open. Her heart skipped a beat and seemed to stop altogether when Jackson appeared in the opening, wearing jeans and a T-shirt and his three-year-old nephew perched atop his broad shoulders. His deep brown eyes widened and his lips parted in shock, as though she was the last person he'd ever expected to find on his sister's doorstep. "Hey," he breathed.

Having the kid watching them from Jackson's shoulders threw her for a moment. "Hi." *So, um, I was in the neighborhood because I wanted to see you so badly I hopped on my bike three days ago and drove here.*

Because yeah, that didn't sound desperate or anything.

Jackson slid the boy from his shoulders, the motion emphasizing the bulge of his biceps and shoulder muscles beneath that snug white T-shirt. "Hey, buddy, go on inside and keep your brother outta trouble, will you? I'll be inside in a minute."

"Who's she?" the little guy demanded.

"This is my friend Maya I told you about. Go on, now."

The boy dragged himself into the house, and Jackson quietly shut the front door behind him before facing her. Her stomach was a hot ball of nerves. She was wracking her brain for something to say to fill the awkward void, convinced she'd made a huge mistake in showing up unannounced, when he suddenly reached for her.

A funny sound came out of her throat. Maya

launched herself into his embrace, wrapping her arms around those broad shoulders and burying her face in his chest, breathing in his scent. Soap, citrus and wintergreen. Jackson hugged her tight, holding her close with a ragged sound that came from his gut. She hitched in a breath and squeezed her eyes shut, praying she wouldn't cry. A shudder ripped through her. After weeks of lonely isolation spent aching for him, she was finally in his arms. The feel and smell of him wrapped around her, familiar and comforting.

"Did you drive all the way here from California?" He sounded stunned.

She nodded, her cheek rubbing over his chest. "I left three days ago. Wanted to surprise you."

"You did. *God*, I missed you, baby," he said roughly against the side of her neck, holding her so tight.

She bobbed her head, fighting for composure. "Missed you too. But I was such a mess. I couldn't come to you until I was sure it was real." She didn't know how to make him understand.

"If what was real?" She could hear the frown in his voice.

"This. *Us*." How could she explain it to him? "My therapist forced me to take a hard look at what you and I had been through. For the longest time I wondered if what I felt for you was real, or if it was just because of how intense things were out there. I had to be sure it was you I wanted, not just the sense of security you gave me because of the captivity. And then I had to figure out if I wasn't imagining that you wanted me too. Otherwise it wouldn't be healthy."

He released a hard sigh. "God, of course I want you. You seriously doubted that, for even a second? Christ."

He squeezed her tighter, his arms so strong and protective she almost melted. "I wish you'd said something sooner. I hate that you went through all of this alone."

She shook her head. "It was better this way. I didn't want you seeing me like that." She'd been a shadow of her former self. A frightened, insecure woman afraid that Khalid had broken something inside her. A woman afraid to sleep without a light on, jumping at every strange noise, questioning everything about her life. "I'm not the same person I was before all this. But I think I'm better for it. A lot of that is because of you, by the way. Hearing your voice every night helped me a lot." It was so much easier saying all this with her face pressed into the solid curve of his shoulder. Didn't mean she wasn't still shaking inside though.

His arms tightened fiercely. "I would've been there for you if you'd let me. Dammit, I would've *been* there."

She hugged him back. "I know you would have. But I wasn't ready." She never wanted to be a burden to him.

With a sigh, he released her and cupped her face between his hands, forcing her gaze up to his. His eyes were misty. "You know this is real now, though. Right?"

Gazing up into those warm, dark eyes, she nodded. She loved him. She'd never been surer of anything in her life. A sudden lump filled her throat, and it was growing by the second. She swallowed hard. "So, how are you? Really." Her eyes dropped to his belly where the T-shirt hid his scars.

"All healed up, just missed you like hell." His gaze traveled over the length of her body with concern and interest. Then he frowned. "You look thinner."

"I lost some weight when I came home, but I'm gaining it back. I've been working out again too, so that's helped me put some muscle back on." The mundane conversation was killing her. *Say what you need to say.* She exhaled and gave a shaky laugh. "I changed my mind about coming here a dozen times. I almost turned around in Tucson."

"I'm glad you didn't." He was still holding her face, as though he couldn't bear to stop touching her.

She gathered her courage. She didn't want to have this conversation out on the front porch where anyone might overhear it, but too bad. "I wanted to come see you before, but I couldn't until I was strong again."

He tilted his head to study her. "I don't like it, but I guess I can understand. Sort of."

The lump was all but choking her now. "I missed you every day." It came out a rough whisper.

"Ah, baby, I know. C'mere." He tipped her face up to his. After searching her eyes for a moment, Jackson lowered his head and kissed her. A tiny sound escaped her, half gasp, half whimper. She threaded her hands into his silky soft hair and drank him in, reveling in every single sensation. He tasted like sweet tea and smelled of warm, clean man. And she'd missed him every single minute they'd been apart.

He kissed her deep and hard, one arm wrapped around her back and the other holding her head still. When his tongue slid into her mouth, she was ready to climb him like a tree just to get closer, frantic to feel more of him. Before the kiss could get completely out of hand, he pressed his mouth to hers one last time, firmly, like a stamp of ownership, and eased back. His eyes smoldered with the promise of more to come later. "Come on inside with me."

Maya hesitated. His eldest sister was in there, and her children. This was their home. She didn't feel right barging back into Jackson's life and meeting his family yet. It was too much pressure for everyone. "I don't—"

"No way, baby. You found the guts to drive that bike all the way from California to see me, you can see the rest of it through. Come inside." He took her hand and tugged her toward the door.

Since he wasn't taking no for an answer, she followed grudgingly into the foyer and up a short staircase to the main living area. In the bright cozy kitchen, the boy who'd been on Jackson's shoulders was seated at the granite island and a striking woman with long, dark hair and bronze-toned skin stood at the stove. She could easily see the family resemblance between her and Jackson.

The woman stopped stirring something on the stove that smelled like spicy heaven and blinked at them. "This is my sister, Angela," Jackson said. "Ang, this is Maya."

Angela set down her spatula and smiled at her. She didn't hold out her hand as Maya expected. No, she wrapped her arms around her and pulled her in close for a hug instead. "Hi. It's so great to finally meet you. Jackson's told us all so much about you."

Maya awkwardly returned the embrace. "Hi. Thanks. Great to meet you too."

Angela pulled back, still smiling, eyes a little misty. "Are you hungry? We're just about to eat. My husband's flight got delayed so we're eating without him."

She glanced at Jackson. "I..."

"She'd love to stay. Right, buddy?" He ruffled his nephew's hair. "This is Eli, by the way. Lucas is upstairs, perfecting his latest Jedi training."

"Hi, Eli."

"Hi." The boy regarded her seriously for a moment. "I thought you'd be taller."

Maya didn't know how to respond, but Jackson grinned and said, "Gotta love kids. Guess I made you sound ten feet tall when I told them about you."

He ushered her to the table in the eating nook and handed her a glass of white wine, refusing her help in the kitchen. She made small talk with them while he helped fix everything with Angela. Not only was the man sweet and heroic and beautiful, but he obviously knew how to cook. Her head was spinning. How did things stand between them? That wasn't something she was going to ask him in front of his family members.

Dinner was delicious and enjoyable, despite her nerves. She hadn't eaten very well over the past few weeks. It was clear how much the family loved each other. Watching them together filled Maya with a wistfulness that made her heart ache. This was how she'd always imagined her and Pili would wind up, hanging out at each other's house with their kids.

They kept the conversation light through dinner, focusing mainly on Eli, who seemed a lot older than he was, and his five-year-old brother, Lucas. When the meal ended, Angela shared a secret look with her brother then scooped up Eli and Lucas. "Bath time for my guys." She shot Maya another smile. "It was really nice meeting you, Maya. I hope we'll get to see you again soon."

Maya didn't know what to say, so she nodded and

returned the smile. "Thank you for having me, especially without any notice."

Angela waved her thanks away. "You're welcome anytime."

As his sister carried the boys upstairs, Jackson took her hand and pulled her to her feet. "Let's go out back and sit on the porch. I'll get you another glass of wine."

"I shouldn't. Have to drive back to the hotel later."

"I'll drive you there on your bike." He leaned in to kiss her temple, his warm breath making her shiver. "I think I want you a little tipsy."

Her belly fluttered but she raised her eyebrows. "You think I trust you with my Ducati?" she said to cover her nerves.

"Yeah, I think you do."

He was right. She did.

Once he had her settled on the white wooden porch swing, he brought her that next glass of wine and sat beside her to pull her tight against him. Her whole body sighed at the contact. She rested her head on his shoulder and closed her eyes, relaxing into him. If she died right now, she'd die happy.

Jackson stroked his fingers through her jaw-length hair. "When did you cut it?"

"As soon as I got home. Couldn't stand all the snarls and knots in it."

"I like it, it's sassy. Suits you."

She blushed at the compliment. Looking out over the tidy backyard with its green swing set, she didn't know what else to say. *I love you. I love you with everything in me.* It was almost impossible to hold the words back. "You told me you were all healed up, but I wasn't sure if you were lying." Unable to resist, she slid a hand to his belly, pulling up his shirt so she could see the scar. It was about five inches long, the angry red incision fading to purple.

Jackson covered her hand with his, rubbed it slowly over his skin, all warm and silky under her palm. He let her pet him like a cat, stroking him while his muscles twitched against her hand. Instant arousal pulsed through her body.

"Recovery was pretty easy," he said at last. "I had Ang and the boys to look after me when I got discharged from the hospital. I can't stand knowing you went home alone." He shook his head in annoyance.

She tipped her head back to meet his eyes. "I managed fine." Well, okay, not *fine*, but she'd made it through. "My therapist says I'm doing great, all things considered. Panic attacks are few and far between now and I'm sleeping better at night. Hardly any nightmares now." Down to a few a week, rather than a few every night.

"Then you'll sleep even better with me beside you," he said in a smoky voice that made her toes curl. "And I'll sleep better knowing you're next to me tonight. Right after I wear you out so much you won't have enough energy to dream later." The look in his eyes told her he wasn't just teasing. Then he grinned and gave the swing a push with one foot, setting them in gentle motion as he bent and nuzzled the side of her neck. Goose bumps rippled across her skin. "Now hurry up and finish your wine."

Like she was interested in wine after that comment? She reacted to his nearness on a chemical level. The anticipation of what might happen tonight was the most exquisite and frustrating torture. She sipped her wine while they talked about a lot of different things. The Air Force agreeing to grant her an honorable discharge. His plans to write the MCAT in the fall once he finished his enlistment. Haversham putting in a good word for her when she decided to apply to the FBI in a few months.

"You want kids someday?" he asked suddenly.

Startled, she set her glass down before answering. "Yeah, maybe someday." A wistful smile broke over her face. "I guess I've always dreamed about having a family of my own. A real one, like you've got."

His expression thoughtful, he nodded and kissed the top of her head. She didn't know what to make of that and didn't want to press. All she wanted at the moment was to find a private place where she could peel those clothes off him and kiss and lick every inch of his body.

As she swallowed the last sip of wine, he took the glass from her, eyes dark with hunger. "So. Ready to take that ride with me?"

She almost swallowed her tongue at the heavy throb that set off in her body. "Yeah."

"One thing." His tone held a warning note and she stared at him expectantly, wondering what he was going to say. "When we get to your room, this time you're letting me run things."

Instant desire and nervousness exploded in her belly. She had promised that, hadn't she? Back when they'd been locked up in those cages. Many a night she'd lain awake, imagining what it would be like to give him control in bed. The idea turned her on more than anything ever had. But could she actually let herself go like that? She'd never let herself be vulnerable to a lover before.

She stalled. "I only have one helmet—"

"I've got one. Meet you out front."

She stood by her bike as he came out of the side of the garage with a helmet in his hand, battling the lingering nerves eating at her. "I've never ridden on the back of a bike before," she admitted, feeling off balance.

He titled his head, eyes twinkling. "No? Well, just think of it as foreplay."

What? He leaned in for a hot, deep kiss before she could say anything. She moaned low in her throat and reached for him, but he pulled away to throw one long denim-encased leg over the bike and straddled it. My God, he was sexy like that. All-American hero meets badass biker. Her heart fluttered and her knees went a little weak.

He tossed a grin at her before putting on his helmet. "Climb on." He fired up the engine.

Maya strapped on her own helmet and settled on the seat behind him. She leaned forward and wrapped her arms around him, immediately struck by the intimacy of it. Her breasts, stomach, hips and inner thighs were all pressed against him. Jackson set a hand on hers where they were clasped against his belly and squeezed once before putting the bike in gear and pulling away from the curb.

The drive to her motel only took about fifteen minutes, but it felt like an eternity. Her body was already gearing up for what was coming and reminded her of it every time either one of them shifted or leaned into a turn. Her open thighs hugged his hips, pressing the hot glow between her legs against him. Tiny shocks of sensation traveled through her, turning her nipples into tight points that pressed against her T-shirt inside her leather jacket. By the time Jackson pulled into the parking lot and killed the engine, she felt dizzy with arousal, a little breathless.

Inside her helmet, her breathing sounded overly loud. Her heart drummed in her ears. Between her thighs, she was wet and aching for him. The intense need kept growing, heightening until she could barely contain it.

He pulled off his helmet, stood and quickly restraddled the seat to face her. Maya tugged her helmet off and swallowed at the flare of heat in his dark eyes. Reaching up to tuck a lock of hair back behind her ear, his fingers trailed down her jaw, triggering a shower of sparks in their wake.

"You're nervous," he said, sounding surprised.

There was no way she could deny it. "A little." She wanted this to be perfect and was worried she wouldn't meet his expectations when she was the one on the receiving end of things. It was a role she was completely unfamiliar with.

An adoring smile formed on his lips. "No need to be. C'mere."

Those strong hands closed around her hips to tug her forward, lifting her to practically straddle his lap. Catching her breath at the show of easy strength, Maya set her hands on his broad shoulders and tilted her head back as he leaned in, one hand on her ass and one sliding into her hair. She shivered at the controlled hunger so evident in him. He kissed her slow and deep and she let him, mentally testing the idea of handing him the reins during sex. It was tempting. It was terrifying. Her heart knocked against her ribs.

Her hands crept into his hair as the kiss grew hotter, more demanding, their tongues caressing. She broke away to catch her breath, gauging the look in his eye. They were almost black with desire.

"I can't wait to be inside you," he said in a low voice. "Show me where your room is."

The words made her breath catch. Gathering her rattled composure, she got off the bike, her legs surprisingly shaky. Up at her room, she unlocked the door and stepped inside. He followed, sliding past her as she closed the door and turned the dead bolt. She reached for the sliding chain with unsteady hands, dropping it twice with a metallic rattle against the door before she finally got it in place. Jesus, she'd never been more turned on in her life, yet it felt like she was on the verge of another panic attack.

She sensed him approach from behind, then the heat of him licked along her spine. She had only a second to tense before his hand closed over hers where the chain attached to the door. His long fingers wrapped around hers, trapping them against the wood. He pressed his chest against her back, the hard ridge of his erection nudging the top of her buttocks. She drew in a startled breath when he bent to nuzzle the delicate spot where her neck met her shoulder, sending a cascade of shivers through her. His warm breath brushed over her bare skin in an intimate caress, and her knees wobbled.

"Just turn around and give yourself to me," he murmured against the top of her shoulder. "That's all you need to do."

Maya closed her eyes. He made it sound so easy and it wasn't. It *wasn't*. She was caught between an intense yearning that made her want to whip around and devour him, and a terrible, cringing fear of being rendered emotionally bare. Her heart was pounding and her breathing was erratic. The ravenous sexual need amplified every tiny piece of sensory input. She was acutely aware of the feel of him pressed against her, waiting, all that coiled strength begging to be turned loose, the quiet hum of the air-conditioning unit beneath the windowsill.

Taking a fortifying breath, she gathered herself and pivoted, launching herself at him. He caught her with a low growl as they collided, their mouths fusing together. The kiss was wild, full of pent-up need. Jackson drove her back against the door with a hand on her nape and one on her ass, forcing the aching flesh between her legs against the hard outline of his erection. She whimpered and strained in his grip, struggling to get closer, nipping and licking at his mouth. His kiss was forceful, demanding, and she was right there with him. But it wasn't nearly enough. She was starving for the feel of his naked skin on hers, for him to slide deep inside her, to make her his.

Urgency and impatience drove the lust higher. Seams popped and material ripped as they tore at each other's clothes. Her groping hands met bare, heated flesh. She gripped his back, glorying in the raw power in those bunching muscles. He undid her jeans and wrenched them down her thighs while she clung to him, walked them the few steps over to the queen-size bed without breaking the voracious kiss. He reached past her to yank the covers down, and she released him long enough to scramble up toward the pillows while shucking her jeans, leaving her in her black bra and panties.

He gazed down at her with a possessive look that made the breath back up in her lungs. His jaw flexed as he stared down at her, as if he was struggling for control. "Lie back and don't move."

TWENTY-FOUR

THE LOW COMMAND seemed to shock her. Jackson didn't miss the uneasy ripple that moved through her body, but she stayed still for him. It was incredibly hot to have her lie there, complacent, while he removed her bra and drew her panties down her legs.

His heated gaze devoured every inch of the naked skin he revealed. He tossed the scraps of lace to the floor and prowled up the bed to straddle her calves, still wearing his jeans. The last time they'd been naked together in that tent, it had been too dark for him to see her body. Now he couldn't help but stare at her. She was all smooth, silky skin overlaying sleek muscle, and he couldn't wait to explore every inch of her with his hands and mouth.

Before, it had been wild and hungry. Now he took it slow. So slow he feared his heart might pound its way through his chest. Maya watched him in silence, her eyes full of heat yet tinged with uncertainty. He knew how hard it was for her to remain passive like this. To let him look his fill while she lay totally exposed to him, allowing him anything he wanted. And, given her history with her sister, it made sense that she'd never allowed herself to be vulnerable during sex. Her show of trust now moved him.

"You're so beautiful," he whispered, shaking his

head in reverence. She sucked in a sharp breath when he reached out and cupped her breasts in his hands, brushing his thumbs across the hard, dusky-brown centers that seemed to beg for his touch.

"Jackson." She reached for him, unable to stay still a moment longer. He didn't protest or try to restrain her, merely leaned forward to take a nipple into his mouth, sliding a hand beneath her spine. Her back bowed, her body trembling under the onslaught of sensation. She locked her hands in his hair, urging him to give more, take more, demanding that he did.

She tasted of soap and the sweet musk of her skin. Delicious. He pleasured her nipples with teasing flicks of his tongue and the tender pull of his mouth, switching back and forth while her gasps and cries filled the room. She moved restlessly beneath him, almost edgy, as though the building sensations were becoming unbearable. He wouldn't let her panic or pull away.

He trailed one hand down her belly in reassurance, over the curve of her hip and thigh, back up the inside. The texture of her body fascinated him, smooth and firm with toned muscle. The feel of her—a contrast of strength and soft femininity—was the sexiest thing he'd ever experienced.

Nuzzling her baby-fine skin, he pushed her thighs up and out, making room for his hand between them. She tensed, waiting for that intimate touch, maybe even a little afraid of it, then closed her eyes and bit her lip. The muscles in her belly and thighs quivered, the trembling becoming more noticeable with each pull of his mouth. She was more than ready.

He let his fingers drift higher, skimming the sensitive place where her thigh met her hip. She went still, seemed to be holding her breath. Rather than prolong the moment and give her anxiety a chance to grow, he slid two fingers deep inside her. She was so wet, her inner muscles closing around him.

Her breath caught in her throat. She shuddered once and lay still, waiting to see what he would do next. The pulse in her throat throbbed more visibly now. With her head turned away from him, she raised her hips in a silent plea for friction. Her hands stayed locked in his hair while he kissed his way down her belly, and he knew she was fighting her body's instinctive reaction to close her legs in a last-ditch effort to protect herself.

But she would never need to protect herself from him.

Without a word, he continued kissing his way south until he reached the soft curls covering her mound, letting her feel the heat of his breath against her sensitive folds. She swallowed. Nervous, fighting the need to struggle.

Splaying a hand low on her belly, he added pressure with his palm, rubbing in gentle circles, anchoring her. "Breathe, Maya."

She forced out a shaky exhalation.

"Been dreamin' about doing this," he murmured against her.

Her head turned and she opened her eyes to stare down at him. Her expression was guarded. "About what?"

"You lying there so quiet, trusting me with your body. Letting me make you come with my mouth."

The look in her eyes turned soft with longing. She relaxed a little.

With her eyes on his, he pressed slow, openmouthed

kisses down the length of her sensitive flesh, then gave her a slow stroke with the flat of his tongue. She gasped and grabbed his hair, as though the pleasure had caught her off guard. God, he loved that flare of shock in her eyes and knowing he was making her feel good. He zeroed in on her clit, drawing languorous circles around it until she whimpered and shifted beneath him.

"Shhh," he soothed, twisting the fingers buried inside her. He found the hidden source of pleasure there and rubbed it while he lapped at her sensitive bundle of nerves.

A low, shocked cry spilled from her lips. An articulate sound of pleasure and need. The muscles in her belly rippled beneath his palm. He licked deeper, increasing the pressure slightly, watching her every reaction. Her trembling thighs parted farther, encouraging him to move deeper between them. His cock pulsed in near agony, straining against his jeans. She was almost there, starting that final climb to ecstasy when he raised his head and removed his hand.

She shook her head and pulled his head back toward her. "No—"

"I want to feel you come around me." He rolled to the side to strip off his jeans and tear open a condom.

His reasoning seemed to take her by surprise. Her eyes were glazed, heavy with pleasure and frustration. He could tell she wanted to flip them over and ride him hard and fast, but Jackson was having none of that. He shook his head and lowered his voice to a soft growl. "This time I want you on your back, staring up at me." *This* time it was going to be face-to-face in the light, him on top so she wouldn't be able to hide. This time he'd get to see every expression that crossed her face

as he made love to her. Because that was what he was
doing, whether she was ready to accept it or not. And
he wasn't giving her a chance to overthink this.

As soon as he rolled the condom on, he stretched out
over her and settled deep between her thighs. When
she reached for him, he caught her hands to pin them
to the mattress on either side of her head. The muscles
in her arms flexed once in protest, but she didn't fight
him. She stared up at him, breathless, her eyes wide
and pleading for an end to the torment he knew was
every bit as emotional for her as it was physical. The
molten heat in her eyes made his heart leap, and that
tiny flare of uncertainty beneath it brought all his protective instincts roaring to the surface.

The throb in his groin was almost unbearable. He
wedged his hips in the cradle of her thighs, bringing the scalding length of his cock against her tender
folds. "Wrap your legs around me," he said in an urgent whisper.

Shivering, she did as he told her, her expression
a mixture of hope and yearning. The need twisted
harder inside him, clawing for release. But Jackson
didn't tease her. Holding her hands firmly in place, he
shifted his weight and slid the head of his cock inside
her. Maya made a soft sound at the back of her throat
and tilted her hips, the muscles in her thighs straining
to pull him closer, force him deeper.

Poised above her, he shook his head, fighting a
smile. "You're not the one in control this time," he reminded her. He wanted her to remember this for the
rest of their lives. Every single detail, from the heat and
vulnerability to the knowledge that he would always
take care of her. That she was safe with him, even when

she was defenseless. He knew that was really what un-
settled her. The lack of control.

Jackson reached deep for his self-control. He vowed
that after today she'd never again be afraid to let go
with him. Above all else, he wanted her to know exactly how much she meant to him. She might not be
ready to hear the words, but he could damn well dem-
onstrate them with his body.

Gazing down into her wide sea-green eyes, he held
back the driving urge to plunge into her and find relief
from the tortuous throb in his dick, waiting as the tension around her mouth eased and the tiny lines above
the bridge of her nose disappeared.

His heart thudded, the muscles in his arms trembling as he gave her the words he'd wanted to tell her
for so long, praying she'd give him all of her in return.
"Just let me love you."

MAYA'S THROAT TIGHTENED at the words and her heart
turned over.

He did love her. She could feel it in his touch, hear
it in his voice and see it in his eyes. No man had ever
treated her with half the tenderness or consideration
for her pleasure. And when he drove forward at last,
burying himself deep inside her with one smooth, in-
exorable thrust, the knot of emotion she'd kept locked
away deep in her heart suddenly tore loose.

Her head tipped back on a guttural moan of relief.
She felt him shudder, bury his face in her hair as though
the pleasure of being inside her was too intense for him
to bear. The lack of control over her body was scary,
mingling with the swollen ache between her thighs.
She struggled in his grip, caught there with no hope of

escape. It was exhilarating. Terrifying. Her legs tightened around his hips, holding tight while he pulled
back and plunged deep. He took her hard and fast, his
rhythm demanding, urgent. Exactly what she'd wanted.

Only when she was writhing and twisting beneath
him did he release her hands. She reached up blindly
for his shoulders and hung on, her fingers digging deep
into the muscles there, lifting into every thrust. *Dios*,
he was strong. It turned her on even more to know he
could overpower her if he wanted to.

He levered up on to an elbow to squeeze his hand
between them, his clever fingers finding the aching
nub at the top of her sex. She shivered at the sensations
building inside her. Jackson pushed her higher, relentless in his quest, destroying her resistance. She made a
helpless sound and held on tighter, shaking with need.

"Don't fight it," he whispered roughly, his lips right
against her ear. "Not with me."

Squeezing her eyes shut, she buried her face in his
neck and let out a shaky breath. Nothing had ever felt
this good. She was drunk on the pleasure he gave her,
on the sensation of those muscles shifting beneath his
smooth skin, his clean, masculine scent. The orgasm
she'd been struggling toward suddenly built deep in her
belly. Her heart burst open, spilling its closely guarded
secrets to him there in the darkness. "*Te amo. Te amo...*"

Jackson moaned and shuddered in reaction. He
pressed his face deeper into her hair and pounded into
her, the headboard thudding against the wall, but his
touch was so careful between her thighs as he took
her up on the dizzying climb to orgasm. It rose up and
slammed into her like a blast wave, sending her flying, leaving her helpless and clinging in his arms. She

barely heard her own loud wail echo through the room, lost in the intensity of the pleasure.

It ebbed slowly. Jackson drove deep once more and stiffened, his head tipping back on a tortured moan of release, face twisted in ecstasy. She loved that he let her watch him fly apart in her arms. Those wide shoulders bunched, his whole body shuddering as his climax took him.

Maya wrapped her arms around him, hugging him as tight as she could and breathed in his scent, the mixture of lemony cologne and male musk. He snuggled deeper into her embrace, clearly enjoying the closeness. A feeling of utter contentment stole over her. It thrilled her that he was so tactile, allowing her to hold him like this and touch him at will as he recovered. She took advantage of the opportunity, exploring the ridges and hollows of his muscles with her fingertips, following the deep indent of his spine to the cleft at its base. His back and shoulders were slick with perspiration, and she opened her mouth to taste the salty essence of him.

After a few minutes, Jackson stirred and raised his head, coming up on to an elbow to stare down at her. His eyes were dark, intense. "Tell me again."

She didn't even pretend to misunderstand him. Setting a hand on the side of his face, she cradled his cheek in her palm and met his gaze head-on. "I love you."

His answering smile was so beautiful it made any lingering traces of vulnerability evaporate. "You know I'd do anything for you."

She nodded, because she did know. He'd comforted her, been there for her when all hope had seemed lost, had seen her at her worst and still fought for her, end-ing up taking a bullet to shield her with his own body. He'd even killed to protect her. "And I'd do the same for you."

That smile widened, filling her with the warmth of his love. "You have no idea how unbelievably hot it is hearing that, especially since I know you can back up that claim."

A grin tugged at her mouth. "Glad it turns you on that I can kick ass. And speaking of asses..." She trailed a finger over the strong line of his jaw. "I want to see your tat now."

"Oh, all right," he huffed. Sighing in mock exasperation, Jackson withdrew and lay on his stomach beside her, propping his head on his folded arms. "Go on, then. Have a look."

Unable to resist, she pushed up on her forearm and gazed down at the muscular curves of his ass. Sure enough, high up on his right cheek were the two green footprints. And not just any old footprints, because they were set on a background of the Texas flag. She traced the design with a fingertip, unable to stop the husky laugh that escaped. A Texas boy to the core. "You were right, it *is* pretty special."

"I knew you'd like it," he said smugly, pulling her to him and rolling them so her cheek was pillowed against the firm pad of his pecs. His arms encircled her, his fingers stroking through her hair and across her shoulders.

Maya sighed in bliss and closed her eyes, soaking up the tender affection he lavished upon her. "You're gonna turn me into an addict with all this lovey-dovey stuff," she murmured, feeling relaxed enough to float away.

"That's my plan." He kissed her forehead, his lips lingering there for a long moment.

They were quiet for a while, enjoying the peace of the moment and the new closeness they shared. Letting him see her softer side wasn't scary at all anymore.

"I didn't think men like you existed," she admitted hoarsely with a slight shake of her head.

"What, decent ones?"

She nodded, even though he was so much more than decent. She loved that he was as humble as he was brave and caring.

His arms tightened, bringing her even closer. "We do. Just like sexy ass-kicking female Security Forces superheroes exist."

She raised her head to frown at him. "I'm not a superhero."

His hand drifted over her bare back. "Are too. You're *my* hero, anyway."

The man killed her when he said things like that. She huffed out a breath and poked a threatening finger into his chest. "Don't you dare make me cry."

He grinned. "No, ma'am. Wouldn't dream of it." With one hand he pulled her head back down to his chest, sighing when she snuggled into him.

God, she could really get used to this. Only she wasn't sure if she should let herself get used to it. He hadn't said anything about what he wanted in terms of a relationship with her. Love didn't fix things like logistics, distance and separations during deployments.

"So, what are you doing next week?"

The sudden question threw her and it took her a moment to mentally recall her schedule. Next week she had more therapy sessions scheduled, and she'd planned on getting her resume ready for submission. Nothing she couldn't push back until later if it meant spending more time with him. "Nothing. Why?"

"I made you a promise. I still want to take you to Kauai."

She closed her eyes, the memory of that conversation while in their cages not nearly so sharp and painful anymore. "I'd love to go there with you." She swallowed the lump in her throat and searched for something light to say. "I'd even put out while we're there."

He laughed against her hair. "I'm relieved to hear that. Know what else?"

She shook her head, tilting it back to see him better.

"I love you too."

Though she'd already known that, for some reason hearing the words out loud made them more real. Irrefutable. Despite herself, a pleased flush crept up her neck and into her cheeks. She hid her face against his chest. "I already promised to put out," she teased.

"I know. But I've been waiting a long time for you to be ready to hear me say that to you."

Maya kissed his naked skin, running her hand over the taut plane of his abdomen. What had she ever done to deserve a man like him? "I don't...I'm not sure how this is supposed to go. I've never done this before." She was so afraid of screwing it up.

"Me neither, darlin'. But don't worry, we'll figure it out together."

Knowing he would be there for her filled her heart so full she was afraid it might burst. And she felt ready to open herself up to him even more. Because there was something else she'd never done that she was suddenly desperate to.

She rolled over to lie atop him, her breasts pressed against the hot skin of his chest, bracing her weight on her forearms so she could see his face. He reached up to sweep a lock of hair back from her cheek, and the gesture made her throat wobble. "I love you. So much," she whispered.

His tender smile bolstered her courage. "I know you do. But I'll never get tired of hearing you say so."

Good, but she had to get this out while she still had the courage. "I'd like to...show you." God, why was it so hard to say what she wanted?

But somehow he understood.

The hand on her face stilled, his expression turning serious as he realized she was asking for the chance to make love to him, take away the regret she'd felt from her first time with him. His eyes heated, and she realized he was already hardening against her abdomen. "Baby, you never have to ask permission for that." His voice was a sensual purr, the vibrations of it echoing in the pulsing flesh between her thighs.

Her heart leaped in relief. "So that's a yes?"

His strong, capable hands slid into her hair as he shook his head. "That's a *hell* yes." Jackson lifted his head and drew her down into a deep kiss.

TWENTY-FIVE

THE WARM WATER was a clear, crystal blue as Jackson swam toward the surface in a rush of bubbles. Just a few strokes above him, Maya surfaced first. She was treading water, wearing a huge grin when he joined her above the waterline. She took the regulator out of her mouth and pulled off her goggles. Her dark brown hair was slicked back, and the sheer joy shining in her eyes filled him with happiness.

He cocked his head. "Well? How was that for a first dive?" He already knew the answer because he'd seen her reaction the moment she'd dropped over the side of the boat into the water.

"It was *amazing*." She laughed, the sound brimming with joy. "Everything I ever hoped it would be and more."

He smiled. "You're a natural." From the very first time he'd introduced her to scuba in their hotel pool, Maya had taken to it easily, without any fear. They'd practiced buddy breathing and other important things over the past four days in preparation for this dive. Seeing her underwater earlier, delighted by everything she saw, was beautiful to watch. This was exactly what both of them had needed—a stress-free vacation in paradise to help put everything that had happened in Afghanistan behind them. Every day he could see her getting stronger, the lingering signs of trauma lessening.

"You look hot in that wet suit, by the way," Maya told him with a naughty grin.

He quirked a brow. "Yeah? Wanna peel it off me once we get back on the boat?" Just the thought of it made him hard.

"I do. Wanna race?" Before he could answer, she turned away and began swimming for the catamaran bobbing behind them in the gentle ocean swells. He caught up with her within a few strokes and together they swam side by side to the boat. After taking care of their equipment and getting out of their wet suits, they relaxed on the deck with a beer with the other passengers until the sun began to go down.

While the faint beat of reggae music floated up from the cabin, Jackson led Maya around to the front and sat with his back against the window just aft of the trampoline centered between the two pontoons. He pulled her down to sit between his upraised knees, wrapping his arms around her to hold her close. She laid her head back against his shoulder and snuggled into him, enjoying the view. They were only a couple of miles offshore. The Kauai shoreline was studded with coconut palms and volcanic rock formations that the waves crashed and exploded against in bursts of white foam. A salty scent tinged the air, made stronger with Maya's sea-damp hair wetting the shoulder of his T-shirt.

"You were right," she said after a while. "It's paradise here."

It was, and he'd loved showing her the island. Every morning they'd gone for an early run on the beach. Except today, when Jackson had woken her with soft kisses up her legs until she'd begged and he'd concentrated on the soft, secret flesh between them. He'd teased her for a long time with his tongue, then made her come twice before letting himself find release inside her warmth. Afterward they'd fallen back to sleep, sated and tangled around each other.

Bending his head to kiss the sensitive skin beneath her ear and earning a smile, he saw the look on her face and his heart swelled impossibly full. Her expression was one of complete serenity. She was happy, totally at peace with him here. Their first night she'd had a bad dream and he'd been right there to hold her. They'd stayed up for a few hours after that, lying together in the darkness talking about what they'd been through. That shared experience made a huge difference. He knew they both had a long way to go before they'd dealt with everything, but at least they were moving forward, rather than getting stuck on the past.

Jackson hugged her closer. She felt so damn good in his arms. He'd never get enough of holding her. It thrilled him that she'd already become comfortable with displays of affection. Now she initiated cuddling and fooling around almost as often as he did, telling him she craved the closeness as much as he did.

Maya's face was soft and almost dreamy, bathed in the rosy light from the setting sun as she stared out over the waves toward shore. Suddenly she sat up, pointing excitedly. "Look!"

He glanced up in time to see a large humpback whale breach the surface of the water. It turned its massive body in the air so its pale belly faced them before slamming back down into the waves, sending up a huge eruption of water.

Maya's delighted laugh was like music. "God, that was the most beautiful thing I've ever seen!"

No, *she* was. Jackson knew what he wanted and he couldn't wait one second longer to go after it. Setting a hand on the side of her face, he cupped her cheek and turned her head toward him. Maya tipped her head back to look up at him, that gorgeous smile still on her face. It faded a little when she saw the intense look on his face.

"Will you marry me?" he murmured.

Her expression went blank with shock. She straightened and swiveled around to face him, absently tucking a lock of wet hair behind her ear. "What?"

"Marry me. Here. Tomorrow. I'll find us a justice of the peace, and we'll get married on the beach at sunset."

She looked incredulous. "You're serious?"

He nodded, trailing his thumb across her parted lips. "I love you. I want to spend my life with you and have a family together someday. I'm going back to Bagram in ten days and when I do I want to do it knowing you've taken my name." Maybe that was territorial, but he didn't care. Maya was his, and he wanted the world to know it.

She searched his eyes as though she still couldn't believe what he'd said. "But I don't know what's going to happen with my job. I'll be out of the Air Force soon and I don't know where I'll wind up. You want to go to medical school."

"I don't care where we end up, as long as we're there together." He could go to med school in a lot of different places.

Her face softened and her eyes warmed in that special way that told him he'd touched her deep inside. She raised a hand to touch his cheek. "What about your family? Won't they be upset if we elope?"

That sounded like an almost yes. He pressed. "You've already met my family and they're all in love with you. We can do a church wedding later. I want to make you my wife tomorrow, just the two of us and an official on the beach."

Her lips quivered slightly and her eyes turned damp. She sighed, seemed to struggle with her composure for a moment. Finally she shook her head and spoke. "God, on top of everything else you're a romantic too?"

Her reaction made him chuckle. "Yes, ma'am."

That quiver in her lips turned into a full-blown smile. It bloomed slowly, and the soft glow in her eyes was the most beautiful thing in the world to him. "I would love to marry you, Jackson," she whispered.

Sheer relief almost tore a groan out of him. "Tomorrow?" he prompted, wanting to make it real, to lock it down.

"Tomorrow is perfect," she agreed with a nod, and hooked a hand behind his neck to pull him down and seal her promise with a kiss.

* * * * *

ACKNOWLEDGMENTS

I WOULD LIKE to acknowledge several people for their help not only with Lethal Pursuit, but for the entire series as well.

First, my wonderful and supportive critique partner, Katie Reus, whom I could not do without. Thank you for being such a supportive and caring friend! I love you bunches.

And of course, I couldn't have made the stories shine without the patience and insight of my wonderful editor, Rhonda Helms.

Also, one man in particular deserves a huge shout-out, because without his help I could never have given these books the sort of realism I wanted. Research is a wonderful thing, but having a trusted go-to source who's actually "walked the walk" is invaluable.

To David A. Weaver, U.S. Air Force (Ret.) (former Pararescueman)—you rock my socks, sir. Thank you so much for always taking the time to respond to my many questions, and for taking me seriously even after you knew I was using the info in steamy romances. I am so proud to "know" you.

On a final note, any errors or inaccuracies that exist in the book are my fault.

PJs are such unsung heroes; it's high time these quiet professionals gained more recognition and respect for what they do.

ABOUT THE AUTHOR

Kaylea Cross writes edge-of-your-seat military romantic suspense. Her work has won many awards and has been nominated for both the Daphne du Maurier Award and the National Readers' Choice Award. A registered massage therapist by trade, Kaylea is also an avid gardener, artist, Civil War buff, special ops aficionado, belly dance enthusiast and former nationally carded softball pitcher. She lives in Vancouver, British Columbia, with her husband and two sons.